# GHOST MUSIC

He was halfway down the hall to his room when he heard it again. *Rock-br-r-ring Rock-br-r-ring Rock-br-r-ring*. Kyle twirled and froze.

The light under Lisa's bedroom door shone like a wicked yellow finger. The sound of the rocking continued as Kyle started slowly for the door. His trembling hand began to reach for the glass doorknob when the music began to play from the other side of the door. "Mares eat oats, and does eat oats, and little lambs eat ivy . . ." the lady on the record sang.

Kyle's throat twitched compulsively. He listened for a moment for Lisa's voice singing along in a high, lilting manner, but heard nothing. Thank God.

He hesitated, then called out in a tone that shocked him because it was so familiar. How many times had he used this tone of voice with her? A thousand, at least. "Lisa," he said, "Go to sleep. It's late, Lisa. Go to sleep."

The rocking sound stopped. Kyle felt a tinge of relief. Then, he heard a familiar patter of footsteps start toward the door. Kyle opened his mouth wide and sucked in air. If that doorknob turned, he would scream. The footsteps stopped at the other side of the door. Kyle stared at the doorknob.

It began to turn . . .

## TERROR LIVES!

**THE SHADOW MAN** (1946, $3.95)
by Stephen Gresham
The Shadow Man could hide anywhere—under the bed, in
the closet, behind the mirror . . . even in the sophisticated
circuitry of little Joey's computer. And the Shadow Man
could make Joey do things that no little boy should ever
do!

**SIGHT UNSEEN** (2038, $3.95)
by Andrew Neiderman
David was always right. Always. But now that he was
growing up, his gift was turning into a power. The power to
know things—terrible things—that he didn't want to know.
Like who would live . . . and who would die!

**MIDNIGHT BOY** (2065, $3.95)
by Stephen Gresham
Something horrible is stalking the town's children. For one
of its most trusted citizens possesses the twisted need and
cunning of a psychopathic killer. Now Town Creek's only
hope lies in the horrific, blood-soaked visions of the MID-
NIGHT BOY!

**TEACHER'S PET** (1927, $3.95)
by Andrew Neiderman
All the children loved their teacher Mr. Lucy. It was aston-
ishing to see how they all seemed to begin to resemble Mr.
Lucy. And act like Mr. Lucy. And kill like Mr. Lucy!

# DEVIL'S MOON

## William M. Carney

**ZEBRA BOOKS**
**KENSINGTON PUBLISHING CORP.**

ZEBRA BOOKS

are published by

Kensington Publishing Corp.
475 Park Avenue South
New York, NY 10016

First printing: July, 1988

Printed in the United States of America

*for*
    *Mom and Dad*
    *Who taught me the meaning of Love*
        *And the value of Dreams*

# ACKNOWLEDGMENTS

Steven Spruill, Ph. D., a fine novelist and friend, offered his expertise on this book from outline to final draft, and to him I am most indebted;

My agent, Sharon Jarvis, is a writer's dream: good judgment, a discerning eye for story content, and a nice human being, too;

Little brothers are good for something: mine read the manuscript for matters police, and arranged for me to go on patrol with the Los Angeles Sheriff Department. Thanks, Kevin, and thanks to the L.A.S.D.;

Wendy McCurdy, my editor, and the nice people at Zebra Books get personal "thank yous" for publishing my first novel; And the following people are mentioned for various reasons (all of them good): Lee Vaughn, Joan Zyda, Craig and Leslie Powell, Curt and Ann Hart, Dr. Nancy Lyon Spruill, Tim and Margaret Alyea, Paul J. Smith, Ann and Jeff DeWolfe, Marcy and Ken Petersen; and Jean, William, and Carolyn Carney, who would have been proud.

# Excerpts I

# July 1948

*All excerpts are taken from the personal journal of the noted anthropologist, Professor Nancy Lyon (1915-1981) as read into the public record during the Governor's Special Investigative Committee's inquiry concerning the mass murders in Briggs City—a.k.a. the Briggs City Massacre—convened January 7, 1982, Sacramento, California.*

July 26, 1948

I asked Holy Eagle what was Ravana and he said that It was the darkest of the Dark, an evil thing from the very middle of hell itself. "The Devil," I offered, and he said, "No. You must understand: Ravana is the Devil's Devil—It alone can destroy the world, that is why it must be faced."


July 27, 1948

. . . my God . . . and now I believe in prophecy, and I pray that it does not occur in my lifetime . . . but who will believe me? I believe because I was there . . . It all begins with *Heytah-nee*, the Traitor, and Devil's Ground, the trees . . .

*Heytah-nee*
Shame on thee
The moon's gone bad
The world's gone mad
You've set *Ravana* free
*Heytah-nee*

—Child's taunt,
Laikute Indian tribe

# Prologue

*Devil's Ground, 1965*

The boy stood on the white dividing line of the deserted country road, his hands on his hips. The night sky arched high, dark and cold, above his head. He faced east toward his destination; he'd come from the west, his shack of a home. To the north, ten miles up the road was Briggs City, California, population 23,000. To the southwest seventy miles lay Santa Barbara. The boy was sixteen and had never been there.

He knew two places on earth: the town Briggs City, and the reservation. He hated them both. In Briggs City they treated you like a second-class citizen, and if you lived on the reservation, you knew you were one. He was too proud for either situation. Tonight he would prove his equality—with the help of Old Man Pickers's daughter, Cathy. Old Man Pickers's *white* daughter. That'd teach her Injun-hating bastard father!

Her old man would kill them both if he knew what they were going to do tonight. His sweet, blond-haired angel getting laid by an Indian, full-blooded, of the Priest clan, greatest of all the clans of the Laikute tribe.

The boy frowned as he thought about his tribe, and Old Man Pickers. There had been bad blood between the tribe and the Pickers brothers since 1949 when they had stolen the Indian land using white men's law, and made it their ranch. And with the steal had come the trees, Devil's Ground, as sacred to the Priest clan as any white man's church anywhere in the world.

11

It was to this place that the boy's grandfather had come, and his father too, before his death, to face the Devilthing, to face Ravana and save the world. It was sacred, holy land to his tribe, and Pickers had taken it with a shuffle of papers and money tucked up tight white assholes.

The boy could feel years of hatred swell up in his gut like wet black cotton. He touched the talisman at his neck and thought of his grandfather, a brave noble priest-warrior who had danced before Ravana, shaking the charm of the Spirit Elders' bones, hundreds of them, strung on a leather thong right in the Devilthing's face and defied It to take his life, to possess his soul; and the old man had lived.

He was a great man in the tribe, and it was he who had told the boy the secrets of the Great White Spirit and Great Black Spirit, and how it would be up to him one day to face Ravana and save the world from its evil.

He looked both ways on the road. It was near midnight and there was no traffic. In the distance he could hear cattle bellowing somewhere on the range. He would have to hurry now. He was meeting Cathy at midnight and he wanted to be there on time. But before he left the road, he pulled the thong holding the talisman up off his neck and onto the outside of his army-green field jacket. The bones rattled in the night. They seemed like small white stones, but were bleached pieces of bone: the tip of the left little finger of every Laikute Priest to face Ravana, including one untested yet. Even now the second joint on his finger was still scarred with red temporary tissue and throbbed with the beat of his pulse; a small price to pay for the power and prestige of a Priest.

He cocked his head to the moon with a challenging look. Gone bad, he thought. Moon's gone bad. He didn't think a white man could tell, no. White man's eyes see only things themselves, not the spirit of things.

But the moon had gone bad—Ravana's moon: the moon's color had changed fully to a glowering burnt orange, and had surrounded itself with flat lifeless clouds. A small, black puffed floater lingered across the very center of the orb like a pupil to give sight to the unheavenly eye. A bad sign. A bad sign that he knew his grandfather would not have ignored. But Pickers had to pay, and the boy was hot for Cathy now.

And if Ravana came?

If It came, the boy would vanquish It. He had the bones and of them the Devilthing was afraid—if, and only if, the wearer was brave, truly worthy of priesthood. He knew he was brave, and worthy, too.

He ran to the barbed wire fence and used the wooden fencepost to vault over. He landed on his feet and looked south at a gray box shadow a half of a mile away. Pickers's house. No lights on, a good sign. Cathy was going to meet him by the old scrub oak in the center of Devil's Ground. Her old man should be asleep by now, so she probably got out of the house with no problem.

Devil's Ground was straight ahead half a mile. The tall trees lay a solid black wall in the dark night. The boy started toward it at a ground-eating pace. The field he ran through was overgrown. Once it had been harvested, contributing to the fortunes of the Pickers, but since the taking of the old man's wife, Cathy's mother, Pickers had let the place go to hell.

The vegetation changed as he got closer to trees. The bushes became more dense and their thorns seemed to grab at him like hands of the dead, making sinister scratching sounds on his blue jeans as he kicked through the field.

As he reached the trees a weeded ditch appeared as if by magic and he was forced to jump, arms pinwheeling, legs scrambling-dangling suddenly in midair. He landed with a jarring compression of bones and muscles on the slope of the opposite bank of the ditch, his boots a half an inch into some putrid water, his knees jammed into sandy dirt, his hands clenched in rough, grassy topsoil sod. A massive wave of pain gripped his body, then was gone. Every joint ached and his wounded finger screamed in pain.

"Shit!" he yelled, the word absorbed by the curtain of

13

eucalpytus trees before him.

He took a minute to catch his breath, then looked up the incline to the trees. They stood sixty to seventy feet high like giant fingers raised in praise to the evil eye of the moon. A feeling of dread overcame him and for a second he thought he might turn back, but he clutched the bone necklace at his throat instead and scrambled his way up to the level of the trees. Puffing, he stood erect. The pungent odor of the eucalyptus carried with it the smell of rotting garbage that cloyed in his throat.

He would have to walk through the woods. Devil's Ground itself was ringed by tall, thick trees that formed an unnatural eerie stockade some one hundred feet deep. It was said that the light of day never touched ground inside the woods, and that dark, soulless things were lost forever within its bounds, stalking and walking, guarding their unholy master, Ravana. It was dark in there, a textured darkness of shadows and forms. Dark, pernicious forms.

He caught his breath, wiped the dirt from the ditch off on the sleeve of his field jacket, and then took several steps into the black veil of Devil's Ground. So far, so good, except it was black in there. He fished a flashlight from a zippered pocket and clicked it on. A puddle of urine-colored light played on rotting leaves on the ground. He cursed himself. He hadn't thought to check the batteries in his hurry to get out of the house, and now he had a light that was shit good for nothing. It would have to do, though; he wasn't going to miss humping Cathy for nothing.

He moved quickly through the woods, not liking it at all. Halfway through, he thought he heard footsteps off to his left, then his right. He stopped and listened. Had he heard it or not? It didn't matter now, he decided, because if something was moving, it didn't need a flashlight, and that meant it could see in the dark. Shit! He'd debate the reality of the noises later.

He ran, hoping his sense of direction was correct.

Damn it! How far away was the clearing!

It could only be a few yards; it might as well be miles. He felt something slap against his back, a branch maybe, or . . . or, worse. Another slap, harder this time, but he wouldn't turn around to look, No . . . No . . . suddenly he felt a tug at his foot, something had him, and then he was flying into the air, free from the trees and tumbling head over heels down a dry dirt embankment, landing prone, his arms out in front of him still clutching the flashlight, his legs splayed like a supplicant. He lay like that, stunned for a moment, then scrambled around to face them, the creatures that had chased him . . .

Nothing.

Nothing but the blank, uncaring boles of the trees.

Could he have imagined it? He had panicked, he could admit that to himself. He was panicked and they had just been branches slapping at him after all. Just branches.

He laughed nervously, relieved, then sat back on his heels, his knees punched into the dirt. His heart was beginning to slow down and he took large, gulping breaths of air. That had been damned scary, that's for sure. He shook his head rapidly, shaking his fright off, and replaced the light in its zippered pocket.

The bones, he thought, and reached up and touched the dry remnants. He'd forgotten about the bones. If he had just held them out, this never would have happened. If there was anything there in the first place, that is.

He brushed the dirt from his hands and blue jeans, stealing distrustful peeks at the high black wall of eucalyptus trees. He realized an odd contradiction: on the other side, this ring of woods seem to be there to keep him out; on the inside, to keep him in!

He began to notice an uneasy silence.

All natural noises had stopped. Not just quiet, but dead silence as if smothered in a heavy blanket of nothingness. And there was light here, orange light from that devil's-eye moon, bathing the acre and a half of ground like a glow from hell.

Where the crap was Cathy?

15

He stood up and did a little dance to sort the pains out in his body. He would live. But it was too quiet, too eerie. He realized that Cathy couldn't be here, not when it was like this, when the moon had gone bad. He scanned the ground. It banked down all around the perfect ellipse of trees into a flat area of coarse sand. Through that area a small creek flowed and pooled into a black miniature lake. He estimated the pond to be sixty feet at its widest point. On the other side of that dark, oily water stood the scrub oak, gnarled and leafless, with twisted limbs clawing for the sky like some deformed horror in a grade-B fright flick that chases crazy teenagers and strangles them. In the body of its trunk was a hole, the kind left where a limb has been severed. Only this one was hollowed out, slightly larger than a decapitated head; and black inside, ungodly black.

Slowly the boy slid down the bank. Cathy had told him that she would meet him by that oak. She had been here once before with her father, and was forbidden by him ever to return here. It was from this tree, the gnarly scrub oak, that her mother had been found hung (taken by Ravana, his grandfather had said, though the Law called it a suicide), when Cathy was a little girl. But that fact didn't seem to bother her. Her father finding them bothered her more, he guessed. He wouldn't look for them here, she said, and they would be safe and could love one another.

He walked to the water and jumped the four-foot span of creek at a place where it flowed into the pond. He approached the oak tree cautiously. The orange moonlight set trunk and limbs vibrantly aglow.

Cathy wasn't here. It was past midnight. Where was she? He tried unsuccessfully to quell a thought: maybe Old Man Pickers was here. Maybe he caught her leaving and beat her bloody to find out why. And he was out there, in those trees, a double-bladed ax clutched in his hands, waiting to get close. To take a full swing in the light of this mad moon, and hoot and holler as the sharp wedge of the ax split his Indian skull, cracking it open like a nutshell, sinking deep into

16

his brains . . .

Hands grabbed his shoulders, and he screamed.

David Pickers's eyelids popped open out of a cold, dark sleep. Something was wrong. He felt it.

Lying rigidly on his back, every muscle tense, he forced his gaze, widening with fear, to the floor beside his bed. Bleeding through the open window and fluttering gauze curtains, moonlight pooled burnt-orange on the hardwood floor.

Pickers leaped out of bed, ignoring the cold wood against his flat feet, and padded to the opened window. He stuck his head out into the night air, his chest heaving.

The moon. He had seen the moon like that only one time before, the night Emily had killed . . . been killed, he corrected himself. She had been killed, all right. She was a country girl, too sensible for what everybody said she had done. That orange moon had shone on that awful night too, five years ago when he had awakened in the dead of night and found her gone. He still ached to this day. For eleven years of nights Emily's body had been either beside him, in the kitchen, or, with little Cathy . . .

Cathy!

Pickers ran to her room and slammed open the door. She was gone!

"Oh, God, not my little girl, too," he said.

He ran into the living room, pulled his shotgun from its mount over the fieldstone fireplace, and burst from the house into the night, barefooted. His red-striped nightshirt whipped up and around his long chickenlegs as he ran frenziedly toward the eucalyptus trees half a mile away. In his mind he saw Emily, swinging from that damned scrub oak by a black sisal rope, her milk-white neck stretched long, and the golden hair skewed to match the unnatural angle of her head. As he reached her body, the face swung so that he couldn't see it. He stopped her swinging with one shaking hand, her naked back to him. He turned her around, the body twitching under his guiding hands. He convulsed as he saw her face, those eyes bloated out of their sockets, and that rigid black tongue that seemed to punch outward through the puffed lips like a wooden stake speared through a piece of raw meat.

That face.

It filled his vision now as he rushed through his field toward Devil's Ground under this August moon gone bad.


It's good for her she hadn't laughed when he yelled or he would have punched her in her white mouth. She had jumped back, startled; then looked ashamed. "I'm sorry. God. You all right?"

He said nothing, jumped to his feet and grabbed her arms above the elbows, and shook her so hard that her teeth collided with brittle, chipping sounds.

"Stop it," she said. Fear rippled in her blue eyes. "It hurts."

He stopped. "I wasn't scared," he shouted. A warm flush seeped under his skin. Slowly he got his inscrutable look back. She had seen through his armor and that was never allowed. Awkwardly he slipped his arms around her waist and pulled close.

"I'm sorry," he said, kissing her the cheek. "I love you so much," he lied, and kissed her full on the mouth, pressing her supple body into his.

He moved his right leg forward so that his thigh caught her between the legs, and kneaded her into a warm heat. For a moment he shoved the strange light, silence, and baleful moon out of his mind.

Her lips lingered eagerly as he broke the kiss. "Me too, me too," said Cathy.

"Your old man sleeping?" he asked, eyeing her chest, the big jugs. He ran his hand across her skirt, caressing her stomach, creeping low, but not too low. He would touch her there later.

"Un-hunh. Besides, he'd never come here." She kissed him

18

on the lips and looked at him intently. "I want you to know that I'm only doing this because I love you, because you won't believe me unless I do. I'm not like Daddy at all. I don't hate Indians. And I love you. We'll get married one day and that'll make this okay."

"Yes," he said, "this'll make everything right."

She smiled happily and glanced around. "What is it?" she asked, and glanced around. "Why is it so quiet? And the moon?" She looked over her shoulder at the orange circle. He looked too. It was halfway hidden by the gnarled oak, and its light eerily lined the tree's armlike branches. The oak towered over them.

"You can see the orange?" asked the boy incredulously.

"Yes," she replied, "it's hard to miss, isn't it. Look, this whole place looks orange. I've seen the moon look like that before. It's . . . it's weird, I guess."

He looked at her speculatively. She wasn't supposed to be able to see the light, it was a spirit thing, only for Priests. "Gone bad," he said.

"Is it going to rain?"

The dark clouds had gathered ominously.

"Nah. Moon's gone bad. Devil's moon. It's out tonight, but don't worry, I got this." He proffered the talisman around his neck.

"What's that?" She reached for the bones. He jerked the necklace back covetously. No white should touch these!

"Indian. Indian," he said. "You wouldn't understand. As long as I got it, there's nothing going to harm you here. Don't be afraid."

"I'm *not* afraid," she said. "I don't believe in the devil."

"Don't be afraid," he repeated, the words of this white girl not worthy of hearing. He feigned a loving look and squeezed her playfully. "Are you ready?" he asked, and leaned forward into a long kiss, working his knee into her once more until she moaned.

"Yes. Yes." She clutched at him, her soft lips close to his

19

ear. "If you care. If you really love me."

It was a question that demanded an answer, so he murmured that he loved her while his hand dropped low this time and held her between her thighs where seconds before his leg had been. He kissed her at the same time and she yielded, undulating against his hand as he pulled up her skirt and shucked down her panties. He rubbed her hard now and she began moaning. His hands moved out from under her skirt, found the zipper and the clasp, expertly undid them both, then pulled the skirt up over her head. He grabbed the sweater and pulled it up, catching at the armpits. She raised her arms to the sky and he pulled it off her. She wore no bra. Her large young breasts stuck out to him and he caressed them and clutched her to him, his mouth finding hers, his hands running down to her butt.

He closed his eyes only after she did. He began rubbing her again until he was into some serious foreplay. She was moaning and groaning, and he was as hard as a rock. In his heat he ignored the noise, a rhythmic rustling sound. With what he was feeling now, who cared? He reached around her ass and poked deep between her cheeks. She pulled away and said harshly, "Don't." He liked to finger the asshole before screwing her. "C'mon, Cathy," he coaxed, but she was having none of that. He moved his hand between her legs and she began pumping again. "Okay, okay," he said, "let's do it . . ." He stopped and listened. What was that sound?

"Look!" said Cathy.

"Shit," he said softly. The ring of eucalyptus trees were swaying in unison, making the leaves rustle.

"God!" Cathy squealed.

The ink-black water of the pool began boiling violently, steam rising off its surface.

"Crap!" He twisted his head and stared into the black hole in the trunk of the oak tree. Two iridescent yellow eyes glared back at him. The eyes shifted as if taken with the naked back of the young virgin. They watched the twist and curve of her spine as she undulated against the boy's hand.

20

*His little snake must not enter her*, rasped a voice in the boy's mind; somehow he knew it came from the intelligence behind those eyes. *Come forth, my children, come forth*, commanded the voice.

Lightning shattered the sky with lingering yellow threads, and ear-splitting thunder followed.

He pulled away from her and looked briefly to the heavens, then to the swaying trees. From the darkness between the waving eucalyptus stepped skeletons. Ragged, putrid meat still hung on their bones. Maggot-ridden eyes stared at him and Cathy. They drew closer in a tightening circle, their lipless mouths fixed in permanent grins.

A low moan fought its way out of Cathy's throat, then she screamed.

With a yelp, the boy ripped the talisman over his head. He stuck his arm out, defending against the approaching skeletons, his back to the steaming, black water. Cathy stood naked, screaming. Her chest shuddered, jiggling her full, white breasts.

One of the glowing yellow eyes in the black hole of the tree winked out. The other floated to the center of the hole, glared, then winked out too. The bonemen were now fifty feet away and closing in ragged, jolting steps. The reek of rotting flesh from the corpses festered in the boy's nose and throat.

"Stop them! Please stop them!" pleaded Cathy. She began to scream again.

A monstrous blast of heat scorched their backs. He saw their shadows loom on the ground in front of them, born out of the light of the fiery pool behind. He whipped around. Cathy stopped screaming and the boy thrust out his charm over at what he saw rising out of the conflagrated pool.

He watched It rise slowly from the dark roiling water. Grampa had never told him It was so fucking tall, thirteen feet, at least. And shit, you couldn't see nothing but . . . Christ, was it cloth? or—

*Oh, shit!*

21

The bonemen behind the robed figure stopped at the edge of the lake and leveled their arms in front of them, their bony fingers reaching out as if to say, "I want you, to touch you . . . and rip you apart." And their mouths opened and moaned, the grief of the lost souls of hell.

Cathy whimpered.

The Thing glided over the burning black water and through the hellish flames toward them. Its eyes vibrated with cruelty and cunning, and It laughed—a predatory sound that circled the living creatures and died. The bonemen picked up a shrieking mockery of their master's voice and wailed in gleeful torment. Lightning flashed to Devil's Ground in blinding whiteness, but Ravana's form seemed to absorb the light.

It kept coming at them.

"Back Devilthing!" screamed the boy. Shaking the talisman he began chanting an Indian incantation to ward off the Evil One.

It stopped, just at the edge of the fiery pool, the flames spurting high about its head. The bonemen ceased their wail. The noise of the rhythmic sway of the dark trees ended, though their motion continued. All sounds ceased.

The hateful eyes gleamed.

The boy began to falter. He stopped his chant. He realized that Ravana was ridiculing him with silence. All those eyes staring at him, and especially those big yellow ones. They seemed to take him in and talk to him. Yes. Talk only to him, inside him. Vile words. Hateful words. But he was so afraid, so afraid. His gut felt like jelly and his bowels were loose. He felt like he was going to shit his pants right there. In front of Cathy and everyone. He was afraid, so fucking *afraid*.

The voice kept talking.

Cathy watched him as he lowered the charm. He nodded, acknowledging the private conversation between himself and the Thing.

"We have a deal, then?" rasped its inhuman voice, not a question, but a statement.

The boy's lips began to quiver. Tears welled up in his eyes. Shame deformed his face. He brought the necklace close to his lips and spit on them. "Yes," he replied, his voice breaking.

"What?" asked Cathy in a stupid whimper, turning her eyes to the boy. "What? What does it mean?" She grabbed his arm and shook it, shifting her eyes from him to the Thing. "What does it mean?"

Shame paralyzed his voice.

The dark form floated forward, lust in its eyes.

Sudden understanding twisted her face.

"No! No! No!" she cried. "No-o-o-o-o!"

He broke Cathy's grip and pushed her toward the Thing. She sprawled at the foot of the black figure. She looked up. Iridescent yellow eyes, the size of grapefruit, glared down in lustful malevolence.

"Oh God, no!" she shrieked. *"No-o-o-o-o-o!"*

The boy ran, knocking past two of the filthy bonemen, and headed for the woods. He scrambled up the bank, then tripped, falling flat on his ass at the edge of the ring of trees. The scene burned intensely in his mind: where had Old Man Pickers come from? He was being held by bonemen, his back to the boy, being forced to watch as Cathy—Oh, God, poor Cathy—stripped naked, her feet dangling, opened, unresisting legs, was held high in the air by Ravana, at an angle, then slowly brought forward, the crux of her thighs aimed toward its head, the Devilthing miming a man, head tilted back, about to wolf down an appetizer. Old Man Pickers wailed, and the boy nearly swallowed his own tongue, when Ravana began to feed.

The boy jumped to his feet and ran into the woods. It was his fault Ravana was loose now. Free to grow. Free to fulfill the Prophecy, to end the world.

# Excerpts II

# August 1948

## August 4, 1948

It is now close to midnight. Holy Eagle and I spent a long time around the fire tonight, discussing my concerns for his people versus my duty as an anthropologist. As I thought, he would help none but myself . . . told him that I would write about the culture, but not my personal experiences, and he seemed pleased . . . When I told him that would write my paper on their beliefs then return again, he told me that I would never again come back here. I must confess to being both shocked and hurt; I have come to care for this old holy man. . . . He told me that the Spirit Elders told him this . . . promised to speak to me about *Ehkeh-Heh*—the Fallen Warrior, the Chosen One, tomorrow.

August 5, 1948

*Ehkeh-Heh* follows *Heytah-nee*, Holy Eagle explained. First the traitor betrays his people and the world and sets Ravana free, the beginning of the end of the world . . . the end of the world does not occur all at once, he explained; Ravana is weak, and in order to gain strength he must face an opponent. The stronger the opponent the more power he gains. Before the Traitor, the Priests choose the opponent, and each time It is faced and defeated It becomes weaker . . . When asked the difference after *Heytah-nee*, he said that before the betrayal the Priests picked the opponent; after the betrayal, Ravana picks his own . . . how It will chose *Ehkeh-Heh?* Holy Eagle said that he did now know . . . When? He said that he did not know that either, that it could be a second after the betrayal or a hundred years, the choice not being a simple matter of finding just anyone. He must be brave and strong, yet weaken at the sight of the Devilthing. Ravana will do anything to get this man.

I told Holy Eagle that I would hate to have to be *Ehkeh-Heh*, the Fallen Warrior, the Chosen One, and he told me that *Ehkeh-Heh* will hate it too.

# Book I

# 1

Kyle Richards knew it wasn't necessary, but out of an old habit, which he really hadn't needed now for going on two years, he chose the last booth. He made his way down the narrow, empty diner between counter stools and emerald-green tabletops, then slid onto a worn bench facing the door.

As he reached for the metal ashtray with one large tanned hand and gathered his Pall Malls with the other, that same old valued feeling of safety came back to him; he was okay now, his back to the wall and the greasy length of the diner stretching before him like a no'man's land. No one could enter or leave without coming under his scrutiny. It was a small town, true, with little chance of an old acquaintance with a beef walking in. But good habits survive on practice. As he tucked the nonfiltered cigarette in the corner of his mouth and lit it with a well-worn Zippo lighter, Kyle felt the pleasant return of emotional normalcy. He savored it along with the smoke in his lungs. Normalcy. It had been a long, long two years, and now, normalcy was just what he needed; that, and a home. Maybe he would find both of those today.

He watched the middle-aged waitress with scuffed white work shoes move toward him, smiling yellow teeth through bright red lips, a glass bulb of steamy black coffee in one hand. She waddled down to his table, and as his mind absorbed the mundane fact of sitting in a small-town diner, a long-awaited voice of hope spoke inside his head: *Maybe it will be all right after all. Maybe Leo was right. Maybe I can make it.*

"Coffee?" she asked, pouring the black, oily liquid before

29

Kyle could answer. He waved off the menu with a smile.

"Sausage, scrambled eggs, juice large," he ordered.

The waitress ("Lucy," her name tag announced) scribbled with a stubby yellow pencil onto a pad of tickets and, taking a deep, nervous breath, said, "I could've told you that."

Jesus, she's flirting with me, thought Kyle, staring at the furry red polyester creature that had curled up on top of her head and died. "How's that?" he asked, as if surprised.

"Big man needs a big breakfast," she said simply. She bit her lower lip softly as if the words had just slipped out by themselves, blushed, and scooted toward the kitchen, leaving in her wake the rhythmic scratching sounds of the leg panels of a Maidenform girdle attacking one another.

Kyle chuckled to himself. He gulped the dark brew, staring through the diner's window at the large, red brick building across the town square: city hall.

That's what it's all about, today, he thought.

Most men Kyle knew would be too nervous to eat a big breakfast before an interview; but not him. Never had been nervous, at least in the standard sense of the word, because he had the secret that old Leo had taught him: "Be prepared. Preparation is everything, Kyle, if you're gonna get ahead. And if you're prepared, then there ain't no reason to be dumbstruck nervous. Don't be so overconfident that you blow it, but don't be nervous either." And he hadn't been. Not back at LAPD, and not now. He was prepared. Three days' prepared. Three days of looking at the town, and he knew it up and down. And if he was a bit nervous, it had nothing to do with the town, but was of himself and his past.

Kyle saw a brown arm produce his breakfast plate through the service window. Lucy took it with a "Thank you, Raoul," to the cook. She smiled a bit too cheerily, a gesture Kyle guessed was for his benefit. As Lucy walked toward him Kyle noticed that she had let her zipper slip down to cleavage level. He hid a smirk behind his hand. She sat the plates down in front of him. She bent over a little more than necessary to place his juice, so that when her uniform fell away from her chest Kyle was served with the view of her enormous breasts, held in restraint by two overworked C-cups.

Kyle felt stirring of desire in spite of himself and fought hard to restrain the laughter behind his lips. It had been a long time, but not that long, thank God.

Normalcy. Yes, this was normalcy, and for that reason when Lucy stayed around to chat, he didn't mind it too much, though he would have preferred her to leave him in peace.

"You a policeman?" she asked, her brown eyes flicking to the gold-handcuffs tie tack, then running across the length and breadth of his shoulders.

"Used to be," answered Kyle, accustomed to that question. He didn't mind having the "look"—having people recognize him as a policeman. It was good to show your colors; that way, people who choked up at the sight of the law knew to stay out of your way, and those who found some sort of thrill about the job (and they were few and far between these days) could make their way forward.

"Police chief was killed less 'n month ago, down in niggertown. Never caught him, though, the one that did it." She smiled conversationally, then continued, "Lord know what the world coming to these days. You know what I mean?"

Kyle had just forked a bite of fluffy eggs into his mouth. He swallowed hard. The goddamn interview hadn't spoiled his appetite, but this waitress had. Yes, he knew about the murder of the chief. Leo had given him that little tidbit right off the bat. It would get first priority as soon as he landed the job. It was that kind of club, being a policeman, whether a *gendarme* in Paris, or a bush-ranger in Kenya, when one dies they all die. Policemen, the smallest minority in the world.

He swigged a mouthful of hot coffee, wishing the watiress away with a squint. But she stood there and smiled, then continued. "Yessir. Dead as a doornail. Loretta, over there"— her hand flipped toward the front window, and Kyle assumed she meant city hall—"said they had a man coming in today.

31

Mayor's all hot bejesus for him. 'Spose to be something special, Loretta said. No local boy this time . . .''

Kyle let her drone on for some time, pushing his plate away. No appetite any more. He watched her face, wondering when she was going to make the connection. Suddenly she stopped, her mouth opened, her red lips forming an O. For just a second he saw the pink muscle of her tongue convulse with excitement. "Oh, oh, oh." Her brown eyes grew wide. "You, you, you're the one; you're the new chief, the new chief."

"Not yet." He smiled weakly. "May I have my check, please?"

"Uh . . ." She stared at the plates still heaped with breakfast, and started to ask him about that when the cow bells strapped to the front door jangled and a street bum walked in and sat down.

Kyle noticed he took the stool nearest the register, the best spot for a till-tap artist. "Take care of him first," ordered Kyle. Lucy turned and said, "Oh, shit. Another one," and marched in quick, dreadnought steps behind the counter and down to the indigent. Kyle stared at the man for a moment, then relaxed. The man was okay, no problem. Just in for something to eat, or whatever.

"What do you want, anyway?" demanded the waitress, her cheeks flushing with irritation.

The man removed a tattered felt hat from his head and placed it carefully on the stool beside him. From his position Kyle could just catch the profile of a hard-featured man.

"Well, whattaya want?" she repeated. "I ain't got all day."

A slow heat rose up Kyle's neck. Give the man a break for Christ's sake, he's on the skids as it is.

"Coffee," said the bum. He scratched his stubbled beard and looked hard at the countertop.

"Lemme see the money. Forty-three cents." She glared at him.

The man dug through the pockets of an old tweed sports coat, and then to his khaki slacks, while Lucy balled up both her fists and planted them fiercely on her trussed hips.

The man placed the money on the counter. "I've got forty-five cents," he said hesitantly. Lucy stared at the money in disbelief.

"That ain't enough. Ya gotta leave a tip. I don't serve for no two-cent tip."

She glared at the man triumphantly. "Now get out!" She pointed toward the door with a flourished hand.

"I'll pay the tip," Kyle's voice boomed. "In fact, I'll buy this gentleman breakfast. Give him what I ordered, the juice, too."

Lucy stood in shock for a moment, then her face went loose and mobile, quivering in disgust and rage. She recovered, then looked hard at him, as if hurt and betrayed by a friend. The cook, a young Chicano, stuck his head through the service port and smiled gleefully at Kyle. Apparently Lucy could be a pain in the ass to a lot of people.

"Hey, *Loo-cee-ee,*" he said, "I'll have it up inna minute." He smiled joyfully at Kyle again, then his head disappeared through the rectangle.

Lucy stomped off into the back room, the swinging doors flapping angrily behind her, and for the first time the man looked at Kyle. The years of outdoor foraging had weathered the face into a rough, haggard tan, but beneath that, as Kyle's mind sorted out the effects of the derelict's life from the man himself, the sharp features of a relatively young man appeared, thirty-eight years old, maybe. My age, thought Kyle. And the brown eyes, so deep and somber, as if the man were looking out from some gloomy crypt.

He hesitated under Kyle's gaze, and then nodded his head in thanks and turned slowly back to the counter. He fumbled in the big floppy pockets of his ragged tweed sports coat, pulling out a small, hand-sized book, opened it and began to read, his lips moving but no sound issuing forth.

Kyle felt relieved that the bum hadn't tried to strike up a conversation.

Leo would have given me hell, thought Kyle, telling me for

33

the umpteenth hundred time that I'm too soft for my own good. Kyle sat back, realizing he had no control in some situations (like this one). It had been his way since he was a kid, taking on a bully hectoring some smaller boy, or giving money to someone so they could buy milk at lunchtime. He had felt a *need* to help, to offer a friendly hand. Hell, that's why he had become a police officer; he wasn't ashamed of it. He told anyone who asked the all-important Why? that he liked to help people, and that's what being a policeman was all about. Unfortunately, most people didn't see it that way (and most cops, either), but that was their problem, not his.

The cook appeared and placed the food in front of the indigent, then walked back to Kyle and fished out a white bill.

"Loo-cee, she ain't comin' out." He beamed a toothy smile. "She's a real bitch, man," he said, still grinning, handed Kyle the check, and went back in the kitchen.

Kyle stood at the register some minutes later. The cook came out and took the money for the meals, then called back after him as he made his way back to his table: "You gonna leave a tip, man, you crazy?"

"Guilt," responded Kyle. He left Lucy ten percent instead of his usual fifteen, deducting five percent for what the cook called being "a bitch" and dumping on someone more unfortunate than herself.

"Shee-it." The cook waved, and disappeared into his kitchen once more.

Kyle walked past the bum.

"Thank you, officer." The tone of the man's voice was deep and refined, not hesitant at all as it had been with the waitress.

Kyle turned, his hand on the door, and looked into the man's somber, dark eyes.

"You're welcome . . ." *Father?* . . . Why had he wanted to say Father? "You're welcome," he said again, then saw that the man had pulled out all the napkins from the dispenser and had been writing on them with a red Flair pen. Kyle suppressed an urge to shake his head in disapproval, and pushed his way to

34

the outside, toward city hall.

The derelict watched the tall policeman cross the street, and he was certain that a moment before, two lost souls had been in this diner instead of just one. Somehow the man now heading toward the white bandbox in the town-square park seemed so alone and solitary—that cold central California wind blustering against him as if to knock him down, and him leaning against it. It brought to mind a strong tree standing stiff-angled against some invisible but tremendously violent storm.

He looked after the cop for a second longer, then turned back to his meal. He saved the hash browns for last. He smothered them with ketchup and savored the golden brown potatoes. Bounty from God.

Yes. Of course it had been the kindness of the tall policeman, but he knew God works through such men, and as each well-chewed portion of potatoes slid down his throat he thanked God for his unexpected generosity. Beside the actual eating of the food, he savored the intent of the provider, the brooding, broad-faced man, who had spoken out so strongly for the plight of his fellow man. A voice out of kindness, not pity. Too many times in the past two years—yes, it had been that long since he'd been out on God's mission—had bounty been provided out of fearful pity. That sort says feed this man, perhaps it will not happen to me if I feed this man. Simple kindness, such as this big centurion had demonstrated, was more holy.

The bum sighed to himself as he finished his potatoes; there were things to do here. He dumped more ketchup on his plate and spooned it between his wind-chapped lips. Nutritious, he thought, I'll need strength here. He craned his neck to look outside once more. Yes, this is the place. Somewhere out there, somewhere near, he could feel the Devil's presence.

Finished, he gathered up the excess napkins taken from the holder and hesitated a moment. It was stealing, wasn't it? Yes.

35

God forgive me, he thought, and stuffed them in his other coat pocket. Small sins like this could be atoned for in time, there had been many along the way. But his true penance was yet to come.

Here, somewhere, *It* was here. He shuddered at the thought.

Through the kitchen service window he heard the waitress's voice berating the cook. It was time to move on. Slowly he looked outside and grimaced in anticipation of the cold wind; it cut into you here like a freezing straight razor.

He turned back to the serving counter, pulled out a small, worn missal, and began to pray. He prayed for the cook, the waitress, the kind policeman, and lastly he prayed for himself.

Finished, he craned his weathered neck once more and spotted the policeman, standing up on the bandbox, the wind having at him mercilessly. He was just standing there, staring at the municipal building, city hall. In a flash of insight the indigent was guided to understand that the man out there was part of his holy mission, too, so he smiled. He did not feel quite as lonely anymore.

# 2

The derelict had bothered him at the end, that enigmatic soul-flame rekindling briefly in his eyes, then dying as he turned back to his meal. Kyle let the thought drop out of his mind. He was standing on the bandbox, trying to ignore the cold wind harassing his back and light another cigarette at the same time. He gave up and walked toward city hall. It was fifteen before ten and he was starting to get The Jitters. The Jitters was one of Leo's euphemisms for any situation when all signs were go, but something undefined made you nervous. The Jitters, and Kyle had them, with a modifier: he thought he knew what was wrong—himself. He just wasn't ready for the responsibility, not yet.

He found a telephone booth just outside city hall and closed the door, locking the frigid wind outside, then dropped a quarter in the slot and lit a cigarette. When the operator came on he billed the call to his home telephone. He waited a minute while the earpiece whistled and chattered its electronic jargon, then made the connection and started the ringing. The secretary picked up on the second ring: "Chief Brumagin's office." Her voice was crisp and cheery.

"Hi, Gladys, this is Kyle, is Leo there?"

"Maybe, Kyle. Don't I get a 'hello,' a 'how-are-you'? or have you got a new girl instead of me? Nifty Sixty and rearing to—"

"If I tell your hubby that, he'll nifty-sixty my behind, Gladys."

"Small price to pay for a vintage wine, Kyle."

Kyle chuckled. "When I get back, I promise."

"Promises, promises. I'll get the chief for you. Hold on, handsome."

A few seconds later Leo picked up: "What's up, Rookie?"

Kyle smiled at the nickname. Leo had been calling him that since Kyle had been a rookie and Leo a sergeant at Hollenbeck for what seemed a lifetime ago. If Kyle were in Leo's office right now, he knew what he would be facing. Leo held to his styles. Right now he was in his telephone chat position, leaning back in his brown padded desk chair, held there by both small feet, a cigar tucked in that wide mouth, and staring at the little pattern of holes in the ceiling squares.

A feeling of comfort eddied over Kyle.

"I've got The Jitters, Leo, with a capital J."

"You know the rules, Kyle," said Leo, his tone going deep with concern. His elbows would be on his desk now, the cigar out of his mouth and cocked to the side in his right hand. "You wouldn't be there if I didn't think you could do it."

"I'm not sure that I can," Kyle said.

"You can do anything I tell you you can do. Who knows you better than your own mother, Rookie?—Leo the Magnificent, that's who, and don't forget it."

Kyle said nothing. That was Leo's warm-up, the pitch was to follow, and it wouldn't do any good to try to interrupt.

"Did you prepare?" he asked.

"Yes," Kyle said, "I've been here three days—and I've researched this town from one end to the other, I've got its history down, its commerce, the demographics—"

"What about questions? Did you do your homework, in front of the mirror, like I taught you?"

"Yes, I did." Kyle felt like a little boy being questioned by his older brother. One of the things Leo had taught him about interviews, or review boards, or any kind of panel discussion, was to think up your own questions beforehand and do a little rehearsing. Kyle had done that, practicing until he could deliver a good cogent answer to any question that he was likely to be asked without it appearing to be rehearsed.

"If you're prepared, scoped out the joint, and played question-question, what's the problem, Kyle? You scared?"

"Shit, yes." Kyle paused, and watch a piece of newspaper roll by in the wind. City hall stood there, not a hundred feet away. "I couldn't ask myself one question, Leo." The man on the other end was silent, waiting. "I couldn't find an answer for . . . for the Tragedy, Leo. What about the Tragedy, if they know, I mean? Do they know? I can talk to you about it, but I—I—I can't talk with a stranger about that. I—I don't think I'm ready yet, Leo, and Christ, that resume, even a barnyard dolt is going to spot something fishy when he reads the reason for leaving the department."

Kyle let the last word hang and was silent. Leo had written the resume, and it had been his idea to give that reason for leaving. Leo was an assistant chief, in charge of personnel; it was he who had gotten Kyle to resign, and it was he to whom any inquiries about his service record would be processed.

"It's a flimsy excuse, the way it was meant to be, Kyle. Since when do you question me about getting things done, huh? Who pulled you out of Woodhaven, boy? Who?"

"My, God. Do they know about Woodhaven?"

"If they knew about Woodhaven, you wouldn't be interviewing today, Rookie!" Leo's voice was heated. Now he would be chewing on his cigar. "Nobody knows about the Tragedy but the mayor; I had to tell him about that, Rookie. That excuse for resigning was meant to be seen through, you big baboon; then, when I talked with Neil and he saw through it, I explained the circumstances—"

"The Tragedy . . ."

"It worked for you, not against you. Compassion. The man had compassion for you. Listen, I went to college with Neil Gathers. He's uglier than shit, and used to getting his own way. He's a politician, Kyle, just like the assholes we've got here. But Christ, the devil himself would have a hard time not feeling compassion after what happened to you. The Tragedy got you that job if you want it and don't fuck it up. You're prepared, so the only thing standing between you and it is *you*, Rookie!"

"If he mentions the Tragedy, I can't handle it—"

"I think you can," stated Leo simply. End of conversation, but Kyle pressed it.

"You're not me, Leo."

"Look." His voice became patient, suddenly calm like the air in the absence of a sudden gust of wind. "As long as he knows the reason for the phony excuse, he can accept it. It's a sensitive point with you, and it would be rude to bring it up. He wants you, Kyle. You've got everything he needs to make his town safe. He needs you."

That thought touched Kyle's soft spot, and if anyone else had said it Kyle would have questioned it, but Leo was a straight shooter, especially about police work. He would never have set Kyle up for the interview if he did not believe Kyle was ready to take on the job.

"What about Woodhaven?" Kyle asked softly.

"Taken care of, Kyle." Leo's tone indicated that he knew he had reached Kyle. "Nobody but you and Dr. LeClerc know who you really were there. Nobody can find out; I covered it, Kyle."

"You really think I'm ready, Leo?"

"Transitory psychosis, isn't that what the doctor said, brought on by stress—the Tragedy was the greatest kind of stress, Kyle. You went to the edge, but didn't fall in—"

"I almost fell in—"

"They wouldn't have wanted you to fall in."

Kyle's heart rose suddenly in his throat at the intimation of their names: the image of blood and mutilation appeared in his mind, and the smells, cloying gushing blood, the porcine smell of human flesh burning. The sound of snakes hissing swelled in Kyle's mind. Tragedy, think Tragedy, he ordered himself, and the hissing sounds diminished, then finally stopped.

Kyle fought his hearts pounding until it subsided, saying nothing. Leo was silent too. No doubt he was thinking he had come too close. Damned right, too. Leo had made the rule and now he had broken it. He had been the one who had checked Kyle into the Woodhaven Sanitarium in Alberta, the one who had flown up to Woodhaven when the time was right and whispered in Kyle's ear, *"Tragedy.* Forget everything and use that word. That's the only thing you have to think of when thinking about what happened. Anything that had to do with that, think, and see, the word 'Tragedy,' and it'll take the charge off of it," he had said; and Kyle, unsure at first, did just that, and slowly his depression lifted, his psychosis transmuted next to a recurrent dream, a nightmare, but he could handle that. Then one day, Leo had come and taken him back to Los Angeles and set him up in a guest house of some friends in the San Fernando Valley. That had been almost a year ago. And Kyle had gotten better, a lot better, and in his heart he knew that he was ready to do battle, ready to work again. The dream would cease in time . . .

As if reading his mind, Leo asked, "How 'bout the dreams?"

"I haven't had the dream since I've been here," said Kyle, realizing as he spoke that for the first time in almost a year he had slept three nights in a row without the night terror of that dream.

"That's great, Kyle! Now, that is a definite sign, Rookie. A goddamned definite sign. Didn't Dr. LeClerc say it was natural and that it would go away after a while!"

"Yeah," Kyle said, a little puzzled that until now he had not been conscious of the absence of the dream in the three days that he had been studying the town; it was if he were meant to be here. "You know, Leo, if I really think about it, it's pretty nice, here—"

"They need a man with your qualifications, Rookie."

Kyle swallowed. How do you tell a man like Leo that you love him? "A night doesn't go by, Leo, that I don't thank God you're my friend."

Leo would be back in his telephone chat position by now, and when he spoke it was with all the modesty of Muhammed Ali—"Leo the Magnificent, that's what they call me, Rookie,

41

Leo the Magnificent. Now, you get the attitude, and go in there and mow 'em down."

Kyle checked his watch, two minutes to ten. "Yeah, Leo. Gotta go now."

"You're better than you think."

"Gotta go, Leo, and thanks again."

"Piece of cake, kid," and Leo hung up.

Kyle recradled the receiver, opened the door, and stepped into the gusting wind, heading for city hall confident that he could take this one . . . as long as no one mentioned the Tragedy.

# 3

Edgar Griffith knew that the city government had become corrupt when Mayor Gathers had come to power seven years ago. That is why Edgar had read Kyle Richards's resume at least four times each day since last Wednesday. Mayor Gathers had personally delivered it to *The Review*, slapping it down on Edgar's desk with a pleading, "This is our man, Edgar. We're lucky to get him, if we can get him. Don't scare him off, huh?" This was Monday. That made it twenty times read. He started to read it again.

"Got something there, Edgar?" asked the mayor from the center of the long, curved oak bench that served in common the four-member city council. His voice echoed slightly around the old town hall, accentuating the blank emptiness of the pews.

Edgar looked up, puzzled. "Pardon?"

"The envelope." The mayor nodded toward the manila envelope that lay on the press table an inch from Edgar's arm. The other members of the council, Old Judge Baxter, Jack Lewis, and Leia Conway, ceased whatever they were doing in midmotion and looked at Edgar.

"At the proper time," he said, thinking that the mayor had tipped his hand when he had personally delivered the resume. It meant three things: one, the mayor really wanted Kyle Richards; two, the mayor had confidence that the resume was flawless; and three, the mayor recognized the power of the press, Edgar's newspaper, *The Review*. *The Review* had put the kibosh on more than one of his pet projects. The fact that

43

Edgar himself was covering the interview instead of one of his reporters let the mayor know that Edgar had more than a passing interest in the hiring of a new police chief. Edgar knew that if the press's right to be present at affairs such as this was not ensured by law in the city charter, the mayor would have "closed-door'd" the whole affair.

"If it has bearing on this interview, the proper time is now, Edgar." The mayor's voice boomed through the large room.

The old newspaperman simply placed one finger on the envelope as if to hold it against the wind of the mayor's voice.

A blotchy red colored the mayor's face. He was a big man whose shape reminded Edgar of a giant Pillsbury doughboy, but whose face resembled an anemic blowfish, a nose too short and turned up for its face, and puffed cheeks, a small mouth with protruding, fat little lips. His black hair was styled in a prim way, the dry look attempted at age forty-seven without much success. And his eyes? Cold, fish eyes that could silence and chill people with a glance. Few people could stare into his eyes without succumbing to the urge to look away.

Edgar Griffith could stare into the mayor's face until the cows came home, didn't bother him. He'd faced many a fat-cat son of a bitch as a reporter on the *Chicago Sun-Times*, from politicians to blood-loving gangsters; he could always look them straight in the eyes and ask them the questions that had to be asked, no matter what the consequences. Of course it had gotten damn hairy at times, but that came with the territory.

"Edgar," said the mayor, "I've gone to a lot of work and sweat to get this man to even *consider* taking this job. If you harass him off . . ." the mayor began waving a long, fat finger at him, stopping short of making a threat, ". . . it will . . . it will damn well show what I've been trying to point out to you: that you are unconscionably contentious, and counterproductive to the good and well-being of this community at large."

Edgar smiled up at the mayor, a predatory smile. "Can I quote you on that, Neil?"

The mayor snorted indignantly, and stabbed again at Edgar with his finger. "That was off the record and you know it. This is an interview session of the city council and that interview has not started. Off the record, Edgar." The mayor pulled in his finger and sat back.

Edgar sighed. He had enough friends and supporters in this town that he was a man to be reckoned with, and a quote like that, published in *The Review*—which he owned—would start a row county wide; bad for the mayor. Edgar knew that the mayor had looked into starting a rival paper, but the costs were prohibitive. *The Review* had been in existence since the late days of the last century, in the Griffith family for the last fifty years. (After Edgar had worked out his need for big-time experience and excitement in Chicago, he had come home to take over the family business back in 1964, when his father had retired. He had been editor ever since.) "Oh, for God's sakes, Edgar," said old Judge Baxter, "Keep it clean. Keep it . . ." The ancient jurist's words hung in the air, and his left hand, which had made palsied circular motions while he spoke, froze in a wrinkled claw. He had forgotten what he was going to say.

How the old man was reelected every term was beyond Edgar. He nodded patronizingly at the white-haired old man and turned back to the resume.

He had mixed thoughts on the man this resume represented. Everything was right, too right. He had been able to tell that the first time he had read it—this man, Kyle Richards was perfect, a perfect policeman. Perfect for the town; too damn perfect: a war hero, bronze star with oak-leaf clusters, Vietnam, 1964; returned from service 1965, entered UCLA in the fall of that year, graduating spring, 1969, with a B.A. in History, and had gone immediately into the Los Angeles Police Academy. He had been a model officer, and was promoted very rapidly. He had numerous citations for bravery and competence, and the letters of reference that were attached to the resume spoke in glowing terms about Kyle Richards—there

45

were even letters signed by the mayor of Los Angeles, and the chief of police.

Edgar had one question, though: If Kyle Richards was so damned perfect, what the hell was he doing here, in a small town like Briggs City, looking for a job?

This question, mingled with a distrust of the mayor, made Edgar telephone his old friend, David Cornish, a reporter for the *L.A. Times* and ask him to go through the clips and see if he had anything on Richards. Two days later, last Friday, when Edgar had gone home to Clarice's tuna casserole, he'd found a manila envelope sitting in his plate where his dinner should have been. Edgar pulled out a wad of Xeroxed clippings held together by a huge silver paper clip. David Cornish had attached a handwritten note about Kyle Richards: *Good w/press,* it read, a stroke in Richards's favor. The majority of the clippings (so many for just one officer) had substantiated what was touted in the resume, but an article near the last clip had headlines and could be what he was looking for. He'd blinked hard one time and read the article. The details were gruesome and he'd held them back from Clarice. After dinner, he'd told her, "Grisly business. Grisly." Clipped to the back of the article were a few more follow-up pieces that Edgar read hastily and compared with what he did know about Kyle Richards. The dates were the important thing.

Still, after it was all over, Edgar wondered, why hadn't Richards gone back to LAPD to work? Why was he here instead? Could that be the flaw? A flaw in the perfect policeman? Couldn't handle it when—

A rear door opened, and his niece Michele entered and waited for him at the back. Edgar was puzzled until he was halfway down the aisle and Michele held up a small case— blood-pressure medicine.

Didn't she make a picture, though? Pretty woman, in her early thirties, honey-colored hair and blue eyes.

"Aunt Clarice said to tell you that you would forget your

head if it wasn't attached," Michele said, and handed him the case.

"You're gonna be late," cautioned Edgar.

"I *own* the store, Unk. I can't be late." She looked past his shoulder. When does the interview start?"

"A few minutes."

She leaned forward, and spoke softly: "Aunt Clarice said you were being paranoid again."

"I'm not paranoid," he said quietly. "The facts are that in the last seven years since the mayor's been in office, the city council has become a rubber stamp for him. Even the feisty members have succumbed. A lot of questionable things have happened that you are not aware of, Michele. With Chief Nelson murdered, Gathers has lost one of his all-time flunkies—now, he brings in a sterling candidate that appears flawless, and I'm naturally suspicious."

Michele grinned. "What you're saying is, because the mayor is for him, you're against him."

"I've never known the mayor to hire a man he didn't own. And this man Richards reads like a white knight."

"Maybe he is, Unk. Maybe the mayor just wants what's best."

"I'll be fair, Michele. But if there's a chink in his armor, I'm going to find it. Now run along." Edgar pointed to a side door. "Go that way. And then straight out the exit. You may still make it to work on time . . ."

"Bye," she said, and left, while Edgar went back up to the press table and sat down.

He glanced at the large round clock on the opposite wall. It read ten o'clock. The double doors at the rear of the hall opened with an echoing sound. Kyle Richards entered. He faced the council, smiling warmly.

Edgar thought wryly to himself that he was about to meet the one man in the world who could pick a fist fight with Godzilla and walk away the winner. He picked up the envelope

47

before him and put it in his pocket. He knew everything that he had to know to ask the questions that would satisfy himself that hiring this man was indeed serving the best interest of the public.

He watched Kyle Richards start down the aisle toward the council bench.

# 4

As Kyle pushed open the double doors and stepped in onto the carpet of the large hearing hall, he felt himself come alive.

Leo was right, he thought. All I need is to get back on the firing line.

He listened for the snakes from his dream that, even when he was conscious sometimes, hissed into his thoughts. They were silent, all but forgotten. Kyle moved in his medium now, fueled with confidence, ready for battle.

The council room, like many he had been in since he joined the police department, reeked of organizational officialdom. On either side of the long, curved bench, holding the four members of the Briggs City Council, stood the traditional banners: the American flag on the left, and that of the State of California on the right, adding a dash of color to the dreary room. Raised on a dais the council members sat at the bench. The path leading to these superhumans was an aisle bordered by twenty rows of oak benches, like pews in some old-time church. The same worn, wine-red carpet that Kyle stood on now paved the aisle. Oak paneling skirted the four walls, and the portion above that was painted an off-white aging toward yellow.

Three men and a woman sat behind the bench. To the side, manning a short table at a right angle to the council, sat a small elderly man, whose function Kyle couldn't determine at this point.

It's all the same, reflected Kyle, no matter where you go, no matter what the scale, it's all the same. And suddenly he felt very comfortable, and exhilarated. He wanted this. He needed this—so badly that he knew he would fight bare-knuckled to get the job.

He strode up the blood-colored carpet to the bench and Mayor Gathers. Before he had reached the back row of benches the mayor stood, raising his hands: "Welcome, welcome, Commander Richards." Kyle's face did not change, but he knew from the tent-show-barker pep of the mayor's voice that he was wanted by this town; wanted in the worst way. Leo must have really done a job on the mayor, Kyle thought. He was close enough now to read the black plastic sign in front of the old man at the side table: Press.

"Come right up," the mayor urged. "Step right up. Yes, sir, right up here."

The mayor reached down over the bench to shake hands. "Neil Gathers, Captain. Leo Brumagin has told me all about you."

Kyle reached up and grasped the offered hand. The mayor's grip was firm, hinting of surprising strength in those long, chubby fingers. He looked into Gathers's face, found the man's eyes disquieting, so he reverted to the policeman's trick of looking "through" a person's face to some imaginary point in the back of his head—a gaze that neither challenged nor looked away.

The mayor introduced the council, starting with the judge and working across the board to the opposite end. Kyle unobtrusively studied each of the faces as he shook their hands: Judge Baxter was a grape, he decided, the telltale thin river-delta lines of blue and pink veins across the nose and cheeks a dead giveaway. The judge simply nodded, and Kyle moved over to the next man, who smiled guiltily—Jack Lewis, a lawyer, he was told. He crossed in front of the mayor and took the hand of a black-haired attractive woman in her early forties, "Leia Conway," the mayor said. "She's one of our most successful realtors here in Briggs City." The woman flushed when he took her hand, and he thought he saw a touch

50

of yearning in her eyes, an invitation, perhaps. Kyle smiled warmly, broke hand contact. She sure beats the waitress, he thought, and walked the eight feet over to the press section.

The man stood to meet him. "This is Edgar Griffith, the publisher of *The Review*," Mayor Gathers announced. Kyle thought he caught a snag in the mayor's voice. The man's face bore an uncanny resemblance to Popeye the Sailor, an aging Popeye, with 1957 spectacles. Kyle met the man's inquisitive blue eyes. Griffith's grip was formal. "A pleasure," he said, his voice as thin as copy paper. Something about this man brought Kyle's guard up. As he turned back to the podium, he thought; *keep an eye on this one.*

The mayor waited as Kyle gained the podium, following his movement with smiling admiration. Once Kyle stepped behind the lectern and faced the council, the mayor said, "I believe in honesty, Commander Richards. So let me be perfectly honest with you. All of us here"—he spread his long arms out like tentacles, his head moving slowly from left to right, and then back to Kyle again—"are very impressed, and pleased, I might add, to have you here today. Your record is outstanding"—he smiled generously—"and my old and trusted friend, Underchief Leo Brumagin, assures me that you are the best of the best; and that is exactly what we are looking for here in Briggs City. Let me assure you, Commander, that Briggs City is a thriving, growing community, and that it deserves the best of the best.

"Now . . ." He paused and settled back with a magnanimous expression into the black imitation leather of his chair. "Of course, Commander, there are a few routine questions that must be asked. I hope that you will bear with us." The mayor looked down at a buff-colored folder on his desk. "Let's see, it says here that . . ." and the questions began.

Thirty minutes later Kyle decided that the mayor's adjective "routine" was nice, but "whitewash" would have been a more accurate choice. The questions followed his resume: military service, schooling, his entry into the LAPD and his ad-

51

vancement; and had all the depth of cheap veneer, pointing only to his strong points and ignoring any probe that might uncover a ragged edge. It was too easy, and things too easy bothered Kyle. Each of the questions was carefully constructed to make the most out of the information given on his resume.

When they got to Reason for Leaving; "to write a book, on policemen, American policemen," the mayor displayed glowing admiration for this goal, deeming it both worthy and generous, "showing Kyle's concern for the brotherhood of policemen of this great nation." He asked if Kyle had finished the book yet. Kyle said no and braced himself for the obvious question, the question that Kyle and anyone else would have asked who was giving thoughtful consideration to hiring Kyle. Instead, the mayor commended him, commenting that it was a true mark of a leader that the commander just could not stay "out of the saddle," that he just had to get back into action, "the telling quality of a true public servant."

Edgar Griffith cleared his throat at this and all eyes turned to him. He raised his hand in apology. "Sorry," he said, "a little congestion," but his gaze lingered skeptically on Kyle.

The mayor began another glowing oratory about Kyle, with all the intonations and pacing of a man summing up a favorable decision. Kyle listened politely, noting the things that he had learned during this interview. There was no doubt who the Big Boss was here. Mayor Neil Gathers had asked most of the questions. After Kyle's reply, and the mayor's inevitable favorable remark, Judge Baxter would nod, Jack Lewis would emit a throaty, "Yes, yes," and Leia Conway would say, "Impressive. Yes, impressive," in a warm, coddling manner. The only dissent radiated from the side of the bench—Kyle kept catching it out of the corner of his eye. The newspaper editor did not, or, Kyle imagined, was not allowed to ask questions. But this did not deter him from expressing disapproval of the proceedings. He sat forward, his hands clasped together, his forearms resting on the table, his eyes darting from one speaker to the next. A lipless frown arched his mouth.

Kyle knew that his former self would have felt a touch of contempt for the mayor's syrupy charade of an interview. Even now there was a small taste of it in the back of his throat. An interview was to judge a man, ask him those questions that brought out his weaknesses so that it might be determined if they would disqualify him for the position. But Kyle felt a crosscurrent of relief, too. He needed this job. Needed it to maintain his sanity. If it was whitewash, he would take it and be thankful.

The mayor was concluding, looking left and right at his peers: ". . . then, if there are no further questions, I think—"

"I have questions, Mr. Mayor." The newspaper editor's voice sliced to the bench.

The mayor sucked air. "Edgar, first of all, you have a legal right to be present, but not to question the applicant. Secondly, I think it's clear in everyone's mind the competence and character of Commander Richards here. I really don't think—"

"What's on my mind, Neil, is the competence and character of some of the members of this council . . ."

The mayor jerked back as if slapped in the face. A hostile murmur rose from the other members on the bench. Kyle turned and faced the editor, a small, wary smile on his lips. Warning bells rang in his head.

The editor continued, ignoring the outrage of the council. He turned to Kyle. "Now, Mr. Richards, do you mind answering a few more questions, and I'm afraid you're going to find that these have a little more grist to them."

"More than happy to answer any questions that you might have, Mr. Griffith, grist and all." Kyle realized he *didn't* mind. Edgar's challenge was rekindling an old fire—confrontation in debate. Adrenaline streamed through his body, exhilarating him. He would tear the editor apart if he had to, but he could still admire a man who spots bullshit and calls it bullshit.

"Commander, you do not have to answer this man's questions; and, Edgar, I warn you . . ." The mayor's threat hung for a moment, long enough for Kyle to interject, "Mr. Mayor, I have nothing to hide. Mr. Griffith, please, feel free, I understand the needs of the press."

The old man nodded in approval. He glanced down at the resume, the neon lighting gleaming on his pink, freckled scalp. He looked up suddenly, his blue eyes boring into Kyle.

"First of all, let me welcome you. As the mayor has said, your record does speak for itself, and it is a pleasure to have you here." He spoke in an earnest, businesslike tone. His eyes never wavered from Kyle's.

"I trust your drive down here this morning has not tired you out too much?"

Kyle saw at once that it was a question that was asked to be answered. "My drive up was quite enjoyable, thank you." He smiled, leaving out the fact that he'd come up three days ago.

"Good . . . the thought that runs through my head when reading your resume, Mr. Richards, is here is a very competent, brave man, who's been promoted as fast if not faster than humanly possible, who has everything going for him, an obvious career ahead of him, perhaps that of chief of police of one of the finest police forces in the country, say, one day in the future, and that same individual *quits*, and for what reason? Not to move on to an equally prestigious position, or, say, to take over the reins of a financial empire left by inheritance, but *quits* to write a *book?*" The old man brought the last word up in pitch and left it sitting there for a few seconds, then, answering his own question, he said, "I think not. No, no, I think not. Now, please, Mr. Richards, for the benefit of everyone, shed some light on your departure from the LAPD."

The man was good, Kyle gave him that, and whatever it was he was planning had yet to show its ugly head, so Kyle stood firm. "I have four chapters written, if you wish to see them, Mr. Griffith." Not an untruth, Kyle had been planning to write a book for the longest time; that is what had given Leo the idea to use that on the resume, having all the earmarks of a great lie, the mingling of truth with fiction.

"Four chapters in eighteen months? Please, Mr. Richards, that is taxing credibility."

Kyle forced a light, almost condescending laugh. "The research in such a task is no small matter, Mr. Griffith."

Griffith sighed, reaching in the inside pocket of his jacket, retrieving a manila envelope. "In here"—he waved the envelope slightly in Kyle's direction—"I have copies of news clippings that speak very highly of your career, Mr. Richards." He stopped and laid the envelope down on the desk; his voice became low and conciliatory, the expression on his face changing to one of a man very much opposed to what he must say next. "Please excuse the following, Mr. Richards. What I want you to understand . . . let me change that . . . what I know you understand, having been a public servant yourself, is that it is a job fraught with serious responsibilities, including making sure that those that join our ranks are indeed qualified to serve the people; and when we find one flaw, it is necessary to look even deeper to make sure that there are no others. Please excuse me, but I have in these news clippings the reports about a tragic event in your life, the brutal . . ." He hesitated here, looking up at the council as if he could barely bring himself to say it. ". . . the brutal murder of your wife and daughter . . ."

*You fucking asshole!*

". . . and isn't it a fact that this tragedy was the cause for your leaving the department . . ."

*I'll rip your fucking throat out and shove it down that big hole of a mouth of yours!*

". . . and that tragedy was just too much to bear?"

*Fucking asshole!*

"Edgar, that is enough!" shouted the mayor.

"My God, Edgar!" Jack Lewis said.

"Keep it clean, for God's sake, Edgar," Judge Baxter warned.

55

All that the woman was able to utter was a shocked "ooh-oohing" sound.

The outbursts allowed Kyle time to regain his mental and physical composure. Kyle's body screamed to be let loose, to trample the small man, but years of training held him fast. His scalp at the back of his head seemed to tighten, shrinking, pulling his scalp back, while the skin under his chin seemed to tighten too—his face stretched taut like parchment. He heard the hissing of the snakes, rising in a crescendo, writhing in a frenzy in the branches of that tree, the flicker of their tongues actually touching his brain like light passes of the scent of death. But the council's outrage had broken that image. Kyle, still hot, came in on the mayor's words: ". . . bringing up that is irrelevant, Edgar. Completely irrevelent, and inexcusable. It was a tragedy, Edgar, not to be mentioned!"

The word *Tragedy* erased the image of the snakes as if by magic. Tragedy. That's what this old fart of a newspaperman was talking about. What Leo would have said whispered through his mind: "Kyle, you've handled a lot tougher. So talk to the man. Make him look bad. You're good at that."

Kyle opened his mouth, and it was as if someone else were speaking, someone distant from himself: "Mr. Griffith, let us cut to the bone, please. It is your main concern—and correct me if I am wrong—that the . . . that the tragedy that occurred in my life will adversely affect my performance as chief of police, is that not correct?"

The old man, flushed slightly from the outburst of the council, nodded his head. "Basically, yes—"

"Fine. Let me assure you that a tragedy such as that is not a pleasant thing, nor an easy thing to have in one's past, especially if one is a policeman. And yes, you will have to forgive my not going into detail on the resume about that tragedy, and yes, it did adversely affect my performance on the job—*but not so anyone but myself would notice,* Mr. Griffith, as you know by the newspaper clippings concerning my resignation!

56

"There, in the clippings, which you have not seen fit to share with the members of this body for whatever reasons of your own, lies your answer, Mr. Griffith: What they say is that I resigned, not in disgrace, but in honor. There was a certain speculation that the tragedy might be the cause, but no one knew for sure because everything seemed normal to them. *I* was the one who made the decision. *I* was the one that recognized the problem and took corrective measures—and I can assure you that that was the most difficult decision of my life. I had already lost the two things most precious to me—my wife and daughter. Then I had to face the fact that I could no longer serve the community and my men in the manner that they deserve. It ripped my very heart out to decide that I must step down, but I did it!"

From the corner of his eye, Kyle saw that the council was frozen in awe. It gave him a rush of confidence. "Any man who can make that kind of decision, Mr. Griffith, can make a sound judgment as to when he is fit to return to work!"

The mayor beamed. "I think that settles that!"

The council assented as a body.

Kyle turned back to Griffith. "Any more questions?"

"Just one," Griffith said, his voice now thin and labored, obviously deflated by Kyle's speech. "Suppose, Mr. Richards, that right this minute, this very minute, you were offered the job. Would you take it?"

What was the old codger getting at? "With a satisfactory tour of police station under my belt, I would say yes without hesitation."

The man looked down at his clasped hands, then up briskly at Kyle. "I must confess that I am very suspicious of anyone who would take a job so quickly without careful consideration to where he would find himself living after not one, but we would hope many, many years. It seems to me that perhaps you are grasping at this job, without taking a good look around you. After all, how much could you have seen in a ride through town this morning. Maybe you're just a little too eager for this job—"

"Mr. Griffith, I have been in town since Friday, and have had ample time to consider the living conditions here. They are far from harsh: the mountains for camping; a lake nearby for fishing; and an hour's drive or so for the beach. The people are pleasant. It could help me find a home away from painful memories. What is more important—and I say this with all humility—I am really quite good at my job; I love police work. I have no doubt, if I decide to do it, that I could serve your community with utter loyalty and pride."

Before Edgar Griffith could answer, the sound of the mayor pounding the bench top with his fist resounded through the room with glee. "Well said, well said!" He rose and walked behind the bench, past the newspaper editor, and up to Kyle. "The rest of you talk it over," he said over his shoulder, guiding Kyle toward the rear of the door, "you can call me over at the police station. I already know what my vote is going to be. He's the one for me."

He turned his attention to Kyle. "Chief," he said, placing his hand on Kyle's shoulder as they walked, "let me give you a tour of the station like you wanted while these good people talk this over, and Edgar wipes the egg off of his face." He smiled sweetly at the newspaperman. Then, happy as hell that the old geezer hadn't found out the real skeleton in Kyle's closet, he led his applicant from the room.

# 5

Kyle walked the jail corridor alone, glad that the mayor had been called to the telephone. It gave him time to think. Would he take the job? Probably. It felt right. It felt better than sitting around doing nothing, although he already suffered a vague uneasiness around the mayor—a distrust. Nothing he couldn't handle, though.

Kyle reached out and touched the steel bars. Cold. Why did the bars always feel cold? He continued down the corridor. The jail was empty. The county bus must pick up the jailbirds early, he thought, or maybe in such a small town they just didn't have any arrests last night.

The tangy smell of disinfectant hit him as he reached the end of the row. He stepped past the last cell and looked down an offshoot hallway. The back door was propped open, and just inside the door a small black man put a mop into a bucket and leaned the handle against the wall. "There," he said to himself, then noticed Kyle.

"How are you doing?" said Kyle.

"Fine," he answered. "Gonna rain, though."

"Looked clear when I was out." Kyle admired the man's deep voice. But where the heck did it come from? The man was not taller than five feet, and looked bird-boned. His body seemed practically lost in his green jumpsuit.

"My knuckles hurt. Always rains when my knuckles hurt."

Kyle looked around. "You do a nice job," he said, and stuck out his hand. "My name's Kyle Richards."

"George Carver, but I'm called Coogle. He shook Kyle's

hand firmly, gazing at Kyle intently as if making some unknown point. "You the new chief everybody and his uncle's been talking about?"

"I'm deciding right now. What's it like living around here, anyway?"

"Okay, if you like quiet."

"I like quiet."

"You're gonna be real happy then," Coogle said, and smiled.

Something about the smile relaxed Kyle. He grinned back. "What you're saying is that it's *real* quiet around town."

Coogle nodded and pulled a small cigar from an inside pocket of his jumpsuit. He lit up, and Kyle asked him how long he'd worked for the city.

"I don't work for the city. I work for the mayor, Gathers Market. Loomis is sick today, and the mayor wanted the jail looking spiffy. So he told me to clean it up. I don't mind. I get paid for it."

"They'd never put somebody from the outside in like that in Los Angeles," said Kyle.

Coogle puffed on his cigar, and looked furtively past Kyle, as if someone might be listening. Satisfied, he said, "Just between you and me, Kyle: In this town, working for the city and working for the mayor is about the same thing. You know what I mean?"

Kyle said that he did, realizing that his own instincts about the mayor had been right. No problem, though. Los Angeles had its share of men like the mayor; dealing with their type came with the job.

Kyle heard approaching footsteps and stuck out his hand to Coogle. "Nice meeting you, Coogle. Hope to see you around."

Coogle shook his hand. "Mutual," he said.

"Well, Kyle"—the mayor's voice was jovial—"there you are. Got great news." He paused and gave a quick smile to Coogle. "Good job, Coogle. You can wrap it up now."

Kyle caught the flash of resentment in Coogle's face before the man turned away, walking toward the back door.

The mayor guided Kyle back into the main jail corridor, and stopped. He smiled. "It's yours if you want it."

"What was the vote?"

"Unanimous. You have the full support of the council. Besides, I'm police liaison for the council. Everything goes through me, anyway."

Now that it came down to it, there was really only one decision he could make. Christ, I need to work, he thought. I really need to get back into the action.

"Well," prompted the mayor.

"I'll take it," said Kyle.

The mayor's grin reminded Kyle of a shark.

# 6

The mayor asked Kyle to lunch with the rest of the city council, an affair that left no doubt in Kyle's mind that Mayor Neil Gathers ran the city. Although the other members spoke separately, the words all seemed to come from one mouth, the mayor's—Gatherisms, Kyle coined the phrase, biting the inside of his cheek to keep from laughing—that spoke of "Potential for Progress," "Growth," "Business Hub of the County—the State! in just a few years," and on and on, until Kyle thought, *Enough already*.

Perhaps their ramblings were caused by the liquor. Kyle noted that before the main course arrived, Judge Baxter and Leia Conway had sucked down two double gin-and-tonics each, causing the old jurist to slur his Gatherisms, and the real-estate broker to accent her opinions with openly seductive glances at Kyle. Jack Lewis glared at the two as if in pain, and took every opportunity to feed leading questions to the mayor in an apparent attempt to minimize the damage he thought the other two might do. The mayor sat stoically sipping his one martini, taking Jack Lewis's questions one at a time, engaging Kyle with his eyes as much as possible.

At the end of lunch Kyle thought, What the hell, he would take the ride as far as it went, and if it wasn't for him, he'd hop off. He'd be no worse off than he had been, that was certain. He made a mental note to call Leo when he got home and thank the short fat fart for pulling him out of the fire one more time.

It was raining when the mayor drove Kyle to his blue Ranger truck. Kyle agreed to start work in two weeks, and two o'clock in the afternoon he was driving home. Once out of Briggs City the rain fell off drastically, and by the time he pulled into his own driveway three and a half hours later, the early January darkness showed a cloudless, star-filled sky.

He called Leo right away, but no one answered, so he showered in welt-raising, hot water while drinking an ice-cold beer. He dressed, made a sandwich of bologna and cheese, and tried Leo's number again—still no answer. Must have a new girl, Kyle thought with a smirk, then was overcome with deep feelings of appreciation for the man—a guardian angel if God had ever made one, and a good friend.

Kyle tucked himself in bed by ten o'clock. For a while sleep consumed him in black, undreaming arms, and then he was standing in the entry hallway of his own home that godawful night two years ago, sickened by the smell of the blood and feces emanating from the living room. But this time he would not go in there. No, because it was too terrible to be lived again.

Instead he turned and entered the hallway closet and closed the door. Darkness prevailed for a second, then purple light radiated from above, and Kyle looked up and saw that the "sky" was in reality the top of the inside of his own skull. The purple light shone down through a membranous material webbed with vines. He realized the vines were blood vessels and capillaries, bright glowering red and dull throbbing blue, casting an ephemeral sheen over the ground.

Kyle looked down. Of course it wasn't ground. It was his own convoluted brain matter, shimmering purple, red, and blue light. He was walking on *his* brain. His shoes, flat black in the weird light, punched down as he walked, in rubbery steps that left slippery tracks behind him like smears in wet clay.

He saw that he was walking toward a gnarled black tree whose branches bore the writhing of a hundred hissing snakes, their bodies as thick as Kyle's leg.

Kyle felt himself being pulled closer and closer to the tree. The hissing grew in intensity. With horror, he realized the full implications: those snakes *were* the snakes of insanity, knotted

63

in a big tangle, dangling over his brain. If they were to become untangled, and fall, they would burrow into his brain and fester until the demons of insanity emerged and he was crazy forever, never to escape the way he had the first time.

He slogged forward, against his will, as if being pressed through invisible clay. The fear pressed in his chest. His body began to tremble as he approached and stood under the tree, near the massive knot of writhing serpents, that hissed *louder, louder, until he thought he could not stand it anymore! But as long as the snakes stay in the tree he'll be okay, because if they fall he'll go insaaa-nnnnnnnne!*

Kyle closed his eyes and suddenly felt relieved, and then thought that he would be okay . . . but when he opened his eyes giant hands appeared in front of him, folded, as if prayer. Then their gray fleshy fingers unfolded and reached up, untangling the snakes. First one, then another and another, so that they hung down from the tree limbs and dropped, slithering around until finding a nice convoluted fold and burrowing deep into his brain. And he began to scream because he could feel each one tunneling through his gray matter and driving him, bit by bit, totally, irrevocably insane . . .

He awoke to his screams filling the blackness of his bedroom, the howl of the insane and the damned. He was sopping wet with sweat, shuddering. Finally, when his shaking subsided, he staggered to the bathroom and dried himself with a thick crimson bath towel, then sat on the edge of his bed and began to cry. Tears came from the depth of his soul, because in that dream he'd recognized the hands that untangled the snakes of insanity and pulled them down.

They were his own hands.

## 7

After dropping off his newly acquired police chief, the mayor guided his silver Mercedes sedan through the thundering rain onto Main Street and drove to the eastern edge of the town proper to Gathers Corporation Boulevard. He turned right and drove on the corporate-owned road one half mile up a hill to a towering (by Briggs City standards) four-story building of smoked glass and black steel. A fractured spray of lightning cracked the dark potbelly of a cloud as he pulled into the parking lot. Slithering bolts of light reflected ominously in the windows of the block-shaped building like bursting capillaries in a demon's black eyes.

A curse rose in his throat when he saw that someone was parked in his parking place, then dissipated just as rapidly as the image of his Christa's little red Alfa Romeo Spider registered on his brain. Seventeen years old and just like her mother; how many times had he told her not to park in his space, and how many times had she said, "Yes, Daddy." Kids, thought the mayor and pulled into Leonard Phael's space. Let *him* take a walk.

The mayor danced through the rain, his briefcase flapping. He cursed himself for not having the foresight to have an umbrella in the car. He reached the lobby of the building at the time that his gray suit had dark freckles of rain drops evenly distributed over its surface. Instead of going up to the fourth floor to his office, he circled around a couple of corners until he came to an office marked Rentals. He opened it and stared at the young girl sitting behind the desk. Whatever anger he had managed to salvage dissolved under Christa's giggling. "Daddy, you look like a wet puppy." She covered her mouth, her brown bangs bouncing, mahogany eyes, large and searching her daddy up and down, cute face, pert sharp features, like her mother—thank God, like her mother. He had feared any of his children looking like him. Christa had escaped that fate, Little Neil had not. This job was a work/study through the school. Christa was a senior this year, USC in the fall, and that was going to cost a bundle.

"Christa Marie," he said, his voice lacking the sternness he wished, "how many times have I told you—"

"Not to park in your space, right, Dad?"

"That's right." What's a father to do?

She tilted her head down and stuck her lower lip out in mock sorrow. "It was going to rain; if I parked out in the lot I'd get soaked, Daddy, catch cold, maybe die even, and then you'd be sorry."

The mayor gave up. If he had a soft spot it was his kids and wife, and the very softest of that spot was sitting behind that small desk right in front of him.

"Tell your mother I'll be a little late tonight," he said just to change the subject.

"Okay, Dad." She was back entering checks and writing receipts before he had left the room.

The mayor took the elevator up to the fourth floor thinking that there was more to his business than his daughter knew, or that he would want her to know, for that matter. He had realized that it had to be that way when he had started out fifteen years ago to build his empire. They were playing hardball out there in the business world. Somebody was destined to win and somebody was going to lose. And that was fine with Neil Gathers as long as he was the one that was winning. It was true that he had built his multimillion-dollar empire "by hook and by crook," as he liked to say, and in the world of the Beast and the Sheep, he knew that he could never be the Sheep, no matter what the cost.

66

"Any messages?" he asked Lydia, his personal secretary. Her neatly coiffed gray hair complemented her blue two-piece skirt suit and white silk blouse—the epitome of Ward's catalogue fashion, as always. Her eyes were clear blue, her voice high and penetrating.

"Mr. Gathers, there are *always* messages." She smiled, holding up a handful of pink message slips, which he grabbed in passing. "No calls," he said, and closed the office door behind him.

He spent the rest of the day in the office administering his corporation, and by six o'clock he felt physically and emotionally drained. Lydia was long gone by five, and he had taken one telephone call, his wife, wondering why he would be late this evening. She had understood immediately when he'd answered "Work"; it had meant he was in a brooding mood; he knew it and she knew it, and she was sensitive enough to his needs to let it drop.

As the rain-pouring clouds fell under the black hand of night, his mood and thoughts turned dark. This mood came more frequently now, and for unknown reasons. He tried to sort this one out. It wasn't Edgar Griffith, although lately he was becoming much too much to bear. If his attack on Kyle Richards had cost the mayor his new police chief, then that would have been a different story. For a number of years now the mayor had been trying to get something on the old bastard, but Edgar Griffith was so damn clean it was inhuman.

The mayor believed in the motto Charles Colson, Richard M. Nixon's pal in the White House, had tacked up on his wall: "When you've got 'em by the balls, their hearts and minds will follow," and had used that philosophy with his takeover of the city council: Judge Baxter had a fancy for thirteen-year-old girls, and if anybody doesn't believe, behold! the mayor had pictures to prove it; Jack Lewis, embezzlement and fraud, the mayor had stepped in in the nick of time and saved a grateful Jack Lewis (the mayor often wondered if Jack Lewis would be so ingratiated to him if he knew that it was he, Neil Gathers, who, recognizing Jack's greedy nature, had purposely put too much temptation in the man's way—yes, he had him by the balls, too).

As for Leia Conway, she didn't have any balls (to the best of the mayor's knowledge), but she did have tits, and to borrow from another Watergate hero, John Mitchell, and paraphrasing a little, Leia Conway had gotten her tit caught in a big wringer—land-fraud scheme—and who was there to bail her out? Neil Gathers, of course. She'd given him a little trouble on the council up until then; after that, she'd been as docile as a kitten, and had turned to drink and screwing (discreetly as possible) as many men as she could find.

The mayor believed in research. Research on anybody could turn up something, and if not, you could manipulate the circumstances, or manufacture something on anybody. Anybody, that is, except Edgar Griffith—goddamn, he ran a tight ship!

In all the mayor's dealings over the past fifteen years, he'd maintained a visible yet silent asset in the person of Leonard Phael, who helped on the seamy side of matters in the rise of Neil Gathers's fortune from one grocery store to a multi-million-dollar enterprise.

By hook or by crook—Phael served as the operational end of the crook, and for this the mayor paid him well. He earned bonus payments too, for little "extras" like killing Buddy Nelson, the former police chief of Briggs City, who'd had some damn notion that he could put the squeeze on the mayor for some extra cash.

Once, the mayor had thought of having Edgar Griffith killed—his investigative reporting, a series of articles entitled "Who Really Owns Briggs City," nearly cost the mayor an election. But Griffith would be more trouble than he was worth dead; he'd turn up a damn martyr. And a frame on the old man would look too much like a frame. The mayor could live without that.

Thunder clapped, lightning wracked the sky, and the mayor moved from his huge, dark wood desk to the giant wall mural of Briggs City. The city limits on the mural were set out in a thick, money-green dashed line that showed the body of the city to be shaped like a closed fist with an index finger pointed east. That finger ran out some seven miles from the body of the fist, a long, thin, accusing stretch of land whose fingertip ended just past the large undeveloped acreage of David Pickers, the land that the mayor wanted for his new shopping center . . .

"That's it!" he said aloud, finding the cause of his depression: time was running out for the old man to sell. I need that land, the mayor thought.

He paced in frustration. He was a man of deadlines, and once one was fixed in his mind, he did whatever was necessary to meet that deadline. That finger of land was mostly farm and cattle land, dotted with oil wells; that accounted for that strip of land being included in the city limits: the city fathers of old weren't anybody's fools, and they'd recognized that they could tax oil wells within the city limits.

But the mayor's interests were not the oil wells; the land that he sought was twenty miles from Harristown, twenty-two from Evansville, and eighteen from Minnatta City. What he proposed to do was put in a large shopping center, a mall, with every name department store he could find, shops, movies of every kind, a true one-stop shopping center. Around this he planned eventually to have restaurants, motels, and industrial parks.

What this would do would be pull money into Briggs City from the other three towns. An average of twenty miles or so wasn't anything to drive—what? twenty minutes, twenty-five at the most. The kids could play, while the parents shopped. It would be the only mall within sixty miles, and it would be a money maker.

The mayor already had acquired the land that he needed, except for that acreage old crazy Dave Pickers owned. The

Pickers property was special land, because the mayor had his eye on it for the headquarters store for Gathers Foods. It was a dream that his dead father had had, to own a huge chain of supermarkets.

The headquarters store would be set away from the main mall by a half mile. It would have a huge warehouse space and be a model store. From there the buying for future stores opening first countywide, then statewide, then nationwide, would be done.

And where that model headquarters store would be built, was right on Dave Pickers's land. That's the way the mayor saw it and that's the way it was going to be. The old man was going to sell one way or another.

The lightning slashed the night sky again, then the thunder. The mayor thought he might need Phael on this one, though a new consideration was in the picture, Kyle Richards—he was nobody's fool. But then again, neither was Neil Gathers: his old friend Leo Brumagin hadn't pulled the wool over his eyes, not at all.

The mayor had hired one of the best Los Angeles private investigators, a former LAPD detective, and with some digging the man had found out all about Kyle Richards. The investigation included a trip to Canada, and a discreet talk with the doctor in charge. Kyle Richards was recovering. He was okay. God, wouldn't any man go nuts over a thing like that?— the mayor understood that, right off: he loved his kids and wife, and if what happened to Kyle's family had happened to his, he would've gone nutso, too. God, how gruesome.

So if anything the mayor was sympathetic, and all that he cared about was that he was getting a Super Cop who could turn Briggs City's force into a professional, crack police force. As for the temporary mental setback, well, the doctor said that Kyle was fine, and functional. But the joy to the mayor was that Kyle Richards obviously wouldn't want that stint at Woodhaven revealed.

And the mayor knew how to use that information.

Woodhaven would never come up, unless it was really needed. He knew that with a man like Kyle Richards, it was best to have him by the balls without him knowing it until it was time to squeeze them—then, squeeze 'em real hard, and the chief's heart and mind would follow, anywhere the mayor wished to lead.

# 8

Less than two weeks after Kyle had accepted the job, he moved to Briggs City, arriving on Tuesday. He picked up the key and address from Councilwoman Leia Conway's real estate office, and, feeling the first real sense of adventure since the tragedy, drove off toward his newly rented three-bedroom house, his blue Ford Ranger truck stuffed and lumbering under the weight of his post-sanitarium possessions (comprised mainly of history books, a few pots and pans, clothing, and his weight-training set).

He drove up the gently sloping street, admiring the walnut trees lining the road. Three-seventy-five Eskay Street. Easy enough to remember and to find. Small town, Kyle thought to himself, and that was fine with him.

He was pleased with the house. It was one story, with a shake roof, redwood siding, white trim, and an expansive front porch enclosed by a low white railing all around. The sight of it brought pictures of rocking chairs and old creaking porch swings to mind. The yard was freshly mown, green with the February rains, and fenced in by red brick and black wrought iron. Kyle guided his packed truck up the cement drive, stopping before becoming flush with the house. The garage was set separately, at the end of the drive, in back of the house, and if Kyle's guess was correct that backyard was nice and big. When Leia Conway had called and offered the house to rent she had said that he would like it. He had taken it sight unseen, and Leia's choice of homes for him confirmed one thing in his mind: whatever else Leis Conway may be, she was a damned good judge of houses.

Kyle sprang from the truck, walked around to the front of the house, and grinned at it. Perfect. The smell of the new-cut lawn rose in his nose; he took in a deep breath of it just for the flavor. His eyes feasted on the house for a moment, then he mounted the short flight of steps to the porch and let himself in with the key. The living room was large, white, with a powder-blue carpet. Kyle's eyes were first drawn to the brick fireplace, then to the white telephone sitting on top of an amazingly thin telephone book.

He moved further into the room to get the feel of the place and noticed that near the telephone, printed on the same yellow paper as his address had been written on, was a message:

> Kyle,
>     I took the liberty of having the power turned on and a telephone (unlisted) installed. Please give me a call if there is anything else I can do.
>                         Leia
>     P.S. Call if you need company, too. I'm in the book (and on my card).

Kyle looked at the business card that he had picked up along with the note. Leia's home number was on that, too.

"No thanks, Leia," he said out loud, and the echo made him jerk his head up.

The dining room ran freely from the living room, but Kyle's real delight came from the many-windowed, sunny bright kitchen. It was long and narrow with a breakfast nook, bathed in sunlight whitened by sheers, and speckled in yellow and white tile.

At least he would have somewhere to eat, thought Kyle, admiring the positioning of the nook. He had no kitchen table. He had decided against having his old furniture taken out of storage. Too many memories, and too much chance of those nightmares coming again.

73

He stopped a minute in the dancing sparkle of the kitchen, reflecting on that last and, he hoped, final nightmare, the one that he had had the night he returned from the interview. The most remarkable thing about that one was that the next morning he didn't remember it in detail at all, and he had not had another one since.

The slap of the morning paper against his front door awoke Kyle on Friday. Kid's a damn good shot, he thought as he raised up on his elbows out of his brown sleeping bag to investigate the noise. He did a quiet double take as his head cleared and he remembered that he hadn't ordered the paper.

"Leia," he muttered, throwing the unzipped half of his sleeping roll off and standing up in his Fruit of the Looms in the middle of the living room. Last night he had opted for the living room for his sleeping place, the carpeting more inviting as a mattress than the hardwood floor of the bedroom. Debris of a night's reading lay around his bag: his robe, a tensor lamp, the procedure manual, an empty glass, an ashtray, cigarettes alongside it.

Kyle put on his red tartan robe then retrieved the paper.

He read *The Review* in the bright light of the breakfast nook, while sucking down cup after cup of freshly brewed coffee. His two pieces of toast had been devoured two cups ago and he sat now, still trying to remove the remnants of the toast crumbs by wiping his hands off on his robe, as he stared at his own picture on the front page.

He was shown with his right hand on the Bible, his left hand raised, facing Judge Baxter as he gave the oath. Mayor Gathers stood in the background, smiling proudly. The headlines read simply, NEW POLICE CHIEF TAKES OATH.

When Kyle had first opened the paper he had sought the text of the article with eager eyes, skimming quickly to see if that old newspaperman editor had railroaded him in any way, most specifically about Susan and Lisa, and the Tragedy.

He was pleased to find that the article was factual, and even complimentary in places, and that the old man had not

74

mentioned anything about the death of Kyle's wife and daughter.

Kyle placed the newspaper down on the yellow tabletop for just a minute, and wondered if the mayor had put any undue influence on the old newspaper editor. He shook his head and picked up the newspaper again. That old fart couldn't be kept from saying what he wanted to say short of death; Kyle had picked that up in the short time he had been in the interview. No. Edgar Griffith had gone easy on him. Kyle recognized that. The old man could have used the article as a vindictive weapon (after all, Kyle did leave him with a slap in the face), but instead he had been fair, unbiased, giving Kyle the benefit of the doubt, and because of this, Kyle's harsh feelings for the old man softened. Good relations with the press would be a plus. Maybe he could salvage them after all.

A heavy knock at the front door pulled Kyle out of his thoughts. He opened the door with a big How Are Ya smile, and then his face fell, and even a little shiver ran up his neck tingling his ears.

Two men stood at the door. One a tall, burly older man, the other short, squat, and younger. They were dressed in white jumpsuits, their names embroidered on the fabric directly about their hearts in green thread. The big man's said *Jack*, the squat fellow read *Mike*.

"You Mr. Richards?" croaked Jack.

"Yes," Kyle confessed; his voice was faint, as if in admitting that much, he had signed his own death warrant. He stared, close-mouthed, his eyes settling on the moving van with the big green letters spelling BEKINS in an arc.

"Got some furniture," said Jack.

"I didn't order any furniture," Kyle answered, his eyes riveted on the truck. If it was what he thought, he wasn't ready for this.

"We're the movers, Mr. Richards. With your furniture. Here." He shoved a clipboard at Kyle, and Kyle grabbed it and stared indignantly at the paper. He scanned the page quickly, and when he reached the bottom, under an open space titled "Please Note" printed in black ink was a line in type: *Leo Brumagin acting for Kyle Richards—delivery approved.*

Leo! He still had power of attorney for Kyle, and he had done this! Doesn't he realize what he's done!

"Sign here," said Jack, handing him a Bic pen.

Kyle signed mechanically, then handed the clipboard back to the man and grunted.

"Okay," smiled Jack, taking Kyle's grunt for some sort of strange approval. "Let me just have a look around." He moved toward Kyle, and Kyle, still stunned, backed up a little, not taking his eyes off the huge white tractor-trailer hogging most of the street. Both men walked through the house quickly to get a view of the layout, then with a lilting "Okay" went out to the truck and began unloading.


"Why in the hell did you do it, Leo? I mean, you didn't even ask me, for God's sake." Kyle sat at the nook, his right hand clutching the phone to his ear, his left one running through his hair. He could hear the movers grunt as they eased a couch through the door.

"You can take it, Kyle. You're ready. Have I ever led you wrong, huh, Rookie?" Brumagin's haunting voice exercised its usual cooling effect on Kyle. He stopped stroking his hair and took a sip of lukewarm coffee, then spoke more calmly now: "This is the first time, Leo, but you're wrong, my friend. Dead wrong!—"

"You're not having the dreams anymore, right?"

"No, but—"

"And what are the movers doing right now? Tell me."

"They're unloading the *fucking* truck, for chrissakes, Leo. What in the *fuck* do you think I'm yelling about, for chrissakes!"

Brumagin said in a simple voice, "Did you tell them *not* to unload the truck, Kyle?"

76

The question hung between two hundred miles of telephone connection static.

"No," answered Kyle quietly, easing the air out of his lungs. "It's still gonna bring back memories that I'm not ready for, Leo. I can't handle it, I'm telling you."

"Then why didn't you send the truck away, Kyle? Answer that for me."

A dead silence between them lasted a full ten seconds, then Leo spoke: "Because you can handle it, friend." He spoke softly, "Because down inside you know you can handle it, that's why, Rookie. You know it's true."

"And the coffee table, Leo? What about the coffee table? How am I supposed to handle that one? You tell me that, or don't you know?"

"Threw it out, Kyle. Out in the trash."

"You've got an answer for everything, don't you?"

"Don't forget who pulled you out of the looney bin, sonny," snapped Brumagin. Even over the long distance his voice had a brawling effect. "And took care of your ass from snot-nosed rookie up to captain! Now straighten up, Kyle! I mean *now!*"

Kyle's green eyes flared a little, then he tilted his face into the phone receiver and sighed in resignation.

"Leo?" his voice echoed in the mouthpiece, devoid of any hostility.

"Yeah, Rookie?"

"The canopy . . . Lisa's bed; is it still there?"

Kyle heard the static and knew what the answer would be.

"I cleaned it up, Kyle. It wasn't really that bad. It'll be all right."

Kyle paused a moment. "Leo, I don't think I can handle her bed, I really don't." Kyle was almost pleading.

"In your own time, you'll be able to handle everything, believe me, Kyle. All you have to do is face it."

A stomp of leather boots on the kitchen floor turned Kyle's head around, his eyes still moist and wide. He raised his hand to the mover, Jack, signaling him to hold on. "Listen, Leo. I got

77

to go now. Thanks a lot, I mean that. You're the best."

"Everybody has to have somebody," said Leo, and the tone of voice was so familiar that Kyle could see that flabby-faced smile of his. Kyle thanked Leo and hung up, then directed his attention to the mover. "Yes?"

"The bedroom stuff, what goes where?"

Kyle ran his fingers through his hair, thinking how much he needed to clean up. "Take the big bedroom in the back for the adult bed," Kyle said, "the middle one's for the den, and . . ." he hesitated, and looked at the foot of the refrigerator considering how to cope with Lisa's furniture, ". . . the little girl's things . . . there's a white bed, with a canopy, and matching chest of drawers . . . anything that is for her, you put in the far bedroom. Don't bother putting it together. And once it's all in, if you don't mind, would you please be sure to close the door?"

Kyle's voice had been soft, distraught at the end, and the mover seemed to listen to him with increasing discomfort. Kyle realized the man must have picked up on his pain.

"Sure, mister," the man said sympathetically, "I'll close the door real tight."

Kyle feigned a smile and nodded his thanks. He sat on the back porch steps to smoke, and let the movers bring in the next test for his sanity. He lit up, gripping his robe closed against the cold.

When they came to the little girl's furniture Jack stopped a minute. "I think this little girl's stuff . . . I think she's dead," he said. "Maybe leukemia or something."

"Is that why we're rushing like hell?" asked Mike.

"I don't like it here," Jack said simply. "Now be careful with that canopy, it's delicate."

Mike pulled the white curved canopy for the child's bed out of a protective container. "What—oh," he said, grabbing Jack's attention immediately.

"What is it?"

"Looks like mildew, I think," said Mike, leaving it at that. He just hoped to hell that tough-looking man inside didn't go through the roof.

Jack leaned over for a look. The creamy white curving plane of the silk was dotted with rustlike stains, blotches in some places. Around several of the larger marks a patina of rusty pinpoints formed a macabre splattered pattern.

"Not our fault. Stains," he declared. "Besides, I'm telling you, he ain't going in that room. Wanted me to shut it tight, I tell you."

Mike suddenly felt that Jack was right, maybe they should bust their humps and get this over with, he was hungry for lunch anyway.

Both men worked fast, taking the proper furniture to the proper rooms, the proper boxes, marked at the time of the packing, to the proper rooms, and worked as fast as they could. At that pace anyone could make a mistake, and take a box marked *Den* into the dead little girl's room. Anybody could make that mistake, and in their hurry not even notice it at all.

When the mover came Kyle was still sitting on the back porch, a scattered spray of crushed cigarette butts on the bleached cement slab at his feet. The man shoved the same clipboard at Kyle that he had earlier.

"I already signed," said Kyle.

"Signed first for permission to unload, then to say you got it all," said Jack.

Kyle signed. The man took it back with a thanks, and a look that said he was glad as hell to get away from this move.

Feeling's mutual, thought Kyle as the man left.

Kyle sat for a while considering the ramifications of going back in the house. He could go crazy. What this morning had been a bright airy place of serenity, billowing with hope and the achievement of normalcy, had at this time, just before noon, become a trial marker, and obstacle course of unknown hazards.

*You have to face it, Kyle.* Leo's words formed a thick white line in his head. He crushed his cigarette against the side of the steps and, aiming it like a bombardier, dropped it between his legs to the scatter below.

Feeling numbed, Kyle raised himself and entered the house. Make it or break it, he decided. "I'm going to make it," he declared firmly. He stalked through the house staring at the ghostly furniture of years ago. Memories tried to insert themselves, but he forced them out of his mind. It was furniture, with no past—as long as he could remember that, he could handle it.

He decided against going in Lisa's room, though. He wasn't ready for that, yet. Kyle returned to the kitchen and stared at the kitchen boxes. Yes. Yes. The kitchen boxes were safe. Safe. He could open them. And if he could open them, why not the others, in time.

Over the next two days Kyle straightened the house and began his evaluation of the Briggs City Police Department, stopping by the station to pick up personnel files, manpower reports, and the like, trying to get a feel for the station.

During all this time he was a happy man. Happy and mindful about his healing mind, like a man near-drowned is about his saved life. The house became a home to him, except for just one space, the threshold to his bedroom. There, where the bedroom's hardwood floor ended in the small rise of blue hall carpeting, Kyle stopped each time he left his room; he stopped and stared at the closed door to Lisa's room at the opposite end of the hall with its white surface and cut-glass doorknob. When he could walk into there, he would really be cured. He'd think that, then go on his way to the living room and about his business.

# 9

Sunday night Kyle sat in his den at his dark oak rolltop desk, washed in the yellow glow of a hanging lamp he had put up to serve as a desk light. He tipped back in his chair, fingering a pile of personnel folders that he had just finished reviewing, and wondered how tomorrow would go—the first day on the job. He was excited, like a kid thrilled with the prospect of going back to school after a long, boring summer. He'd already made preparations. His black briefcase sat ready near the door. His daily uniforms, black serge pants, light blue shirt with black pockets and black epaulets bearing a single gold star, hung in the den closet next to his dress blues.

His new Sam Browne, the gunbelt issued by the Briggs City Police Department, sat glistening in the tweed fabric armchair, ready and waiting for his baton, extra ammunition, handcuffs, and gun. All ready. Just get up in the morning, slip into that nice new uniform, put on those shiny black shoes, wrap that Sam Browne around you, and voilà!—Super Police Chief rides again!

Kyle got up and picked up the Sam Browne. He fingered the black stitching on the holster, savoring the smell of the fresh leather, and remembered when he had recommended a change of firearms for the LAPD. He had suggested a Colt .45 automatic, instead of the .38 special, but the high brass had shot his ass down in one quick hurry. They cited the problems that the department was already facing over police shootings. Kyle wanted to give the street soldiers, the guys who are putting their lives on the line daily, a sidearm that would

81

actually stop a gun-wielding scrote in his tracks. Early in his career, he had witnessed a bank robber "take a lickin' and keep on tickin'," killing two good cops in the process, only stopped when Kyle emptied a couple of loads of buckshot into him. It was a shame, for the dead cops, their family, and the department.

On impulse he detached his holster from the belt and went to the boxes stacked together in the corner of the room. He rooted through them looking for his guns. He was the police chief in this town, and if he wanted to carry an automatic he would. He found nothing, and stood briefly in the middle of the room, reasoning. Either Leo still had his guns or they were in another room in the house. The box itself should be marked *Den,* he knew, and that summoned forth an unsavory possibility. Earlier that morning he'd gone from room to room, checking each box's marking and stacking them neatly in the closet or corner. Each and every room except Lisa's bedroom. And there was no box marked *Den* in any of those rooms.

He stood in the doorway of the den looking down the hall at the door to Lisa's bedroom. The glass knob glinted in the hallway light and the planes of the door shone with creamy brilliance.

*You have to face it!*

He found himself standing at the door, a finger's grasp away from that antique doorknob, and his dead daughter's things.

I don't have to open this door at all, he thought, I don't have to prove a thing.

The glass knob was cold to the touch. The door swung away slowly from his push. The light from the hall spilled in around Kyle's shoulders, shadowing a hulking monster half across the floor and up upon a topple of boxes in the center of the room. Kyle grasped at the wall plate, killing the darkness and the monster shadow with the light. Lisa's furniture, the disassembled canopy bed, the chest of drawers, the little nightstand, the rocking chair, the school desk—all of it little-girl white, delicate and loving—waited on two sides of the room's walls. Kyle felt the tears coming on. He pressed his palms against his eyes, then dropped his hands and let the tears come. He knelt and wept, letting the waves of his angry pain break over the rocks of his soul. He cried for a long time. Finally, he stopped. His breath became small gasping sobs. "My wife and my child are dead," he said in low, halting tones. "I . . . I . . . uh . . . dead. I can't change that. I have to go on with my life, now!" He thought about how much he missed the soft comfort of his wife hugging him when he came home from work, and asking how his day went; and how his darling little Lisa had always giggled as she kissed her daddy good-night.

But that was all gone, now. Forever.

Kyle sniffled and looked at the furniture. The pieces of the bed rested against the far wall, the stained white canopy mounted on the outside of the leaning so that the speckled rust-colored stains showed. Kyle gazed at these a second, then at the chest of drawers against the near wall, and the white rocking chair that he had painted himself, decaling Little Bo Peep and her lost sheep on the high cross-piece of the back. On the left rocker of the chair was attached a small metallic box with a lever pin that extruded to be pushed in as the rocker rolled back, to make a tinkling sound. And oh, how she had loved that, rocking for hours on end, her favorite doll, Annabelle, clutched in her tiny soft arms, her blond little pigtails bouncing in gentle rhythm to the rock and her little song, "Mares eat oats, and does eat oats, and little lambs eat ivy, a kid'll eat ivy, too; wouldn't you?"

Kyle wrestled the ache of his loss down into his mind. Time to move on with my life, he reminded himself.

He moved to the rocker, testing with a tentative, restive hand the rock of the chair. He smiled hesitantly at the light *br-r-r-ring* of the bell. I faced it, Leo, he thought.

Kyle washed up and put on a pair of blue jeans and a tee shirt and made a dash out into the cold night to get his tool box out of the truck. Back in the house he assembled the canopy bed, put the chest of drawers in a proper place, and set the rocker in the corner. Near that he placed the school desk. It had been an unconscious act, he realized, but the furniture sat now just as it had been in Lisa's previous bedroom. Kyle then began unpacking the boxes. He halted at times, wondering if he was doing the right thing, then continued. Her clothes, so small, so delicate, conveyed so much of daddy's little girl that the ache of loss returned.

Tears rolled down his cheeks as he hung up her small dresses and put away her small shirts. Lovingly, he folded her play clothes and placed them gently in the drawers. This done, he began to put up the pictures and decorations of Lisa's room. He opened up Lisa's pink and white phonograph and put on her favorite record, but did not turn it on. He pulled Annabelle out of a box filled with stuffed toys and set her in the rocker, then moved to the center of the room, his fist on his hips, and stepped around in a dancer's circle—it was just the way it had looked when his Lisa was alive. He could handle it, he smiled wanly, choking a little at the thought.

He hefted up the one full box remaining left, marked *Den* and weighing a ton with the guns and ammo inside. He decided to get up early in the morning and open that one then, because, God where had the time flown.

Kyle reached out for the light switch when he heard *rock-br-r-r-ring rock-br-r-r-ring*, of the small rocking chair. He snapped around, his eyes flaring for a second. The red yarn pigtails and powder pink face of Annabelle smiled up at him from where he had set her. He had brushed against it probably. He moved to the chair and stopped it, staring at the doll almost as if it were alive. He looked at the rust stains on the canopy, and left, turning out the light, and closing the door.

In bed Kyle reviewed the day's events with a satisfied deliberateness. He had a house he could live in, a job he could live with, and a past he could live to forget. Not too bad, not too bad at all. He had Leo Brumagin to thank for most of it, and he wondered how that short fart had gotten so smart.

\*          \*          \*

Kyle awakened in the middle of the night totally alert, ready for danger. Somebody was in his home, and God help them. He swept the covers aside quickly and quietly, catching the time in red digital numbers: 3:25 AM. He pulled a snub-nosed revolver from the night-table drawer and gained his feet. A sound foreign to the house had awakened him. But he did not know exactly what sound. He strained in the dark, listening.

*Rock-br-r-ring Rock-br-r-ring Rock-br-r-ring*

That was it. The son of a bitch was in Lisa's room, and making noise. What an idiot.

Kyle stood in the doorframe of his bedroom, looking down the darkened hall. Yellow light seamed the foot of the far bedroom. The intruder was in Lisa's room with the light on, for God's sake. A stupid asshole.

Kyle moved quickly down the hall, threw open the door, crouched and aimed, all at the same time yelling, "Police! Freeze!"—into a darkened room.

He searched the darkness quickly, then reached over and snapped up the light switch, illuminating the room. Nothing. He checked the windows. They were closed and locked. He checked the closet. Clear.

Now what the hell?

Had he been dreaming? He knew that he had heard the rocker. He looked at it now. Annabelle's black-button doll's eyes stared at him. The rocker was still. The light had been off when he entered, yet he had seen it on at the crack of the bottom of the door. It could have been a dream. Sleepwalking? Could be, though it had never happened before. After all, it had been an emotionally charged evening for him; he had faced his fear of Susan and Lisa's deaths. No easy task. Perhaps he had been dreaming. But the light? Kyle reached over and jiggled the light switch—loose wiring? That was out. The light switch worked perfectly. He flicked it up and down. Its clicking noise echoed emptily in the quiet of the night.

Kyle turned the light out and closed the door behind him. Tomorrow was his first day on the job, and he could figure this out later. But just to be sure he checked the rest of the house, the front and back doors, and started back down the hall to his bed. He needed his sleep.

He was halfway down the hall to his room when he heard it again. *Rock-br-r-ring Rock-br-r-ring Rock-br-r-ring* Kyle twirled and froze—

The light under Lisa's bedroom door shown like a wicked yellow finger. The sound of the rocking continued as Kyle started slowly for the door. This time he stopped cold outside the door, then burst in—

The room was dark.

Kyle's heart pounded lightly and he found himself listening for the hiss of the snakes, his craziness acting up. He could cope with that. No snakes hissed in his head.

His throat thickened as he backed out of the room. He closed the door. He stood staring at the darkened surface, afraid to look down. Finally, as if against his will, the muscles of his neck bent his head down so that his eyes could stare at his feet, and the bottom of the door. The light was on. The rocking sound began its constant rhythm: *Rock-br-r-ring Rock-br-r-ring Rock-br-r-ring* It was a rhythm Kyle recognized. He raised his eyes to the glass doorknob, and his trembling hand began to reach for it when the music began to play from the other side of the door. He recognized the song, and the tinny sound it always had being played on little Lisa's pink and white kid's phonograph. "Mares eat oats, and does eat oats, and little lambs eat ivy, a kid'll eat ivy, too; wouldn't you?" the lady on the record sang.

Jesus Christ!

Kyle's throat twitched compulsively, and the soft, meaty underpart of his jaw felt ponderously heavy. He listened for a moment for what had always accompanied that song, Lisa's voice singing along in a high, lilting manner "Mares eat oats . . ." He strained his hearing to the limit, but heard no voice. Thank God. His heart triphammered in his chest. He hesitated, then called out in a tone that shocked him because it was so familiar. How many times had he used that tone of voice with her? A thousand, at least. "Lisa," he said, "Go to sleep. It's late, Lisa. Go to sleep."

The rocker sound and the bell continued, the rhythm unbroken.

Kyle waited. This was nuts, yet somehow it felt right. He breathed shallowly for a few seconds more, then lifted his chin and spoke again: "Lisa, honey, go to sleep." His voice resounded gently down the long hall, and died.

He leaned toward the door, his hand cupped to his ear. The music stopped. The rocker sound continued.

Kyle gathered his breath and said scoldingly, "Lisa. I said go to bed. Now go to bed."

The rocking sound stopped. Kyle felt a tinge of relief. Then, he heard a familiar patter of footsteps start toward the door. Kyle opened his mouth wide and sucked in air. If that doorknob turned, he would scream. The footsteps stopped at the other side of the door. Kyle stared at the doorknob. It began to turn.

"Lisa!" yelled Kyle, "You're scaring Daddy! Turn out that light and go to bed like I told you to!"

The doorknob kept turning.

*"Right now, young lady! Do you hear me!"*

His heart pounded. His Adam's swelled in his throat.

*"Lisa!"*

The doorknob stopped its rotation.

Slowly, it turned clockwise back to its rest position.

"Good girl," said Kyle, breathing raggedly. "Now turn off the light and go to bed."

Kyle heard the snap of the light switch and saw the light at the bottom of the door extinguish. He heard the tiny footsteps diminish in volume as they moved away from the door, then the swish sound of covers being pulled aside and the squeaking sound of bedsprings, a settling sound. Then silence. Dead silence.

# 10

Rick Jaeger shifted his Chevy into fourth, took in the night air, and cursed Sue's mom. She's the one that had spoiled it.

Somehow, by the powers that mothers have, she had guessed that Rick and Sue weren't going to the library this school night for a study date. And just to throw a monkey wrench into their mid-week makeout session she had sent along Sue's younger brother, Tom, and his friend, John Stahl, to make sure it was a study date after all.

Rick thought both of them were fifteen-year-old dorks of the first order, but with one saving grace—they didn't want to go to the library either.

He squeezed Sue's hand to let her know he was up to something, then looked in the rearview mirror. "Listen, guys," he said, "I'm going to cruise by the library. We're gonna wave at it, and that way we don't have to lie about whether we went there tonight. Okay?"

"Okay by me," said Tom from the back seat. "What are we gonna do, though?"

"Go cruisin', Tom," said Rick, formulating a plan to get rid of the two of them for an hour or so. Shit, there wasn't much time. He had it. He turned on Main Street and gunned it out of town onto Highway 28. Ten minutes later they were out in the country, with the darkness and the cold night air. Rick started decelerating, and craning his neck. It was around here somewhere.

"Hey, where are we, man?" asked Tom. John joined in: "Yeah, where the fuck are we?"

Rick slowed the wheels down to a crawl. Darkness swelled outside the car. Checking his rearview mirror for headlights and searching ahead for the same, he made a slow left across the deserted highway and drove down a short cut of dirt road. The headlights picked up a barbed wire fence with a gate stretched over steel cattle-guard bars inset in the road. The beams of the light came to rest on a sign—Gathers Investment Corp, No Trespassing—wired to the fence.

"It's the old MacInnes place," said Rick. "Nobody'll look for us here."

For a moment, everyone was silent, peering out into the darkness.

"Ain't that next to the Pickers place, Rick?" asked Tom, the nervous edge on his voice just what everyone else was feeling.

"Crazy Dave, himself," answered Rick as if he were proud of the fact. "No one's going to look for us here . . ."

"Except Crazy Dave," interrupted Sue gloomily.

"Get out and open the gate, Tom." Rick eyed Sue's younger brother in the mirror.

"It's probably locked," said Tom; he hadn't moved.

"Go open the gate, wimp."

Tom got out of the car and opened the gate.

Rick eased the car through, telling Tom to close it behind them in case a cop came by and saw it opened. He pulled the car around a scrub oak so that he could spot the road, and killed the lights. By the time Tom caught up, everybody was out of the car.

"We're gonna take a walk, all of us. Over there." He jabbed toward the south, and started walking. They fell in step behind him and Sue, and he led them over to the barbed wire fencing separating this graze from Pickers's Ranch—Crazy Dave's ranch.

"What are we doing, Rick?" Sue asked.

"You know, what I told you before, hon'." He gave her a meaningful squeeze on the arm that told her to play along with him. She was good at picking up on stuff like that.

"What?" Tom belched, and the sound was swallowed by the night.

"What?" John croaked, a little wire of anticipation snagged in his voice. Of the others he was the only one staring ahead, past the dark textured landscape of Crazy Dave's graze to the wan porch light, as still and cold as the winter night air, that marked the Pickers place. Rick could not remember a time passing down that road at night and not seeing that unblinking light aglow.

"They say he uses it to get his bearings when the moon's dark," said Tom. He had picked up on it, too; his voice had a strange, distant quality to it, and now the four stood by the fence in tableau, faces still and pensive, sheened by the glow of the crescent moon.

"Yeah, right," said Rick to break the mood. "Up and over." He mounted the wire carefully, using the top of the post for balance. "Come on, Sue." She started to protest, but he rationed out a grin to silence her. "Come on. Just like we did the other night, remember?"

She caught it. "Oh, yeah." Even in the dim moonlight he caught the mischievous widening of her eyelids. "Like the other night." She picked her way carefully over with Rick's help, and of course, Tom and John couldn't help but follow.

Among furtive questions and rumblings from the two clods, all of which Rick ignored, he led them a hundred feet or so toward the inpenetrable blackness of the trees and stopped dead.

"Okay. You two have got to do what we did the other night."

"Yeah," taunted Sue proudly. She hugged in closer to Rick for warmth.

"You two"—he jabbed at them for emphasis—"are gonna go to the other side of the trees. Me and Sue tied her scarf, the red one, by the inlet of the stream. Where it goes into the trees, know what I mean?"

Both of the boys knew, but they stared blankfaced for a second.

"I'm not going over there or anywhere," John choked. "That's crazy. Crazy Dave is walking around out there."

"Look, pussy, if you don't want to, don't." Rick gawked at him, then turned up his nose and looked at Sue. "I told you he was a pussy. And I'm gonna tell everyone at school tomorrow, too."

"Now wait a minute," said John, but Rick had moved on. "Tom," Rick said patiently, as if his whole confidence had been on Sue's brother during the entire conversation with John. "I knew it'd be you. You've got balls. You'll go get it, won't you? Hunh? Ain't nobody can call you a pussy, Hunh?"

"My brother's no pussy, are you, Tom?" Sue squeezed Rick playfully, though the tone of her voice had the proper mix of pride and indignation in it that no brother could refuse.

"No. I'm no pussy," he said half-heartedly, "but you're going with me, meatloaf." He prodded John's brown nylon jacket with his fist. "I'll tell everyone, even Nancy, what a faggot pussy you were if you don't."

"Move it, then." said Rick.

The two boys grumbled a little, then took off toward the trees. Rick and Sue watched until they couldn't see them anymore, then Sue turned to go back to the car.

"No." Rick took her hand and pulled her to him. He cupped the back of her neck with his free hand and bent down slightly to kiss her heavily, his tongue forcing her lips apart and ravaging the inside of her mouth while she sucked on it like it could come. He dropped his free hand down off her neck, stroked her left breast on the way down to where the action was, then cupped her there hard for a second and began to rub hard and fast like he was trying to start a fire by friction.

"Let's go to the car," she said, her voice soft and gooey.

"No. If they chicken out they'll go straight for the car." He grabbed her hand and led off into the field.

Both of them walked in silence, Tom irritated with his sister for hooking up with a prick like Rick, and figuring John had shut up because he was pissed off at being dragged along out here. Well, Tom didn't like it either, but—

"Whoa-a." John planted both boots heavily in the wet, rank grass. "I'm not going anywhere," he said. "Especially not in there."

Tom only heard the "Whoa-a" and had been walking with his eyes cast sullenly down at the ground in front of him. He stopped immediately and spun around, lighting into the bozo. Didn't he *understand*? "Listen, Fanner. You think I wanna be out here? Hunh? You know what happens if Rick runs around *telling* everybody we're chickenshit? Hunh? Be like when he went on about Waller, right? Nobody'd talk to him. He was shit. Now he has to hang around with Turner and those dorks. Shit!"

Tom talked up into his friend's face in that harsh whisper that grabs hold of a guy's voice when it's dark night and everything is spooky still. John's fat face was cushioned in the collar of his black nylon jacket, seemed to float in the night air by itself, bodiless. It caught the moonlight just right so that his right eye seemed to glow, staring past Tom into something shadowy and cold. "I don't care if they do call me chickenshit," he stated absently, "I'm not going in there." He nodded his head so that the glowing eye found darkness for a second, and Tom realized that his friend meant behind him, and then suddenly the sense of "where he was" fell upon him like a net of cold, wet rope on his bare skin.

*Crazy Dave's land.*

Those damn words waved stiffly at his mind. *Crazy Dave's land*: where he walks, like a zombie, with his shotgun; where he's killed and eaten kids, and even some adults.

And where was it that John didn't want to? It was behind Tom and he wasn't afraid to turn, not really, but he'd turn very slowly, because goddamnit, he didn't like being here, not at all, and most of all, not in the trees. It was dark in there. Those trees were almost black, and they rose high, too high. They formed a sullen, dark wall, the kind of dark that Tom knew too well, the inky shadows that you find late at night when you were all tucked in your bed safe and warm, but mostly safe, and then you look out into that gray twilight zone that your room has become and it's almost okay except for the closet. Why didn't you remember to close the closet door, because now it stands open, a gaping black mouth, and that'd be okay if it weren't for the clothes that hung in there, because they seemed to move. Not a lot, just a little, or did they, or were the clothes clothes at all, but maybe something scary and alive and inhuman, having a need, a real *need* to come out and visit you, *feed* on you . . .

"I ain't going in there," said John for the third time.

"I think I saw something move in there, Johnny."

"No." The word caught in his throat.

"Maybe. Yeah." He paused a minute, thinking. He had to satisfy Rick and Sue, and not let on to John that he was chickenshit at the same time. John wouldn't be any problem, because he was the first to crap out, so that left Rick and Sue, and besides he really *did* see something move in those trees; he thought so, anyway. The best thing to do would be to get away fast. Back away from the trees, back away from them, and . . . yeah, he had it.

"All right, you just follow me, John."

"Where're we heading."

"Goddamnit, just let me handle this, hunh? Let's get away from the trees first, then have a smoke, okay? Okay?"

John assented with silence. Tom heard him trudging along behind as he led them away from the trees, skirting over to the side where the weak moonlight had shown a dark ribbon running across the land, a shallow rain-wash arroyo, dry now with the lack of precipitation since that big downpour several weeks ago. A cow bellowed in the distance, across the road on the Indians' land, but besides that there was only silence, and the night noise. With a careful eye on the gray landscape, Tom led them toward the darkened arroyo, which now gained more substance of gray as they closed in on it.

"Just remember," he told John, as they both slipped down into the gully, "keep your head down and we can smoke and mark some time." They settled into the ditch, their backs resting against the side. He was pleased with himself. The gully was about four feet deep, and if John would just keep his head down, this little ditch would provide them with the cover they needed. It was far enough from the trees to be safe, and down low enough so that Rick, if that jerk was checking, which he doubted, wouldn't get wise. Ditto for the real danger, Crazy Dave.

Tom fished down into the soft cotton of his jacket pocket and retrieved his Kools. He liked the menthol, it bit into your tongue when first lit up. The pack was half full; he shook a small filter-tipped bungle partly out of the pack and selected one for John, let him know by the short-stroke gesture of his arm that he didn't exactly like the idea of giving him one of *his* cigarettes, that the cheap bastard should buy his own. Then he brought the pack up to his mouth, gently pinched his selection between his lips, and pulled the pack down decisively, completing the important act properly.

Pocketing the cigarettes, he fished around for his matches, lit up his smoke, pocketed the matches, and puffed the cigarette twice, casting a glow on his face. He then passed his cigarette to John, and waited while John fired up his smoke. He and John were sitting, crouched in the arroyo, half leaning, half sitting against the dirt side of the culvert. A little dirt trickled onto his shoulder from above. He brushed it off absently then took back his smoke from John, and they squatted for a moment like two soldiers in a foxhole, contemplating their smokes.

"What are we gonna do about Rick?" asked John during a thoughtful, histrionic exhalation of smoke.

"All right. All right. What we're gonna do . . ." he paused a moment, a little more dirt had come loose up top and run down on his shoulder and he brushed it off, "we tell Rick that we

94

went over there. Now we'll wait here for long enough to seem like we went there, but fuck him."

"What about the scarf? We're supposed to get it."

"Like this, we went over, it wasn't there. Crazy Dave must of got it. Something like that."

"What if he goes checks? He'll know we're lying."

Tom sighed, exasperated. "Can't you figure anything out for yourself? It's nine o'clock about"—he checked his watch—"there, nine-ten. We wait here for another twenty minutes. We gotta be home by ten, so he's not gonna have time to go check. And besides, I don't think he'd check, anyway."

"But what if he *does* check, Tom?"

More dirt trickled down on Tom, but he ignored it this time. How could such a big guy as John be such a pussy? "Look, you big ba—"

"After what I do to you, he won't come to my land," said a hollow voice from above.

Tom sensed John stiffen. For a moment he felt a bubble in his own heart, but he knew that voice. It was Rick. More dirt rained down on him, as he turned, half raising to look up over the ridge of the ditch to cop out to Rick, tell him to fuck off, then he froze. It wasn't Rick. *Oh God! It wasn't Rick!*

The figure, black and towering into the cold twinkling firmament, loomed over them—the figure of a man. It could only be one man. And that shaft, outlined in the man's right hand against the night sky, could only be his shotgun.

"Get off my *land!*" howled the voice from the dark. "Off my *land!*"

John flashed past Tom, gurgling and gobbling half-choked sounds of fear. This broke Tom's momentary paralysis. He heard a warbling cry, shocked as he realized that it came from his swelling throat, but he was running now, fast, very fast, oh yes, through the ditch, the car must be up and over there and please God—

*"Get off my land, damn you!"*

The sound carried so well that Crazy Dave's own lips seemed

inches from Tom's ears, so that when the first sharp *Boom!* of the shotgun split the night air, he was sure he'd been hit, but he kept on running, howling in fear as a second report with its cannonlike boom filled the night air, a pause, then another *Boom! Boom! . . .*

When the screaming started, Rick stopped kissing Sue. She pulled away and yelled, "Tom!"

Tom and John ran past them, screaming, "Crazy Dave, Crazy Dave."

The shotgun boomed, not fifty yards away.

"Oh, shit!" Rick blurted out, his mind suddenly stark and clear with understanding, "let's get the fuck outta here!"

He ran. Sue was right behind him. They reached the fence and hopped it at the same time. Tom and John were already at the car.

"Get the gate!" Rick told Sue. They were off Pickers's land now, but his shotgun could still reach them. Rick fired the Chevy up and popped the clutch. The wheels spun, chipping at the dirt at first, then caught, and they accelerated down the dirt access road. Rick zoomed through the gate, turned onto the highway, and would have left Sue if Tom hadn't grabbed his shoulder, pinching through the heavy nylon jacket, "Hey, stop! Wait for Sue!"

The tires squealed, the car stopped abruptly, rocking wildly from the raised rear end. She gained the car and pulled the door open with an insane jerk. "You fucker!" she screamed.

Rick didn't care what she thought.

He popped the car into first and pressed the accelerator to the floor, then clutched and shifted again, then again, then again, he was in fourth and cruising the hell out of there. Forever, if he could help it.

# 11

His grandfather, Holy Eagle, had told him as a child that when Ravana took a soul it was like stealing a turtle from its shell—people could see and touch the shell, but the turtle wasn't there.

The Indian boy, now a man, knew that to be true. Ravana had taken his soul that night, and left the empty shell. It was worse than being dead.

He squatted near a small fire at the base of the sacred mountain, wishing he were worthy to ascend and call forth the Spirit Elders, and plead with them to help him reclaim his soul.

His pleas would fall on deaf ears, this he knew. He was *Heytah-nee*—the Traitor, a soulless piece of shit. But there must be some way to regain their favor, he thought. He shook his head in self-pity and stirred the fire with a stick. He watched the angry embers glow in the night.

He pulled a worn leather pouch to him and removed the sacred talisman of finger bones—his grandfather, the great Holy Eagle, had gone and fetched it from Devil's Ground that night, but it was too late to change what had happened: Ravana's time had come.

And what did that mean?

He had expected horrifying things immediately. But none had come. Instead, years had passed, Holy Eagle had died, and as far as the Indian knew, nothing had happened. There were other of his tribe, but he was the last of the Priest clan, and Ravana had already taken his soul.

What Holy Eagle had explained to him about the facing of

Ravana was that his clan kept the balance between good and evil, and that after Ravana was set free, the nature of the world would change to that of darkness and evil, that all things good would die, and that Ravana would rule, in one form, or many forms. This evil change would start from this tiny place on earth, and in the end the earth, moon, the stars, would cease to be.

It sounded like a lot of bullshit to a white man, but the Indian knew it to be true.

He gripped the talisman and shook it at the starry night, and shouted, "Grandfather! Help me to steal back my soul!"

He sat still and listened. The wind brought no reply. And then he lay down before the fire and slept, and dreamed: A large eagle landed near the fire, and the night became the day, and the eagle spoke to him.

"He has come," said the eagle.

"Who?" said the Indian.

"*Eh-keh-Heh*—the Chosen One, the fallen Warrior."

The Indian sat up and stared hard at the eagle. "Where is he, O great bird?"

"In the trap," said the bird, extending a silvery black wing toward the north. Briggs City appeared there, and superimposed over it was Devil's Ground.

# 12

Kyle awoke with his head full of mixed emotions, the strident excitement of starting a new job, jarred by the sobering events of the previous night. He had to make a choice, however, before he got out of bed: accept last night for what it appeared to be, or consciously ignore it.

He chose to ignore it.

Making the right choice was how he had gotten out of Woodhaven in the first place, and he never wanted to go back.

Inspection was at eight-thirty. At eight-twenty-five Kyle walked with the mayor into the maintenance yard behind the station. The patrolmen stood at parade rest in a long blue line, eighteen men, three women. Dwight Koger and Craig Powell, the only plainclothes on the force, stood off by themselves, talking. Parking enforcement stood by their scooters, four women, one man. The black-and-whites, cleaned and waxed, glistened in the morning sun. The five sergeants waited in a group talking until Lotito, the duty sergeant, spotted Kyle and the mayor, and poked Gurnell, the acting station commander. The sergeant started toward them. He was tall, and his belly jiggled as he walked. His haircut, GI flat-top, looked the same as it must have when he got out of the army in the late fifties.

"Ready to start, Chief?" asked Gurnell.

Kyle caught the edge on the sergeant's voice. He looked at the sergeant, and recognized the problem instantly. It showed in Gurnell's eyes like fire, in the tone of his voice like grit stuck in his vocal cords. Gurnell resented that an outsider had been brought in.

"Yes, Sergeant," answered Kyle, and the man turned and walked back to the assembly.

"With Buddy Nelson killed," said the mayor, "and the lieutenant's spot open, I think Gurnell was expecting your job."

"There can only be one chief," said Kyle. "I've been promoted over older men before. I'll bring him around."

The mayor walked beside him to the front of the assembly.

"*Ah*-ten-tion!" commanded Gurnell.

The blue line snapped to attention, saluting. Kyle returned the salute. "Stand at ease," he ordered, and the troops came to parade rest in a rustle of fabric and the squeak of leather.

He chanced a glance at Gurnell. Resentful pride was swollen on his face.

How would he handle the sergeant? He needed to bring him into line, without turning him into a problem. If Kyle just got heavy with him, that would only worsen the situation. No, the best way with a man like Gurnell, whose pride had been wounded by being passed over—and Kyle sympathized with the man—was to make him doubt himself. Now, how would Kyle do that? His mind's eye flashed reports in his head; Kyle looked at the chief's car—he had the answer. But first he would address the men.

"I am not one for long speeches. I am pleased to be your new chief. I will speak to each one of you on an individual basis sometime during the next two weeks. You will notice that I'm wearing street blues. I am not an ivory-tower administrator. I am here to help you in any way that I can.

"There are no major changes in policy in the immediate future, so go about your duties as you have been doing." Kyle turned to Gurnell and nodded.

"*Ah*-ten-tion!" Gurnell's voice carried like a bullhorn. "Pree-sent arms!"

The troops drew their pieces, and held them out, the cylinders swung out and empty for inspection.

Kyle walked the line, stopping twice to examine the pistols,

Sergeant Gurnell at his side. They looked good, he had to hand it to the sergeant. Kyle knew that all the man's pride was wrapped up in this inspection. It was his way of saying, *See, everything's perfect, I should have been made chief, I could handle it!*

That pride would be the lever Kyle would use to turn Gurnell's resentment into utter loyalty.

"Sergeant, secure arms," said Kyle. He walked to the front of the assembly.

Gurnell secured arms and put the troops at ease, then walked to Kyle.

"Fine-looking troops, Sergeant."

"Thank you, sir," he said, his tone spiced with bitters.

Mentally Kyle sighed. Time to handle the problem.

"Sergeant Koger," he called.

Koger walked over, his black wingtips chopping the asphalt, the picture of a successful Wall Street broker, in an expensive, black three-piece suit. He was handsome, with brown hair, mustache, and aggressive brown eyes. "Yes, Chief," he said.

The robbery detective made Kyle feel underdressed. Kyle pulled out the keys to his police car that he had received only this morning, and handed them to Koger. "Would you pull my car over here for me?" he said.

Koger took the keys. "Yes, Chief."

Gurnell's face screwed up in puzzlement.

"Something wrong, Sergeant?"

"The vehicles are clean, sir. I had 'em wash 'em up."

"Yes, I can see. I read in the log you were driving the chief's car for a while."

Gurnell flushed lightly; his lips formed a straight line before speaking. "I stopped about two months ago."

"Why?" *Because the mayor probably got on your ass, that's why.*

"I was just running it to keep the battery charged up, Chief."

"Oh. I trust you were the only one driving it, Sergeant."

"Uh . . . Yes, as station commander . . ."

Koger pulled the car up and opened the door and started to get out.

"Wait a minute," said Kyle. "Pull the shotgun for me, would you, Koger?" He glanced at Gurnell. His face was screwed up in the "Oh shit" look, and Kyle knew that he'd hit the bull's eye.

Kyle took the weapon, and jacked the slide, ejecting unspent cartridges onto the blacktop.

"Sir . . ." Gurnell began, but Kyle tilted the gun muzzle to the ground. A small pile of cigarette butts, matches, and paper formed at the sergeant's feet.

"First shot'll blow that right outta there, Chief—"

"Or, blow the gun up, and me with it!" Kyle disassembled the weapon, and handed the pieces to Gurnell, keeping the barrel. He shook it, turned both muzzle and breech end to the ground to make sure the dirt was out, then pointed it to the sky, and looked through the tube—blocked. He then put the barrel to his lips, held it like a blowgun, and tooted on it. Five Reese's Peanut Butter Cup wrappers flew out and fluttered slowly to the ground. A ripple of laughter wafted from the ranks. Gurnell's face burned red with embarrassment.

"Not satisfactory, Sergeant," said Kyle. "Clean this weapon after assembly, and report to me. Dismiss assembly." Kyle turned and walked over to the mayor.

"How did you know?" asked the mayor, smiling.

Kyle didn't like explaining himself, but said, "Old habits die hard. Patrolmen treat their units like big garbage cans. The shotgun barrel is a favorite place for trash. He ordered the car cleaned but forgot about the shotgun because it was the chief's car, not a patrol unit. Easy enough mistake to make when you're in a hurry."

"You don't think that's going to alienate him a bit?"

*Why don't you fuck off,* thought Kyle, but told him, "He was responsible for the inspection, and he knows it. It was he who blew it, not me. Nobody works harder for you than somebody who wants your respect."

The mayor smiled, impressed. "I can see I got the right man for the job." He put his arm around Kyle's shoulder and guided him toward the door.

Kyle heard Gurnell dismiss the assembly as he thought how he hated the touch of this man.



Kyle's inheritance from his predecessor was a boxy office that smelled of fresh white paint. An oak desk and chair with two visitor's chairs occupied one half of the room, two gray metal file cabinets and an oak bookshelf the other half. The ubiquitous walnut paneling that seemed to be the symbol of Briggs City officialdom skirted the walls at a height of four feet, so that Kyle, as he sat behind the large, flat plane of his desk, and stared straight ahead, seemed to be looking over a barrier into a distant white infinity. A few pictures would fix that, he thought. The last thing he needed was a long look into infinity. Not now. Because he felt great. Safe and comfortable in the finiteness of this office, the familiar confines of his position.

A man needs his work, he thought. His work, and his family.

His family. A feeling of sadness passed briefly over him; he dismissed it by standing up and leaving this year's budget gaping open in its blue binding on his desk, and walked over to the window that gave out onto the service yard. He cranked the casement windows wide open, breathing in the fresh morning air. It tasted of the lingering cool of the early morning—a pleasant relief from the cloying paint odor that still hung in the room.

The yard was idle except for Jimmey Rodriguez. All that Kyle could see of the mechanic was the bottom half of his blue overalls, the rest of him swallowed by the open hood of a black-and-white. A *tink-tinking* sound rang out clearly in the midmorning air. The sky was brilliant light blue, a beautiful sky, a beautiful morning.

A high, scouring voice shot through his open door. Kyle

heard Sergeant Gurnell's dull tones in reply.

"Oh, Edna," said the sergeant, and Kyle picked up the familiarity in his voice, that subdued tone reserved for normally friendly people when they're chastising the hell out of you.

"Don't 'Oh, Edna' me, Randolph," the woman cautioned sharply.

Kyle hooked his heavy white china mug off his desk and emerged from his office ostensibly to get a cup of coffee; he had to see this.

"That madman shot, *shot*, at my babies, and that is all there is to know about it, Randolph! I want him arrested right this minute, do you hear me!"

The sergeant had braced himself for the onslaught by pressing his big hands flat on the black formica countertop, holding his arms stiff as if to hold up his massive weight. His belly hung over his Sam Browne like a blue bag of sand. His face, already suffused in red, flushed almost purple.

Trapped, Gurnell hitched up his breath, and blew out like a blowfish. "Do you want to file a complaint, Edna?" he asked.

"'Do you want to file a complaint, Edna?'" she mimicked. "Of course I do, you boob! How Aunt Carrie had you, I'll never know. Of course I do."

Sally Gonzalez, the dispatcher, giggled, causing Gurnell to grimace. The sergeant's color was fast approaching postmortem lividity. Kyle watched as "Randolph" ushered his cousin into a small partitioned area and began to take the complaint.

Kyle took a deep swig of his coffee, and winced in pain as he verified once again one unvarying Universal Truth: stationhouse coffee always tastes like crap. As the hot brew ate away at his stomach he pondered why Gurnell hadn't seemed that alarmed over the incident. If . . . Edna? yes, Edna's kids were being shot at, that would make it Gurnell's relations, yet the sergeant seemed unperturbed. Kyle could step in, of course, but one of his cardinal rules of good management was to never take a man's handle away from him unless absolutely necessary. He would wait until Edna left, then ask him about the matter. Maybe Edna was a little "off," or something. Who knows.

As Edna unleashed another scathing attack on "Randolph's" mentality, Kyle slipped back into his office and jailed himself in the confines of the up-and-coming budget. He had promised the mayor a report, a state-of-the-department white paper, complete with proposed changes and improvements. Kyle's specialty. He had been looking for a name for the project, but it had escaped for some time now. There would be a lot in the name.

He rocked back in his chair and looked at the ceiling for inspiration. What was it he was going to do to the department? Basically, bring it up to date, upgrade it. That was it! He rocked down in his chair and picked up a pen, pulling a clean sheet of white paper out of a drawer. He printed carefully, in large, block letters: PROJECT UPGRADE. Catchy, and a banner to run the changes in the department under. Project Upgrade.

He felt pleased. It was the perfect name. But oddly enough, the first phase of his program of change, Project Upgrade, would require a seemingly contrary element, no change: no action, nothing, except observation. Every one of the people out there in the department was expecting immediate changes. The New Chief says do it this way, the New Chief says do it that way. But Kyle knew that could cause a lot of unnecessary resentment, and unnecessary resentment was bad. Instead, he would come in slowly, observe the situation as it existed in the here and now, and accomplish two things: one, become smoothly accepted as the leader of the team; and two, initiate in a metered manner the changes necessary for a more efficient department, a dose at a time, with increasing doses as the people became more amenable and trusting. Kyle felt that trusting, happy people do a better job for you in the long run.

He was engrossed in cost analysis figures when Gurnell rapped on the doorjamb with the beefy right hand holding the complaint form. Kyle nodded and the sergeant stepped in. In his left hand he carried the riot gun that had been his downfall at inspection this morning. It glistened blue-black with fresh gun oil.

"The gun, sir," he said, "do you want to inspect it?"

"Step in and close the door, Sergeant."

Gurnell did so, awkwardly shutting the door with his elbow. Apprehension showed on his face like a movie on the silver screen. Kyle pulled a heavy brown folder from the corner of his desk and opened it. "You know what this is, Sergeant?"

The big man eyed it and nodded. "My jacket. Mine?"

Kyle nodded, then eyed the shotgun in Gurnell's hand. He patted the personnel folder and said, "Your jacket says you've got twenty-two years of service in this department. Twenty-two good years. And on my first inspection I find a dirty piece in my *own* car. Do you know what that makes me wonder, Sergeant?"

"No, sir," Gurnell said, the resentful tone in his voice this morning gone. Kyle decided to go easy on him.

"Makes me wonder where your head was at. You can slide on it this one time, but this is the last time." Kyle lowered his voice as if embarrassed for the sergeant. "Frankly, Gurnell, I was surprised, a man of your experience, getting caught like that." Kyle patted the personnel folder. "No need to put anything in here. We'll start over with a clean slate, understood?"

"Yes, sir," Gurnell said gratefully.

"Excellent. Now what's that?" Kyle pointed to the papers in the sergeant's right hand, but before Gurnell could answer, he asked, "Is it that woman's complaint? The shooting?"

Gurnell lowered his head slightly in embarrassment. "Yes. Cousin Edna. She says Crazy Dave's been shooting at Sue and Tom—those are her kids."

"You don't seem too excited about that," Kyle said.

Gurnell blew like a blowfish, a habit Kyle was coming to understand accompanied any explanation from the sergeant.

106

"Crazy Dave's a recluse, lives out by himself on Highway 28. He's kind of the boogey man around the town. Kids always picking on him. I think he just tries to scare them off."

Kyle noted a sympathetic tone had crept into Gurnell's voice. "When there's shooting, people can get hurt," Kyle said, then, keying off Gurnell's look, asked, "What is it?"

Gurnell shifted from one foot to the other, then back again. His words came out low and slow, as though he was uncomfortable at showing a soft spot. "It's just that I knew Mr. Pickers before he went *odd*, and . . . I just think that when a man's wife is murdered, and his little girl butchered"— Gurnell's face twisted up in revulsion like the face of a rookie cop watching his first autopsy—"he has a right to go crazy. Don't you think, Chief?"

An invisible mallet hammered into Kyle's chest. He felt his jaw hanging open like that of an unstrung puppet. "What?"

"I said that he's entitled to go a little crazy, his wife's being murdered, and his little girl getting butchered. Don't you think?"

Kyle stood up. He felt sick. He found his voice and told Sergeant Gurnell that, yes, he did agree, then in dreamlike steps, he walked around the desk, took the shotgun from the sergeant, and asked directions to the Pickers place. He would take this call himself.

# 13

The cold air rushing in the open car window helped. He pulled it into his lungs in gaping mouthfuls. He could just hear Sergeant Gurnell telling the others, "He went as white as a fucking sheet, and zipped out the door like nobody's business," and then they would suspect him; look a little too deep and they would find out, *know*, know about his past and how his wife and his daughter were—

Stop it!

He gulped the air down and then forced his breathing to be slow and regular. Main Street turned into Highway 28, and the steel springs in his body began gradually to uncoil as the scenery took over. Soon the feel of the automobile calmed him, the smooth rolling grip of the tires on the road soothing him, making him aware of how much he loved to be riding alone in a police car. He had always loved that feel, the knowledge that you were the law, the protector. That meant that he was responsible for any situation in which he was in charge; and responsible was what you were just before you went crazy over the edge—probably why this guy Pickers, who he was going out to see, had taken the slip, gone over to Wonder-Wonder Land. Of all people, Kyle knew how that was, now, didn't he?

*Yes. And if I don't keep my mind on my business, I could end up dead,* he reminded himself soberly. The thought had come from nowhere, strong and immediate, and Kyle felt relieved because of it—the street cop in his mind pulling him back to reality, a part of him readying itself, standing guard over his mental ramblings.

The man Kyle was going out to see was crazy . . . emotionally disturbed, he corrected himself (when you've been on the other side of the line, the distinction is somehow important). Pickers was disturbed and armed, although judged by Sergeant Gurnell to be harmless. Well, Kyle had seen a "harmless" seventy-three-year-old woman put a butcher knife the size of a scimitar across the blue belly of a veteran patrolman with such force that his guts came spilling out over his Sam Browne gunbelt. Kyle shuddered, remembering the sick look of surprise on the dying cop's face.

And how harmless can a man be if he's shooting at people? Should have asked the good sergeant that, Kyle thought.

Kyle began to be angry at himself. He hadn't followed procedure. He should have called Pickers up and asked him to come in to the station. That would take the edge off any sort of confrontation: not a man of the law "invading" another man's property, but a citizen voluntarily coming in at the request of the law. A big difference; and most people, crazy or not, complied. But the only thing that had been twirling through his mind like a razorblade since he ran out the door was the words: *Killed his wife and butchered his daughter, so he went a little crazy;* and he'd come flying out here like a victim of an unnatural catastrophe trying to find some other survivor, someone who had shared the same terrible experience. That was the real reason he was out here, wasn't it? A voyeur who wanted to watch another suffer the way he had suf—

"Shut it up!" he said. Realizing that he had spoken out loud he repeated the command more softly, and tried to relax again by forcing himself to appreciate the scenery.

Just outside the town proper, the banking row of southern mountains came out to nudge the road. Kyle noticed that the recent rain held effect: the grass sprouted green, the shrubs verdant, though where the land had been sliced to make an even bed for the road, the clay and dirt had dried a tan and dun color. He found himself compelled to catch glimpses of the low, rolling plains to the north. They rippled green waves in the fresh breeze. Cattle grazed here and there, and occasionally ranch houses appeared, disappearing as Kyle rolled on by.

The view soothed him so much that when the distant hissing of snakes (still safely contained behind those cast iron doors in his mind) began, he was surprised. He chose to ignore them, but the hissing intensified as he approached a bend in the road where the base of the mountain shouldered out to meet the asphalt. The snakes had been silent for so long. Why now? Wasn't he rid of that part of his life? The sibilant sounds became very loud as he rounded the big shoulder of the base of the mountains, where the range ran back, away, as if in fright, from the road opening up both north and south to grazing land. The land, magnificent, beautiful, scenic, the bright sunlight picking up every color of the panorama and the—

"Those damn trees," he said, again out loud. They were like a smudge on a beautiful photograph. Kyle made a jerky search across the panorama of grazeland trying to shake the magnetic draw of his eyes to those black trees.

The hissing stopped suddenly, leaving Kyle's mind blank. He shook his head as if avoiding a gnat about to land on his nose, then felt himself slide back into reality. This was the place. Sergeant Gurnell had said that where the road ran into open land, there was an old yellow ranch house and a stand of trees, and there it was.

Kyle slowed and made a lazy left and drove through the space in the barbed-wire fence where the gate should be. He followed the tan-colored ribbon of dirt road that ran up to the low-roofed ranch house. He felt irritated for no reason and looked away from the house and toward the trees. *God*, he thought, *how the hell do trees get that black?* He peered for a moment and realized the dark, swamp green of the leaves only showed now because of the bright sunlight. *They're ugly*, he thought, and forced himself to study the house as the car rolled slowly toward it.

It sat neat and perfect except for the yellow paint with the white trim. Once bright and gay, years of sun and neglect had faded the color to a ghost of its earlier hue. Other than that it was in good repair. The roof had a few new shingles on it, the porch that ran the length of the front was clean, and held a white rocking chair and white porch swing. A screen door, closed, gave a dark hazy view into the open front door. Kyle could not see inside it.

Some two hundred feet from the house sat a barn, the same faded yellow as the house, its large hulking doors firmly shut, as if to keep in the secrets of the damned. In between, in stark contrast with the other two structures, a bleached-yellow henhouse stood, alive and bustling, with several dozen chickens. Other than that there was no sign of life.

With the ease of old habit, Kyle plucked the mike out of the clamp, pushed the red plastic transmit button, and spoke: "Car One, code six Pickers call, Highway 28, over?"

Sally's pert young voice cleared the static off the channel; "Car one copy code six Pickers call Highway 28." The transmission ended abruptly, and Kyle popped the strap on his holster almost without thinking about it. Yet, with that action he felt a vital focusing of concentration.

He slid out of the car and pulled his baton from the clamps on the car door and slid it into its ring on his belt. He was suddenly very conscious of the squeak of new leather and the fact that he was back in action. Excitement tingled up his spine. No one had come to the door yet. He had already started toward the porch when a movement caught his eye. He turned, his hand resting near his gun, his body loose in a very alert manner.

A tall thin apparition of a man glided from the henhouse in Kyle's direction, a galvanized bucket dangling from one hand, his faded denim overalls flapping around his skinny legs. His face was lean and seamed with a deep work tan. Shadows hung under his eyes like dark half moons, insulating hard blue eyes from the fragile shell of his body. His hair was flaxen white. Pickers stared at him, his eyes cold with hate. Kyle saw in the bucket some yellow straw and near to a pailful of good,

111

fresh eggs.

"You the mayor's new puppet?" Pickers spat, then walked past Kyle.

Kyle followed. "No, I wouldn't say that. And I wouldn't step up on that porch, Mr. Pickers. This is official business, not a social call."

Pickers stopped and turned slowly around. "Get off my land." His voice rattled.

"The funny thing about the law," Kyle said, "is that the second you break it, your property rights don't mean a damn thing."

Pickers blinked rapidly as if washing away a dirty film from his eyes. "I ain't broken no law."

"You shot at those kids."

"I did not."

"They say you did, Mr. Pickers."

"They're lying, then."

"Then you're denying that you shot at them."

"Yes, I am."

Kyle took a breath. The old man was stonewalling pretty damn good. He spoke as if he wasn't lying, but there was just enough emphasis in that haunting voice to give away his game: Semantics.

"Did you discharge your weapon last night, Mr. Pickers?" asked Kyle.

"I didn't shoot at those kids," he stated flatly.

"But you fired the weapon?" Kyle was unsure of what was fired, handgun, shotgun, rifle, or what.

"If I'd been shooting at them they'd be full o' buckshot, you can believe that, puppet! Now, get off my land!"

Kyle stepped up to the old man so fast that Pickers's face jerked back. "When I left for here," Kyle said, "they told me I'd be talking to a madman. I've looked in your eyes and I don't see a madman. So why don't you take a look into *my* eyes and tell me if you see a puppet."

Pickers broke eye contact and came back, looking long and

hard. He backed away, his bucket of eggs dangling loosely. "What do you want?" he asked, resigned.

"The first thing you could do is let me have a glass of water, Mr. Pickers; then we can sit down and talk this out like two sane men. There's an answer somewhere. I'm sure we can find it."

He turned and walked up the porch, opened the screen door. "You can come in," he said gruffly as if his mouth had trouble forming those words. Kyle warmed to the old man. Pickers probably hasn't said those words in fifteen years, he thought, so they might just be hard to say.


While Dave Pickers got the water Kyle sat uncomfortably in a hardwood maple chair, staring out the dining room window at those damn trees, trying to conceptualize his approach to the problem at hand—keeping Dave Pickers from hurting someone by accident.

The old man put a tall glass of tap water on the pitted maple table before Kyle and sat down with his back to the window. The trees sat framed through the window over Pickers's left shoulder, and Kyle fought for control of his attention as the blackness of the trees repeatedly drew his eyes. What was it about those trees? Finally Kyle turned his body and angled it toward the narrow kitchen, looking at the man occasionally as he talked.

"Mr. Pickers," he began, "let me say first that my name is Kyle Richards . . ."

"I can read," said Pickers shortly. Kyle saw the man eyeing his name badge.

"Fine," said Kyle. "I'm new around here, so I don't really have any biases yet. Why don't you tell me what the situation is from your point of view first? We'll start from there."

Pickers sat, his big bony-knuckled hands laced and resting on the maple tabletop, his eyes cushioned by the dark, baggy rings, eyeing Kyle for a long moment. "People trespass on my

113

land. Kids mostly, comin' to bother me, so I scare 'em off. That's all to tell."

"Mr. Pickers, if a man can't be let alone to live in peace, then there's something wrong there, and that's my job, to make sure you get some peace and solitude. It would make me mad as hell, too. But—" Kyle righted himself in his seat and glanced uneasily at the trees out the window, "but if those people break the law, by trespassing, and you break the law by shooting . . ."

"They're on my land," Pickers said fiercely.

"You're right, Mr. Pickers; but if one of those trespassers is killed, or even wounded by your shooting, and I mean by accident—I believe you when you say you're not shooting at them—then you go to jail, pure and simple. It's just like that . . ."

Pickers rose quickly and walked past Kyle into the living room. Kyle turned and felt a shock of adrenaline. Pickers was headed for his shotgun mounted over the fireplace.

Kyle stood and pulled his own gun, holding it down at his side. "You're not going to shoot me, are you, Mr. Pickers?" he said as if kidding.

"No," stated the old man, his back partially to Kyle. He reached for the shotgun. Kyle raised his own gun, watching Pickers hands.

The old man breeched the weapon and removed two shotgun shells. He snapped the weapon closed and put it back on the rack.

Kyle returned his own gun quickly to its holster before Pickers could turn around and see that he had had it out. Kyle relaxed, his legs trembling, bleeding off the effects of the adrenaline. He gathered his breath to speak, but held back until the beat of his heart slowed. It took some time. That old man could have just as easily intended to swing around and pull the trigger.

Kyle sat down, while Pickers busied himself with one of the shells. He silently pulled a small pocket knife from the kangaroo pouch at his chest, fingered open the blade, and began prying at the creased star closure at the business end of the shell. It opened blossomlike to Pickers's grim smile of satisfaction. Without saying a word he turned the shell over and the load fell to the table in a white, gritty rain.

Rice. Uncle Ben's Converted rice. That was the load.

"Now tell me that I'm gonna kill some kid with that," said Pickers.

"Well, I guess you can't. Not at a distance, anyway," answered Kyle, then picked up the other shell and fingered the rounded moldings that the buckshot makes on the red plastic tube of the shell, "but this can."

The old man wrinkled his nose in disgust. "That's not for the kids. It's for the trees. I use the rice to keep the damn kids off my land. They all want to go into the trees. I scare them off so they won't go in the trees and get themselves hurt. Load those kid-chasers away myself, too, and don't go telling me I might 'accidentally' go shooting 'em with the buckshot either. Been around guns too long for that flaming horseshit."

He emphasized his point with a sharp nod of his head and sat down.

Probably the longest speech the man had made in years, Kyle thought.

The old man sat the knife in the pile of rice. He laced his hands together on the table again and waited for Kyle to respond.

"What's in the trees?" Kyle asked. His question surprised himself.

The old man's gaze faltered, then sharpened in defiance. "The Devil," he stated flatly.

A dark feeling shot through Kyle like a chill. Let that answer pass, he thought. Lots of people believe in the devil. I've made progress with the guy, don't blow it now by making him talk crazy.

"What I propose," Kyle said, "is signs—"

"I got signs."

"Not with my name on it, you don't. Those little paper 'no

115

trespassing' jobs aren't going to cut it."

"It won't help."

"You can call the police when the little devils" (*Oh god, why did I say that?*) "come around, and I'll make sure damn quick somebody's out here, I promise you that!"

"I ain't got a telephone," said Pickers.

He sat stone-faced once more, his eyes erratically scanning the table.

"I'll get the municipal numbers for the signs and bring them out to you," Kyle said, "you can paint them yourself."

Reluctantly, the old man nodded his head. "Okay," he said, "but I don't think it's going to do much good."

"The law's for everybody, Mr. Pickers," Kyle said cheerfully.

"You *are* new around here, aren't you," he said.

Kyle made a mental note of it. The old man didn't trust the law in this town and he certainly hated the mayor. Not for the first time a nagging doubt about the mayor wormed itself across the back of Kyle's mind.

Now wasn't the time to think about it. Kyle asked to use the bathroom. In the bedroom hall he stopped to admire a painting. It was of a beautiful blond-haired woman—must be the old man's wife. In the corner of the canvas in an elegant hand were the initials DPP. David Paul Pickers, maybe it was Peter, now the damn middle name would pester him the rest of the day. Son of a gun, what was it about the old man that intrigued him so? The most obvious answer was the similarity of histories, and although he hated to admit it, there was some comfort in knowing that someone else had . . . *is* . . . traveling the same road as he. Like me, Kyle thought, the old man isn't crazy but he hasn't fully adjusted either.

He found the bathroom and started to enter, but spotted a door at the end of the hall and stopped.

The door, a bedroom door, was closed and locked with a steel hasp and padlock. Kyle blinked and twisted his head back the other way. The bedroom door, first one on the right was open.

116

He had passed it, and seen a four-poster bed, and matching dresser; definitely the master bedroom. His mind hung there for a minute, his head twisting back and forth between the two rooms. It was just like at his house, little Lisa's room and that room not twenty feet from him, now. His bedroom was as far away from it as he could make it, and evidently Dave Pickers had put himself as far away from that room as possible—and put a damn boxcar-sized padlock on it.

*To keep something out or keep something in?*

Cool it, Kyle thought, and went in and used the rest room. It didn't do him any good to think of such things; thoughts he had now all had to do him some good. That was his rule.

Dave Pickers walked Kyle out to the car as far as the porch, and stood there silently as Kyle slipped into his car.

"I'll get you those code numbers, Mr. Pickers. And remember, no more shooting, okay?"

When the old man said nothing, he said, "Think about getting a telephone, will you?" Kyle waved and drove off.

After clearing the Pickers call with the station, he checked his watch and saw that it was eleven-thirty and decided to take lunch and try to find that book on Douglas MacArthur he'd been looking for. He had seen a used bookstore over on Main and I Street, wasn't it?

The locked room in the old man's home nagged at his mind as he drove away.

*Why did that bother him? The similarity of that and Lisa's room? Could be.*

Other things about this call were troubling, too. Sure, he could tell himself not to think about them, and maybe even fool himself into believing that they had no validity, but his instincts had spoken, twice in one day: first, to say that Dave Pickers wasn't crazy; and second, that when Pickers had said there was a devil in those trees, he wasn't lying.

And that just didn't make sense, not at all.

*       *       *

117

The bum sat tucked away up on the hump of hill, half hidden behind some brush. He ducked down as the policeman's car pulled out onto the black asphalt road and then he sat up when he heard the big man's car roar by. He put the battered field glasses to his eye. The right lens was shattered but, though the view was distorted, they were serviceable.

The old man had gone back into the house, so there was nothing to see, but he hadn't really been watching the house, no. How could someone live so close to something so evil? Did it mean that he was evil too?

Slowly, he pivoted his head until the trees were in sight. Black and foreboding, brooding and evil. So Evil.

He dropped the glasses suddenly and crossed himself. *"Lord* have mercy," he incanted. *"Lord* have mercy."

He fumbled around in his sack and pulled out a large leatherbound Bible. It was scarred and pitted. He dug some more and came up with a rosary and put its cross to his weather-chapped lips. He pressed so hard that he split his lips even more; they bled slightly. Then he began to pray to God for the courage, and for mercy, because he was a lowly sinner and afraid. "God, puh-puh-please," he beseeched. "Please. I'm so afraid, afraiaid! I can't go in those trees, I can't." Tears began to roll down his cheeks. His lips were red and white; slivers of skin clung to the sores like spits of brain. "Ha-ave mercy, God. Oh, God, have mercy." He was crying fully now, and lay back against the sloping earth and buried his face in the twigs and dirt. "Puhplease have mercy!"

And when he had cried and recovered, he sat back up and brought the broken binoculars to his eyes. They were still there, of course, the trees . . . and he would still have to face the evil in there. It was waiting for him.

# 14

Michele McKinney took a last sip of her coffee and placed the china mug, with MOM stenciled on it in bold red letters, next to the register. She glanced at the circular wall clock. Eleven-forty, it read; and no one in the bookstore. This had to be the slowest Monday since she opened The Bookworm, eight years ago.

It was different then, she thought, as she folded the newspaper, catching a glimpse of the new police chief on the front page (*New Police Chief Starts Today* read the caption). Back then, it wasn't so easy getting started in business if you were a woman, especially a widow with a little boy. For her efforts at obtaining a loan, she earned negative answers, and a feeling that the establishment would rather she *be* on welfare, than make something of herself, become financially independent and free.

Well, thank God Uncle Edgar was a progressive thinker, that's all she could say. It had burned her no end to be forced to have him co-sign on the loan application, but it had been the only way to get the money. The question now was, Had she beaten the system or become a part of it? Beaten it, she decided. Showed them that she could build a lucrative business with her own smarts and hard work. Now she was part of a woman's network that helped other women get into business, including obtaining loans.

Her own loan was almost paid off, thank God and a lot of elbow grease. Now, The Bookworm provided her with a comfortable living, and a desire to expand, perhaps in nearby

Vickston, though that was still a few years off.

She sighed; time to go back to work. She walked down the aisle between the tall wooden bookshelves, and squatted down beside a heavy cardboard box that in its previous life had held oranges for shipment. In it were her newest batch of finds from Ellen Hall's attic.

She reached in the box and grabbed a handful of the books and marked them with a black price gun, sorted them by author, then placed them back on the shelf marked Harlequin.

She grabbed more books and shifted her position, sweeping the long black wool skirt up on her legs to aid in her mobility. She shifted forward and felt the big silver O of the buckle of her black patent-leather belt bite into her stomach, reminding her ungraciously that she had forgotten to do her sit-ups this morning. Although, if she did say so herself, she had managed to break even on the battle of the bulge. Not bad for a gal thirty-two years old, she thought. Do a few exercises, and dress right, and she just might make it to age thirty-three.

This morning she had chosen her white blouse, opaque with its silklike sheen. Her hair fell shoulder length and was the color of honey. Every morning when she faced herself in the makeup mirror, she patted down that pert little nose, gave those blue eyes a dash of eyeliner, the cheeks some blush, and that was it—not too bad looking, if she did say so herself and . . .

. . . And she still didn't have a fellah—except for Curtis.

She stopped working. Her eyes misted lightly at the thought of her son. *Thank you, God, for that little boy. He made life worth living, even without a man.* Sometimes she felt very guilty about not having a father for him, but she could not justify marrying someone she never loved just to give the boy a father—it had to be right for her as well as for him, otherwise it was no good for either of them. She had done her best to raise the boy to be a man, and maybe worried too much about him portraying a masculine image; she didn't want him to be a sissy, but she didn't want him to be a bully either; violence is bad, that's how

120

John had died, violence, the Vietnam War, when Curtis was just a baby. Now Curtis had no father.

The cowbell at the front door jingled. A customer, she thought. She stood up, dropped the marking gun and books in the cardboard box, and made her way past thousands of shelved books, turned the corner, and fell in love.

She stopped abruptly and hitched in a breath, her heart racing. She felt flushed. Did it show? Get hold of yourself, Michele!

This must be what Nana had meant, when she told Michele, "When I first saw your grandfather, it was at a picnic. The moment I laid my eyes on him, I knew we would marry. Your Aunt Clarice, the same with Uncle Edgar; your momma the same with your dad—it's a family trait, I think. We all got hit by Cupid's arrow."

Well, if that were so, Cupid had just emptied his quiver into her. Oh, she wasn't thinking marriage, but some serious dating was in order if she didn't stumble all over herself. He was beautiful, in such a masculine way. Tall, and was that ever tall. She gazed at him as he stood, backlighted by the noonday sun.

Don't just stand here, she chided herself, go on. She walked toward him, her heart still beating fast, and resisted an urge to fuss her hair into place. She put on her best smile, the same one that she used in all business dealings, calm, politely serious, and smiling all at once. She stuck out her hand, saying, "Chief Richards, I'm Michele McKinney. I'm very pleased to meet you."

She detected a small shock in his green eyes as he took her hand and shook it. His hand was warm and dry, and enfolded hers. "I recognized you from the newspaper," she explained. How gently he released her hand.

"Oh." he said. His voice was a gentle rumble.

Though she looked directly into his eyes, she was aware of the broad blue wall of his chest, and the star over his heart that gleamed dully in the neon light. He twisted his neck and looked back over his shoulder. "Michele McKinney, Proprietor," he

121

read. Michele tilted to the side around him and saw the large plate-glass windows and the reversed black letters under the large green ones that said The Bookworm, along with a logo, an erudite bespectacled worm poking half its body out of an apple, holding a book.

"The one and only," she said, smiling; there'd been no derision in his voice. There were still men who couldn't stand for a woman to make something of herself, but this didn't seem like one of them.

His eyes moved over the store quickly without missing anything. He said, "I always thought running your own business was probably the toughest job going. You must put in a lot of hours, huh?" There was genuine admiration in his voice and Michele felt that schoolgirl flutter suddenly subdued by her own pride.

"I enjoy it," she said matter-of-factly, "but yes, it is a lot of work." Do I sound like a martyr? she wondered. I hope not. He's divorced? . . . No, widowed, that's what Uncle Edgar said. And he has no children ("No family," was the way Uncle Edgar had put it). Now, how do I let him know that I'm available without making it sound like I want to do it right here and now?

Before she could think of anything he said, "I'm going to browse if it's all right with you."

"Go right ahead. That side is fiction, and this side is nonfiction." Damn. Was he interested, or wasn't he? She was sure that he was. She'd been watching around, no, *looking for*, the right man, a long time. The big problem in a small town like this was the very small selection of her kind of man. And just what was her kind of man? Well, ladies and gentlemen of the jury, her kind of man was that kind of man just disappearing down the aisle marked History.

She felt a momentary twinge of guilt. Was sex what it was about? After all, it had been almost over two years since her breakup with Mike, and even that relationship had been short-lived, no more than three months. She had felt something for him, but not enough. And since then, nothing, no one; not that there weren't plenty of suitors. There had been, and still were, plenty of them. It seemed to be a game with them: who could get into her pants. Not that she was a prude about sex, no, just a little bit old-fashioned; it had to mean something, that was all; and it couldn't possibly mean a damn thing if she wasn't interested in the man, and in this small town, face it, there just weren't that many eligible (her kind of eligible) men around. So she could just make do by herself, thank you.

Until now.

She hesitated about what to do while he browsed. She looked out the window and saw the stirrings of lunchtime traffic go by. Mrs. Alton, Bob Alton's wife, parked between the slanted lines in front of her husband's barber shop and got out of the '68 Chevy wagon. She came every morning at this time just to bring him his lunch. It touched Michele to see the middle-aged woman hand him his plate covered with tin foil and kiss him on tiptoes. Now that was love.

He put the books on the counter. Two of them. *American Caesar,* by William Manchester, and *Thomas Jefferson, an Intimate History,* by Fawn Brodie. Not a paperback porn reader like the old chief of police, Buddy Nelson, had been, that was for sure.

"Did you find what you wanted?" she asked.

"The history section, that's all you have, right?"

"What were you looking for?"

"*A Distant Mirror,* by Tuchman."

The name rang a bell. The collection that she had picked up at an estate sale. "Let me check. I just got some in. I seem to remember . . ." She left him for a moment and went down an aisle.

She found the five boxes and took an educated guess, the third box, and began plowing expertly through it. Finally near the bottom (where else) she pulled it out, *The Guns of August,* Barbara Tuchman. The author's name had keyed her, same author, but wrong title. She pulled it anyway. Then she hesitated, wondering if he would think her too pushy. That had been most men's major complaint. *What the hell? I'm interested; if he can't take me the way I am, I don't want him.* She hesitated a minute, stood up, then dropped the book back into the box. If he wants it he'll tell me. I'll just mention that I have it. That's not too pushy.

"Well, I have the author, but it's *The Guns of August,*" she said regaining the counter, "not the title you wanted."

She heard the jangle of the back-door bell, then the open and close of the office door. It wasn't time for him yet, she thought. "Hold on," she told the chief. She turned around and depressed a teardrop lever on the small gray metal speaker box. "Curtis! Are you there?" she said.

"Yes, Mom." His small voice sounded tinny through the com-box. She heard the office door open and suddenly Curtis appeared.

Michele noticed that with the sight of her eleven-year-old, his blond head canted to the side, his arms extended out, hands trailing along the fourth shelf of each row of books and looking everywhere but at the two grown-ups, the chief grinned. A relaxed warmth radiated from him as he watched Curtis approach.

Curtis was wearing his black Pittsburgh Steeler shirt with a big blocky yellow-gold number twelve on it. It hung limply around his thin, willowly frame. Thank God he was wearing his new blue jeans, not the old ones. He trundled toward them on blue Adidas tennis shoes.

The chief said, "Hi," and Curtis pushed his glasses back on his nose, and said, "Hi" back.

She felt pride well up in her chest as Curtis took in a deep breath, walked straight up to the chief, and extended his small hand dutifully. "My name is Curtis McKinney. Pleased to meet you."

A little mechanical, but just as she had taught him to do. The chief shook his hand firmly. "Kyle Richards," he said. "You like the Steelers?" He released the handshake.

"Yessir."

124

The chief fished a yellow pack of Wrigley's Juicy Fruit gum out of his shirt pocket and shook out a couple of sticks, offering it absently to Michele then to Curtis. Curtis glanced up at her for an okay. Michele nodded and he took a stick, opened it up, and stuck it in his mouth.

"Giving up smoking, been going through a lot these." He glanced at Michele, then turned back to Curtis. "You don't smoke, son, do you?" he asked, smiling.

Curtis's head jerked back. "Nossir," he said, and then, seeing the chief was teasing him, cracked a big toothy smile. How long has it been since he's smiled like that? Michele wondered. A long time.

"Good," he continued, "it's tough to kick once you've started, and it's bad for your health."

The chief turned to Michele. "How much do I owe you?"

Michele pulled out a receipt book, then opened *American Caesar*—four dollars—and Thomas Jefferson—five dollars—and added them together. "Let's see, that'll be nine-fifty-four with tax."

The chief slipped out his billfold and selected a ten-dollar bill and handed it to Michele. She punched up the amount of purchase on the green keys of the register, made his change, and counted it out into his broad hand. Calluses, the hard bumpy kind, knobbed up where the fingers joined the palm; this man did some work with tools, too. Gardening?

"You know what you forgot, don't . . ." But he didn't finish the sentence. From outside the screeching sound of brakes and tires was counterpunched by the gut-wrenching crunch of Detroit steel on Detroit steel, followed by the annoying blare of a jammed horn.

"They're playing my song," said the chief. He retrieved his books from the counter before Michele could hand them to him. "Save that *Guns of August* for me, will you?" he said as he headed for the door. "And, Curtis, you come down to the station . . . better call first, make sure I'm there, I'll give you a tour. How 'bout it?"

"Sure!" Curtis's little eyes bugged out of his head.

And the chief was out the door, the warning bell jangling after him.

Curtis ran to follow, but a sharp command froze him in his tracks. "Stay inside. Just because other people are ghouls, doesn't mean that we're that way."

"Oh, Mom." Disappointment pulled at his little face.

"Indoor ghouls, then." She laughed and ran from behind the counter. "We'll watch from the window."

Curtis pressed his face against the plate glass, tenting his blond bangs up above his head. Michele sensed that his excitement was more than just the prospect of a car accident; the new chief had made quite an impression on the boy. Most men that Michele had known had taken an interest in Curtis only in passing, a sort of obligation to be had in order to curry favor with the mother, and all that that entailed. Bed, mostly. Sometimes men made her so mad. But with the chief, if anything, the roles with Curtis would be reversed in this play. There was no faking the enthusiasm in that man's face, almost a craving for an interchange with Curtis that made the chief's face glow. And that's exactly what Curtis needed. Someone to take an interest in him— and maybe take an interest in his mom, too, if she was lucky.

"You liked the chief, didn't you?" she asked, stepping beside Curtis and looking out between the THE and BOOKWORM painted in huge green letters on the storefront window.

"He's strong, Mom. Did you see how big he is?" Curtis said excitedly, not budging from the window.

"Yes. Yes, I did. And smart, too."

They watched the chief. He opened up his car door and put the books in and grabbed the microphone and stood one foot on the bottom of the door frame, looking over the hood at the accident. Finished, he threw the mike into the car and closed the door and headed over to the melding of cars.

A new silver Cadillac with a black landau top (Wasn't that

Leonard Phael's car—oh, God) had run into an ancient beige Dodge (Now, that could be Mr. and Mrs. Finney's. Yes, she thought it was). People had started to gather, and traffic was jammed; a few horns sounded in irritation. And there was the chief, tall and confident, moving toward the noonday mess. A blue pickup truck blocked Michele's view, but it made its turn, revealing the accident even more. Yes, it was Leonard Phael, and he was mad! bending over and into the poor elderly Finneys' car and screaming. His long arms reached out and pounded on the roof of their little Dodge, scaring them half to bits, she bet. Leonard was a big man, almost as tall as the chief, and had a very bad reputation for drink, woman, and fighting. And when he got mad everybody stayed out of his way.

She felt concern for the chief. She had one time been at The Alibi Club with a date when Leonard, in one of his drunken states, had picked a fight with two big, burly oil-rig workers, and had left both of them cut, bleeding, and unconscious. That was before Phael had started working for Mayor Gathers's company.

Her heart flopped over with worry as she saw Kyle step up behind Phael, standing relaxed, but attentive, and talking to Phael's back. Phael continued to lean over, screaming into the elderly couple's car. Kyle's mouth opened a little wider. She could really hear nothing except the distant screech of Phael's screaming. Then, without warning, Phael turned blindly and threw a haymaker punch at the new chief, and it was like tossing a match on gasoline.

# 15

*"You doddering old fart! That's a fuckin' twenty-thousand-dollar car you wrecked, you doddering old fart!"* Phael screamed into the window of the old car, emphasizing each word with a thump on the top of the car, and continuing the invectives in choleric rage.

"All right, knock it off!" said Kyle in his fogcutter tone of voice, guaranteed to get the attention of anyone unless they were too far gone. "Over here. I want to talk to you."

Kyle was still twelve feet from the man, and moving closer, and the dumb ass hadn't budged, hadn't stopped screaming or pounding the top of the roof of that old gray Dodge. He was far gone; his back still to Kyle. He was wiry tall, and by the breadth of black cloth of his sports coat across his shoulders and his flailing arms, he would have a good reach, and power to do some real damage. The long legs were covered in light gray double-knit slacks; and he was wearing black patent-leather loafers. Kyle could not see the man's face, but his hair was carrot red, dry and brushed back like feathers, blocked sharply at the collar of his white shirt.

Kyle pulled his baton from its belt ring, then dipped down to get a look at the driver. An elderly man and his blue-haired wife. That explained it. A man as angry as this red-chested vulture was looking for easy meat, but the Dodge's driver was too old, so to take out his frustrations he was pounding the car. What he really wanted was somebody to pound, and Kyle knew that as soon as his words cut through to the man, he'd be that person.

He stopped six feet from the man. *"You! Back away from the car, turn around, and shut up!"*

His broad, bony hands froze in midair, just about to drop. Kyle angled over to the side and caught a glimpse of the side of the man's face. It was rugged and mottled a scarlet red. He had heard, and hesitated. "Step back," Kyle said, "Back here. I want to talk to you."

Suddenly the window of the Dodge started to rise. Kyle saw it. The man saw it, and began pounding on the window with his bare fists, starring the glass, screaming, *"Open up, you old bastard! You fart! Open up before I break your fuckin' nose!"*

Kyle moved in fast. He grabbed the man's left arm up above the elbow, stopping its pistonlike punch at the window. He pulled at him. He felt an instant meaty tension and then a flash as the man swung around and wildly punched. Kyle sidestepped, dodged the blow, and drove the baton deep into the writhing man's back. He kicked him hard in the crook of the leg, driving him down on both knees. The man's face mashed against the glass of the driver's window. Kyle rammed him again with the point of his baton, planning to ride him down and cuff him—

Until he saw the shoulder holster.

He mashed the man down, dropping his baton to get a better grip. He jerked the man's arm around his back. It gave with a sickening, wet popping sound. The man screamed. Kyle didn't care. The shoulder holster was in plain view now. Kyle grabbed for the man's gun, popped it out of its holster, and knee-dropped him in the kidney. The man screamed again. Kyle slammed the man's red head into the rough asphalt, and put the round hogleg of the revolver to the man's temple.

"Don't move!" he said. The man's body tensed, his eye, a sickly pale green, glared at Kyle, then his strength left him and his head sagged to the ground.

For the first time since the fight, Kyle became aware of the noise around him. The crowd was golly-geeing and murmuring. Someone yelled to his friend, "Hey, Bob, you missed it. The new chief just beat Phael silly. Jesus, ya shouldda seen it. Phael didn't have a chance."

As Kyle cuffed the man he looked briefly at the crowd and there, standing short and studious, his reporter's notebook open, was Edgar Griffith, in gray tweed jacket, tan slacks, and maroon bow tie. Next to him, squatting down on haunches shooting pictures like machine-gun fire, was a young sandy-haired kid. Kyle had seen enough of that in his lifetime to recognize a Jimmy Olson, a cub reporter/photographer for the *Daily Planet*, when he saw one. Shit. Just what he needed, his picture all over the front of the morning paper, shown beating hell out of some dumb asshole. It could go two ways. One, the citizens appalled by the violence on their city streets; the other, citizens grateful for an action-type police chief. It all depended on what this hothead's story was. And if Kyle could have his druthers, he'd druther no pictures be printed in the damned paper.

A three-wheeler pulled up, and the meter officer got off and, with a nod of her double chin, waddled toward the encroaching mass of onlookers, flapping small white flipperlike hands like she was shooing kids. She ordered in a strident voice, "All right. Let's break it up. Move on back. Move on back."

Two patrolmen, John Black and Tracey Higgins, pulled up near the scene of the accident in separate cars. They got out of their units, red lights still flashing.

Kyle stood and for the first time noticed the broad streak of blood from the Dodge's window down to the wheel well of the car. That would be the man's blood; Kyle had been uninjured.

"Roll it down," Kyle said gently to the old man behind the wheel. He repeated it twice more before the man complied. The old man and his wife, both over seventy, were shaking. The poor bastard could speak only in hoarse, unintelligible words.

Kyle wooed him as he might a child. "Everything is all right now." He smiled at the old woman who sat worrying both ends of a black shawl and staring at him with rheumy, brown eyes. "Everything is going to be fine, ma'am. I'll have someone here

130

to look after you in a few minutes." He raised up and called to Higgins, "Need an ambulance here." Higgins ran back to her black-and-white to take care of the matter.

"I wouldn't want to be you, Chief, when Phael's feeling fit!" someone catcalled from the crowd; a bray of communal masculine laughter followed.

Kyle jerked up. There were several men gaping at him. It could have been one of them, they looked the type. He turned back to the couple and comforted them.

For an hour Kyle, Black, and Higgins took statements during which time an ambulance came and rendered aid to Mr. and Mrs. Tyler Finney and Leonard Phael. Finally, Kyle directed Higgins to transport the prisoner to the station, and as the short blond-haired officer took the prisoner, Kyle waved Black over. He came in a fluid motion like he was skating.

Black was an Indian, handsome with smooth dark skin and oily black hair. He never looked Kyle in the eye for more than a second at a time, but that was no weakness in Kyle's book. The man moved with a great deal of self-assurance and Kyle liked him. In his stoic mannerisms he reminded Kyle of his own younger brother, Tom, and just as he had known his brother's moods, he had picked up on the uneasiness in this twenty-five-year-old Indian, like the calm stirrings of water deep in a pool. Something about this call was bothering Black.

"What is it?" he asked simply, and Black's dark eyes skittered to his for their brief second, then found a point in infinity to rest on, then answered in a soft voice, "That man. Leonard Phael. He's bad news, Chief."

"Well, we'll put him away for a while."

"No." Black's eyes began their flight again, this time catching Kyle for more than a few seconds. Kyle felt the young man's intensity. "He's the mayor's main man, Chief. He's bad news."

"Does he have a license for the gun."

The Indian's eyes were gone again, looking at rooftops. "I doubt it. Never needed one. He's the mayor's man. Mayor's not

131

going to be too happy about this one. Neither is Phael."

"What are you trying to tell me, John?"

"He's the mayor's main man," he said firmly, as if explaining it all, his gaze now dancing on the asphalt.

"So?"

"So, you'll be lucky if Phael doesn't try to kill you, Chief." Black's line of sight shifted sideways up to Kyle, and a grim look showed a row of crooked white teeth. "Mayor's man," he said, and headed for his car.

# 16

Edgar Griffith rushed back to his office after the big fight. He told Harvey to get ready for some great action shots of the chief and Leonard Phael going at it toe-to-toe. Bob Duncy had the film in the soup before Edgar finished telling Harvey that he was going to have to move the Gathers's Grainery reopening story from the front page to page two, next to the Briggs City Woman's Club piece on the corrupted morality of today's youth. Then, shunning the use of a car, Edgar began a nice, reedy quickstep down to the police station to get the story, and see if the new chief knew exactly *who* he had done *what* to. And, if the chief had any trouble with that, Edgar would be glad to fill him in, not to mention the consequences of tangling with a man like that hoodlum Leonard Phael.

Edgar paused momentarily outside the smoked glass doors of the police station to regain his breath and composure. Without realizing it he had almost trotted the three blocks from the *Review*'s building.

He held his green reporter's notebook in one hand, and with the other he tried with flat-handed strokes to lay order to the few gray hairs that were the last defenders of his pink freckled pate. Inside those doors lay the answers to some pretty hefty questions that he had been asking himself since that embarrassing day of the interview; questions that had made him reconsider Kyle Richards and make some investigative telephone calls. Calls, by rights, that he should have made *before* that interview three weeks ago. But he'd been so sure, so damn, damn sure about the nature of the mayor, that he'd judged and hung Kyle Richards before giving him a chance. Well, not all of his questions had been answered concerning the character of Kyle Richards, but one thing was certain: every single person that he had spoken to had nothing but the highest regards for the man as a policeman, as a leader, and as a human being. When you get that kind of feedback it's time to reconsider your position.

And then this comes along . . .

Griffith grunted: Whatever happened now on the other side of those smoked glass doors would be the final proof of Chief Kyle Richards.

Griffith pushed his way into a press of park locals. They were all here to see Phael. A bunch of old men who spent their time in the small park in the town square, waiting for the grim reaper to make his harvest. The thought gave the old newspaperman an inner shudder. Not him. Never him. He would die with the printer's ink still fresh on his hands, or be found slumped over an editorial—never a living death like that.

"Morning, Edgar." It was the colonel; he'd lost the use of a leg in the Korean War and walked with a pronounced limp.

"Colonel. What seems to be the event?" As if he didn't know.

"A little recon on the working of the taxpayer's police department, Edgar. Yourself?"

"A story, Lee. Always looking for a story." He nodded at the veteran and issued quiet "Hellos" to the others as he made his way through to the desk.

The "desk" was in reality a long counter that acted as a barrier into the inner office. To its right side was a small locking gate. Griffith nudged his way up to the counter and placed his forearms, one folded on top of the other on top of the cool Plexiglas that protected the counter's plane from harm.

Whoever was working the desk wasn't. Sergeant Mead was over at the switchboard talking to Sally Gonzales, his beady eyes dropping to her mammoth chest every time hers would

134

flick to answer a call. Ken Hart, their newest patrolman, was typing at the desk, intent on the report, trying not to make a mistake.

The new chief was nowhere to be seen, and Edgar was content to just observe for the moment. That moment proved very short. Kyle Richards emerged from his office at the same time that John Black brought Leonard Phael in from the back. The mayor's "executive," Phael, wore bandages across the left side of his face and his right arm was wrapped in ace bandages and resting in a sling. A spasmodic scowl gripped the exposed right side of his face and his carrot-red hair flamed up comically over to his surly, mottled face. A murmur rose from the town locals. The new chief studied the group with impassive eyes, then turned away and said something to the sergeant that Griffith couldn't hear. Mead's beady eyes canted up to the gaggle of senior citizens. "Right," he said.

The murmuring subsided a little. The sergeant rolled toward the desk with bad news in his eyes. Then Sally turned toward Richards and chirped, "The mayor's on line one for you, Chief. It's important!"

The geriatric crowd loved that.

The chief glared at them, and turned back to his office.

"Chief." John Black nodded toward his redheaded prisoner.

"Book him," Kyle snapped, and disappeared into his office.

Sergeant Mead hand-signaled to Black to wait. "That's interesting," said the colonel. Edgar watched the other men nod agreement. That's what this whole thing was about anyway, wasn't it? Obviously, the new chief had just not understood who he had tangled with, who it was that he had wanted to book. After his conversation with the mayor, that would all be changed. Wouldn't it? All Mead was doing was looking after his boss, like any good sergeant should.

"You'll have to leave, unless you've got some business here," Mead said to the crowd, then added to Griffith, "Press stays."

"Chief want to talk to me, Bob?"

135

"I guess so." The sergeant pushed a button under the desk and the gate buzzed. "Step on through and wait here, Edgar."

Griffith glanced at Phael as he entered. Phael now sat on a bench near the hallway leading back into the bowels of the station. He sat unmoving, glaring at the door of the chief's office where this minute the mayor was laying into the man who'd been stupid enough to bring him down.

Behind him, Griffith heard the colonel say, "But we do have business here, Sergeant. My men and I would like to fill out applications to become policemen."

"We're not taking applications at this time, Colonel," replied Mead, to his credit not mentioning age or the obvious disabilities of the old man.

"And why not?" asked the retired military officer. "Yeah, why not," chipped in his "men."

"Because . . ."

"Because you're discriminating because of age, aren't you, Sergeant?"

The sergeant shook his head woefully. "Coffee's over there, Edgar, help yourself," he said from the side of his mouth.

Edgar suppressed an urge to tell Mead to give up; the colonel would find some way to prolong his stay in the station long enough to see what happened when the chief came out of his office.

Edgar pulled a styrofoam cup off a stack and poured himself some of the black liquid. He loaded the cup with sugar to kill the bite of the acids and oils, and sipped it sparingly as he waited for the chief to come out of his office. It would all be right there, right on his face, and Edgar would be there to catch it.

Halfway through the cup, Edgar couldn't stand it any more and he placed the cup politely to the side of the maker along with other rejects. Kyle Richards stepped into the room and immediate silence.

All eyes beheld the chief.

Leonard Phael was the first to move. He stood up self-

136

righteously, turned his upper body, so that he could thrust his handcuffed hands out as far as he could from his back. *Undo these, you son of a bitch*, he seemed to be saying. The chief ignored him, and swung his gaze to the colonel and his group, and stared for a moment.

Griffith studied the chief's face. Beneath his ruddy coloring lay a flushed undercoating; his eyes were hard and filmed over. Griffith surmised that this was about the limit for the chief before he lost his temper. The battle with the mayor must have been a doozy.

"Sergeant, I said get those people out of here," he commanded, then turned to Black. "Black, do you understand the words 'Book him'?"

Black straightened up. "Yes, sir," he replied.

"Then do it."

The colonel and his regiment murmured in wonderment. "Well, it's about time," one of the old men said, as Sergeant Mead, on the other side of the desk now, ushered them out the front door of the station. Black had taken Leonard Phael back, disappearing into the hall that led to cells, to be booked. Griffith stood, openmouthed. Damn my eyes, he thought.

Chief Richards turned his attention to Edgar. "Mr. Griffith," he said. "Do you wish to see me?"

"Yes, I would, Chief," he replied, then nodded in the direction that Phael and Black had disappeared and said, "Quite a show."

"It wasn't meant to be 'a show,' Mr. Griffith." The chief pointed toward the coffeepot. "Would you like some coffee?"

"No, thank you." I've had the privilege, he thought.

The chief indicated his office with a hand. Edgar stepped into the man's private domain.

The chief indicated one of the oak chairs opposite his desk. "So what can I do for the press today?" he said.

Edgar gazed at the man thoughtfully for a moment, "Came for the story, Chief. The incident with Leonard Phael. I'm sure that you're aware that Mr. Phael is a high official in the

Gathers Corporation, not to mention a personal friend of the mayor." That's the way, bait him. Press him a little bit further and see if you can expose a vein.

The chief didn't take the bait. In fact, he looked like he was cooling down. The flush undertone of his skin was gone now.

"Mr. Griffith," began the chief, "I am aware of Mr. Phael's position. It has been pointed out to me all too many times by numerous people . . ."

"Including the mayor?" asked Griffith sharply.

The policeman rose gracefully and walked around to the front of the desk and leaned against it, his butt resting barely on the edge, his long legs straight and reminding Edgar of two telephone poles nicely wrapped in blue serge. He gazed directly into Edgar's eyes for a moment as if he were looking right through him.

"Mr. Griffith"—his deep voice was deadly serious—"I respect the mayor's confidentiality. My conversations with him remain safe with me, just as my conversation with you is none of his business. Now, what is it you want to know?"

"What charges will be filed against Leonard Phael?" he asked simply.

"Reckless driving, disturbing the peace, and assault on a police officer . . . Oh, and yes, carrying a concealed firearm and carrying a loaded gun in public. We're talking four misdemeanors and one felony count—the assault on a peace officer."

"You mean carrying a gun *isn't* a felony?" asked Edgar incredulously.

"That's the law, Mr. Griffith."

Edgar flipped open his notebook and quickly wrote down the charges in a cryptic notation that he had devised himself many years ago. "You know of course, Chief," he said, looking up from his notebook and staring straight at him, "that Leonard Phael will never go to trial for this? You do know that, don't you?"

Edgar watched the life go briefly out of the chief's eyes. His shoulders sagged. He exhaled a long, slow, tired breath. "I want this off the record. Agreed?"

"Agreed," Edgar said, and tried to convey an openness in his expression.

The chief studied him thoughtfully. "Is it really that bad in this town?" For a second, all Kyle Richards's defenses were down and Edgar could see into his soul, a man pleading to know what exactly it was that he had gotten himself into.

"Oh, yes, Chief. It's worse than that. It's rotten to the very core."

"And that's why you tried to nail me at the interview? You thought I . . . that I was a puppet?"

Edgar noticed the odd emphasis the chief placed on the last word. "Yes." What else could he tell the man, but the truth.

"Do you still believe that?"

"Jury's still out, but I predict a verdict in your favor."

The chief toyed with some papers on his desk for a moment, then said, "Fair enough. I'd like to ask you a favor, if I may?"

"What's that?"

"I'd like to avoid the stormtrooper image, if I can. The pictures you took . . ."

"They stay, Chief. I'd be doing less than my job if I pulled them." The chief's face was impassive. Edgar continued, "You did your duty, in a timely and professional manner, that's how it happened, and that's how it'll be reported—I'm not going to paint you a devil. Fair enough?"

The chief did not look completely satisfied, but he nodded, and shifted in his seat. "Fair enough," he said.

"Okay. Now, I'd like the rest of the details of the incident . . ." Edgar took down the facts, and at the end, stood up and shook Kyle Richards's hand. "Remember," said the chief, "Phael didn't get let go on my end."

"I'll remember that," replied Edgar, and felt hope; perhaps now he had an ally in this town.

139

# 17

"Chief. Bail's posted for Phael."

Kyle looked up from his notes on Project Upgrade. "Okay," he told Gurnell.

"He wants his gun back."

"No way." Kyle waved Gurnell out of his office and checked the time: ten to four. He shuffled through the notes on his desk and grunted. He hadn't gotten as much work done as he had wanted; but what did he expect from himself anyway? His time had been tied up pretty damn tight. Edgar Griffith had stayed until two. Then, Kyle had immersed himself in Project Upgrade to ward off the bad thoughts and feelings about today's events that kept jabbing at him.

*But how much good has it done me?* he wondered. *Not much. You just can't hide from a day like today.*

The mayor's call had been the worst of it; disgusting would be a better word, he decided. Disgusting because he thought he could get Kyle to kick Phael free. Kyly had answered the mayor's demand for Phael's immediate release with a firm "Negative, Mayor. Phael broke the law and Phael has to pay."

The mayor had sputtered at that, so Kyle pleaded the mayor's case back against the mayor. "Neil," he'd said, "let me tell you something. Edgar Griffith is out there snooping for a good corruption-in-government story. Now, is that what you want to read tomorrow morning when you're eating your Wheaties? 'MAYOR'S MAN ABOVE THE LAW', is that what you want your voting public to read? And how am *I* supposed to explain releasing him? You tell me that. He assaulted me in front of fifty witnesses. Griffith has pictures, for Christ's sake."

He'd shut up after that, and listened to a few seconds of telephone static that seemed like hours. Finally the mayor spoke. His voice was hard and whispery with anger, and all that he said was one work, "Okay," and then he'd hung up.

A small victory for Kyle, the outward appearance of his authority still intact, like the glossy red skin of a delicious apple, but when you looked deeper, bit into the fruit, the meat of it was dark and spoiled with rot.

The mayor was that rot.

Kyle spun viciously around in his chair and looked out the window.

"Let it go," he said out loud. "Let it go." The important thing to remember was that Leonard Phael had not left that jail without being booked and charged. Kyle had to remember that. As a policeman, he had carried out the responsibilities of his position. He couldn't blame himself if the rest of the system was corrupt, could he?

And that's what his question to Edgar Griffith had been about, hadn't it? *Is it that bad in this town, Mr. Griffith?* And what he'd been hoping for was a quizzical smile on the old man's face, a reply of "What are you talking about, Chief?" But it hadn't been like that. No, not like that at all. The old editor had sat there looking at him, his small blue marble eyes, the eyes of judgment, and told him that it was worse than that, *rotten to the very core,* he'd said. And at that point Kyle knew that it was rife corruption he was dealing with, and, what's more, Griffith knew about the mayor. Now the newspaperman knew that he knew, because for once Kyle hadn't been able to hide his feelings of abject disappointment. The old man had spotted it and in a way that made a tenuous bond between them. Any definite decision on the nature of that bond would have to be postponed for the future, however.

Kyle called it quits at a quarter to six, and by ten till he was steering his truck the short distance home up the gentle slope of Elm Street, enjoying the fresh darkness of the February night and trying unsuccessfully to keep the events of the day from wheeling in his brain like so many steel truck ball bearings.

He pulled into the drive and went directly to the back yard, snagging a flashlight and a fresh blue-and-white bag of Kingsford charcoal starter, remarking to himself with a silent smile the absolutely useless warning on the flammable liquid's can: DO NOT SQUIRT DIRECTLY ONTO IGNITED COALS. Kyle couldn't think of one person he knew that didn't juice up the process a little with an extra squirt or two.

His mouth began to water at the thought of the New-York-cut steak he had bought to celebrate his first day on the job. Well, there were things to celebrate. He had a job. He was back on the road to a normal productive life. And, of God, how he had waited for this day, after so many months of troubling thoughts.

In the bright white light of the kitchen, Kyle, still in his blue uniform, slipped a big cream-colored plate from the cupboard. He savaged the plastic wrap around the steak, laid the meat on the dish, and proceeded to punch it full of holes, on both sides, with a kitchen fork. This done, he slit the short rind of fat to prevent the choice cut from curling on the fire, then bombarded both sides of steak with every seasoning he could lay his hands on, sending spills of onion powder, garlic salt, dried parsley, black pepper, and many other varieties all over the plate and the counter.

Kyle dashed out the back door to check the coals. The barbecue set, he dashed back for a quick, bracing shower.

He stripped quickly in his bedroom, hanging his uniform neatly in the closet, then treated himself to a hot shower. He used two of the big brown towels to dry off. He let them lay where they dropped on the bathroom floor and walked into his bedroom. In five minutes he was dressed in jeans and a blue plaid shirt and out cooking his steak in the dark, flashlight in his left hand, long two-pronged fork in his right.

He sat in the breakfast nook and ate the steak with a tossed green salad and cold can of Pepsi. As he ate, he thought of Phael. The physical confrontation had been exhilarating in a way. He still hadn't lost his touch, and Phael was no pancake pushover. As for John Black's warning, Kyle had given it the same consideration he had a hundred other threats that had been issued to him over the course of his career.

The dishes went unwashed into the sink and Kyle felt his restlessness buzzing throughout him like the hum of high-tension power lines.

Pressure. Of an odd kind, he thought, because all those other things, the mayor, Phael, Griffith, the vile nest of corruption that his job made him sleep so close to, it was none of these that had haggled his mind the most. It was that old man Dave Pickers.

What was it about the old man that
(*Somebody butchered his wife and daughter*) made Kyle feel so *close* to him? And those haunting eyes. The sadness in them. So total. So complete. And that was why
(*Someone butchered his wife and daughter*) Kyle wanted to be near him, to help him. No, tell the truth. To help *yourself*, like a survivor of the Holocaust wanting to be with other survivors of that same hell because only they would understand the horror
(*Someone butchered his wife and daughter*) the horror . . .

He found himself in the hall closet pulling out a tan leather sheepskin-lined jacket. His throat felt suddenly dry, and way back of those cast-iron doors those snakes hissed faintly.

Choices, that's what sanity was about. He chose to ignore those sounds. That's what Dr. LeClerc had said. Choices.

He retrieved his backup gun, a Smith & Wesson Model 60 stainless steel Chief, from the bedroom, and using his ankle holster knelt down to fasten it to his right ankle. As he looked up he saw his daughter's bedroom door, and thought of the other night and the noises and the light, and the footfalls . . .

The hall light caught the oil-based paint (all the doors had been freshly painted before he moved in) and reflected off it.

For just a moment it seemed to waver and the fear started to rise in the gorge of his throat, but he swung his head around, twisting his body, and looked at his own bedroom door, open and reflecting the illumination from a small night-table lamp by his bed out of his direct line of sight. The paint was so fresh he could see a dark splotch that must be his bed reflected on its surface. He looked back at the closed bedroom door glistening dully, like an oily skin.

He arrived at the station close to eight o'clock and parked out front, finding John Black working a double shift, handling the desk. The station was empty and John was seated, bringing a meatball submarine sandwich to his lips when Kyle walked in. "No, stay put," Kyle said to him as the young officer rose to buzz him in, "I think I'm still young enough to do this." He mounted the counter, butt first, and swung long legs over and slipped on his seat and dropped to the other side.

It was a little too easy, he noted, and that would go into his report to the mayor and the city council. His report would request better security for the station and that would include a bulletproof glass screen across most of the desk, preventing such a simple entry to the complaint area.

"Still wouldn't want to be me, John?" he asked jokingly as he pulled a straight-backed wooden chair over to Black's desk, turning the back so it faced the Indian, then straddling it.

Black's gaze went everywhere, anywhere, but Kyle's face, then lit on his meatball sandwich. He grabbed it with both hands and smiled suddenly in understanding. "Oh, Phael, you mean. Yeah"—he laughed absently—"I guess I still wouldn't want to be you." He paused for a moment, starting to take a bite of his sandwich, then jerked it back in a half-poised position, moving his eyes directly into Kyle's. "But, I'll tell you one thing, you made a lot of friends today bookin' Phael. He's a real son of a bitch, and he ain't seen the inside of a jail since he's been with the mayor." His gaze hopped back to his dinner.

"The old chief would of let him go, unh?"

144

"Buddy would of *helped* Phael stomp on that Finney couple, then bought him a beer."

"That bad, hunh?"

"Worse."

*It's worse than that. It's rotten to the very core.*

The thought made Kyle uneasy, and he shifted in his seat and crossed his arms gripping opposite forearms firmly.

Black had managed to get in a bite and chewed it thoughtfully, following the swallow with a swig of Hires root beer.

"I had a call today. Dave Pickers. You know him?"

Black aborted an attempted second bite and his eyes started counting holes in the acoustical squares in the ceiling. "Hates Indians," he said matter-of-factly. "He's a little crazy. Kids always bugging him. His wife and daughter died so close together, within two years I think, it really got to him. I was just a kid at the time. It was ugly, *real* ugly."

"Gurnell says Pickers blames the local tribe for his wife's death," Kyle offered, letting the word "death" hang in the air speculatively.

Black's eyes snapped to Kyle, burning holes into him. "We get blamed for a lot of things around here"—he lapsed suddenly into a broken English—"but no Laikute touch Pickers's wife or his kid."

Kyle rocked back slightly as if to let some of the heat of Black's tone rise in steam from between them.

"I wasn't making an accusation, John," he said, eyeing the man steadily. Black's facial skin loosened slightly and he took a bite of sandwich, his gaze took off for parts unknown as he chewed noncommittally, and a stony silence ensued.

Discomfort wormed its way up from Kyle's belly. He had not meant to offend the young officer, but in matters of race, it was sometimes hard not to offend. Evidently the Indians were held in contempt by at least some of the townspeople, and it was a damn touchy situation, to say the least. Finally, to ease the tension Kyle asked a question: "Who do you think did it,

John? A transient, maybe?"

Black tilted his can of Hires and washed down his bite of sandwich, then momentarily glanced at the chief and said apologetically, "Sorry, Chief." His good-natured smile returned. Kyle acknowledged it with a nod. Black said, "You don't want to know . . ."

A harsh bell sounded, and both men glanced immediately toward the front desk.

The front door was closing slowly behind a huge man. He was an Indian, very tall, and even taller with his cream-colored cowboy hat on. The hatband was a ring of silver ovals, in the center of each a smooth, shiny piece of turquoise. A large oval belt buckle matched the hatband, splotched in the center with large piece of the semiprecious stone. His hair fell straight and black down to the roll of his massive shoulders that were struggling valiantly to stay inside a mammoth fur-lined jacket. The man's eyes were wide and bloodshot, and the malty smell of scotch rolled across the administration area like a billowing fog.

Kyle shot a look at Black and then back at the big Indian, who now raised a half-empty quart bottle of Johnny Walker Black to his lips and tilted it to the neon lights, blinking with heavy lids as he guzzled.

Good taste, thought Kyle, and a cast-iron stomach.

"Wolf, what in the hell do you think you're doing?" demanded Black, then followed that statement with more words in a language Kyle didn't understand; apparently their native tongue.

From Kyle's angle of vision, the big Indian's head seemed to sit on top of Black's head and his dark eyes steadied a moment. Black said something else in the Laikute tongue, the rich consonant sounds rebounding through the empty room in an alien rhythm that was pleasing to Kyle's ear.

"Don't give me that shit, Black Horse," the big Indian said. "Wasn't me changed my name, was it? Hell no! Hell *no!*"

With a frown he screwed the cap back on the bottle and

146

presented it to Black as if he were going to hit him in the chest with it. Instinctively Kyle stood up and moved forward, visually patting down the big Indian for suspicious bulges that might indicate a weapon.

"It's all right, Chief," said Black without turning his head; his voice was level and atonal. "Wolf here wants to sleep it off, that's all." He took the bottle of scotch and slipped it on a shelf under the counter, then pressed the door release. The buzzer made an irritating sound all the more noticeable in the night quiet of the station.

To Kyle's surprise the big man moved as quietly as John Black, his blue jeans seeming to hide comparatively spindly legs, and at a closer view he noticed that the face of the silver-and-turquoise belt buckle canted, with the help of a parabolic stomach, toward the floor. The Indian had to be either in his late twenties or early thirties, it was hard to tell.

The newcomer walked quietly within three feet of Kyle, stopped, and raised a meaty right hand, "Ugh," he grunted.

"Knock that shit off, Wolf," said Black. "You don't, I go call Dove and tell her where you at."

"Ah, shit, no!" exclaimed Wolf, the fumes blasting Kyle so that he turned his head in self-defense.

"Now, go sleep it off."

Wolf ignored Black. "Me Chief," he grunted to Kyle. "You Chief of paleface long-knives." He thumped his chest, making a muted whacking sound. "Ugh."

"Ugh, yourself," said Kyle. "Now straighten up or we'll straighten you up, Wolf. Take your choice."

Kyle watched a wildfire somewhere in the reaches of the man's soul through the blitzed lenses Wolf was trying to pass off as eyes. Then the fire extinguished, and the man did his best imitation of sober, and offered his hand.

"Wolf's the name."

Kyle glanced at Black, who seemed relaxed enough, so Kyle took the hand. "Kyle Richards," he said.

"Black Horse is my brother-in-law," he slurred, and

wrapped a massive arm around the other Indian's shoulder, who quickly brushed it off.

"Not for long if Dove finds out you're boozed up again. Now go back there and sleep it off."

"Ain't sleepy."

"Get sleepy." He spoke in their native tongue again, and Kyle noticed that when Black spoke to Wolf they always held steady eye contact, as if more than words passed between them.

"Okay, okay," said Wolf, and turned to Kyle, raised his hand again, and with an "Ugh" turned and disappeared down the hall toward the cells.

"Who's back there?" asked Kyle.

"Nobody. Tanner's out to lunch. It's okay, Wolf comes in to sleep it off. He knows the way."

Kyle nodded. At least the man had sense enough to be off the street when he was ripped to the gills.

Kyle stretched his head. What had *he* come in for? Ah, yes. "Do you know where the Pickers girl's file is? That was a long time ago, wasn't it?"

To his surprise Black knew instantly. It was upstairs in the storage files, first bank on the right. When questioned how he knew exactly where, Black replied that everybody has to get a look at that file, and it's pulled out at least once a year by some of the department ghouls, just to look at the pictures.

Black went back to tuck Wolf in and Kyle found the access door to the stairway behind the booking cage. A master key jangled out from his key ring opened the locked door. Kyle entered, found the switch, and flooded the stairwell with a pale yellow light from a low-wattage bulb. He mounted the stairs and was confronted immediately by several rows of gray metal file cabinets, all with a heavy coating of brown-gray dust on top.

After a few minutes of reading once-white drawer tags now in various shades of yellowed age, he squatted in front of the bottom drawer of the eighth cabinet in the first bank. The tag insert read Homicide—Unsolved: 1963-1973. The drawers were unlocked and slid open easily without a sound. Kyle wrinkled his nose as the musty smell of old paper mingled with the dusty stale air of the low-roofed room. Kyle reached by instinct for the Pickers file. The quantity of paperwork had been so great that the file had been placed in a dun-colored expando-file and wrapped with three large elastic bands. There were only five other files in the drawer, another reminder that he was in a small town. If he took any ten-year period in Los Angeles and stacked unsolved homicides, they would reach from the floor to the moon. Crazy world.

Kyle lifted the weighty file out with one hand and placed it on its back on his upper thighs: File No. 000-65-001: Catherine Eve Pickers, the tag read. Kyle slid the drawer home and walked downstairs, the file riding securely under his left arm.

Black was back at his desk taking down information from someone on the phone. Kyle selected an empty desk in the corner of the room and sat down. Black passed him on his way to the dispatcher's console where he made a routine call and tagged it "Maple Street call." Kyle ridded the file of its bands, and in a massive fistful pulled out its contents: photos, police reports, investigative reports and county supplementals (the County had been called in on this one. Have to be a biggie for that, Kyle surmised).

He sorted the various reports from the photos. He found it useful to see the pictures before the unintentional biasing that the report reading introduced into his mind. He picked up the stack and set it in front of him, then lifted the first eight-by-ten black-and-white glossy up gingerly by the edges and gasped audibly. "Jesus Christ," he said out loud.

"What?" said Black, and he moved over beside Kyle, his presence felt by Kyle like soft cotton on one side of his face. The picture repulsed him. He had been in police work almost twenty years now, and even that had never hardened him to some of the bestial actions of one human being on another.

"I know," agreed Black to an unspoken statement, "it's pretty gross."

The texture of the photo's print was sharp and clear, blacks, grays, and whites, but the inhumanity and terror that the girl must have felt could not have been more graphic even if the snapshot was in living color. Her head had been severed and stuck in a large hole in a tree. This particular picture was an extreme close-up showing what, even in its agony, had been a pretty face, light hair, her eyes bulging out of their sockets, her mouth open in rictus as if in terror of the final scream torn from her throat. The severed area of the neck was ragged and looked almost as if it had been chewed off. The area below the hole that held the young, pretty girl's head was one big black drip, blood in black and white. But what disturbed Kyle the most was the tongue, the totality of the mouth itself. It was odd, unnatural. The tongue (if that's what it was) stuck out from the mouth like a black wooden stake and seemed to be sticking through something stuffed in her mouth. Something that looked like her—

"Her snatch," stated Black, reading his mind. Kyle watched a tanned finger jab a rough circle around the tongue. "He scalped her snatch and stuck it around her tongue."

Kyle slammed the photo down on the pile and laid both his hands over it. The queasiness rose from the very gut of his being as he fought it back. *Dear God!* And this is what the old man had seen? No wonder he went over. No wonder. *Had he seen them do it? I hope not.*

He pushed the photos aside for now, and picked up the reports, purposefully reading slowly, concentrating, removing his mind from sickening thoughts that circled like vultures in his head waiting patiently for something innocent to die so that they might feed. Dave Pickers had been found the morning after the butchery, lying by the side of the road screaming about devils and demons. After an extensive search the head of his daughter (and only the head) was found in a hold in a tree. The marks around the neck were determined to be teeth of undetermined origin (*Jesus, her head had been chewed off?*), the tongue was found to be filled unnaturally with dried, coagulated blood, the pubis area of the skin removed from the groin region of the torso and placed in the mouth surrounding the stiffened tongue. The report read in its final paragraph that the murder was committed by perpetrator, or perpetrators, unknown. Dave Pickers remained under heavy sedation for a period of time, and when finally in a condition to be questioned still stuck to his story that the Devil had done it (*He had broken. It's understandable. Every man has his breaking point, hasn't he?*)

Kyle looked up. Black had returned to his desk and Kyle hadn't even noticed. "Pretty grim, hunh?" he asked.

"No shit. I just about tossed my cookies when I looked at those pictures, Chief," said Black.

Wolf emerged from the back, looking no better than he had going in.

Kyle looked at him and continued talking to Black. "Pickers still sticks to his story that the Devil did it," said Kyle, buying some time before he had to return to the photos.

"That's all hor'shit!" exclaimed Wolf.

Kyle looked patiently at Wolf, then back to Black. "What do you think, John?" he asked quietly. Wolf stood motionless, the tenseness in the air somehow cutting through the remaining fog of his drunk.

"I think," said Black, "that Wolf better go lay down and sleep it off." He rose and started herding Wolf down the hall.

"John," Kyle spoke sharply. Black stopped and turned around slowly, staring at Kyle, waiting. "What do you think?" repeated Kyle.

Black exhaled deeply, hitched up his pants, and stared Kyle straight in the eyes. "I think Pickers is right, Chief," he said lightly, "but don't listen to me, I'm just a superstitious Indian."

"Bullshit, hor'shit," said Wolf from down the hall, and Black turned to take care of his charge, leaving Kyle alone to finally face the other pictures. He pulled the stack over reluctantly and shifted through them almost absently, observing but trying not to look too closely at first as if his mental distance could keep his stomach in line. There was a shot of the group of tall trees. He spotted Sergeant Gurnell, a young patrolman then, with a thinner body but that same fat face, and some more close-ups on the poor girl's head (*God, how had it been to be the man who pulled the head out of the tree? Who got the job? Jesus!*), and then a full shot of the area . . .

Kyle froze. He held on to the one photo as the rest cascaded as if in slow motion down on the tabletop. The picture began to shake as his hands trembled. It couldn't be.

His mind began to tell him a thousand reasons why it couldn't be.

But it was . . . Oh, yes it was . . .

The full shot of the tree that sucked that little girl's head into its bowels so mercilessly, its twisted lifeless limbs so cunningly beseeching the dome of the sky, the dome of his skull, was his tree. The tree in his dreams!

# 18

Dave Pickers stood on the porch and stared after the police chief as he drove away. There'd been no puppet in that man, that was for sure. Nothing but strength. And finally, thank God Almighty, someone could look at Dave Pickers and not see a madman.

*If I can trust this man* . . . Richards, he thought wistfully . . . Kyle Richards, the name tag had read. He pondered the name for a moment. Not a biblical name, he decided, and turned slowly to enter his house. The sight of the screen door brought him out of his reverie as he touched its handle and stepped inside. He felt compelled to go to the room, though his body cried out for sleep.

Not this time, he decided. He would get sleep first, then, if there was time, the room. He had been in there once already today, in the morning, after his rounds, as he always did, every day since he had arrived home from the hospital after that devil took his baby. But not this time.

He started down the hall, but when he tried to turn into his bedroom his body refused. Instead, his legs began to move against his will. He found himself walking in stiff, long strides down the worn hall runner past his own bright paintings from better days. His body stopped and turned in halting, exact, robotlike movements so that he faced the entrance to the room, the tip of his nose an inch from the surface of the closed door.

*Oh, Jesus God. Turn and go in the bedroom and sleep. Do it!*

He tried to turn, but with the attempt he felt the last vestiges of his will wash from him and he relented to whatever drove him to do what he did. It must be the will of the merciful God he prayed to every day. Yet, what he did in there, they were so . . . so hideous . . .

His arms felt stiff as he brought his hands up to grope under his shirt for the stainless steel chain. He pulled it out of his shirt, feeling the angles and the edges of the key scrape along his hairless chest. As it freed the shirt, it popped out dangling from the short stretch of links between his curled fists. He stood staring at it at eye level, his elbows and forearms flush against the door. "Okay, okay," he said aloud, and the flooding sensation of relief completely relaxed his muscles as if some giant magician had thrown a switch cutting his power from the mechanical dummy.

How long had it been since he had been his own man? What, fifteen, sixteen years? Since that night. Since that night he'd felt dominated by a power, or powers, unknown, caught like a stick in the rapids of some dark river, buffeted and twirled, sucked under and spit out, but always moving, always moving . . .

The Yale padlock gave with a *click* as the well-worn key sunk home and turned. Dave removed it from the hasp, pulled the flange free, and opened the door, stashing the lock in the bib pocket of his overalls as he walked in. He closed the door behind him.

The room was twelve feet square, lit by a center ceiling light fixture. Two exposed one-hundred-and-fifty-watt Sylvania light bulbs bathed the room in a white sheet of light. The frosted, etched glass bowl that should have shielded the bulbs sat now on the broad worktable by the window, serving as a repository for crumpled tubes of oil paints. The window was covered unceremoniously with three large strips of black tar paper hastily attached to the wall by nails bent over and pounded erratically into the plaster of the wall. Unframed paintings ran stacked in a four-canvas-thick border around the perimeter of the room. They all were covered with gray-brown croaka-sac potato bags. The smell of old paint, turpentine, and dust scraped the membranous linings in Dave's nose insensate, then settled in his lungs. He really should air the room out, but the thought of what it contained possibly being exposed, even for a second, to outside eyes was unthinkable. Since coming home, he had never left the door open longer than necessary for him to enter or exit.

He moved slowly to the workbench, pulling a four-legged stool across with him, raising a scream of wood on dusty wood floors. He sat down, not really knowing why he was here, and placed his arms folded across one another on the flat pitted surface of the old table. Directly in his line of sight, placed between rough stones as bookends, were the two books that meant the most to him now: a big, leather-bound Bible; and a cloth-covered daily journal that covered every day of his life since he had gotten home from the hospital. He had already done his entry for the day. God, how he longed for his bed, to get some sleep before tonight.

Suddenly, he rose, feeling his body move independently of any conscious will on his part. He recognized the feeling, and for a moment felt helpless and sad—*Not again,* he pleaded silently, but already he was moving, bending, picking up a large blank canvas (*stilt-walking, that's what it feels like*), and moving toward the empty easel and placing it down in the bottom runner, lowering the upper clamp and making it tight with a turn of the screw so that the canvas lay lengthwise.

Broad, he thought. Forty-eight by thirty-six. That's big. None of the others were this big. Jesus . . .

His hand reached for a number-three charcoal pencil from a small wooden supply table beside his easel that held his brushes, fresh tubes of paints, rags, and medium and turpentine (both kept in closed clear jar containers). He began to draw, while he stood rooted in the floor, his arm and hand moving numb and independently of any conscious effort on his part. He watched as he had so many times in the past, feeling a spectator, then a voyeur, then an entrapped participant in something unholy.

After a while his breathing became labored. His lungs ached and sweat popped in small protesting beads on his forehead and soaked his armpits. His leg, back, and neck muscles screamed to be set free, feeling as if they were impregnated with hot rods. And even with this he was able to concentrate enough on the tracings on the canvas to recognize some of the elements of the sketch. In fact, he realized, he was familiar with almost all the elements of the sketch except one, the last one. But as the hand moved to fill that in—and somehow he knew that it was important that he see that one—the burning-hot rods that were the muscles in the rest of his body exploded into white-hot spikes, forcing him to squint in pain. He grimaced as his body, suddenly free after the hand finished the sketch, dropped like a sack of nails to the floor. He groaned and passed out.


Dave awoke lying on top of his bed. A hazy memory, like electric noise, hung in the cavity of his mind: after lying on the floor for so long he had managed to crawl to the door, raise himself using the doorknob, and stumble out into the hall. (*Had he . . . Yes, he had taken the time to lock the room . . . Yes, it's locked. It must always be locked*). His legs had somehow moved him to the bed and he'd fallen face first onto the mattress, and slept until now.

He heard a moan, low and ugly, from somewhere, from someone alien. As the throb in his head subsided, and the dull pain passing in waves throughout his body began to withdraw, he realized that the sound was coming from himself. He made a conscious effort and the noise stopped. He lay there for several more minutes, then, groaning, he rolled over and sat up and held his thrumming head on his broad forehead with the palms of both hands, the bones of his elbows dug in just above his knees. After a few minutes he felt strong enough to go into the kitchen.

The low golden slant of the sun's rays bathed the long kitchen, reminding Dave of the nearness of dusk. "Damn," he swore. There would be no time for a shower, nor a decent meal before walking those trees. Damn. He broke three eggs in a pan dabbed with butter and scrambled them, thinking about how his nightwalks had changed over the years. In the beginning, when he was fresh out of the hospital, he'd rise about ten o'clock at night, get dressed, and make his rounds until about one o'clock, pitch black in the dark, rain or shine, didn't matter. He'd be there. But over the sixteen years the doings out there had started taking place a little earlier and ending a little later. Not that they happened every night, but the nights they did happen . . . Well, it was like they were *growing,* and now the ruckus started right at dusk and went on all the way to dawn. And it scared him. If it's growing, that means it's getting bigger and bigger, don't it? Well, so far, they hadn't come out of the trees, and he wasn't going in (and no little thrill-seekin' kids were going in either—they just didn't know. If they only knew, they'd leave him alone; they wouldn't be within miles of this place. What happened to his Cathy wasn't going to happen to nobody else's child; he'd see to that).

He finished his eggs as the rays of the sun turned that somber golden glow, just before the big orb slipped down so far that all was left was the half-light of its gift in a gray, gauzy wrap over the earth.

There wasn't much time, so he left his plate on the table and found his dark-blue navy peacoat and wrapped himself in it. Then he donned a black rainslicker that he wore every night, rain or shine, because it got wet out there in the brush, the night's dew clinging to the branches and grasses. He pulled a black knitted stocking cap over his head and the matching black rain hat whose brim he turned up like the sides of a boat. He patted the sides of his slicker and found the reassuring lumps of shells in both pockets—the left pocket, rice for the damn kids, and the right held double-O buckshot for anything else that wanted to get in his way.

157

He grabbed a pair of leather gloves from the top of the closet along with his flashlight, then lifted his double-barreled shotgun from its horseshoe mounts above the fireplace. Placing the gloves and flashlight on the mantel, he breeched the weapon and the glistening copper eyes of the shells stared reassuringly at him. He closed the gun with a snap of his wrists and held the piece in the crook of his arm as he shimmied on his gloves. They felt warm immediately, and he grabbed the light, stuffed it down deep beside the shells in his right pocket, and grabbed a small pocket-sized Bible off a sideboard and stuffed it down on top of the rice-filled shells in his left pocket. He always walked with the Word of God, because he knew only God could help him get what he wanted most.

The screen door slamming behind him, he began his praying out loud in a low monotone as he walked in the graying dusk toward the dark, towering trees. His voice seemed not to carry on the air, but rather stopped dead six inches from his face. He prayed: "Dear God, Oh, my God, forgive me, for I am a sinner. I have sinned against Thee though I know not why or how. For whatever my sins are I am sorry and repent in Jesus Christ's, your Son, the living God's, name. Please, God, hear my prayer: I'm pleading not for myself but for my daughter, Catherine, but a child of God, and a Christian child, that the Devil has taken, and thrown back her head like a bone to the dogs. Please, God, please bring the rest of her body back to me. Please deliver her body and her soul from Satan. Oh, God do this for me, your lowly servant. In your name I pray, God. Amen."

He repeated the prayer over and over until he reached the path that circled around the ring of trees, worn smooth by sixteen years of his boots. He stopped and eyed impassively the massive wall of trees. They stood tall and pernicious in the meager light offered by the yellow crescent moon; unmoving in the cold, still night. They're out tonight, he thought. Though he saw nothing, he could *feel* that odd sensation of foreboding, like candle wax dripping over the inside of his skin.

It made him shout out loud to the trees, "God will punish you, Satan!" But these words, too, the night enfolded into its darkness.

For the first few hours Dave walked, resting every half hour for five minutes. He had found over the years that he could last longer that way. Later on he would rest ten minutes out of every thirty, scanning alternately with his line of vision the trees or the road. Along the backside of the trees Dave moved faster. He was out of the line of sight of the road and that's where the kids would park; he could always tell because of the lights. They never dimmed their lights soon enough. He could always pick them up from their lights, unless he was behind the trees, so he made that stretch as fast as he could.

The smells started just before midnight. The stink of dead, ripe meat, two, maybe three days' spoiled, rode the night wind, faintly at first; then, as if in waves, the vile odor radiated from the evil trees, bringing with it the porcine smell of roasting human flesh. Dave knew that smell, that roasting stink, from his army days in World War II (he'd carried a flame thrower). He wrinkled his nose, unintentionally catching a noseful of the powerful stench. It smelled hot and fresh . . .

And then the screams began.

Human cries of anguish it sounded like (*My Baby! My Baby! Oh, My Poor Baby!* his own mind screamed) but distant, maybe not human at all.

Dave stood frozen for a moment, on the road side of the trees, listening. The screams vanished; there was silence for a moment. He leaned into the trees, cupping one gloved hand to his best ear, straining to hear. There was something being . . . chanted. That was it, chanted. His face contorted, as if pulled back by thin unnatural fingers, in his effort to hear. Yes. Yes. He could hear faintly, the chanting of the dead, *"Child, Higgums! Child, Higgums!"* in a slow death-beat rhythm. At least that's what he thought he heard, but he was straining and could not be sure. Not without moving closer.

He stood indecisively frozen for the moment, his hand

159

cupped to his ear, listening. He did not want to go any closer to those trees, no. But, to hear, to be sure, he would have to.

Without thinking again for fear of not doing it, he moved closer to the trees. The brush thickened as he came closer, the witch grass more rank until he was within thirty feet of the black wall of boles that towered high into the cloud-speckled heavens. The stench gagged him at this distance, and from deep in that terrifying, textured blackness the chant was clear and throbbing like the beat on a giant drum. Its intensity became greater, louder, so very loud, that it mesmerized him for a moment. He stood dead still in his tracks listening to its beat and its rhythm and its words. He understood those words, but what could they mean?

From the dark weave of the tree trunks a set of glowing amber eyes appeared, low and feral. He froze, his shotgun clutched unmoving in his hands. Another set of eyes appeared, these glowing iridescent red. Then another set, and these were large and a burning iridescent yellow. And suddenly the whole wall of the woods was blanketed with glowering eyes of red and green and yellow, in sets of twos and threes. Thousands of leering, hateful, inhuman eyes, watching him, wanting him—to come to them! Be one with them!

A scream rose in his throat. He heard a booming crack and looked up. The tree directly in front of him began to totter, then fall slowly forward, gaining momentum—falling on him! Other cracking booms filled the night air. The sounds jolted him out of his shock. He jumped to the side. The first tree crashed down beside him. But more trees were falling! They would hit and kill him! He bolted at an angle away from the woods. He heard the cracking of the splitting wood, the *whoosh* of air rattling the leaves and branches, the thundering crash of the giant trunks as they struck the ground just beside him; another falling next to it, to crush him. He made spry, long-legged strides away from the woods, the trees crashing to the ground behind him. Only twenty feet to go and he would be out of their range. Ten feet. Five feet, and he felt the scratchy slap of death's branches on his back and suddenly was thrown forward into a roll, landing flat on his back. He looked up just in time to see the giant black tube of another tree falling, falling right on top of him—

He rolled quickly to his right, yelling, and kept yelling until the tree crumpled next to him and drove the winds from his lungs with the thinning lengths of its outer branches.

He gasped for breath and pushed madly against the branches, scrambling to the safety of the open land. He sat up with difficulty. His ribs ached. He raised his gloved hand to his face and felt fire. Even in the weak moonlight he could see the black liquid—blood from a nest of scratches on his face.

He sat that way for a long while, staring at the fallen trees and the massive black wall of their brothers beyond. No smells now. Nor sound. All was quiet. And finally he raised himself painfully to his feet, still feeling stunned. He fished his flashlight out of his pocket (he had landed rough on it and hoped it still worked) and turned it on. He was in luck. Keeping a careful eye on the stand of eucalyptus he searched through the fallen trees and found his shotgun right where he would guess he was knocked into a roll. He picked it up and retreated quickly to the safety of his well-worn path. For a minute he stood staring coldly at the eucalyptus stand.

You came close tonight, Satan, he thought, but God is my protector. Praise God.

He pulled the small Bible from his slicker and, leaning the shotgun against his side, held it in both hands. He repeated his prayer for Cathy, adding a "thank you" for delivering him from the maw of the Beast.

Finished, he tucked the book away and continued on his rounds until dawn, when he trudged the quarter mile back to his home, went in, and fixed himself breakfast. By seven o'clock he was in the locked room, sitting at the workbench entering the night's events in a steady even hand, black ballpoint ink on the stiff white pages of his clothbound journal. Behind him was the sketch of the painting. Before he had sat down he had taken a good look at that and seen the last element that had been denied his eyes the day before (he would start the painting sometime today, he was sure of that), and now it all made sense. He wrote everything that had occurred that night in the journal, and on the last line of the entry wrote, *A decent man would warn him, but I cannot. He is the only way to bring my baby back to me. Thank you, God, and may God forgive me for doing this to him.*

He folded the book closed. It made a quiet whispering sound as he slipped it in next to the giant brown leather-covered Bible. But that sound was nothing, swallowed meanly by the throbbing in his head, the throbbing sound of the chant. The chant of the dead. At first he had thought the incantations *Child Higgums. Child Higgums. Child Higgums.* But when he'd gotten close enough, he'd heard what was really being chanted, and the name clicked right away. The legion of the damned were chanting, *"Kyle he comes! Kyle he comes! Kyle he comes!"*

# 19

Kyle declared the first Saturday after his first week of work a personal holiday, putting aside the status-report project on the department until next Monday, and found himself buying paint at Wagon Wheel Hardware on the west side of Main Street at nine-oh-five in the a.m., being serviced by none other than the big Indian Wolf.

"How are you doing this morning, Wolf?" he asked, just a little too loud, enough to make the man wince. He smelled of whiskey, and the mummified expression on his face told Kyle he was up because he had to be up, not because he wanted to be.

"Ugh," replied Wolf, sounding more like he was barfing than acknowledging Kyle. "Don't talk so loud, okay? My head."

"Sure. So this is where you work, hunh?"

"Own," corrected the Indian softly, almost like he was moaning. "What can I get you?"

Kyle told him, and Wolf disappeared back in the aisles for a moment and brought back a full gallon of white and two small pint cans each of red and black. "Seconds," he told Kyle, "Latex. Fast-dry. Half-price." Kyle took them, paying the man with a twenty, and pocketing his change. The gallon was too much paint, but the price made it right. He could always use it later.

Wolf placed the cans in a shallow cardboard box, lowering them gently so as not to jar any of the whiskey-soaked nerves in his body. He shoved the box toward Kyle.

"Thanks a lot, Wolf," Kyle said. He lifted the box and

smiled cheerily.

"Ugga-fugga," answered Wolf, and managed a weak smile before Kyle turned and walked out.

Kyle slid the box onto the passenger's side of the seat next to another box of brushes and rags that he had brought from home, then gained his seat, started the car, and backed out into Main Street. Traffic was still light at this time of the morning. Kyle looked at the blue sky. It was going to be a beautiful day . . . already a beautiful day, Kyle corrected himself. Physically, anyway. The rest would depend on the reception he got . . . and wasn't he getting forgetful.

He bent slightly to the side of the steering wheel and quickly nudged two toggle switches on the police radio that had been installed yesterday. A burst of static exploded in the cabin of the truck, then cleared as the dispatcher tagged a call on Wilson Street, Unit Twelve-Baker responding. For just a moment, Kyle tried to remember who would be in Unit Twelve-Baker; George Boylan, he thought. Well, enough of that. It was bad enough having the damn radio noise on his day off without worrying about radio-car assignments. The radio was necessary, because as chief of police he was on call twenty-four hours of the day, and in actuality, the radio noise didn't bother him at all. After so many years of it, the static chirping and staccato bursts of police traffic settled quickly to the recesses of his mind, to be heard and not heard at the same time.

He drove through town past the city hall, the shops on the east side, and finally past that marker of the east side of town proper, the Gathers Building. The mayor's silver Mercedes sedan sat parked, solitary in the Saturday-morning emptiness of the parking lot. *No one can accuse the mayor of being lazy,* he thought, then grimaced, and looked back at the road. *Then again, there's no rest for the wicked, either.* For a brief moment a sullen feeling flickered in his chest; he frowned. There had been no mention of the Phael incident by the mayor since it had occurred, but Griffith's prediction had come true. In almost a summary manner, and at lightning speed for a judicial matter, the case was thrown out by Judge Baxter on grounds of insufficient evidence, which was a crock if Kyle had ever seen one.

No. He wasn't going to let that ruin his day. As long as his department was lean and clean he could stay happy. He had decided that sometime during the week. That, and the fact that he was starting to really like it here. He had a home, a good, interesting job, and most of all his sanity. Of course the incident in Lisa's room might make for an argument against the latter, but he had fought it, fought it and won. And the police photo of the tree, the one that he thought was the one in his dreams?—his mind had about exploded like a water balloon on that one. Thank God, John Black had been back tending to Wolf. After a long two minutes of howling hissing in his head he had managed to get control of himself, and had bundled the reports and pictures up in his arms and made his way to his office where he yanked open an empty file drawer and shoved them in. He closed the door quickly and sat there for a full thirty minutes before regaining enough of his composure to leave without arousing Black's suspicions. Later on in the week, after bulwarking his mental defenses, he was able to pull out the reports and the crime photos and look at them again.

He felt sure that much of his adverse reaction had been the surprise of suddenly seeing a tree that *resembled* the tree in his dreams. That one point he had made over and over in his mind. That tree *looked* like the tree in his dreams, was very *similar* to the tree in his dreams, but couldn't possibly *be* the same tree. After all, his tree didn't have a hole in the trunk, and when you're talking about trees, well, hell, a tree's a tree, for God's sake.

Kyle hit his horn. A stake truck, lumbering under the weight of several tons of freshly baled hay, pulled slowly out onto the highway forcing Kyle to hit his brakes. He signaled and passed, wishing he were in a radio car so he could write the dummy a ticket. He gave the drive of the truck his killer eye through the rearview mirror, then settled down to enjoy the verdant scenery of the fields and the roll-and-tuck hills that bedded up against the craggy mountains.

Someone stepped out onto the side of the road. Kyle passed by. He licked his eyes to the rearview mirror. The strange sensation that he was seeing a dark apparition filled him, then it passed—it was the derelict from the cafe. Heading out of town, on his wayward journey to the next town, Kyle guessed. The man disappeared from view as Kyle rounded the bend.

Kyle's attention was drawn immediately to the dark eucalyptus grove. Something was different. Seven or eight trees were down. Now, how in the hell had that happened? Had Dave Pickers pulled them down? They sure as hell hadn't been sawed or chopped down—the damn stumps were raggedly uneven, like they'd been snapped in two: they looked like yellow fangs.

He turned the truck onto Pickers's drive and bounced and bumped his way up to the front of the faded yellow ranch house, revved the engine, and then cut the ignition. He slipped quickly out of the cab and bounced just a little too heartily up the worn wooden steps onto the porch, and rapped on the screen door. The front door proper sat wide open, and though dark inside, Kyle could make out the old man's paintings. The old man had a real talent, Kyle thought.

There was no answer, so Kyle backed up a few steps and looked over at the henhouse where first he had seen Dave Pickers last Monday. Not there. His eyes scanned the barn. Nothing. And the old man's worn-to-the-primer Dodge truck, vintage '65. Nothing.

As if by magic his eyes were drawn to the trees. Nothing there, either.

"Whaddyawant?" asked Dave Pickers. He cracked the screen door and walked out onto the porch. He was wearing the same faded bib overalls that he had been wearing the other day, bleached almost white by so many washings, but his shirt was different, a faded blue Pendleton. The smell of fresh paint, oil paint, hung in a little atmosphere of its own around the old

166

man and upon his hands were smears of black, brown, and crimson paint.

"Doing a little painting, I see." Kyle gestured toward the old man's hands.

"No," answered Pickers.

A lie. Kyle blinked a little and looked over at the trees. "What happened to the trees?"

"Wind."

Another lie. Getting off to a great start, Richards, he thought. He fumbled in his shirt pocket with two fingers and produced a small white piece of paper folded in half. He shook it opened and said, "Got the city ordinance numbers for you." The old man's blue eyes shifted briefly to the note, then returned to Kyle, expressing no comprehension. "The signs we talked about." Kyle nodded toward his truck. "I've got some paint; stencil; took the liberty of bringing a power saw, portable workbench. Thought if you were of a mind we'd take some of that wood alongside the barn and whip up a few signs, nail 'em up along the fence posts and see if we can keep the trespassers out."

The old man remained stone-faced, making Kyle feel uncomfortable, an intruder. Maybe he shouldn't have come; the man just wanted to be left alone, that was obvious. Kyle really could understand that, just as he couldn't help feeling disappointment prickle into his consciousness. All he had wanted to do was help—the old man and himself, too. Kyle needed to be close to another survivor, to know that he was not alone. Well, the old man wanted to be left alone, so the least Kyle could do was respect his wishes.

Pickers brushed by Kyle, heading toward the barn. "Run the power outta the barn. I got a cord."

They worked symbiotically, without conversation. The silence bewtween them seemed almost natural to Kyle after a period of time, and within an hour, he and Dave Pickers had twenty one-and-a-half-by-two-foot sign-sized boards cut and painted with a base coat of white. Kyle knelt down beside the first board now dry and laid it flat on the ground. Pickers stood beside him and watched silently as Kyle pried open the quart can of red paint and the quart can of black paint. Kyle carefully centered the stencil and fixed it to the board with masking tape, then picked up a two-inch brush and coated the first line in red paint, laid down that brush and picked up a second brush, and used the black paint on the lines under the first. He then removed the stencil. The sign read, the top line in bright red, the lower lines in wet black:

NO TRESPASSING
Violators will be
prosecuted. Briggs City
Municipal Code 222-03

"There. That ought to do it," said Kyle, a small bit of satisfaction shining through in his voice.

The old man said nothing. He squatted down in front of the next blank, slid the cardboard box with the open paint cans over to himself, and painted the next sign, then repeated the process on down the line, commanding by a jerk of his bony shoulder and shake nod of his head that he would complete the rest of the signs without Kyle's help.

Kyle stood watching the old man, occasionally turning, stealing a faceful of sun from the bright blue sky. Although not angry with the old man, Kyle would have preferred a little more conversation than the handful of words that had been exchanged between them in the last couple of hours. But Kyle had come to Pickers, not the other way around. And at least the old man hadn't been hostile like he had the first time Kyle had been out to see him. In fact, Kyle had caught the old man's blue eyes looking at him with what appeared to be sadness several times in the last hour and a half. The gaze had made him uncomfortable, however brief it was, and Pickers had turned away quickly when Kyle caught him looking.

Pickers coughed, cleared some phlegm with a hawking

sound, and spat. He said nothing and moved on down the line. He was at the next-to-the-last sign when Kyle spoke. He hadn't really meant to say anything. He wanted to let the old man play the game by his own set of rules, and if Kyle was going to say anything it should be about the weather. But it wasn't.

"I'm sorry about your wife and daughter," he said, "I'm truly sorry."

Pickers stiffened. His gnarled right hand remained rigidly fixed over his bent knees, the brush, freshly dipped in red paint on its way to paint NO TRESPASSING, bled a dripping glob or bright red paint on the faded white of the right leg of his overalls. To Kyle it looked like blood.

Slowly, as if operated on microscopically precise gimbals, Pickers rotated his head up to face Kyle. His pale blue eyes were scorching indictments of Kyle's wrongdoing. His mouth was a seamless hard line, his thin lips pressed hard together making them white, like old scar tissue.

"I know what you're thinking, Mr. Pickers," Kyle began, squatting down next to the man and meeting his hot gaze with a searching, compassionate openness in his own. Where should he begin? How could he begin? Suddenly, his lips moved and he said, "I know what you're feeling. I hurt like you hurt. The saying is, 'Walk a mile in my shoes.' Well, I've walked a mile in your shoes . . . in more ways than one—I read the reports of Cathy's death . . . and, and . . . I've seen the pictures—"

"Oh, you've read the reports, you've seen the pictures," interrupted the old man, the sarcasm in his voice whiny, and bitter like vinegar.

Kyle turned away and searched the freshly painted sign in front of him, not really seeing, not really hearing anything but his own voice, which now seemed distant, disembodied. Could it really be himself speaking, talking, divulging his own innermost horror story, spilling his guts to another human being about that night that drove him over the edge, and made him a stranger in his own mind? Yes. He heard his own voice, speaking in halting, choppy sentences, telling Dave Pickers

169

exactly what had happened that horrible night, just a few short years ago:

The time was fast approaching midnight when Kyle, maybe just a wee bit tipsy, turned Susan's deep blue Volvo into the drive of his home in Woodland Hills, a suburb of Los Angeles. He sat in the car for a moment organizing his thoughts. He'd have to be quiet, Q-U-I-E-T, because little Lisa would be beddy-bye by now. But not Susan. She would be up waiting for him, her white nightgown blossoming down around her long, sexy body, her reading glasses cocked up on top of her fine rich pale-gold hair, a copy of the latest best-seller in her hand, as she walked down the hall from the bedroom to greet him, her ample breasts swaying seductively, and making him want her even in his drunken state. She would not admonish him too harshly, he rarely imbibed, and he could hardly expect to be sober at the celebration party for Leo Brumagin's promotion to Assistant Chief of Police, Personnel Bureau, now, could he? No!

Kyle removed himself from the car interior with tenterhook movements. He closed the car door firmly, then captured a big breath of night air and exhaled. He wasn't so bad off, he decided, and looked up to the double mahogany doors that gave entry to his Spanish-style home.

Now, that was a first. No front porch light on. Susan always, always left that on when he was out. Ah, how soon they forget, he sighed to himself, then laughed stupidly. He'd better get inside and get to bed—kiss little Lisa, and then get to bed, he corrected himself. One night, when Kyle was tucking her in, she'd made him promise that he would always kiss her good-night, even when she was sound asleep and he came home late. It had tickled Kyle. The little angel had made him raise his right hand and swear to God that he would comply. Even now he could see her face, a small oval shape, seemingly filled with bright green eyes that even in their youth held that haunting seriousness of her mother, as she swore him to his word, her fine golden hair falling in braided pigtails over the front of her pink flannel pajamas, her small mouth twisted up in earnest as

170

he completed his oath and bent over to kiss her soft smooth cheek. "I love you," he had said. "I love you, too, Daddy," she had said, then consumed herself in a giggling fit. From that night on, no matter what time of night he arrived home, Kyle had never broken his promise.

He stopped at the front door, grappled for his keys, and inserted the door key in the front lock, turning it to find it rotating too easily. How many times had he told Susan to keep the front door locked? None. She was as cautious as he was, and he had never had to tell her about home safety, never. Some inner guidance began to soak up his drunkenness. It was odd, just odd, he thought. Everyone makes a mistake once (the porch light is out) in a while . . .

Kyle touched the doorknob without turning it. Fear raced up his arm and became a large, furry spider squirming down his throat, and by the time he had bent down to draw his gun from its ankle holster, turned the knob, and pushed the door cautiously open, the creature had grown large and unwieldly, turning over in his stomach and crawling its way up his spinal cord to grip his brain in an eight-legged visegrip of fear.

He had known that creature before in many a terrible place, but never had he thought he would find it in his own home.

He closed the door softly behind him and stopped. Listening. His ears began to ache he clinched his teeth so tightly that he thought the enamel would break. No sounds. Background noise, but no sounds. And then he sensed it—Death! His home was heavy with it! He kept his gun at the ready and moved as if through a thick syrup down the hall, his black shoes making noiseless footfalls on the carpeting. He stopped at the crossroads of the main hall and the bedroom hall. Involuntarily his head rotated toward the bedrooms—there was death down there—but he forced it back toward the living room, because somewhere closer, somewhere just around that wall, into the living room, death was there, too.

How many times had he been in the same situation, entering a home where he could smell the death. And what could he smell now? A porcine smell, like frying bacon. But he was in his own house now, and there had been no fire. Not in evidence, anyway. So all he had to do was step out, step out into the living room and . . .

He stepped out and froze. He heard a crazed screaming somewhere in his mind, but externally he began a low, moaning sob, his right had lowered itself, and his hands went slack. The gun hit the beige pile with a dull *thunk*. Kyle moved slowly forward, toward that wrought-iron-and-glass coffee table that Susan had insisted they buy. He felt queasy, and scared, and finally, grabbing his middle, he doubled over and puked his guts out, falling to his knees near the small utility blowtorch. The smell of bacon was cloying. He retched again. He looked up and saw her eyes. They stared at him. Lifeless. Accusing. Where were you? they were saying. It's your fault, they were saying. *Your fault!* And, of course, he agreed.

The sledgehammer lay closest to her, even closer than the remains of his baton collection. They had chosen several of the rare batons and driven them into her rectum and vagina. She lay now, where she had been tied, over the length of the glass table, face down, her waist bending over one end, her legs strapped to the legs of the table by black electrical tape. She was nude. Her hair was singed as was most of her body, with red, bubbling burns up and down her naked upper torso. Her arms were outstretched and pulled down, taped in massive black ribbons to the other end of the coffee table. Her mouth was open in a scream, a pair of her pink underpants stuffed in it, tied as a gag with her brassiere. In her struggling (or through a vicious blow) the smooth plane of the glass tabletop had cracked into naked, jagged shards and somehow Susan's neck had been severed, almost entirely in two, and her head lay dangling down from her neck above a lake of blood. The slash across her throat was meaty and ragged. And the eyes stared at him. (*Where had he been?—Out with the boys, he says! Out with the boys, he says! Out with the boys while his wife and daughter . . .*)

172

Kyle scrambled to his feet. *"Lisa! Lisa!"* he screamed, and ran to her bedroom. He stood in her doorway moaning over and over again, "My God, my God." They had done most of their dirty work on her canopy bed. The mattress was soaked, the canopy stained, wet and slick, with bright red blood . . . His baby's blood . . .

(*Where had he been?—Out with the boys, he says! Out with the boys, he says! Out with the boys while his wife is murdered and his daughter . . .*)

Hung. Lisa hung by her shiny gold pigtails from the light fixture. Her body was nude and turned slightly away from Kyle. Her skin was smeared red with her own blood that dripped down her legs and formed a sticky pool the size of a small throw rug. Kyle noticed that to make it worse, whoever had done this had made a continuous slit around the outline of Lisa's hairline, and the weight of the body was beginning to pull the skin up, exposing her skull. The blood from that rough incision had flooded down over her face like a veil of crimson, and through that veil, Lisa's eyes were open, too—accusing . . . "Where were you, Daddy? Where were you, Daddy?"

(*Out with the boys!*)

"Stop it!" he screamed. "Stop it stop it stop it!"

He stared at her for a moment. He had to get her down. Get her down before . . .

The light fixture gave, and her young body dropped, in a half turn. It was too much for the scalp. There was a wet, ripping sound and her body splashed into the pool of blood beneath her. Kyle screamed. Dangling from the light fixture by two braided hanks of hair was Lisa's scalp, dripping blood on her white skull below . . .

Pickers was listening as Kyle choked out the rest of it. Tears flowed fully down his own cheeks while those of Dave Pickers were dry. "I sort of went to pieces after that. I needed a break, so I took some time off and then got this job. It's a new start for

173

me. A new start." He cleared his throat and looked at the old man again. The pale blue eyes seemed sad again and turned away. "So, you see, Mr. Pickers, I do know how you feel. It's a little different, but not so different that I wouldn't know how you feel. I've never told that story to anyone . . . I couldn't even face it myself, but I've told you, and God knows why."

The old man still would not face him, so Kyle stood up and walked to the first few signs. He piled four of them on top of each other and walked to his truck. "I better be going. I'll nail these up on the north end, Mr. Pickers." Kyle slipped into his truck. "Let me ask you one thing," he said. "Do you still believe that devils did that thing to your little girl?"

The old man stood up, walked over to the truck, and eyed him hard. No indication that Kyle's telling of the Tragedy affected him showed on his face. "I don't think, I know," he said defiantly. "Yes. And what they did to Emily, too. At first I thought the Indians done it, but after Cathy, I knew it was the Devil in that stand of cursed trees. I *know* it was the *Devil* and his *critters* because I saw them with my own two eyes."

"Well, that's my dilemma, Mr. Pickers. You see, I don't believe in the Devil, and I don't believe you're crazy . . ." Kyle stopped for a moment and searched the tired parchment of Dave Pickers's face, ". . . and I don't believe you're lying. Now that puts me between a rock and a hard place, doesn't it?"

Dave Pickers said nothing. Kyle smiled mirthlessly and started the car and drove off.


Kyle parked on the shoulder of the road near the end of Dave Pickers's property line. He pulled the three signs out of his truck, grabbed a hammer and some nails, and moved toward the weathered fence posts to attach the signs.

He was nailing the third sign in and feeling a little hurt by Pickers's actions. Kyle realized that he had no right to expect any gratitude, or any kind of camaraderie from the old man just because he had had some personal tragedy too. But, damn it, he couldn't help feeling cheated, somehow slighted. The old fart hadn't even said that he was sorry that Kyle's family had died. Hadn't even said thank you for Kyle going out of his way to keep people from bothering him. Hadn't even taken that hand of friendship that he had thrust out there, and by God, the old fart needed it. Needed it as much as Kyle needed it.

The anger burned in him as he placed the last of the four signs he had brought against the wooden fence post, braced a ten-penny nail against it, and drove it home in several mighty slams. He was nailing another one in alongside it when he noticed Dave Pickers's old truck battering up the dirt road on the ranch side of the fence, throwing out roostertail plumes of dry dust up in the air. Kyle drove the last nail home at the bottom of the sign and stood up just as the old truck ground to a halt across the fence from him. Dave Pickers, expressionless, got down from the cab and reached back in and pulled out a small cardboard box, walked up to Kyle and gave it to him, turned around, and walked back to the truck. Kyle looked down. In the box, bedded in straw, were four farm-fresh brown eggs. For the elation that they put in Kyle they might as well have been made of gold.

"Thank you, Mr. Pickers. Thanks a lot." He sounded like a schoolboy, but he didn't care. The old man kept walking toward the truck. "Thanks a lot," Kyle called again.

The man's thin frame stopped and turned around. "Christian name's Dave," he said, and slid behind the wheel of his Dodge.

"I bet these eggs make the best damn omelet in the state, Dave."

The old man started the car without saying a word, turned it around in a wide, bumping loop, and headed down the road toward his house, dust billowing behind him.

# 20

Curtis sat on his bike at the top of Eskay Street watching the new chief of police do his gardening. It was close to eleven o'clock on Sunday morning and Curtis had come straight home from church, changed, and pedaled over the four blocks to see if he could get a glimpse of the chief, maybe even talk to him. He seemed friendly enough, but when his mom had told him that she found out where Chief Richards lived, and told Curtis, she'd bent over in a posture he well recognized, arched her right eyebrow, and said, "And don't you go bothering him, young man," which meant she knew that Curtis really liked the chief.

Well, she really liked the chief too. Or why would she have gone to all the trouble of asking Uncle Edgar where he lived, and why had she been concerned about the chief after that boss fight with Leonard Phael, saying aloud, saying to Curtis, "I hope the chief is all right. That terrible Phael; what an awful man, attacking a fine man like the chief, don't you think?" The only other time that Curtis had heard his mom go on about anyone like that was whenever anyone in the family got sick, like Grandma or Aunt Clarice. And that puzzled him because Mom had just met the chief.

Curtis sighed, contemplating a weighty question: Is it really disobeying Mom if I ride *down* on the other side of the street? Not even look at him, even. Just ride by, real fast? He pondered this for a few seconds, and before he could make a conscious decision he was coasting down the gentle slope of Eskay Street on the east side of the street, opposite the chief's house. He

176

picked up speed and began to pedal, his peg-legged blue jeans smacking softly with the effort. Curtis stopped at the end of the block and looked up the street. The chief was still in the same position, his broad bare back, brown and curved in a gentle arch, squatting and reaching for a weed around the rose bushes. He hadn't *even* seen, and Curtis had given his best fast action. He mad a few more runs down the street, all with the same result. With a nag of caution in his mind he gained the top of the street and crossed over to the chief's side. Now, his mom had told him not to bother the chief, but if the chief talked to him, then he wasn't bothering the chief, was he? And besides, it was a free country, and all he'd do was ride *by* the chief, just once. Just once. That wasn't bothering him, was it? Mom couldn't be mad over that, could she?

He started his run, and just as he did, the chief stood up and turned to grab a box to stuff his fistful of weeds in. Curtis's legs became turbines. He'd show the chief just how fast he could go, a broadie at the bottom of the hill. That would add the finishing touch on a class ride. He raised up off his seat, his small rear grabbing for the sky, his face pushed out over the handle bars staring straight ahead so that the chief wouldn't know that Curtis even knew he was there. Just zooming by minding his own business, not bothering the chief.

He hit the rock just before the chief's property line, his front wheel scooting over into the depression between the grass and the sidewalk and throwing him over the bars in a sideways roll. He landed on his back with the bike partially on top of his body, the wind knocked out of his lungs, so that he had to fight to get the air back in, with a tighter battle of the tears that wanted to pour out. He fought them back because men don't cry, especially in front of each other. And the wall of muscle that was the chief was walking over to him now in his graceful rolling gait. Curtis sat there shriveling in embarrassment as the big man bent over and pried him gently from the tangled wreck, speaking to him in a firm comforting tone, words that Curtis would never be able to remember. All that he knew was that the chief was talking to him, and that his arms were so huge, and so strong, and covered with fine dark hair.

Kyle had noticed Curtis sitting up at the end of the block watching him work some twenty minutes before, but in a fit of good-natured sadism he let the boy make his own approach. Kyle was just about to have mercy on the boy when the kid went over onto the grass strip out by the street.

"Are you okay?" asked Kyle, slipping a thin little leg out from under the front wheel of the bicycle and shoving the two-wheeler away from the boy.

"Uh . . . uh . . ." gasped the boy. Somewhere in his sweatshirt the boy's chest was making like a bellows to get his wind.

"Take deep breaths. Slowly. Try to control them." The boy seemed to understand. His eyes fought back the tears, and his hair, the color of straw, was swept disheveled down in them. Kyle brushed a thatch of unruly strands back off the small, high forehead and lifted him up and sat him on his sneakered feet. "There," he said, and dusted him off. "None the worse for wear." Kyle swung a comforting arm around the boy and picked up his bicycle with one hand and ushered him up to the front porch. Curtis complied willingly as Kyle stopped, kicked the kickstand down, and left the bike upright on the porch as he guided the boy in and fixed him up with a twelve-ounce can of Pepsi-Cola. He grabbed one for himself, then led him back outside. The boy had said nothing to him so far except a muffled "thank you" when he accepted the ice-cold drink, and Kyle understood completely. It was embarrassing to take a tumble like that, especially in front of someone you were trying to impress.

"Here," said Kyle. "Why don't you sit down here and keep me company while you get your wind." Kyle knelt down and began pawing at the dark earth around the rose bushes rooting out weeds. "You took it better than I would have, you know?"

At first the compliment seemed to have no effect upon the boy. He did not answer and was still standing, the red, white, and blue Pepsi can clutched tightly in both hands. Kyle did not think he had taken a sip. Very gradually a recognition came onto the boy's face that he had been engaged in conversation. His mouth screwed up slightly and his eyes seemed to be searching for something to say.

"Am I bothering you?" he asked suddenly in a tone so odd that Kyle laughed.

"My God, boy. No. You're the first friend I've made in this town." Kyle had chosen the words carefully, giving the boy the kind of security that he so obviously needed to relax. In those few words Kyle let him know that he considered their brief meeting a friendship.

The boy responded accordingly, sinking slowly to his knees and smiling tentatively under his huge glasses. Bright blue eyes. "I don't usually fall, Chief Richards," said Curtis. "I think I hit a rock, but I'm not sure."

"You get up good speed, don't you? You were going very fast." Kyle let a tone of appreciation hang heavy in his voice.

The blue eyes looked up excitedly into Kyle's, then away. He reached out with his young hand and pulled a weed and dumped it into the weed box. "I can go a lot faster on a good hill. This one's just a little one."

"Well, I thought as much, Curtis." The boy flashed a look up at him at the mention of his name. *The chief remembered my name!* It was written all over his face and Kyle felt a warm glow of emotion. Most kids nowadays spit on you, and that was if you were lucky. "You've got a real talent with that bike, all right."

"I'm good on a skateboard, too!" he said enthusiastically.

"Really?" Kyle said appreciatively.

"Oh, yeah. I can handstand, but Mom won't let me do it anymore. She says not without a helmet, and that costs a lot of bucks, believe me."

"I believe you. And your mom's right, don't you think? I

179

mean you could get hurt pretty bad. And from what I've seen, all the pros use helmets and kneepads, the whole shot."

Curtis nodded in agreement, jostling his blond bangs across his face comically. They talked for a while about general things. Curtis mentioned that his dad had been killed in Vietnam. He had been a pilot, shot down when Curtis was just a baby, and when Kyle told him that Kyle's brother had died in 'Nam, too, it seemed to lock the boy to him even more than ever. Kyle marveled that from that point on, Curtis relaxed to a level beyond friendship, and Kyle accepted the boy's presence without reservation. For a moment they both sat looking at each other, saying nothing, the heat of the sun warming them both. Kyle felt a little less alone, and that was good.

"How about having lunch with me? Do you like roasted wieners, barbecue beans, buns, and good stuff like that?" asked Kyle.

The boy's face lit up like a searchlight. "Sure!" he said, then he grimaced in disappointment. "I'll have to ask my mom."

"So, you don't think she'll let you?"

"No. She'll think I'm bothering you."

"Ah-h," said Kyle, understanding in full the fear of children of their parents' approval for any activity that might appear fun. "I'll fix it."

"Yeah?" The boy didn't seem to doubt him and was grinning ear-to-ear.

"Sure. I'm chief of police. I'll arrest you and not let you go until you eat lunch. How's that?" Kyle winked, and Curtis's face broke into a million little smiles, interlaced with a windy chortle.

"That's okay with me. Arrest me."

"Well, maybe I'll call your mom and ask her. It would probably be easier than taking you down to the station and booking you. I'll put to rest this 'bothering' business too. How's that?"

"Great!"

Mrs. McKinney answered the telephone on the third ring.

She had a warm and resonant telephone voice. It made him tingle slightly and that made him wary. He just wasn't ready for anything like that yet. To induce her to agree to letting her son stay for lunch, Kyle started the conversation by mentioning that poor Curtis had been in an accident. No, nothing serious. Just fell off his bike. And would you mind if he stayed for lunch? No, she wouldn't as long as he wasn't "bothering" Kyle. He settled her mind by telling her the truth, that Curtis had "brightened his day" and that he "didn't see how such a fine young man could be a bother to anyone." Kyle looked down at the boy, who stood at his feet in the living room, and gave him a big squinty wink. Curtis looked gleefully up at him as if they were both mischievous children playing a prank on his mother. His mother agreed and thanked him for taking care of Curtis after his spill on the bicycle. Kyle said that it had been "no problem" and they rung off.

"All set," Kyle said, "and I didn't even have to arrest you."

Curtis jumped up and down and gave a cheer. Kyle smiled at his new friend. The boy made him feel good. New. Someone had said that "children make all things new" and new was what Kyle was seeking. New life. New emotions. New feelings. This small blond-haired boy with the shy ways and big questioning blue eyes gave him hope and joy, two things that had been in short supply in his life for over two years now. "Curtis," he said, putting his arm around the boy and leading him toward the back, "I've got a good feeling that you and I are going to be great friends, how's that sound?"

The boy said that it sounded great.

They worked as a team, Curtis grabbing the charcoal and lighter fluid, Kyle removing the grill and bedding down the briquettes in a rough estimation of a black pyramid. Kyle soaked the briquettes heavily, delivering his sermon on the dangers of the fluid to an attentive eleven-year-old while praying to God that he wouldn't have to squirt any more fluid on later and make himself a liar-by-example in front of the boy. They left the coals to roast in the flames of the fluid-induced fire and went inside, where to Kyle's amazement the boy moved naturally around, helping by pulling the hot dogs out of the refrigerator and getting silverware out while Kyle found a can of barbecue beans in the cupboard, opened them, and dumped them into an aluminum pan, put the heat on low, and began stirring them. As he did so, he watched in wonderment as the boy's small hands opened different cupboard doors, exploring, looking in an innocent way. There. He found it. Plates, under his gentle guidance, were pulled from their shelf. Four of them—the boy had a head—two to eat on, one for the hot dogs, and one for the buns. A serving bowl for the beans. Kyle smiled to himself. The boy was not being rude, or presumptuous, but rather felt at home with Kyle, and was obviously used to pulling his own weight, seeing what had to be done, and doing it. Kyle admired that especially in someone so young. To Kyle it spoke well of Curtis's upbringing, and without a dad that must have been some chore for his mother.

As the coals became enveloped in gray and their heat was sizzling hot Curtis helped Kyle wrangle all of the supplies out to the redwood picnic table and lay the wieners on the grill. Kyle placed the aluminum pot with the beans on the grill, off to the side of the coals to keep them warm, and then asked a general question just to get the conversation going again with his young partner. "So, do you have a girlfriend yet?"

To Kyle's surprise, Curtis flushed red and said, "Yes."

"Is she pretty?" Kyle decided to pursue this topic with some vigor. The maturity of kids these days was amazing. He hadn't even thought of girls until he was fifteen; now, at that age, almost any girl can give you a twenty-minute discourse on the best contraceptive to use.

Curtis hesitated a minute. "She's pretty. She's really just sort of my friend, if you know what I mean?"

Ah, sweet innocence. Thank you, God. "You mean that you like her, but you haven't dated her yet. Something like that?"

Curtis quietly nodded his head in agreement. "Little Neil, he likes her too," he blurted suddenly. "He's the mayor's son.

He's a bully. He's always picking on me, especially in front of Kari. I think that she likes me better than him. I'd like to beat him up, but he's too big, and besides Mom doesn't let me fight, she says it's 'common' and that I should just walk away. I'd like to pound his head in, but Mom won't let me fight."

Kyle had his own feelings about such things. Every individual should know how to take care of himself. There were always times when there just was no alternative. He wanted to tell this to Curtis, but didn't want to contradict his mother either.

"Mothers are always right," he said, "but sometimes they just don't understand how it is for a kid your age." An idea blossomed in his mind. "Now, I happen to know a certain set of 'exercises' that you can do that keep you in shape and that also can be used to handle yourself should someone drive you to the wall where you have to fight."

"You mean karate? Like you beat up Leonard Phael with?" he asked eagerly.

"I'm not saying that," responded Kyle judiciously. "Let's just say that I teach you a multipurpose physical fitness course, with an understanding that it not be used except when there is no other way out—and I mean that." Kyle shook the tongs at Curtis for emphasis. "The other condition is that it is our little secret. Do you understand? That means don't tell your mom."

Curtis gave him his word and an I'll-take-it-to-the-grave look, and Kyle felt every confidence that the boy meant it with all his heart.

The sound of high heels clicking on the cement driveway made them both look up in time to see Curtis's mother, wearing a green dress, round the corner of the house, a wooden salad bowl covered with tin foil held out in front of her like an offering. Involuntarily Kyle frowned, then caught himself and put on his meet-the-public face.

\*　　　\*　　　\*

Michele knew that it was forward of her, especially at that moment when she'd gained the backyard of the house to see Curtis and Kyle standing there staring at her, both with blank faces. And then Kyle had frowned. Suddenly the salad bowl containing the excuse she had concocted to come over felt like a bowl of lead that made her mind ache to drop the dish and run. Instead, she mounted a smile, and walked forward. "I thought that you two might like a salad to go with your lunch."

Her heart drummed inside her chest. When she had first seen the two together they looked like conspirators, now suddenly they were partners. Kyle handed the tongs to Curtis, who took them naturally although Kyle had not spoken a word to him, and approached her with a public-relations grin on his face. "Excellent," he said. His eyes were working overtime searching her face, and his big hands reached out and slid the wooden bowl gently from her hands. Whatever the frown had been about, it was lost in effusiveness now. "You are just in time for lunch," he said. She meant to say no, but he was standing there, his massive bare chest before her, and she said, "Oh, good" instead, as if she had not been expecting to be invited.

Yes, she had been forward, but even if she had wanted to, she could not have helped herself for following up an opportunity like this. Bless little Curtis for his bicycle accident. Bless him. Since that day in the store when this big city policeman had walked in she had had the thought of him burned into her mind and soul with the searing pain that only love can produce. She had thought about if often, about how her mother had told her that she knew, somehow she just knew, that her father would be the man she married. Michele had never had that feeling with Curtis's father; there had been a good strong love there, but nothing like this. In a way she wished that the chief would just do something, anything, that could make her dislike him—this feeling pained her so.

"Hi, Mom." Curtis was all smiles, too. Eleven years of raising that little rascal told her he was up to something. But his mouth pulled up in the corners and that meant it was a good something. If he were trying to hide something bad the smile just didn't quite make it, the corners of his mouth shooting for his lower jaw in spite of his smile.

In an apparent unconscious agreement, Curtis and Kyle treated her like the guest of honor, seating her at the redwood picnic table with a courtly flourish. Kyle served up beans and two hot dogs, leaving the choice of condiments to her. Curtis rushed into the house and produced three Pepsis for them to drink, and an extra plate, while Kyle served up the salad that she had made.

The feeling of being an intruder was erased completely by the tender care they were giving her, but the feeling that Kyle was keeping things superficial hovered at the edge of her thoughts. He asked her numerous questions, all requiring some thought and discourse, and all, she noted, that somehow kept her at a distance. At least Kyle was paying attention to Curtis, always deferring to him after she had finished answering a question by asking him, "Is that a true story?" and causing her little boy to laugh like she had never seen him laugh before. The marvel of Kyle's technique was that she never felt like she was being interrogated; it was only after a lull in the conversation that she realized that he knew almost everything about her life and she knew nothing about his.

Just as a mild case of indignity arose, Kyle asked her a question that threw her off her train of thought completely. "Do you remember the Cathy Pickers tragedy some years ago?" She said that she did, and mentally admired his replacing the word "murder" with "tragedy" obviously for the sake of Curtis. Without going into the particulars of the murder, she spoke briefly about Cathy Pickers's death, hoping that she was picking out the right details for him. He was interested, that was evident. He leaned forward, staring intently at her with his stark green eyes. His chin rested on his folded hands, propped up as a platform by his beefy forearms. Oh, God, he is handsome, she thought as she spoke.

"It was a very great shock for us . . . the town, I mean. It's a small town . . . much smaller than . . . and Dave Pickers was a well-liked man before . . . You know that his wife 'died,' don't you?" He nodded his head in assent, and she continued. "Cathy was a friend of mine. Not a super-close friend, but we went to pajama parties and the movies and had the same girlfriends. It was quite a shock, like I said, for the whole town."

She stopped. She sensed that she had told him enough. She looked at Curtis, who had not asked one question, but rather gazed calmly between the two of them, somehow sensing himself that this was an area that the two adults preferred to keep to themselves. She felt a wave of pride and turned back to Kyle. "I think we'd better get going; tomorrow's a school day, not to mention work for me. Thank you for everything." She indicated Curtis with a glance.

"Of course," said Kyle. "Listen, Mrs. McKinney . . ."

"Michele, please."

"Kyle," he offered in return. "Curtis is welcome over any time. I've had quite a nice day today, and in these times you've got to count 'em while you can. Curtis and I were planning on doing a little running and some exercises together, if it's all right with you?"

Curtis's eyes gaped wide, pleading with her. My word, what should he be worrying about? she thought, this was one answer to her prayers. "I think that's a wonderful idea, Kyle, as long as he's no bother . . . I mean, of course it's okay." (*God, I'm rambling again, and is he beautiful*).

"It's no bother," said Kyle. She glanced at Curtis, who was grinning ear-to-ear.


In the darkness of his room Curtis knelt beside his bed and said his prayers. As he always did, he asked God to bless Mom, Dad (in heaven), and Grandpa (in heaven), and Grandma, and Uncle Edgar and Aunt Clarice. Then he said a special thanks.

"Dear God, thank you for making the chief my friend, and protect him when he is arresting criminals, and bless him, and please make him like me forever and ever."


Tears sprang into Michele's eyes as she overheard Curtis's prayer. She had been coming to tuck him in, when she stopped at the sound of his voice. She always believed that prayer was a private thing, and past the beginning stages of Curtis's development she only listened to his prayers when he asked her. Occasionally, he would ask her, but not recently. It was another sign that he was coming of age. Pretty soon, puberty, and how would she handle that? His prayer had said it all. Mother that she was, and as much father as she tried to be, the boy still wanted an actual man in his life.

She pushed into his room. "Through with your prayers, dear?" she asked. He was rustling his way down into the sheets.

"Yes, Mom."

She tucked him in, then leaned forward and kissed him, hugging him tightly. She felt the warmth of his breath against her neck. "You made a nice friend today, didn't you?"

"Yes, Mom. He called me his friend, too. He likes me."

"Everybody likes you. There's a lot there to like, kiddo." She kissed him again and retired to her room. She snapped off her light and crawled into her antique, four-poster bed. She had had quite a day, and was thankful for it, and said her prayer of thanks for Kyle's kindness to Curtis, and added a little shot to God about her and Kyle getting together.

She reviewed the day, and thought of how flushed she'd become when she'd first seen his massive bare chest, covered with fine black hair like the chest of a bear. She had actually gotten *aroused*. *My God, did he notice? I hope not. That's all I need, for him to think that I'm a nymphomaniac or something.* And that was the furthest thing from the truth. There had actually been very few men in her life, and even fewer in her bed. She had absolutely no desire to have just *any* man touching her,

187

entering her. *My God, no.* It had always been someone special. And it had been a long time since the last man. A long, long time.

Her hands began to move as if by themselves, lifting her pink cotton nightgown up to her throat. She caressed her own breasts, but in her mind her hands became Kyle's hands. She drew her knees up and out and let his hands fall down her body and between her legs, and as her heart raced and she pulled the second pillow on top of her, it became Kyle touching her, loving her, entering her and making her moan in ecstasy.

Kyle carried a glass of milk to bed with him. He stopped briefly in the hall and looked at Lisa's room. On sudden impulse he walked to it and entered, flicking on the light defiantly and stepping in.

It was as he had left it. Just a room, he told himself. A room with Lisa's furniture in it. He stood briefly, tearing the room apart with his gaze. Just a room, he reaffirmed, with furniture in it. He turned to leave and stopped. On top of the school desk sat some Crayola drawings. Lisa had loved drawing. He stared at the three drawings, all done in red Crayola. One was of a horse, one a flower, and the last a little girl holding hands with her father. Had he pulled those out? He must have. Look, one Crayola, the bright red, lay half used on the desktop. He must have pulled that out, too.

"I left them out myself," he said out loud to the room, then shut off the light and closed the door and went to his room.

As he broached sleep, he thought this weekend a very successful venture. He had two new friends, Dave and Curtis. Dave he would have to work on a bit, but things like that were worthwhile *because* they took time. And as for Curtis, well, there's instant friendship, just add love. As for Michele, she was beautiful, and much too much like Susan in her direct zest for life for Kyle to handle her right now. The problem with her was that he could care for a woman like that, but the time wasn't right. Not right now. He would enjoy having someone to do social things with, but without an attachment—the last woman he'd had an attachment to had been murdered, and as much as he tried to forgive, deep inside he still blamed himself.

He lay quietly in bed for a moment, listening to the night sounds, and the sounds inside his own head. Suddenly he sat bolt upright and shouted, "I left them out myself, goddamnit! I know I did!"

# 21

The Indian awoke in the moonlight, his head needles of pain.

He moaned softly and stared at the dying embers of the fire. He had to get back to town. Since the Eagle had come and spoken to him in his dream, he had tried to summon that spirit back, to ask a favor—the Eagle had not come in a dream, so now he had dared to take the sacred pouch and eat the sacred herbs. He had done that before midnight. Now, by the embers left in the fire, it must be around two AM, and all he had for his trouble was a splitting headache, and the shivers.

He sat up, reaching for the blanket that had fallen from his shoulders, and heard a noise behind him. He turned quickly, and yelped at the two red eyes glaring at him.

The brown bear gave a throaty growl, and the Indian jumped across the fire pit and picked up a piece of kindling. It was the only weapon he had; and that damn bear stood between him and his car. He'd been foolish to come out here without a gun—without a soul, the bear could kill him. If he were not *Heytah-nee*, he could talk with this old bear, and pass by safely.

The bear reared up on its hind legs.

"Holy Eagle!" he cried out, catching the looming shadow of Sacred Mountain behind the bear, "Protect me! Talk to Father Bear!"

The bear came down on all fours and waddled into the fireside. He sat down on his haunches and stared contentedly at him. Only then did the Indian notice the blue-gold aura around the beast. The herbs had worked! It was Holy Bear, an ancient Spirit Elder. "You summon me," said Holy Bear, "and then you cry out to Holy Eagle to save you. You are truly sad, *Heytah-nee.*"

"Forgive me," said the Indian. He felt his body tremble. "I want permission to climb Sacred Mountain, and perform the Rite of Crystal Waters. The Chosen One is in the town. Reveal to me who he is, and I will go to him. And ask him when he faces Ravana to steal back my soul."

"No," said the Spirit Elder. "You may know who, but you will not go to him." Holy Bear's image wavered and then the *Ehkeh-Heh* was revealed to him.

The Indian stared at the image. "He's white!" he said. "I know him. He's the new police chief! How can the Chosen One be a white man, Holy Bear?"

The bear growled. "Ravana has chosen him. If you were not *Heytah-nee,* the Traitor, you would know such things. Do you think that the Laikute people are the only ones on this earth? There are many, many other tribes and religions throughout this world, and each one has foretold the beginning of the end of the world—Ravana is the beginning of the end. And if the Chosen One does not defeat him, then the balance of good and evil will be such that the giant rock of evil crushes the small fruit of good."

The Indian thought about this for a moment, then asked, "Then does he know that he is *Ehkeh-Heh,* this white police chief?"

"No."

"And if Ravana chose him, then he must surely fall."

"No. That which is good, works for him, too. The Spirit of Light works for his good, too. Ravana has chosen well. The man is strong, yet is weakened by his past—it is this that Ravana will use to destory him."

"What in his past, O Great Bear?"

"The policeman blames himself for the death of his wife and child."

"And Ravana will use this to make him fail The Facing?"

"Yes. And to make him cower like you cowered, when the

191

Evil Thing challenged you."

The Indian felt shame engorge his whole being. "Well, then he may run like me. Lose his soul . . ."

"No!" The bear growled, and pawed the ground. "When the time is right, you will know to come to Sacred Mountain; and when the time is right, the Chosen One will know to fight!

"That which Ravana did to make *Ehkeh-Heh* come to this place, and with which It wishes to destory him, is that which will make him stand and fight!"

The Indian shivered at the harshness of Holy Bear's words. The bear's red eyes glowered at him, yet he felt hope: he would be allowed to go onto Sacred Mountain, and beg for his soul. But what was Holy Bear getting at? What did he mean about the police chief? What had Ravana done to him to get him here?"

He stared at the bear and asked Holy Bear to explain.

The bear snorted, then reared up on its hind legs. "It was Ravana that murdered *Ehkeh-Heh*'s wife and child! And when he knows that, he will fight, he will face Ravana!"

The blue-gold aura of the bear intensified, and then the Indian was left with the darkness of the night.

# Excerpts III

August 7, 1949

We discussed Ravana again tonight over the fire. . . .
As they spoke I still shuddered at what I had experienced
the other night. I have never felt so unclean—unclean
not only of body, but of mind, and, most of all, soul.
Should I meet someone who doubted the existence of the
soul, I would submit them to the dark presence of the
Devilthing, Ravana. The soul can be felt, as it fears to be
touched by such an ugly, loathsome force—I shall never
forget that feeling. . . .

Holy Eagle spoke directly to me about the nature of
the Devilthing, as if it were most important that I
understand. He could not find the word, so he asked
Lame Bear, who said the word "Manipulator." Holy
Eagle grabbed that word and tossed it to me. Ravana,
when free, he said, is a Very Great Manipulator, of
events, of people, and of spirits; Ravana will be as the
wind at night, invisible and powerful and dark, so strong
that It will blow the moon, the sun, and the stars from
the sky and cause all living things to die. It was obviously
a metaphor for the destruction of the earth and
Universe; perhaps an Indian equivalent to Armageddon.

But what of *Heytah-nee*—the Fallen Warrior, the Chosen One? I asked this and he told me to remember that Ravana is a Very Great Manipulator, and that *Heytah-nee* is chosen by the Devilthing Itself; that all things around him are manipulated by the Devilthing. At this point I interrupted and asked if the *Heytah-nee* knew that he was the Chosen One, and if so, could he not guard against Ravana's manipulations. Holy Eagle seemed agitated, and looked at me intently, then said that he did know one thing: that *I* would know the *Heytah-nee* when I met him; the Spirit Elders had told him this in a dream; and that I must listen now very carefully to the instructions he would give me, for I would have to remember them for an indeterminate period of time, and the instructions must be followed exactly as given when I meet the *Heytah-nee*. . . . For the second time since I arrived here I am afraid, this time not just for myself, but for all mankind.

# Book II

# 22

The Sunday morning sky was watercolor-gray; Kyle hoped it wouldn't rain.

A dozen daisies garnished with baby's breath and wrapped in waxy green paper lay in the seat beside him as he steered the Ranger out into the country toward Dave Pickers's ranch. He had picked them up last night at Gathers's Market, whose produce department did a thriving business in flowers and plants. They seemed none the worse for having spent the night in a vase. They made him more nervous than anything that he had yet done with Dave Pickers. With them, he was about to tread on the old man's most sensitive spot—and he wasn't even sure why he was doing it. He might be risking their friendship, such as it was, because somehow he needed to get closer to the only other man he knew that had been through the Tragedy. Somehow superficial conversations and games of cribbage they'd played over the past few months weren't enough. Kyle wanted in on the man's pain. Why? He couldn't say, but somehow it felt right to be doing this.

He reached the bend. For a moment, rounding it the first time some two months ago projected itself into his mind. The trees. God, hadn't it rattled him, those damned snakes hissing up a wail somewhere behind that cast-iron door. But, he was sicker then, and now what hissing there was, was far away and he took this as a sign of growing mental health. *This town has been good to me,* he thought, rounding the bend and paying no further attention to the trees. *Leo was right. All I had to do was find a place away from it all, settle down and get my mind working at what I know best. Bless your hide, Leo.* He made a mental note to call his old friend, or at least drop him a letter. *I'll never go back to the way I was in Woodhaven. Never!*

As he reached the drive he debated whether to make the turn and go on with this venture, or just come back later, after the old man had gotten back. Dave's battered gray truck was still there.

He guided the Ranger up to the house.

Dave Pickers materialized on the porch, wearing a somber black suit, vintage 1950s. It looked worn, but well cared for, pressed stiff and rigid. A pencil-thin black tie dangled from his neck, bisecting a white dress shirt yellowed with age but freshly ironed and starched. On Dave's head sat a black derby, and clutched in both hands were two bouquets of violet and yellow wildflowers.

Kyle rolled down the window and mustered a grin. He felt stupid.

Dave Pickers stared.

"Hello, Dave." Kyle got out of the car and stood uncomfortably before the implacable stare of the old man. He was intruding. And damn, he was underdressed. Out of respect he had worn a nice pair of black woolen slacks with a dark green sports shirt. His split-cowhide coat he'd thrown on because it looked like rain. Dave Pickers, on the other hand, looked like a Norman Rockwell character in oil, the painting of a man going to a 1930's Grange Hall Social, dressed to impress (in a somber way) his new girl.

"I'd like to pay my respects"—he waved his hand toward town, the cemetery—"to your wife and daughter if it'd be all right."

The old man stood stonefaced while time crawled. Kyle felt like a kid begging his dad to take him along to the store with him.

He resuced his own bouquet from the truck seat, painfully aware that Dave was holding two. Clutched in Dave's knarled right hand was a small leather-bound Bible.

Dave Pickers looked at his flowers. He descended from the porch, his face marked with the sadness Kyle had seen before only in fleeting moments.

"In times to come, Kyle Richards, remember that you asked to come with me."

Kyle released his PR smile and felt his face mirror Pickers's. "I will," he said. "I want to pay my respects."

"Emily is waiting for us," intoned Dave.

"Would you like me to drive?" Kyle asked.

The old man said nothing, but fumbled the door to his own truck open and placed the flowers and the small Bible on the center of the seat, removed his derby, and climbed in. He turned to Kyle. "Git in," he said.

Kyle got in, ignoring the black electrical tape acting as band-aids for the shredding interior of the old truck seats.

They pulled smoothly away from the house, and out onto the road.

"How'd you know about visiting Emily Sundays?" asked Dave.

Kyle noticed for the second time that Dave had not mentioned his daughter. Kyle looked at the two wildflower bouquets and then up to the old man who watched the road stonily. It was hard to imagine that he had even spoken.

"Someone mentioned it to me," he said, hedging.

Dave said nothing after that and they drove in silence. Dave turned at a crossroad just before the Gathers Corporation building. The road was little used and snaked its way up behind the Gathers building into the foothills to town's cemetery.

Kyle caught Dave glaring balefully at the mayor's head-quarters building. Now, what's that about? thought Kyle.

Dave returned his gaze to the road, and steered his truck carefully up the washboard road until the mayor's building was behind them and out of sight. Soon the ivy-covered brick and cast-iron gates of Ridgecrest Cemetery came into view.

The caretaker, a short, stubby man in green work clothes, waved as the old truck passed through the gates. Dave Pickers raised his hand in greeting, but did not smile. It was the first sign of civility to any person other than himself that Kyle had seen.

Kyle surveyed the cemetery, comparing the jutting headstones here to the bronze markers that lay flat in the more modern cemeteries in Los Angeles. Laid flush for a practical purpose—it made it easier to mow the lawn. For a moment the burning image of two very special markers heated the inside of his brain. Susan and Lisa. God, how he loved them.

Small exploratory drops of rain splattered, disturbing the dust on the windshield as Dave stopped the truck. They were in the section furthest from the front gate. The rest of the cemetery sloped down before them. In the distance, over the ivy bricks of the wall, the town lay below them. Kyle got out of the truck holding his flowers. The heady wet smell of rain mingled with ripe smells of fresh-cut grass; a soft mountain breeze swept his cheeks. A drop of rain hit him. He looked skyward. The large gray patches that were evident on his way out this morning had knitted themselves together into a high light-gray skullcap over the earth. Distant thunder broke, making Kyle wonder how much time they had before it poured.

He looked at Dave Pickers.

The old man's back was to Kyle, his derby now back on his head, and the man was moving away, weaving his way through different colored marble and granite headstones toward a large monument. Kyle caught up with him as he reached the monument. The marker was huge, at least nine feet across by four feet high, with a two-foot thickness of stone. Into its polished gray marble stone was cut the family name:

PICKERS

and below that:

Emily Catherine    Catherine Eve    David Payton
b. 1924 - d. 1963  b. 1949 - d. 1965  b. 1917 -
IN THE HANDS OF OUR LORD

That must have cost a fortune, thought Kyle.

"Emily," said Dave, "this is the man I was telling you about" (Kyle noticed that the old man seemed nervous, almost embarrassed, as he spoke. but nonetheless he continued, his eyes flicking to Kyle, his voice assuming a gruff tone), "Kyle here is going to help us, Emily, going to help us get our baby back."

*What!*

He looked incredulously at the old man, and for the second time that day Dave Pickers let his face express his real emotions. He turned to Kyle, his eyes brimmed with sadness and that strange look that was filled with pity, as if the weary old man thought he was doing something against his will to hurt Kyle.

Dave looked back at the carved letters of his wife's name and said sadly, "She was a good woman, Kyle." He shook his head and bent down and placed one bouquet of wildflowers so that the colored petals touched the marble of the stone under his wife's name, and placed the other under that of his daughter. He dropped to his knees, his body straight, his black coat falling down from his bony shoulders like a shroud. He removed his hat and set it up on the smooth curve of the headstone. He bowed his head as in prayer, then brought the small leather-bound Bible up, opened it, and began to read out loud: "Our verse is from John—11:25. 'Jesus said unto her, I am the resurrection, and the life: he that believeth in me, though he were dead, yet shall he live . . .'"

Kyle felt mystified, a little unreal. Something was going on here. Dave Pickers wanted something from him—perhaps had wanted it all along—and what had he meant, "bring our baby back to us"?

The first spiderweb of lightning flashed in the gray morning sky, followed moments later by a healthy clap of thunder. Rain began to fall.

". . . The Master is come, and calleth for thee . . ." intoned Dave.

Kyle placed his flowers between the two bunches positioned

by the old man. As he set them down, the sound of Pickers's voice droned loudly in his ear: ". . . As soon as she heard that, she arose quickly, and came unto him . . ."

Kyle righted himself and gazed down at Dave Pickers's head. Thin gray hair slicked with pomade poorly covered his freckled pate. From this angle the cloth of his suit showed tired and worn.

Pickers finished his reading and closed the Bible. The rain began to fall. Lightning flashed quickly. Thunder rolled like a cannonade. He looked up at Kyle. The cords of his neck stood out. Tears welled in his eyes. "I want you to find my baby, Kyle," he begged. "I want you to bring her back so that she can rest here at peace with her mother . . . and with me when I die."

"She *is* buried here, Dave," said Kyle.

"No! No!" Lightning gouged jagged yellow seams in the fabric of the sky and the rolling thunder followed in two heartbeats. The rain hit Pickers's upturned face mercilessly. "He's still got her. *He's* still got her. All that's here is her head, Kyle. *He* did all *that* to her and He didn't even leave her body! She needs to be here close to her mother. All of her. I want you to get the rest of her for me . . ." He turned away and looked at his wife's grave, then back up to Kyle, still pleading with his eyes, ". . . for *us,* Kyle. Emily's with you too. Please! Oh, God, please, plea-eas-ease!" He clasped his hands as in prayer and scudded around on his knees so that he faced Kyle and he no longer had to twist his neck. He lowered his voice to a husky, calm beseechment: "Oh, God, *please.* Promise me, Kyle. Promise me?"

Kyle stood speechless. He knew the pain. A proud man on his knees begging him to do the impossible. He had tried to do the impossible before and he had paid the price—Woodhaven—He couldn't do that again. He couldn't expect himself to be a damn savior. When you can't handle failure, when you go insane because you failed at your responsiblities, you just don't make promises any more, because when you do you end up in Woodhaven with you own damned hands reaching, untangling those snakes, and when they fall into your brain you just won't come back to this side of sanity ever again.

"Dave," said Kyle finally, then stopped. The rain pelted them. He felt the cold sting of it in his face like liquid mortar shells. The wind picked up, blowing more rain into his face. He wanted to give this friend, this soulmate, what he wanted; but it was impossible.

"What I want to tell you and what I'm going to tell you are two different things," Kyle began. "I want to say I can help you, but the facts are that I can't . . . Now, just hold on, Dave. I'm very familiar with the case. I've read the file over and over again—for reasons of my own—you know my story. The men back there did everything possible: they dredged the stream; they searched and dug in every possible spot. What you have to realize is that a thing like that eats away at everybody, involved or not involved—it was a god-awful thing that happened. It makes everybody that hears about it sick to their stomachs. Hell, I've seen men in my time work for nothing, overtime, no pay, just to catch the scum that do things like that. Believe me, it was a thorough investigation. They didn't find the body because it wasn't there, and now you ask me to promise to bring . . . find the remains. What I want, Dave, is to be able to say, Yes, I can do it, but what I have to say is, No, I can't. If I could, I would; you know that's true."

"The Devil has her, Kyle . . ."

"I don't believe in the Devil, Dave. I've told you that before."

"But you don't believe I'm lying, either, do you?"

"I don't like my own words thrown in my face, Dave. You're a better man than that."

"I want my baby back. I'll say anything, do anything; I'd kiss the mayor's ass on Main Street, and I'd kill to get her back."

Kyle turned away from the man, looking down the slope of green and marble out over the town. Thunder boomed. The rain intensified.

"Please, Kyle. *Please.*" Pickers's voice rose to overcome the mounting rush of wind and rain.

Kyle turned back to him and stared down. "If there were something new for me to go on, Dave, I could look into it, but ther is nothing new."

"The boy, the boy," said Dave eagerly. "There was a boy."

Kyle eyed the old man, stunned. The rain beat down on them. Finally, Kyle spoke: "What boy? There was no mention of a boy in the reports; not you saying anything about one, anyway."

"They took me away . . . put me away in the loony bin . . . had me drugged up after I told them what happened. I—I was savin' the boy for myself, maybe. I—I just don't remember. By the time I was out, by the time I was out, it was over, and everybody thought I was crazy as could by anyway. No one was listening to me."

I know that feeling, thought Kyle. "Tell me about the boy, Dave," he said, trying to ignore the drenching, the cold wet cling of pant fabric to his leg, and the hair plastered, dripping wet, to his head.

"I came into the clearing and saw what I saw, but just before I was knocked down I saw a boy, I couldn't see much, he was in the trees . . ."

"Could it have been a man?"

"Uh . . . Uh . . . I don't know why I say it, but I think it was a boy. I really couldn't see much, 'cept to know a jacket and blue jeans disappeared into the blackness of the trees."

"Can you tell me the color of his hair? Anything at all to describe him?"

Dave shook his head sending splatters of water off his face only to be drenched by more rain. "Maybe a man," he said. "Could've been a man."

He became silent, staring up at Kyle, waiting for the answer to the unspoken question. For a moment the sky was silent, the wind died down, lessening the impact of the still heavy rain.

"I'll look into the matter," Kyle said finally, "But no promises. I don't make promises."

Dave rose to his feet and glared into Kyle's eyes. "Promise me that you'll do everything you can to find my baby and bring her back to me. *Promise me,*" he hissed.

*Say no.*

Kyle stood for a moment, looking into those tormented eyes and felt he was looking into a mirror. Time was nonexistent.

*Dear God, say no.*

"All right," he said. "I promise you that I will do everything that I can to find Cathy's body."

Relief spread across the old man's face. The release of fear. "Thank you, thank you," he said. He suddenly looked very, very old. And wet.

"We better get back to the car," suggested Kyle.

"No. I have to trim around the stone. They never trim around the stone," said Pickers. He reached inside his waistband and pulled a small pair of trimming shears.

Kyle took them from him. "You go to the truck and get that damned heater on. I'll do this." He lifted the shears in salute.

Pickers began to object, but grimaced instead, and headed for the car.

"What have I done?" said Kyle out loud as he knelt down beside the stone and began clipping at the longer grass close to the gray marble. He clipped fast; the wind had picked up again. Another web of lightning appeared in the storm-gray clouds and Kyle looked up. The clouds were different. Not black, but a light gray. How they could bring so much rain, he did not know. The thunder boomed. He returned to his clipping, paying careful attention to the job, and trying not to think. Finished, he stood up and walked toward the truck slowly, even though the rain poured down on him.

He felt cleansed by the rain, and realized that this promise he had made to Pickers was the first one that he had made to

205

anyone since the death of his own wife and daughter; and there had been no hissing, no snakes behind that cast-iron door crying to be free, crying for his sanity. Still, the promise scared him. But, by God, he was determined to keep it, no matter what.

He watched more lightning flash, listened to the thunder roll, and relished the feel of the cold clean rain pelting his face.

# 23

Kyle stayed at Dave's place until late afternoon, then took a long drive to sort things out. The rain didn't let up, but he didn't care. It had been a good day for him, a growth day. His promise to Pickers still scared him a little. At first, he wasn't sure why, but as the day wore on he decided that it was because old Dave had come to mean something to him, and Kyle didn't want to fail. How could he fail, really? It was a simple investigation, and the odds were against anything turning up. He would give it his full attention, of course, but the fact is, he would probably end up telling Dave that he'd found nothing.

Kyle got home after dark.

After a steaming hot shower and wolfing down two bologna and cheese sandwiches and two tall glasses of milk, Kyle made a dash out to the garage and with a small amount of rooting around found what he was looking for, an artist's easel—it had been Susan's, the remnants of one of her many fad hobbies. He brought it in and set it up in his den directly across from his desk. He directed his lamp to shine on its empty frame. He retrieved a big calendar from behind his desk—1978. He used to draw big pictures of goofy characters for Lisa on the backs of the used-up sheets. Now, that year was dead, and the back of the calender sheets would serve another purpose.

Kyle tore off a page, turned it over to the blank white side, then stapled it back to the rest of the calender so that the cardboard backing could be used for support. He placed the calender in the easel and admired the three-by-two-foot blank page before him. He took a black felt-tip pen from his desk and drew a series of large empty boxes down the center, to the middle of the sheet. The Pickers file was in his office. He would need it later, but not for the preliminary work—he had those events memorized. He printed in the bottom most box: *CATHY MURDERED—AUGUST 15, 1965, APPROX. 12:00 A.M.:* in the box above that he wrote *DAVE WAKES UP—APPROX. 11:50 P.M.—GOES TO TREES, SEES BOY?, CLAIMS SEES DEVIL KILL CATHY,* and from the upper box to the lower box he drew an arrow. That was the flow—something always precedes an event and something always comes after it, that's flow. And when you've got the flow down, a lot of the extraneous pieces just seem to fall into place, and when *all* the pieces are in place, the whodunit of the matter pops out like magic. The problem here is that nobody really knew what Cathy was doing there . . . until now. A boy. That's about as good a reason as you need when you're sixteen and . . . in love?

Kyle capped the pen. He squinted at the boxes he had drawn, the notes that he had made.

And what sixteen-year-old in love could resist telling her best friend? Hell, *he* couldn't resist now telling someone about his feelings for Michele if it hadn't been the—

The house seemed so quiet. He stood listening, using the absence of sound to detract from his thought of Michele and the Tragedy.

Kyle looked at the flow sheet: If Cathy had been in love and told someone then, sixteen years ago, the detective on the case would have caught that too—It was a good investigation, no question; Kyle had read the report over twice; the job had been done on that case; what he'd told Pickers up at the cemetery had been the truth—so either she hadn't told anyone, or she told someone and they didn't tell . . . or couldn't tell . . .

*Now, why had that come to mind?*

*And isn't that going to be fun—sixteen years of time between then and now. Find 'em, that's a big problem, and getting them to remember—hopeless!*

"Nothing is hopeless," Kyle said out loud. His voice

punched the stillness of the night. I'd still be in Wood-haven, he thought, if Leo hadn't taught me there was no such thing as hopeless.

He turned out the light, plunging the room into blackness. Time for bed. "That's the skimpiest damn flow sheet I ever saw," he stated in mock disgust, then felt his way into the hall.

He slept lightly. There was dreaming. A door opening. He was fourteen now and sneaking into his parents' bedroom to steal cigarettes, Camels, just two. Dad would never miss them. His father lay on his side, his back to Kyle, left arm tucked up under his head for a pillow. "Always enter a room like you belong there," his dad said, "'cause when you don't the door sounds like you don't and you wake people up." *The door.* "Yes, Dad," he said; his father still lay with his back to him. "And, Son?" "Yes, Dad?" "Put the cigarettes back." "Yes, Dad." "And, Son?" "Yes, Dad?" (*The door*) "Quit singing like a little girl, will you?" (*"Mares eat oats, and does eat oats, and little lambs eat ivy, a kid'll eat ivy, too; wouldn't you?"*)

Kyle's eyes snapped open. In the quiet darkness of his bedroom he would swear he heard them click.

The door.

In the way of remembering after sleep, his mind forced the facts upon him. He had heard a door opening.

*No, not that door.*

And singing. A child's voice.

*No, Lisa. Please, Lisa.*

Kyle felt his groin tighten. His arms and legs went heavy, resisting movement. His jaw was frozen shut. He could barely draw in enough air through his nostrils to inflate his lungs, because a light came on, now. It reflected off his bedroom door . . . its surface, the light, and now there was a shadow, small, she was down the hall, but

*Oh, sweet Jesus, she's walking down the hall.*

the shadow on the door was growing larger

*Please, Lisa, no, God, no.*

and the singing began, softly, sweetly, his little girl's voice, *Lisa, no, no—no-o-o.*

Lisa's song. The shadow nearly blotted out the weak light on the door. Her voice grew louder, louder, and then softer, echoing . . . from the den? Kyle heard the snap of a switch and the light on the door was white, the shadow gone. He heard her singing. She was in his den. His little girl was in his den, singing, for God's sake. And he couldn't move, he couldn't call out. He just lay there, frozen, like a giant ice sculpture. She was singing, singing singing singing

*Stop it stop it stop it! Sto-o-opppp-iiiiittttt!*

"Stop it right this minute, do you hear me, Lisa!" Kyle heard himself scream, "and go to your room, do you hear me, missy! Go to your room right this instant! Do you hear me!"

Instantaneously the light extinguished and the house was quiet. Deathly quiet. Kyle found himself sitting bolt upright, clenching two big fistfuls of covers, his muscles pulled taut like steel guy wires. His body was awash with the hot nervous sweat of fear, and his heart still triphammered.

He sat until his heart reached its normal beat rate, then he swung his legs out over the bed and sat staring at the darkened doorway. Finally he snapped his bed lamp on. He was going to have to go out there. Shit.

He walked purposely past his den, without looking in, to the middle of the hall and slapped at the wall-plate switch. Light bathed the hall. He stared at the closed bedroom door, and a small flutter worked its way through his body.

*Let sleeping dogs lie.*

He turned around and stood in the doorframe of his den and froze in disbelief.

He snapped on the overhead light and stood gaping. On the floor, under the easel, lay a red crayon. He read the brand name, CRAYOLA, not wanting to raise his eyes, unable to stop himself. He read the flow sheet, stared down the hall at the closed bedroom door, then back at the flow sheet. Scrawled in crayon in the box above the Dave Pickers entry were the words CATHY'S MOMMY. A blood-red arrow was drawn from the bottom of that box to the one below: CATHY MURDERED. Another arrow was drawn from CATHY MURDERED to a box drawn below. In that box was written MOMMY AND ME. Shakily drawn in red, a final new arrow pointed down from that box to another crayoned-in lopsided box containing the word DADDY. Below DADDY was scrawled, in giant red letters, R A and what looked like a partial letter, a V most likely.

The diagram's logic began to stab at his mind: something comes before a murder and something comes after. It flows. And all of it flows in one direction. First *A*, then *B*, then *C*, etc. And that's the way it was here.

Except. Whatever R A V was, was flowing against the grain. Because there, in a thick, smudgy red, was an arrow between DADDY and R A V, but the arrow was pointing against the flow, from the R A V box *toward* the DADDY box. *Into* the DADDY box, actually, sharp and sticking, like a red, and wicked, spear.

# 24

He had done it!

Curtis rolled over in his bed to get a better look at the clock radio on the nightstand. The digital numbers, glowing stark red in the darkness of the early morning, changed from 5:43 AM to 5:44 AM. He reached out and slapped the alarm-off button before 5:45 AM, the time when the radio was set to blast him out of bed to the tune of Queen, or Led Zeppelin, or whatever rock group KSGS was playing this morning.

He rustled his way out from under the covers and sat on the edge of the bed in blue-striped pajamas, and stared triumphantly at the radio. The chief told him Monday that if he instructed himself the night before to wake up just before the alarm went off, he would. Today was Wednesday, and on only his second try he'd done it. They had only been friends a few months, and the chief had taught him a lot of neat stuff like that. Curtis figured falling off that bike had been the luckiest thing in the world. He couldn't remember being so happy. God *had* answered his prayers; not only did the chief like him, he liked him *a lot*. They had already been fishing twice, and camping a time, too!

Curtis slid off the bed and dressed in the silky darkness of the early morning hour. He donned his jogging suit, then put on his socks by standing on one leg like a stork. The chief had taught him this, telling him that it improved your balance. It had taken him a week to learn that one, but now he stood as steady as a fence post on just one leg, putting on a sock and a shoe at a time.

212

He left by the back door, jogged down Wilson Street to the corner, and turned left on Ash. The morning cold began to disappear as his body heat was caught inside his togs and warmed him up. He felt his leg muscles loosen up. By the time he was to Laity Street and turning up the corner (going uphill now—the toughest part of the run), he was feeling good, his lungs billowing in strong sympathy with his efforts. Curtis broke his stride as he reached Peach. He made a turn and at the same time tried to spot the chief. They usually hooked up on their early morning run right about here.

There he was!

The chief thumbed his nose, grinned, and took off in a sprint. Curtis chased after him, all the way to the chief's house. He arrived panting at the driveway, then joined the chief in the empty street, falling in beside him as they both cooled down in a ritual of walking in ever-lessening circles.

Cooled down, Curtis went with the chief up the drive to the garage. The chief opened the side door and ushered Curtis in, flipping on a light switch. The rack of neon lights that the chief had installed flickered on and bathed the stark interior of the garage in its soft sticky light. Curtis had helped the chief change the garage over to a *dojo*. They'd cleared it totally bare except for a few of the wardrobe boxes that they'd pushed into the far corner. All the other extra boxes they had hoisted up in the rafters and this had laid the groundwork for the *dojo*. The chief had a number of tatami mats whose woven dry grass material now covered most of the small garage's floor space. The chief had laid those by himself. In a corner near the big door (which was never opened now—the chief kept his truck outside now all the time) they'd hung a sixty-pound workout bag from the rafters by a large-link steel chain. The first time Curtis had punched it he thought that he had broken his knuckles.

"Okay, we'll have to make it short today," said the chief. "I have to get in early today. I've got that report for the city council at nine o'clock." He motioned toward the mats. "Let's

213

stretch it out first."

Together they did a preordained routine of leg stretches, followed by punches, blocks, and kicks. The garage began to smell of sweat, and the soft whisper of cloth sounded good as they moved in quick, flowing movements. Finally, the chief called a halt and then motioned Curtis to the center of the mat. "Short-form. Falling leaf," he said, then seated himself crosslegged at the edge of the mat.

Curtis took a deep breath, then emptied it very slowly, just like the chief had taught him to do. Then, he began to think about what he was going to do. Think about each piece of the form, then about the form as a whole. The chief had taught him this also. With his mind holding on to its mental image of what he was going to do, he did it, and did it perfectly for the first time, moving about the mat with sliding grace, kicking and punching, blocking and jabbing, sometimes viciously, but always with grace and fluid motion. "Excellent," the chief complimented him. Curtis felt proud. He'd been working on this form with the chief for over two months, and to get an "Excellent" meant he had done it perfectly.

Kyle motioned him to sit down beside him. "Your leg sweeps are a lot better than when you started. Perfect, in fact. Do you remember the rule I taught you?"

"A man fights on his legs," recited Curtis.

"That's right. And take those away and he's down, and with two evenly matched opponents, the man on top has the advantage."

Curtis nodded his head, then asked a question that had been on his mind for a while. "Chief, when I do the forms I'm learning to block and strike for certain strikes and blocks of the other guy, right?" The chief nodded back. "Then, what if I'm getting punched in a way that's different than any of the forms that I'm learning?"

The chief shifted, gently rocking himself around to face Curtis. "What you and I are doing is training our minds *and* our bodies to respond to attack. As you practice these forms

214

your mind stores them, and then when you go free-form, or if you are in a tight spot, your mind and your body put it all together for you to take care of whatever is coming your way. Without you even thinking about it," he added as an afterthought. "Haven't you ever seen red, and just done something automatically without thinking about it, and were surprised that you did it later?"

Curtis shrugged. "I don't think so, Chief."

The chief cleared his throat. "Sometimes it shows when you're mad, so ticked off that you act without thinking. You really couldn't consciously control yourself if you tried. That's seeing red."

"That sounds dangerous."

The chief laughed out loud. "Good," he said. "It is dangerous. That's why it's important to be in control at all times. Control is what I've been trying to teach you. When you see red you lose *conscious* control, but react automatically, and everybody better stand by. If it's life and death, seeing red can save you sometimes. Remember that. You won't have any control over it anyway. You won't be able to help yourself. But practice control, understand?"

Curtis understood and said so. The chief rose and he followed suit. "I'm going to work out some more, okay, Chief?"

"Sure."

When the chief went into the house to shower and dress, Curtis walked to the workout bag and punched and kicked it for a while. He felt guilty. Ashamed. What the chief didn't know was that he didn't have to worry about Curtis seeing red and hurting anyone. He was a big chicken. Yes, he could do the forms and he felt good in here, but when he was outside, near someone giving him a hard time (like Little Neil, *the asshole*) he felt the adrenaline flow into his body, and instead of making him strong, he began to shake. What the chief didn't know, and Curtis couldn't bring himself to tell him, was that if Curtis ever saw red it would probably be his own blood at the end of Little

215

Neil Gathers's fist.

The chief was gone by the time Curtis exited the *dojo*.

Curtis closed the side door to the garage and cut across the dew-wet grass to the back door and let himself in with the key that Kyle had given him. He kept that key with his own house key on a chain around his neck, but *this* key was his favorite. You could say that you like someone, but to give them the key to your house, you almost have to like them for sure, and trust them, too, don't you? Of course the chief had made him make a promise, and Curtis had kept it so far.

He pulled the key out of the lock and closed the door. The sound echoed mutedly and he walked over to the sink, swinging the keys erratically so that they jangled tinnily in the early morning silence of the kitchen. From under the sink he pulled out a small yellow plastic watering can and filled it full of water. Wednesday was watering day. This was one of the jobs that he did for the chief on a regular basis; he also fed the fish and swept the drive, and did other jobs the chief thought up during the week. For this the chief paid him five dollars a week.

Whistling, Curtis made his rounds with the watering can, stopping to "slip a dish to the fish," as the chief would say.

What was that?

He turned toward the hall. A bell? he thought. Raspy sounding, but a bell. He walked to the hall doorway and stopped. It had come from in here he was sure. Puzzled for a moment he stood still, watering can held at chest level, and stared to the right at the closed door. He listened. Nothing.

He hurried down the hall into the chief's bedroom and watered the diffenbachia (the chief had named it Fred) and looked around. No bells in here. Could it have been his imagination? He checked the bathroom next, then the chief's den. Nothing there either. And that brought him back out into the hall to face the closed door and the promise that he had made the chief.

For a moment, he stood just outside the den door, thinking

216

of the promise. The chief had squatted down in front of him right here, right in this very hall, and placed a hand on each shoulder and gazed straight into his eyes. He asked, "Do you know what a man's word is worth, Curtis?"

"No," he answered after thinking about it a little. He really didn't.

"A man's word is the worth of the man." Curtis had never seen the chief look so serious about anything, and it frightened him a little. He wondered if he had done something wrong. "Do you understand what that means, Curtis?"

Curtis thought he understood. "It means that when you say something you should mean it."

"Good," he said softly. "I'm going to ask you for your word on something. I want you to think about it very carefully before giving it, and answer me truthfully. Whether you say 'yes' or 'no' won't effect how I feel about you. But if you give me your word and it's a lie, I will know and you will disappoint me. Do you understand?"

"Yes." His mind began a liquid swirl of fears: if he disappointed the chief, the chief wouldn't like him anymore; the chief would hate him, and not let him run with him, or learn how to fight, and he wouldn't be able to ride in the chief's truck, either.

"Okay," said the chief. "I want you to promise me that if you are ever in this house alone, you will never go in *that* door"—he pointed toward the closed door at the far end of the hallway—"that door right there. No matter what."

"Yes," said Curtis automatically.

"Think about it again, Curtis. The most sure way to get someone, especially when they're young, to do something is to tell them not to do it. I'm not telling you not to do it. I'm asking you if you can keep a *promise* to me not to go in that room, no matter what."

"Yes," said Curtis truthfully. The chief's eyes seemed to fill his whole field of vision. "I could do anything for you, Chief."

For the first time since they had known each other, the chief reached out and wrapped his arms around the boy, bringing his body against his and squeezing him like a bear. He released him, reached into the pockets of his jeans, and gave him the key to the house, offering the job to him at the same time. Curtis felt elated. Whatever he'd said, the chief loved it. And he loved the chief. And he had kept his promise, and hadn't even thought about the room, except in passing . . . until now. But there had never been a bell . . .

*Brrrring*

before.

How had he gotten in front of the door? He didn't remember walking. But he had. The glass doorknob seemed to be begging him to touch it. Turn it. Just one little peek wouldn't hurt. The sound was coming from in there. Maybe something was wrong. Maybe—

"A man's worth is his word!" Curtis yelled harshly to himself, breaking the spell. "I am a man of my word." He whirled quickly and ran to the kitchen. He emptied the remaining water out of the can and replaced it. He had to get to school, and even if there was an old noise in that room he didn't go in that room, because he was a man of his word.

As he stood outside the kitchen door, fetching his key up from around his neck, he felt better. The morning air felt fresh and clean on his skin. He took a deep breath and closed the door. He inserted the key and locked the door, forcing that last bit of information from his mind by telling himself he had to get to school. But as he ran home to change, the thought reasserted itself. He was sure of it. In those last few seconds before closing and locking the kitchen door, as he was fishing for his keys, he was sure that he heard the *brrring* one more time, this time followed by the high sweet voice of a little girl, singing. And a rocking sound. And *brrring*.


By the time Curtis had run home, showered, dressed, and headed for school, he had come to a conclusion about what

218

caused the noises in the chief's room: it was a tape recorder; the chief had left it on. Just the same, Curtis decided not to tell the chief about the noise in case he might think Curtis had broken his word and gone in the room. And by the time he mounted his bike and started pedaling his way to school, the eeriness of the taped voice of the little girl singing and the rocking-*brrring* noise were buried deep in his mind, but not so deep that every so often it didn't raise its chilly hand and wave at him, like a student wanting to be recognized by the teacher. In each case, Mr. Curtis McKinney refused to recognize that pupil. It was safer that way.

Curtis liked to arrive at the classroom at least fifteen minutes before class started because Kari Saunders usually got there about that time and he could talk to her. Today he was ten minutes past that time, and came in panting, having ridden his bike as fast as he could. Mr. Herbert wasn't in the room yet, so Curtis could at least get a little talk in with Kari. He set his books down and pulled out his chair. It made a scraping sound that was drowned quickly by the pre-period murmurs, catcalls, and general ballyhoo of the sixth-grade academically enriched class of Thomas Jefferson Elementary School.

"Hi," he said, slipping into his seat and pulling the chair up close to the table. He was sitting quite close to her: the "desks" in the room were different than in other rooms, in that they were small worktables lined in three rows facing the green chalkboards. At each table there was room for two students. By sheer luck he had been assigned to share this table with Kari, or maybe it was because he and Kari looked like each other. Mr. Herbert said they looked like twins but, secretly, Curtis was glad they weren't twins because you can't be in love with your sister, and he was sure enough in love with Kari.

Kari leaned over to him, and when she did he smelled that fresh, clean perfume of lilac-scented soap that always seemed to be around her. She smelled so . . . so fresh, he guessed, and he love that smell. "Did you get number eight on the math, Curtis?" Curtis leaned over closer to her and pulled the homework sheet she was offering over to him. "It's like this," he said, and a shadow fell across his desk.

Someone sniffed. Once, twice, then said, "Hey, Larry, do you smell shit?" Curtis looked up into the face of Little Neil Gathers, the mayor's son, just in time to see him wrinkle up his piggy snout and sniff again. *Sniff-sniff-sniff.* He leaned over the front of Curtis's table. *Sniff-sniff.* "Yep. Larry, Curtsy Wurtsy's done crapped a big load in his diapers, but that's okay 'cause the chief'll change 'em for him, won't he, shitpants?"

Curtis wanted to belt him good, but he was frozen. He was afraid of Little Neil. Brown hair, white skin, and dark eyes. The mayor's son was a big kid. He was four inches taller than Curtis and outweighed him by at least forty pounds. Curtis wanted to call him fatso, but his tongue wouldn't budge. *I'm frozen,* he thought. *I can't even move. I'm such a coward.* All that the chief had taught him had flown out the window, and Why is he picking on me all of a sudden? whizzed through his brain.

"How's it feel ridin' in the chief's truck, Curtsy Wurtsy? Don't he mind you smellin' like shit?"

Curtis straightened up square in front of his books and stared up at the bully, finding himself looking through his face, just like the chief had taught him. Larry Duquesne was on Little Neil's right, and Billy Markham on his left. They were just smirking. Larry prodded the bully on encouragingly. "Thinks he's Mr. Hotshit, don't he, Neil?—riding around with the chief of police like he owns the town or something?" said Larry in his nasal voice.

"Jealous?" He managed to snap that word out firmly and with a bit of indignity in his voice.

Little Neil sneered cruelly and looked around to see how much audience he was getting. The other kids were crowding around. If this little shit thought he was getting one up on him he had another think coming, his face seemed to say. He bent over the table, balled up his fists, and placed them squarely on the tabletop on either side of Curtis's books, shifting half his weight forward to his arms so he could get down real close to

Curtis's face.

The group of kids around the two boys became silent. Kari scooted her chair as far to the side as possible and its scraping sounded like laughter to Curtis. He could smell Little Neil's breath, sour with this morning's milk. It stank. Mother told him not to fight, that civilized people don't fight. But everyone was watching. Kari. Did she see the fear he was feeling? Why me? he thought. And why won't my arms move like the chief taught me?

"Jealous?" asked Little Neil in an abnormally loud voice, spraying sour spit into Curtis's face, "Ha-ha, jealous." He stared malignantly straight into his eyes. "You know what I heard, Curtsy Wurtsy? Hunh?"

"No," said Curtis. He tried to look away but he was glued to his chair.

The big boy crowded his face even closer. Little Neil still had a yellow, crusty bit of sleep in the corner of his right eye.

"I heard that the only reason that the chief takes you anyplace is because your mother sucks him off for peanuts. Now about that, you little shi—"

Curtis pulled Little Neil's arms out from under him. Hard. The bully's face slammed against the tabletop. There was a splatting sound. Blood began to coat the table in smears as Curtis picked the boy's head up and slammed it *whamwham-wham* against the tabletop. Then he kneed him in the face, reached back and grabbed the bully's belt, hooked his right hand into Little Neil's hair and pulled him over the tabletop and into the table behind him. He dropped him, then descended upon him in a hail of punches. Little Neil was whimpering and trying to cover himself, and he was *crying. Little Neil was crying!*

Suddenly Curtis found himself suspended in midair above Little Neil. Someone was talking to him, telling him to "calm down, calm down"—Mr. Herbert. "Calm down," he repeated. "Calm down. *Calm down.*" The teacher finally set him on his own feet. Curtis jumped on the still-writhing, crying Little

221

Neil. He landed a few more punches before Mr. Herbert pulled him out of range of the mayor's son.

Mr. Herbert managed to keep the boys separated long enough to help Little Neil to his feet and escort them both down to the principal's office. The bigger boy was taken off to the nurse's office, while Mrs. Randolf called the mothers to have them come to school. Curtis finally became aware of where he was, sitting on a straight back in the principal's office, with his mother on the way to get him. The last thing he remembered clearly was what Little Neil had said to him; the rest was all fuzzy, dreamlike, like taking a tumble over the handlebars of his bike: one minute you're riding, the next minute you're on the ground and everything in between is a cartwheel.

Mrs. Randolf hung up from talking with Mrs. Gathers, and stood up and eyed Curtis thoughtfully. Curtis was a quiet boy, an excellent student, and very well mannered. And how he had beaten that big little snot Neil, she couldn't fathom. Little Neil. Now, there's a little boy who'd gotten his comeuppance. She moved from behind the desk and leaned her rear against it, gripping the edge on either side of her as if it would keep her balanced "Curtis, what happened?" she asked.

Curtis stood in shameful silence. His lips were pursed, his eyes were still wet and red from the tears.

"Curtis, tell me what happened." She made her voice stern, and then was silent. Expecting. That kind of pressure worked on every child that she had had in her office.

"I saw red," he said, and nothing more.


Kyle stopped by The Bookworm after delivering his program for upgrading the Briggs City police department to the city council. He was happy. It had gone very well, and he had been given the go-ahead by unanimous vote (even Edgar Griffith in the press section had seemed pleased). And well he should be, thought Kyle immodestly. It was a great plan to completely

222

modernize the department in personnel, training, procedure, and material over a three-year period. The mayor had wanted the best department in the county, and Kyle had delivered him a program for an upgrade that would give him just that.

It was almost eleven when he opened the door, the door's bell jangling his arrival. He wanted to see if Michele knew what Curtis wanted for his birthday. The party was a week from this Saturday and Kyle had been invited personally by the guest of honor.

Michele looked up from taking money from a large woman in a purple muumuu that coughed pink flowers like a disease. She nodded curtly at him and counted out the woman's change. "Thank you, Mrs. Unruh," she said, and forced a smile, then glanced hard at Kyle. He moved out of the way to let Mrs. Unruh pass by, swept by the air pocket of wisteria-scented powder that seemed to hover around her. "Good morning, Chief," said the woman, in passing. Kyle returned her greeting with a polite nod. He didn't know her, but one thing he had learned was that in a small town everybody knew the chief of police.

"Hello, Michele." Kyle saw that her eyes were pinched into narrow slits and her hands were agitating a revolving stand. Had he done something wrong?

"Well, it's happened, just like I knew it would one day." She was biting her lower lip, a habit, Kyle had noted, she had when upset. It made her look sexy, Kyle thought, and though he loved it, he kept his feelings from his face.

"What happened?" he asked.

"Despite all my warning, all my explanations, he finally went and did it! I just can't believe it!"

Kyle felt relieved. Whatever it was, it wasn't him. "Who did what? And why can't you believe it?" he asked, amazed at how involved she was with what she was talking about. He had never seen her like this.

She clasped her hands together with forced patience on the countertop and sighed. "Oh, Kyle."

"Earth to Michele. Earth to Michele," he intoned. "What are you talking about?"

She pointed back to the rear of the shop. "Your . . . Your . . ." She seemed stuck, and for a moment Kyle thought that she was going to say "son," ". . . friend; your little pal, is in the office. He has been suspended, my son has been *suspended* from school for fighting! He beat another boy bloody with his fists. And he is grounded for one solid month, and no birthday party either." She rested for a moment from her tirade, looking from Kyle to the black countertop.

Kyle's gaze was drawn to the square two-way mirror at the rear of the wooden bookshelves. Curtis was in there. His mom had said no birthday party. That seemed a little harsh. Kids could really provoke each other—must be that "Little Neil" character, the mayor's son. Curtis had confessed everything to him, the razzing that he had been taking at school. He felt a wave of pity for Curtis's plight. Michele stared fiercely at him. "I suppose you are going to stand up for him," she stated. "Yes?"

"What was the fight about?"

"He won't say. But he shouldn't be fighting."

"I agree with you, he shouldn't. Is it okay if I talk with him?"

Michele pointed toward the back. "Sure," she said.

Kyle found Curtis with his head down on the office desk. He thought he might be sleeping.

Curtis sat up. "Hi, Chief," he said glumly.

"Hi. I heard about your trouble."

The boy shot Kyle a look of shame. "I saw red, Chief. I didn't mean to. It just happened."

"Why don't you tell me exactly what happened, Curtis. Man-to-man."

Curtis hesitated, but Kyle coaxed him and he confessed everything. When he had finished, Kyle patted him on the head. "I think I can get you off the hook, guy. Just be sure to tell your mom that you know it's wrong to get in fights, okay?"

224

"Yes, Chief."

Kyle found Michele up by the desk. She appeared to have cooled off some; that was a relief. "Well?" she asked.

"Little Neil said some pretty filthy things about you and me. That's why Curtis punched him out."

Michele seemed taken aback. "About us?"

"Real nasty."

"What did he say?"

"I'd rather not—"

"Kyle . . ."

So he told her.

Kyle had to admit, Michele did take it pretty well. She flushed slightly scarlet, but regained her equanimity quickly. He wondered if the information would have the effect on her that he thought it would. After all, how much was her son supposed to take before he defended himself and his mother?

Kyle saw Michele's indecision pass briefly across her face. She went to the intercom and told Curtis that he could have his birthday party, but not to get in any more fights.

When she turned back at him, it was Kyle's turn to flush. She had caught him looking at her with a longing that he hadn't shown in years.

# 25

As the mayor drove he thought how very pleased he was with the plan his new police chief had presented before the city council this morning. Briggs City would be a fully updated police force in just three years, which is just what the mayor wanted. He also wanted a good leader for the force, and he'd sure gotten that. His spies in the station had reported that the new chief was well received by the men and that he instilled confidence and a certain *esprit de corps* in the ranks that had been missing when that good ole boy Buddy Nelson had been in charge.

That run-in the chief had with Phael never would have happened with Buddy, either, but after the mayor's initial anger at Kyle, he'd realized that what the new chief had done was be a damned good police chief (although he doubted that Kyle knew how severely the mayor had to sit on Phael to keep that hothead from seeking Old West style vengeance). Phael had been way out of line; that hair-trigger temper of his was always getting him in trouble. What the chief had advised on the matter had been sound advice—if Kyle had let Phael walk, it would have been smeared all over *The Review* the next morning, undermining not only the chief's credibility, but the mayor's as well. Instead, the mayor instructed Judge Baxter to dismiss the case, and Phael had walked, no fuss, no muss.

All of that seemed forgive-and-forget with chief, and the mayor was humming a tune after this particular session of the city council, which had taken place early in the morning, leaving him time for a little chore he had planned for late morning. He had depended on Kyle Richard's report to be direct and to the point, so he could get out of there on time, but the one thing that he hadn't considered in the later part of this fine Wednesday morning was having to go to school and pick up Little Neil, suspended for fighting. It wasn't the first time, either. Sure, he could have pulled a few strings and had the suspension suspended, but that didn't look good to John Q. Public, and if there was one thing he was sensitive to, it was J.Q.P. He could get you elected, or could bury you. And it always seemed to be the little things in politics that tripped you up, not the biggies. Little things like getting your boy off the hook in school. Damn Griffith would probably run it in big black headlines of *The Review*.

"Dad?"

The mayor looked quickly at Neil and then back over the hood of his Mercedes. They were almost there, now. He hadn't counted on having Neil with him, but maybe he could make a point to old man Pickers by using his son—if the old man didn't think he was bringing him a car-accident victim to use the telephone. He turned his head quickly to look at the half-wrapped mummy head of his son.

"Jee-*sus*, son. How could you let a little twig like that Curtis deck you like that?"

"He sucker-punched me, Dad."

"With what, a baseball bat? It's a good thing he hit you on the head where there's nothing there to get hurt."

"Aw, Dad," said Little Neil disparagingly, sqeezing down into the dark tan car seat, the silence of embarrassment enfolding him.

The mayor checked his rearview mirror, then caught a glimpse of Neil resplendent in his misery, before returning his attention to the road. Sure he'd been hot when he first saw Little Neil, his head bandaged, his lip split, puffy and purple, and those two black eyes! My God, the kid looked like a racoon on a Disney special. But once the principal had told him the other boy's name, that had been that. The mayor had personally awarded the McKinney boy an academic award for fifth grade last year; the kid was a reed, for Christ sakes, with straight A's in his classes and E's for citizenship. No problems with that boy at all, and there had been plenty with Neil. He was hard-headed, loud, boastful, and not a little bit rude at times. Well, time and the heavy hand of reason to his butt would take care of that—he hoped. But perhaps he could teach something to the boy from this mess.

"You have to learn to learn, Neil," began the mayor. Little Neil looked up at his dad with his full attention. "There's a lot to be learned in what happened in school today. Do you think you can tell me what?"

Neil said that he couldn't think of a thing except that he should have just punched that sissy Curtis in the mouth right off the bat.

"No. First of all, number one: never underestimate who you're dealing with; number two: don't use your fists when you can use your brain instead, because violence leads you into trouble if you don't have all the bases covered. For instance, you got kicked out of school today, and you're not getting any allowance this week . . ."

"What! Aw-w Da-ad!" The mayor relished the anguish in his young son's voice.

"Don't 'Aw, Da-ad!' me. Do you think that I'm stupid? Do you think that I don't know who started that fight? Not only that, but you're going to apologize to Curtis, and if you're smart you'll make friends with him."

This raised a wail of protest until the mayor raised his hand like a cop signaling a car to stop. He let the silence reign for a few minutes, then said, "It's the smart thing to do, Neil. If I were in your shoes, sitting right there, that's exactly what I would do—make friends with him. Seriously."

He glanced quickly at the boy. Neil was looking up at him. It was the private communication ritual that they had between them. He told the boy what he would do in such a situation, and Little Neil would do it because to do it would be just what his dad would do.

"Quick wrap-up," the mayor said, as if he were giving the final summation on a business meeting. "It's better to have friends than enemies; and you shouldn't settle your differences with violence." Except as a last resort, he thought. Always as the very last option.

He slowed down and made the turn onto Pickers's drive. Time was running out. The financing was set. The construction company was scheduled and that meant they had to start the project within the next month, or he would lose a bundle. That meant that Pickers had to be off his land, the sooner the better.

Crusty old bastard, thought the mayor, I hope that he'll listen to reason this time.

The fallen trees caught the mayor's eye as he guided his car up to ranch house. He surveyed the rest of the trees. They're beautiful, he thought. Shame they'd have to be cut down, but he knew one great mayor of one great little town who was going to have enough firewood from now to Armageddon.

The mayor slipped from under the wheel wondering what kind of reception he was going to get.

The screen door squeaked discharging Dave Pickers in his white overalls, his double-barreled shotgun crooked in his arm.

Little Neil came up beside his dad and the mayor put his arm around his shoulder, eyeing the shotgun. That had never been out in any previous conversation. He wasn't afraid that Old Dave would use it, but its presence planted a seed of anger that needed very little water to grow.

"Get off my land," the old man said in that dry papery voice of his.

"I want to talk to you," responded the mayor.

"I've said all I want to you. You can't have my land." Pickers's gaze flicked to Little Neil, and he added, "I don't believe in embarrassing a man in front of his kin, so just leave now."

"Mr. Pickers, all that I want is part of the land. You can keep your house. I just need from the far fence to about a hundred yard this side of the trees. All I need is your approval. It's for the good of the community, and"—he shook his boy lightly—"the good of our children . . ."

"As I said, Mayor, I don't believe in embarrassing a man in front of his own! Now, we both know for whose 'good' that land is for, so git! I won't say it again." His tall thin body moved across the weathered porch toward them. His blue eyes, sunk like beacons in a cave, gazed at the mayor with deadly intent.

"Get in the car, Neil." The mayor felt his own anger blossoming. "I don't like to be threatened," he said.

"Then stay off my land!"

The old man stared him down until the mayor threw up his hands in exasperation. He could feel the blood coursing to his face. "Have it your way, then," he said fiercely. "Won't trouble you again, that's a promise." He batted at the air with both hands. "Ah, what's the use." He spun gravel all the way to the highway, slowing only as he headed for home.

"Dad, if we're millionaires, how come we don't have a Rolls Royce?"

"Shut up."

I don't like to be threatened, thought the mayor. No fucking idiot is going to threaten me with a shotgun. Fuck him. I've done everything possible, every last damn thing possible to help him make the right choice. Now it's too fucking late. I got financing, I got my people to think of, my fucking schedule to keep, and ain't nobody going to keep me off that land. That problem with probate's been settled, so either the old coot does the right thing, or he can just kiss his sweet ass good-bye, because he's as dead as a fucking doornail right now, that's for damn sure.

Dead as a fucking doornail!

# 26

Edgar heard a light rap, and the door to his office opened silently. Michele stuck her head in with the same hopeful expression on her face she'd had as a child, and asked, "Are you busy, Unk?" in just the same manner as she had been doing since she was old enough to clamber up on her pink Schwinn bicycle and tool around town by herself.

"Never too busy for my favorite niece; if you see her, ask her to step into my office, would you, young lady?" Edgar smiled fully, savoring those precious words that were the beginning of a little routine that had began . . . Dear Lord, how many years ago? Too many to count, that's for sure . . . twenty-five—she had been seven. That's right, seven, bouncing curls and big blue eyes, carrying a play purse and a world full of seven-year-old-type problems, and she had come to talk to her "Unk" because he understood everything, the kind of things that parents never really understood. Twenty-five years. My, how time does fly, he remarked to himself.

She closed the door softly behind her. "She's right here, Unk."

"Well, so she is, so she is."

Edgar levered himself up from the cushions of his executive chair and held out his arms. The routine was over now except for the hug and the kiss. She threw her arms around him and gave him a wet kiss on the cheek.

He moved back to release her and felt her follow him, holding him tightly. He realized that she was crying. He held her without saying a word until Michele pushed away and said,

231

"I'm sorry."

Edgar picked up his phone and told Mrs. Stratton to hold calls and visitors. He turned to his niece, who was blowing her nose. She said, "I don't know why I let things get to me, Uncle Edgar."

"What's getting to you?" he asked.

She breathed deeply and said, "I let that thing with Curtis get to me. It's not right to fight; not right at all. But I am not going to punish my boy for sticking up for his mom, I'm just not going to do it." She stopped for a moment.

"But that's not what's bothering you," he said quietly.

"No," she sighed. "Aunty Clarice told me once that the first day that she saw you—in Chicago, at the picnic—she knew, knew, that she was in love with you, and she hadn't even met you yet. Mom told me the same thing about Dad; for her it was the same. With Tom it was never like that, it was a gradual thing—I learned to love him, I married him, had little Curtis, and then . . . then, he died. I never *knew* that I loved him when I first met him like Aunty Clarice and Mom. I thought that maybe they were telling me a story like Santa Claus or something. Then a few months ago the bell to the store jangles, I look up, and I know that Mom and Aunty Clarice *weren't* kidding because I fall in love, whammo, just like that. I mean, I *know* that I love him. I think it's hereditary, in my genes or something." She looked up at Edgar. "He's a fine man. He loves Curtis—it shows, it just shows. And I even think that he loves me, but he seems to be holding it back I think, Unk. I'm just not sure." A flush washed over her face. "He even looks at me like . . . you know, Unk . . ."

"You mean like a man looks at a woman?" he asked.

She nodded her head solemnly. "Yes," she said, "like that. When he thinks I don't see. But it's more than that, I can tell, I think. It's like he wants to tell me something, or touch me, but he can't for some reason. Like he's far away somewhere. I want to tell him, 'Hey, you in there, I'm the one for you,' but I can't. It just doesn't seem right."

232

She fell silent for a moment, lost in thought.

"Another woman, maybe," offered Edgar.

"No," she stated immediately, "not that. I checked. Curtis would have known. I just can't think of one good reason why he's so standoffish."

Edgar hesitated for a few moments. He could think of one good reason why, but he did not know whether to tell Mishy or not. He thought the gossip would have gotten around to her by now. But evidently it had not. He began very slowly by asking her if she knew anything about Kyle's wife and daughter. She said that she did not. He explained the brutal murder of the new chief's wife and daughter. He watched her face twist in anguish as he told of the partial decapitation of his wife and the bloody hanging of his little girl. He made it more graphic than normal because he wanted Mishy to fully understand how such a thing could make a man afraid to love another woman, make him hold back. "Maybe that's the reason, maybe not," he concluded, "but I guess I would bet a Pulitzer Prize that that might have something to do with it."

Michele's eyes were wide and wet. Her mouth gaped open. "Poor Kyle," she said, stunned.

"I wouldn't mention it to him if I were you, Mishy. I did. Brought it up in the interview. I have to tell you that I really thought that the mayor was trying to pull one over on us . . . *But* I'm coming around to changing my mind on that one. The upgrading plan for the police department that he presented to the council yesterday was absolutely marvelous. I may have to reassess my position on that Kyle Richards . . . especially if you're in love with him."

Sadness flushed Mishy's cheeks ruddy. Edgar knew that she was very close to tears. "Be patient with him is my advice. Mishy. If what you feel is true, you're just going to have to be patient."

Michele nodded, stood up, and kissed him on the cheek. "I love you, Unk," she said, and sighed. "Don't forget the party, a week from Saturday."

"I won't. And Mishy?"

"Yes, Unk."

"I love you too."


Talking with Uncle Edgar always made her feel better. She started up her Mustang and pulled into traffic. She turned up a side street to miss a minor noontime traffic jam and checked her watch. It was time to relieve Pamela so that she could go to her other part time job at Gathers's market. She thought of Kyle, the terrible loss in his life, and felt sadness fill her. God, he sure hides it well, she thought, I think I would have just balled up and died.

The Mustang approached Peach Street and she braked the car at the stop sign. She heard two throaty young screams of "Death to Darth Vader!" and saw Curtis and another boy flash by on Peach, not seeing her. They were waving those plastic tubes—toy laser swords from *Star Wars*—in slashing arcs while pedaling at a breakneck speed.

She was shocked.

Not that Curtis was out of the house, because she'd decided he'd done nothing to be punished about. As much as she hated violence, that was just one thing no son of hers would have to stand for, even if it meant punching someone out. What jolted her was the other boy that Curtis had gone whizzing by with— Little Neil Gathers.

## 27

The fire sputtered and the Indian shifted slightly. Which Spirit Elder would come this night? he wondered. Perhaps none.

Since the visit of Holy Bear some months before, he had been contented to wait. Holy Bear had said that he would know when to go to the mountain; then he could plead for his *Pehwah*, his soul. Grandfather might help him, *must* help him.

He'd been having dreams lately, of Ravana and that terrible night so many years ago when he had traded Cathy Pickers for his life. Did this have meaning? Were the dreams the sign?

The Elk stepped into the fireside.

"Great Holy Elk," greeted the Indian. "I have had dreams of the Evil Thing."

The Elk stood fast and stared, then said, "The time of the Facing is coming soon. You will know when to come to Sacred Mountain. Holy Eagle awaits you there."

"He knows?" the Indian asked incredulously.

"You have purpose in the plan of things."

"What purpose?"

"A purpose." Holy Elk turned to go.

"What of the Chosen One?—I have a question."

Holy Elk turned back to him and stared.

"O Great Spirit Elder," said the Indian. "*Ehkeh-Heh*, the Fallen Warrior, the Chosen One, how will he know to face Ravana, and what to do when he does?"

"He is being brought to understand," said Holy Elk, "of

Ravana, and the nature of all things evil."

Kyle knew he was in a dream. It had been so long since he had suffered the nightmare that he had almost forgotten, but not now: he chose the closet door instead of going into the living room where his dead wife lay decapitated.

The darkness of the closet enfolded him, and then he was walking once again on the top of his brain, the violet light radiating above from the inside of his cranium, and there stood the gnarled oak, with the snakes of insanity writhing in it.

He felt the panic rise in him, and he wanted to run. "Stop," he told himself. And he did. He stood silently, and closed his eyes and willed himself to wake up from the dream. He said to himself, over and over again, "This is a dream. And when I open my eyes I will be awake! Awake!"

He opened his eyes, and gasped.

Standing near the tree, a tall robed figure beckoned with a taloned claw. Its glowing yellow eyes radiated a terrifying message. *I am pure evil!* it seemed to say, and Kyle began to tremble. He felt the thing's total corruption, of body, mind, and soul. The robed thing beckoned once more and a scream rose up in Kyle's throat, and as he opened his mouth to let it out, he knew that if it came to a choice of going to that yellow-eyed horror, or going insane, he would gladly untangle the snakes of insanity from the branches of that tree himself, and let them burrow into his brain, until he could never regain his sanity again.

# 28

Michele was almost totally pleased with the way Curtis's birthday party was going. The one rub was Curtis's insistence on inviting Little Neil Gathers, primarily because of what the little brat had said about Kyle and herself. She was still stinging over that, but it had been one of those times when good values taught to the young come back to haunt you. Not only had Little Neil come over and apologized to Curtis, but in the mysterious way of kids, they had formed a club called the Jedi Knights, and now claimed each other as best friends. When she had objected to Little Neil, Curtis had pointed out that it was un-Christian not to forgive, especially when a person was truly sorry for what they had done, and Little Neil (according to Curtis) was truly sorry for what he had said and done. There was just no hope in arguing with her son's logic, so she'd given in.

Michele heard an agonized yell outside, and moved away from the boiling pot of hot dogs and looked out the kitchen window.

It was okay. Aunt Clarice had it in hand. One of the boys had fallen down, and Aunt Clarice helped the boy, under the watchful eye of Uncle Edgar, who had parked himself in a lounge chair and was thoughtfully puffing on his pipe.

She loaded the hot dogs into buns and onto a plate. The doorbell rang and she went to answer the door.

"Kyle, you shouldn't have," Michele said. He entered and stood smiling politely. In his hands were three gifts wrapped in bright green paper with racing cars all over it and Happy

Birthday waving on pennants here and there. "Seriously, that is really too much." She felt touched. His generosity with Curtis was almost embarrassing.

"It's not really much," he said. "Where's the party?"

"In the back."

He led the way, and she followed, admiring the tight fit of his jeans and the way the brown cotton shirt molded so closely to the curve of his chest. *Cut that out,* she thought as her nipples began to harden. Did he ever think of *her* in that way? she wondered. Michele grabbed the plate of hot dogs in one hand and a giant salad bowl full of potato chips in the other as they walked through the kitchen.

The kids broke off from the egg-tossing game they were engaged in (under the supervision of Aunt Clarice) and swarmed over to the table when Michele called out, "Soup's on." Michele was pleased to see Kyle give Curtis a big hug and lift him into the air saying, "Happy Birthday, old-timer. How old are you now, fifty?" And all the kids laughed, Curtis beamed with pride, and Little Neil looked wowed.

Michele wondered if Kyle noticed the decorations. She hated to admit it, but she had put a little extra effort, with impressing Kyle in mind. The picnic table was covered in a large white disposable paper tablecloth with scenes and characters from *Star Wars* on it. Balloons—red, blue, yellow, pink, green, and orange—were tied in clusters to every unmovable fixture, including the clothesline. Streamers of red, white, and blue fluttered in the gentle wind. In the brilliant light of a beautiful sunny Saturday, Michele thought the decorations looked pretty damned good.

"The decorations sure look nice," said Kyle, and Michele almost died. He picked up a party favor and tooted it in Curtis' face, then put on a blue-and-white party hat and said very loud and rough, just for the kids, "Oh, boy, let's eat!"

He sat down and ate with the kids after acknowledging Uncle Edgar and introducing himself to Aunt Clarice. After the meal came the cake, a big white two-layer sheetcake with red icing and spaceships and space stations trim and *Happy Birthday Curtis* written across its top in blue thick jelly icing. Curtis blew out the candles and served a large piece for Kyle. Michele heaped ice cream on the plate and handed it to him with a fork and napkin. When he took it from her, saying thank you, she saw it in his eyes—something was really eating at him.

He took his cake and walked over to Uncle Edgar and pulled up a lounge chair and sat down. And they began to talk.

Edgar sat in the lawn chair watching the cake being cut, and trying to map out a diplomatic way to broach the subject of a more cordial relationship with the chief. But he saw that the problem may have found its own solution: the tall lawman was walking toward him. The chief pulled up a chair and smiled. "Nice party," he said.

"Yes, it is." Edgar relit his pipe. He turned to the chief, watching him as he devoured the cake and ice cream, then set it on his knee and wiped his face with the party napkin.

"So, how's your off-the-record ear today, Mr. Griffith?" the chief asked.

Edgar puffed a few thoughtful mouthfuls, then pulled the pipe from his mouth, holding it out in front of him, studying the bowl. "I went to jail one time—spent ten days there—for not revealing a source. That was back in the heyday of the print media. In Chicago," he added.

"Then, I have you 'off the record'?"

"That's right."

The chief sat forward tensely in his chair. *He's upset about something,* Edgar thought.

"Mr. Griffith—"

"Edgar will do . . ."

"Edgar, then. Dave Pickers has asked me to look into his daughter's death. That's fifteen or sixteen years old now. I must say from the onset that it is a waste of time, and I know that. But he asked, and it means a lot to him; I gave him my

239

word that I would look things over for him. What I would like from you"—the chief looked at his lap for a moment, then up again—"is a favor. I'd like to read the newspaper clippings, your file on the events, just to cover the bases. If you wouldn't mind, that is."

"I imagine that the files would be safe enough with Briggs City's chief of police, Kyle."

The chief smiled at him. "Thank you."

Edgar raised his pipe to his mouth but instead let it fall back to its out-of-body position. "And I'd like to officially compliment you on Project Upgrade. I think it will mean a great deal to the safety and well being of the city."

"Thanks."

"I mean it." Edgar stabbed over toward the gaggle of kids. "And unofficially, but personally, I'd like to thank you for taking care of Curtis the way you do. It's very kind of you and it's appreciated, believe me."

"He's a good boy." Kyle looked directly at Edgar. "I want to ask you some questions—off the record—would that be okay with you?"

"Sure. I'm not going to answer, though, if they're not to my liking. Fair enough?"

Kyle nodded his approval. "The fact that you and the mayor are not bosom buddies is hardly a secret, and, well, what's the story there?"

He left it flat just like that and Edgar thought what a great reporter he would make. But how much to tell him? Enough, he decided. "Let me give you a little history lesson, Kyle, civics too, I might add. The mayor was elected to city council ten years ago. At that time each councilman took turn being mayor a year each by vote of the other members of the council. By the fourth year, when the mayor was elected mayor by the council, it came to my attention that whatever the hell Gathers wanted, Judge Baxter and Tom Sweeney—he's dead, now—just went right along with it. When it came time the next year for a new mayor, Benny Baxter's turn, he and Sweeney pushed for the mayor to continue being mayor. Now, there is nothing illegal about that, but I have never known Ben Baxter to let go of anything that even partially resembled power or prestige, and yet he wasn't kicking—the mayor either paid him or had something on him.

"The mayor has been mayor ever since."

"When Sweeney died, the mayor politicked for Jack Lewis to get elected, and he did. He is the mayor's main legal advisor for business and other things. Leia Conway was good once but suddenly she started voting the mayor's way and drinking a lot, too, I might add. He has control over the judicial system through Judge Baxter and that young Mettler, the D.A. He almost has the whole damn city council in his pocket—I'm the rogue, and doesn't he wish that weren't so—and he has the . . . had the police in his hip pocket until that low-brow Buddy Nelson was murdered—"

"And is the jury in on me yet?" interrupted Kyle.

Griffith hesitated a moment. "Yes," he said, "I wouldn't be talking to you now, if I didn't think you were straight."

"Good," said the chief. "But, Edgar, being the Devil's advocate for a moment, I've heard that a lot of good things have come from the mayor too. Government contracts, subsidies, low unemployment—these had been a problem before."

"True enough." He does his homework, thought Edgar. "But what you may not know is that he owns almost anything worth owning in this town, and a lot of the county, too. And there are some people who question his methods of getting what he's got. Sure, there's good associated with the man and his leadership, but the bad is there too, and it's not an acceptable kind of bad. It's the mayor's town, Kyle. And that's not right."

"No, it isn't," the chief replied solemnly. "Boy, when you answer a question, you answer a question, don't you?"

"Don't mean to pontificate."

Michele flagged them with a wave. "Are you two going to

join the party, or what? We're just about ready open the presents."

Kyle said, "Be there in a minute," and turned to Edgar and asked, "Do you know of any cult activity around here, I mean back when Cathy Pickers was killed? Dave swears that he saw devils. I'm going on the theory that he saw something like he reported. Maybe people dressed up like devils. Maybe it's a devil cult."

Edgar thought for a moment, then looked to make sure Clarice was out of earshot. He spoke in a hush: "I haven't seen her for years, of course, but there is a professor at U.C. Santa Barbara who did a study of the Indians, their religion, primarily back in the forties. I was a young cub reporter when I met her. I believe that she did her thesis on the Laikute religion. Her thesis would tell you all you needed about the Devil's Ground and Ravana."

Edgar saw Kyle tense. "Ravana?" he asked. "Could you spell that please?"

"R-A-V-A-N-A, Ravana."

The chief sat thinking for a moment, then stared at Edgar. "Would the thesis be in the library?

"Maybe at U.C.S.B., but not here." Edgar checked for Clarice and said softly, "I can get you her number and address if you want to talk to her. She owes me a favor."

"I'd appreciate it," said Kyle.

Curtis came running over. "It's time for the presents, the presents. Come on!"

Edgar and Kyle heaved themselves up and walked over to the gift-laden card table. The kids all clamored around. "Where's your mother?" asked Clarice.

As if she had heard her, Michele opened the screen door and yelled, "Kyle, phone for you." Edgar followed Kyle for want of anything better to do.

"Probably work," said Kyle. "Same old story as Los Angeles, just a smaller town."

Michele was busying herself with trivial things, waiting to

walk out with Kyle, Edgar guessed. Kyle was speaking very softly, saying "Okay" a lot, and hung up with a grim "I'll meet you out there" to the other party. He replaced the receiver back in the cradle of the kitchen wall phone.

He turned to the two of them. His face had gone stony. His eyes were tight and moist.

"Michele, I would like you to write down the names of all of Cathy Pickers's friends that you remember, and how good of a friend they were. Would you do that for me, please, and keep it under your hat?"

Michele looked at him strangely. "Yes, of course, Kyle." Her voice was questioning.

"I have to go," he said to them both, "please give my apology to Curtis. Edgar, you'll have to take your car. I may be out there for a while."

"What are you talking about, Kyle?" asked Edgar.

"Yes, Kyle, what is it?" Michele's voice was soft with concern.

"Someone's been shot on Dave Pickers's land."

"Was it Mr. Pickers?" asked Michele.

"They're not sure. The face is half blown away. You'll want to cover that story yourself, won't you, Edgar?"

Edgar said that he would.

# 29

It was 5:05 PM the night before Curtis's party and the office of Eureka Finance was Friday-empty. Leonard Phael rose from his desk and strolled over to the front door whistling. He studied the street for any last minute stop-bys. No one.

He returned to his office, closed the door and went to his bookcase. Yessir, every Louis L'Amour western paperback ever printed. He knelt and slid the case aside, exposing a plumbing access panel. He pried off the square piece of wood. With great care, he twisted his body and reached in past the pipes and groped until he felt the plastic he had wrapped it in. He slid the shotgun out of its hiding place and set it on the floor, replaced the panel, and slid the bookcase back in place.

He stood up and placed the bundle butt-first into the metal round wastebasket and dusted the plaster and dirt off the plastic. He undid the twists of wire that held the green plastic on, pulling out his pride and joy—a modified Reminton 870 Wingmaster. He called it Babycakes.

Babycakes and he were going hunting tonight, he thought. He smiled. It was empty land out there at Pickers's place, the boonies, and people were used to the old man capping off rounds at kids. Maybe he'd just empty his whole wad on the old man, make him dance around like a marionette before he hits the ground.

A thought came to Phael: I'll just try to see if I can get all the rounds into him before he hits the ground. I bet I can do it. By God, I bet that I can.

\*　　\*　　\*

At eleven o'clock Phael finished dressing for the night's business. He wondered for a moment why the mayor wanted it done, then shrugged: the ten thousand dollars was enough reason for him.

He wore blue jeans, a heavy green wool pendleton shirt, a wide brown leather belt with a big bronze buckle that read, in large raised letters, DEAD MEAT. He chose an old pair of Adidas sneakers because it would be easier to move without making as much noise as boots and he could toss them after the job (none of that Hollywood "There's mud on his boots" incrimination for him—only a dummy got nailed on the little things. From his closet he pulled a black nylon jacket and placed it on his bed while he put on his shoulder holster. He then slipped his jacket on and left his apartment, the excitement that he always felt on jobs like this just beginning to twang down his spine.

He headed west on Planter Street, then turned north on Calkins, and finally east on Bleier Road that ran on the north fringes of the town. Briggs City fell away completely after a few minutes, then Phael saw the blinking aircraft warning light on the mayor's granary tower. He whizzed by that and ten minutes later parked his car off the road in a grove of oaks, hidden from view from the little-used road. He pulled Babycakes from the trunk, fingering the safety on the shotgun unconsciously with his left thumb to make sure that it was engaged. He didn't want to trip and blow a hole in his foot and give his position away at the same time.

He emerged from the darkness of the oak grove into a clear star-filled night. The moon, its yellow eye halfway open, washed the landscape a grainy pale yellow, with contours of black and darkened shadow.

He started up the gradual slope of a hill with confidence. This back way across the mayor's land was how he'd done most of his surveillance on the crazy old coot. It really hadn't taken much work; in fact, it was a perfect setup: Crazy Dave walked alone in the dead of night in an uninhabited area where no pain-in-the-ass neighbors or witnesses would be around. The road nearest his home was seldom traveled at this time of night, and even if it were, people that lived around here were used to the shotgun fire, just Crazy Dave scaring off some kids.

The only problem was where to ambush him. The old coot made a regular ring around the trees all night long, and the best place to get him would be on this back side of the trees, because then there was no chance at all of anybody coming along Highway 28. Phael had to weigh that risk against the fact that there was no cover along the backside here and old Dave might just catch him at it before he could get a good clean shot off. That old rancher was probably a pretty good shot with that shotgun, you could bet on that. Phael had thought of hiding in the trees, but the problem there was that Crazy Dave's path was tactically out of reach, and sure, Phael could just unload on the man at a distance, but in the dark, if luck was with the old coot, he might get out a round or two off, put up a stand, and then Pickers would be between him and his car and that would be bad news.

He crested the gentle hill and surveyed the slope leading down to Pickers's land. He could barely make out the barbed wire fence separating the mayor's land holding and Pickers's place. But that black smudge out there that was the trees was easily recognizable.

Phael started down.

He had solved the problem of where to stage the ambush by studying a recent aerial photograph of the area that the mayor had—a before shot of the land that would hold his dream, he told Phael. The area around the trees was pretty much bare of cover, as Phael had found out, but in the stretch toward the side facing the road several of the trees had fallen down (Phael had cruised by that afternoon to make sure they were still there and not firewood now), and it would be there that he would hide, toward the top of the fallen trees. Pickers normally walked not ten feet away from them, and it would be like ambushing a deaf, dumb, and blind man, it would be that easy.

Within ten minutes Phael had managed the barbed wire fence and was in position, crouched down beside one of the few large bushes on the back side of the trees, waiting. Now that he wasn't moving he could feel the cold and the last residue of the rain's wetness riding on cool ground eddies. He crouched in closer to the bush as he thought he saw a shadowy movement off to his right. The sight was so quick it could have been his imagination, but then a flashlight flicked on, and Phael watched Pickers check his watch. Yeah, this was right on cue. Once or twice per circle the old man flicked the light on, either to check his watch or to see his way around some obstacle or check a noise out or something. Phael marked his position and then kept a careful eye, straining in the half-moonlight, on the old man as he walked a couple of hundred feet away from him and then past him.

After he had disappeared around the trees Phael followed him, picking up his normal trail worn smooth by years of patroling. He tried to match pace with Pickers, stopping briefly at the bridge of two-by-fours that led over the creek that ran into the trees. Cold wet air enveloped him as he crossed. He shivered. He stopped for a few minutes on the other side, staring into the blackness of the trees, allowing time for the old coot to stop and scratch his ass or whatever, then continued around.

He could see the house, lying dark in the semilight, off to his left. He kept to the path and found shelter in the midst of the fallen trees, nestling in with a rustle of leaves like a viper in his nest. He had a clear field of fire and the asshole would never know what hit him. He figure that he had at least one half an hour to wait, but he clicked the safety off and sat in waiting. He was uncomfortable for a moment without knowing why, then chanced a glance at the moon. The damnedest thing—it was orange, of all things. Must be clouds or something, he thought, and sat and waited.

More than a half hour passed and Phael was getting nervous, when the sound of someone clearing their throat drew him on target. Dave Pickers was less that thirty feet off to the left! God, he moves quietly, thought Phael, and shifted carelessly, causing the bushes to rustle.

"Get off my land!" intoned the old man.

*Damn!* He'd given his position away. The sudden appearance of the old man had startled him, and the bastard wasn't in the right position and he was armed and alarmed, *dammit!*

"I told you kids a thousand times to stay off my land! You think it's funny! Well, the Devil got my daughter in those trees! Now, get out!"

The old man moved closer by ten feet, approaching cautiously. "Get off my land, I said!" The old man flicked on his light and it burned Phael's eyes as he automatically squeezed the trigger and pumped the slide four times. Four explosions split the night with fiery tubes of light from Babycakes's barrel. The light went spinning and Phael emerged in a crouched position from the branches of the fallen trees and hustled quickly up to his kill. The flashlight had been hit by a pellet and was out, and so the body lay too much in the dark from the weird moonlight for Phael to tell where he was hit. He aimed Babycakes at the old man, the muzzle of the barrel not more than ten inches away from the head, and pulled the trigger. It was too dark to see what really happened, but one thing Phael could be sure of was that the old coot was dead.

That, and that there were headlights on the road, heading into town, and the goddamn nosy sons of bitches were slowing down.

Just his fucking luck! Maybe even a goddamn patrol car, for Chrissakes! The mayor didn't have a flunky police chief like he'd had with Buddy Nelson. Maybe that goddamned Richards had . . . Oh, fuck. The car stopped.

Phael thought on the run, choosing the route that would be quickest back to his car. He'd seen the aerial photos. A ring of trees, not a forest. Get in, bust through to the clearing, get across to the other side, out that perimeter of trees and to his car—he'd be safe!

He reached the trees, and the trees took him in.

He ran, cursing out loud at the morass of limbs and slick wet ground of slimy leaves. He ignored the smells and the sounds that he thought he heard. No time to dally. He broke through, tumbling down an embankment, suddenly out in the open before he knew it.

He rolled to his feet and stood still for a precious second, looking for a way over the water. What luck, stepping stones right across the center of this inky black pool.

The orange halfmoon bathed everything in its rusty light, and Phael kept moving. He ran to the pool and padded out on the stepping stones. He was four or five out when the sensation that they were rubbery made its way to his brain. He was two more steps when he heard the watery plopping sounds, like that made when something is pulled under. He took one more step and stopped—

He was on the centermost stone.

His step no longer felt rubbery, more spongy than anything. He glanced over his shoulder. The stones behind him had vanished.

*Plop!*

Phael's head swiveled around forward.

*Plop! Plop!*

Two of the stones disappeared in order, coming toward him. There were only five left to the one he was standing on.

*Plop! Plop!*

Oh, fuck! Three! What were they . . . ?

*Plop! Plop! Plop!*

Jesus! What was going on! What the fuck was he standing on!

He stood stranded in the middle of the inky black pool on a what? He didn't want to look down. He couldn't look down.

The black water began to bubble. He heard things breaking water and looked out—burned, charred corpses surfaced and floated, like dark driftwood. Skulls grinned at him as they drifted by.

He felt something willing him to look down. He couldn't! He was afraid, goddamnit!

The trees began to sway. And dead men, smelling ripe like rotting meat, stepped from behind the boles. More corpses surfaced. The smell of rotting flesh and hot sulfur mixed in his nose and lungs. He gagged. Heat radiated from the pool and suddenly small fires began dancing, cooking the rancid meat. He could taste it. The dead men began to chant.

And still Phael could not look down.

He would use Babycakes if he could, but she slid easily from his hands into the roiling black water. God, he was so scared. *Save me, Jesus!*

The steppingstone moved and he jumped up with a scream and came back down on it. Helpless, he looked down.

It supported him, unblinking, a glowing yellow eye. He was standing on a huge eye!

Before he could scream again, arms, black with rot, emerged from the steaming water, grabbed his legs, and pulled him in.

# 30

When Kyle arrived, Sergeant Mead and John Black were poking around out near the eucalyptus trees. Kyle figured that Dave must have been murdered while making his nightly rounds. That it had happened out on the open range like this meant they would have to search the entire ranch. He unclipped the mike from the dashboard and ordered the reserves called up and assembled at Dave Pickers's place.

Kyle got out of his truck.

Mead ambled over to him through the shin-high grass, his thumbs hooked in his Sam Browne. "It ain't too pretty, Chief," he said.

It never is, thought Kyle, especially when it's someone you know. He looked past Mead at the black lumpy rainslicker lying in the rank grass. From this distance he couldn't see details, but knowing that it was Dave out there dead anguished him. He took a deep breath, waiting while all the old training seeped back to deaden the pain. He would grieve later, after he caught the fucking bastard who did this.

"The van and trailer and backup are coming," said Kyle. "Get on the horn and make sure that they park on the access road there. I don't want a bunch of people trampling this place down to the ground. Keep 'em out of the area, until I say." Mead trudged toward his car and the radio. "And, Mead," Kyle added, "I've got county homicide coming out. And have someone call the mayor. He might want to know about this."

Kyle continued toward Dave's body. He could see the white of his friend's overalls now, hidden before by a small rill in the

251

ground. They stuck out from the rainslicker and bent at the knees like the legs of some giant doll. The soles of his brown work boots pointed toward his ranch house.

Black emerged waving from between two of the fallen trees and trotted toward Kyle. Kyle waved back and, still walking, glanced to his friend's body. He jolted to a stop. "Oh, Jesus," he said. He forced himself to look. Dave had been shot numerous times. Shotgun, no doubt of that. The rainslicker had three large holes in it, each peppered with dime-sized holes around it, the kind of entry a shotgun blast makes at short range. Blood had oozed out of the wounds and dried in large rusty-red pools in the places where it had not been soaked into the ground. Kyle looked at what was left of Dave's face, anger erupting through the anesthetic numbness of his mind. The son of a bitch had just blown it away—Dave's face gone. Couldn't have been more than a foot away when he pulled the trigger. Kyle could see the brains.

He fought back nausea. *How can you tell it's Dave Pickers?* some nasty part of his mind taunted. *He has no face, he has no face, he has no face.*

He looked at the man's hands, oddly gentle now, lying in the rank grass. Kind, strong hands, like Kyle's father's. The old man's shotgun lay a foot from the hands.

Black spoke to him and Kyle was glad to look away. "What?" he asked.

Black offered up a plastic sandwich bag. In it was a lemon-yellow napkin. "This was found in the Bloodhawks' mailbox this morning. Mama Hawk thought it maybe a joke so didn't call right away, but gave a call later. Hunch, I guess. There's writing on it." He handed the baggie over to Kyle.

"The baggie's yours?" asked Kyle.

"Mama Hawk give it to me when I picked it up. I asked for it. Thought it best."

"It's best." Kyle turned the bag over in his hands. The napkin was unused and neatly folded, with a message scrawled in red on it:

Old man by trees dead. Call police. In the name of our Lord Jesus Christ. Amen.

*And where do I remember this from?* he thought. Where? It took a moment, but it came to him. That old bum in the diner, of course, the day of the interview, gnarled and bent over the counter stealing napkins and writing his memoirs in red ink. Kyle stowed the memory away for later use.

"How did you know it was Pickers?" he asked Black. There were a lot of ranches on the outskirts of town with trees and old men on them.

Black squirmed uncomfortably. "Bloodhawk's ranch is the next one over"—he waved in the direction on the out-of-town side of Dave's ranch—"and there were . . . buzzards circling, Chief. Fucking buzzards."

Kyle was revolted. "Were there any on the ground when you got here?" His mind's eye flashed a picture of several huge black-winged birds, tussling long stringy pieces of muscle from Dave's body. One carrion-eater pecking out a chunk of brain and swallowing it . . .

*Stop it!*

Black nodded grimly. "Flushed 'em, then tried to plug 'em with my Ithica, but can't hit shit without birdshot. Just scared 'em off," he said. "Don't know how long they were on him, thought. Not too long, I think."

"Coroner will be able to tell." Kyle turned to walk to his truck and Black fell in beside him.

"There's shells over there, twelve-gauge. I didn't touch 'em.

"Excellent," said Kyle. Fucking buzzards!

"And tracks leading back into the trees."

Kyle stopped.

"Man's tracks. Back into the trees," repeated Black.

Kyle pondered this a moment. "Okay, it's you and me on that one. Let's get the prelims under way first, though."

Kyle strode to his truck and called in to the station. As he waited for the R.T.O. to get the watch commander, Sergeant

Wilson, he watched the blue situation van pull into the drive and Sergeant Mead directing it down to a point parallel to the immediate crime scene. A police truck followed, pulling a medium-sized comfort trailer with food and restrooms; and then more cars came, some police units, some personal cars with reserves in them. And Edgar Griffith in a '65 green Mustang.

Wilson's voice broke through in a sputter of static: "Chief?"

"Put out an A.P.B. on a white male indigent, about five nine, black hair, wearing a baggy brown or olive-green suit coat. I've seen him around town for a couple of months now." He pinched the bridge of his nose up by his brow between thumb and index finger and closed his eyes for a second of relief from the grinder chewing up his brain.

"Can fix you up in a jiffy, Chief."

"Cut the crap, Sergeant."

"I meant there's an 'indigent' sitting out in the waiting room that fits that description, sir. He says he's waiting here to talk to you."

"Ask him if he left a note on a napkin this morning."

Kyle waited impatiently, then Wilson said, "Yessir, he says he sure did."

"Okay. Don't arrest him, but detain him for questioning. You got that?"

"Yessir."

"Did the mayor check in yet?" Kyle asked.

"He's on vacation, sir. Just a couple of days. I have a phone number if you need to reach him."

"No, just leave it. Anything special on last night's duty sheets?"

The sergeant didn't answer him immediately. Why was he stalling? "I haven't got all day, Wilson," Kyle said.

"There was a 'shots fired' reported by a passerby last night out in that area, sir."

"What time?"

"It's logged at 12:37 AM."

254

"And what time did the unit check it out?"

"Not 'til four, sir. It was just Pickers scaring off the kids again, I'm sure that's what they were thinking."

"And it was a real butt-buster of a night last night, Sergeant?" said Kyle sarcastically.

"Uh, nossir."

Kyle was disgusted. If a car had been sent out, they might have caught somebody.

"You working a double shift, Wilson?" Kyle asked sharply.

"Nossir! Gurnell was watch commander last night, sir."

That's right, protect your ass, Kyle thought. He bridled an urge to vent his anger on Wilson, and instead looked at the stand of dark eucalyptus. He was going to have to go in there. "Ten-four," he said, and clipped the mike to the dash, then snatched it back up quickly. "Tom?"

"Yes, Chief."

"Check this guy out—name, where he's from, everything you can get on him, got it?"

"Can do."

"Ten-four." Kyle re-clipped the mike and walked over to the growing line of vehicles and clusters of men on the rutted dirt road.

"Mead," he called out.

"Yessir." The sergeant came jogging over, ready for orders.

"I want you to put up a line around the trees. Use the reserves. Run it from here to the far fence, follow the property line around back of the trees maybe two hundred yards, then up to the house. Nobody in, nobody out. Keep all unnecessary traffic out of the immediate area of the body, understood?"

"Yessir."

Kyle spotted two reservists, the Alyea brothers, Tim and Joe. They were Basque emigrants, short and tough, with a no-nonsense attitude toward law enforcement that Kyle liked. He called them over. "You two take some walkie-talkies from the van, split around the trees, one on either side, and take up

255

positions maybe two hundred feet from the trees. Black and I are going in on some tracks and if we flush something I want you two on it, got it?"

The brothers said "Yes" in unison and jogged toward the van.

Black arrived at Kyle's side with walkie-talkies fixed with straps. Kyle slung his over his shoulder after checking in with the van. "You read me, Slanz?" asked Kyle, releasing the send button. "Loud and clear, Chief," replied Slanz, his voice tinny over the small hand unit. "Chief, out," said Kyle. John Black checked in similarly, and they were ready.

Kyle signaled to Mead to step over again. "When county comes," he said to the sergeant, "point them in the direction of the body, and keep everybody out. It's their handle in that area, got it?"

"Yessir."

"Excellent. Black, let's move."

Kyle and Black turned to go, but Patrolman Boylan stopped them. "Sir, what about Mr. Griffith?" The officer jabbed a thumb in the old newsman's direction. Griffith raised a hand in salutation.

"He's okay," answered Kyle. "An observer. Out of the way, though." He addressed Griffith, speaking loudly to cover distance: "Taking a walk, Edgar"—Kyle jabbed toward the trees—"talk with you when I get back." The old man nodded his head and turned toward the comfort trailer, which was now set up and serving coffee through a service window.

He turned to Black. "Let's go," he said. They got their shotguns from their vehicles and walked back to the trees. Black took the lead. Kyle dropped down after Black into a ditch that seemed to run around the perimeter of the woods. Black led him to a spot where the felled trees crossed the ditch, and pointed to a disturbance in the dirt. "Big man," was all he said, and climbed up the embankment. Kyle followed. They stood where the tree line began, beside the jagged stumps of the eight trees that were down. The height of the stumps was at Kyle's

256

eye level. The trees seemed to have been snapped in two, like a man might pencils. Their jagged tops were sharp. Kyle jabbed at the absolute wall of eucalyptus trees in front of them, and said to Black, "You can track him in that, I take it?"

"Yes." Black stared straight ahead into the dim twilight of the heavy wood. He made no move to press forward.

"What's wrong?" Kyle asked. "Ravana?" The last word had just slipped out?

"How you know?" Black stared at him and Kyle knew from the lapse into broken English that he was shocked.

Kyle shrugged noncommittally. "You said you were a superstitious Indian. And I've heard the legend. Anyway, we've got to go in." In the far distance of Kyle's mind the snakes hissed. With an effort of will, he closed his thoughts to it. I'm not crazy anymore, he said to himself simply. The sounds stopped.

"Ravana's not supposed to come out in daylight," advised Black, "but I hope *It* knows that."

"You really believe in Him?" demanded Kyle.

"*It*," Black corrected. "I've seen the old priests do some crazy shit when I was a kid. Let's just say, I don't *dis*believe in *It*, Chief." He entered the woods.

I offended him, thought Kyle. Damn. I broke my own rule: never discuss politics or religion with the men. And when a man mentions priests, even tribal priests, that's religion.

He followed Black, feeling uneasy the instant he stepped over the first engorged tree root and fell under the shadowy pall of the branches. *I hate this place,* he thought. *I loathe it.* He sniffed and grimace. The place stank with the pungent smell of eucalyptus leaves, slimy and rotting with decay. The odor cloyed in his nostrils as he trailed Black deeper into the wood. After a couple of minutes, Kyle glanced back and saw a solid wall of trees behind him. He felt cut off from the rest of the world. Strips of old bark hung from the tree boles like tatters of dead skin. It was cold in here, much colder than a mere cutoff of sunlight could account for, he thought. Again he heard the distant hissing in his mind and again he forced it out; but another thought came, one that had been gnawing at the brim of his consciousness ever since he arrived: *The tree is here.*

"Where the fuck did *that* come from?" Kyle mumbled to himself.

"What, Chief?" Black whispered. "Nothing." His voice sounded like cannonfire, and he realized why this place was so eerie: There was no noise. No sound of wind through the trees. No birds singing. Nothing.

Kyle pulled his walkie talkie off his shoulder. "You know, Black, we haven't heard any traffic on this." he said, as he brought it to his lips. "Fox One to Mother Bear, over. Fox One to Mother Bear, over."

No response.

Black slipped his from his shoulder. "Mine didn't pick you up and we're five feet from each other." He tested his unit. It was dead, too.

"Nothing we can do about it, now," Kyle said, and started forward. Black grumbled and went back to picking his way through the trees.

Black reached the clearing first. Kyle stepped over a gnarled root and stood beside him, stopping short.

A knot rose in his throat.

The gnarled oak tree was ninety feet away from him, on the other side of the black pond. It could be the tree in his dream, if he discounted the large hole in the trunk, and one other thing.

"Do you see it?" asked Black.

"Yes," replied Kyle.

"Jesus Christ. I hate this place."

"Let's get a closer look."

They dropped down the sandy embankment.

"Let's take it from the left side," Kyle suggested.

They followed the bank of the pool to the outflow stream. Other than the water gurgling lightly, and the brittle shale crunching beneath their feet, there was no noise. And though the sun mounted close to noon high, the light that cut into this clearing seemed diffuse and unnatural. Odd, thought Kyle. How can that be?

The stream strictured at the spot where it flowed out of the clearing and snaked its way through the eucalyptus boles. They stepped over the dark liquid ribbon, using a large rock in the middle of the flow, and approached the oak tree. Yes, thought Kyle, it *is* my tree, *with* a hole in its trunk. Now that he was under it and looking up, he knew it for a fact. Except this tree was not in a dream, it was real. If he wanted he could reach out and touch its crusty, rotting bark. But if he did that, he would have to be careful not to disturb the evidence, because stuffed in the hole in the dead trunk of this twisted oak was the severed head of Leonard Phael.

"I thought you needed a blood supply in it to make it hard?" said Black.

"You do," said Kyle. "The coroner couldn't 'explain it in Cathy Pickers, either. Called it unnatural—found dried blood inside her tongue making it stick out straight—didn't know how it could happen."

"Yeah. But it was only her tongue, Chief."

Kyle agreed, this was worse. Phael's dead eyes glared open at them from his fish-white face. His lips were pulled back over his teeth. His mouth was jacked open in rictus as if to scream, and jammed inside it were his cut-off testicles and penis, the shaft hard and stiff and dried-blood black, slanting up at the faces of Kyle and John Black, like an unholy erection.


When they emerged from the trees, Kyle saw the county sheriff's homicide team hovering around Dave Pickers' body. Kyle introduced himself to the investigators and filled them in on the find inside the trees. The search for the rest of Phael's remains would be organized after the coroner removed Dave Pickers's body, and the team had finished here. Then they would move in to take care of the head, and men would enter and search the wood and stream for Phael's body. Kyle placed a call to Chief Daniels, the fire chief, and asked for assistance in the search; he had a thriving volunteer fireman force that could be brought into play, and their participation would ensure that the search would be complete by nightfall.

After the phone call Kyle ordered Mead to handle the gross search of the ranchland and then, dodging Edgar's summons, got into his truck and drove up to the ranch house.

What was he doing here?

He'd felt this urge (a hunch?—no, it was too strong for that) since he'd left that stand of trees, to come here and . . . and what? Kyle wasn't sure, but he wasn't going to find out sitting in his car.

He killed the engine and entered the house. Kyle felt bombarded with the empty feeling that the finality of death always brought to him. He shielded himself from the feeling by concentrating on what he was doing. He walked down the long hall runner and stood outside the locked room. The Yale padlock hung securely through the hasp, its steel gleaming dully. This was it. What secret was Dave hiding in here? In one swift motion Kyle kicked the door by the metal flanges of the lock. The lock held, but the wood cracked. Another kick and the door banged inward against the inner wall. Kyle walked in.

The room reeked of fresh oil paint. Kyle thought: Dave lied to me. He hadn't given up painting. He'd told Kyle that he had given it up. Why should he lie about painting? wondered Kyle. There were a hundred canvases or more on the floor turned to the wall. Over by the workbench was another painting— Dave's most recent, he would guess—on an easel. Lined up on a bench, against the wall, were a number of books.

Kyle was puzzled. Why would Dave keep this room locked?

He walked over to the bench. The books were mostly about painting, one on Colt revolvers, a large family Bible, and a green cloth-bound book with *Journal* imprinted on it in fading gold-letter relief. He pulled it out. It whispered softly as it slid. He opened it randomly and laid it flat on the desk between bowls of tubes of paints. He turned the pages and spot-read the entries. In a firm, neat hand, Dave had kept record of his days since returning to the ranch after the death of his daughter. Some entries were short, comprised of nothing more than "all went well tonight," others were long and detailed. Kyle shifted from random reading to an organized search. His radio chattered. They needed him now.

"I'll be right there," he said into the radio. He closed the book and picked it up. He would examine it later.

He started to leave, then on impulse he reached out and pulled the white sheet cover off the painting.

He stared in shock, swallowing, swallowing, struggling to keep hold of reality. The book turned to lead in his hands. Hissing filled his ears, loud and virulent. Dear God, he thought. It's the tree—from my dreams!

He could not tear his gaze from the painting.

At the center was the familiar gnarled oak. In the foreground was a man's face—Oh, God, Kyle thought, it's me! Around the tree's perimeter hulked nightmarish creatures. Near the tree, stood a darkly robed thing—that creature, that Thing, whatever it was, was the same robed figure that motioned toward him in his last night-terror. Dave had painted it with burning yellow eyes, too. And like Kyle's dream, the robed figure here had an arm extended—from the folds of its black robed sleeve a greenish-black claw protruded beckoning toward Kyle. The Kyle-face reflected in the flames of the painting, was twisted up in stark, boldfaced terror.

A burst of static from the radio startled him from his shock. He threw the sheet over the painting and carried it and the journal out to his truck. They shook from the trembling of his hands as he set them on the seat. With an effort he got hold of himself. He'd take care of this later. Right now, he had an investigation to conduct and an old bum at the station to interview.

# 31

He was sleeping when they came for him, the second time. The first had been midafternoon and they had been county men asking about the killing. He had told them everything he knew.

Now, the doe-eyed sergeant was gone. The one yelling to get up, and unlocking his cell, was tall and fat, with beady eyes tucked in a flabby face. "Out," said the sergeant, "the chief wants to talk to you."

He picked up his crucifix and his Bible. They had let him keep them, but had searched him and taken everything else. They had read him his rights, but had not arrested him. He was being held for questioning, they said.

"What time is it?" he asked.

"Time to go see the chief," answered the sergeant.

It had to be late at night. There were no windows to tell, but they had fed him dinner and he had prayed for a while, and then curled up to sleep on one of the gray vinyl sleeping pads in the cell. He fought the grog of half-sleep as he was taken down the hall and put in an interrogation room.

He didn't like the room. It was cramped, and lit by cold fluorescent lights. A rectangular wooden table and two chairs took up most of the space. He looked at himself in a large mirror that seemed glued to the wall, with a speaker box under it. He hardly recognized the brown weathered face and scraggly black hair of the man that stared back. He turned away and saw that the opposite wall held another door, closed.

"Sit down," the sergeant ordered.

He obeyed and heard the door behind him close and lock. He put his Bible in front of him, the crucifix beside it, then touched them both for comfort as he began to pray for the soul of the man killed last night, the man near the trees.

The door opposite him opened abruptly. He recognized the man who entered. The tall man had changed since the first time he had seen him. He looked tired, now. Probably worn down with responsibility and worry, he thought.

The policeman carried a manila folder in his hands. He closed the door and sat down opposite him.

"Mr. DeNapoli, I'm Chief Richards," he said. "I'm here to ask you questions concerning the murders out at the Pickers ranch. Have you been read your rights?" His tone said that he already knew the answer.

"Yes, I have," he responded.

"Did you understand what was read to you?"

"Yes, I did."

"And do you understand that they apply at this time also?"

"Yes, I do."

"Do you wish to have an attorney present during questioning?"

"No," he said, noticing a sadness in the green eyes of this man who was once so kind to him in the restaurant. "I've already told everything."

"You're going to tell it again, Mr. DeNapoli," said the chief. He laid the manila folder flat, opposite the Bible and crucifix, opened it halfway, and pulled out a plastic bag with the yellow napkin in it that he had written the message on. "Do you recognize this?"

"Yes." The horror of discovering the old man's body unfolded in his mind. So much blood. Such a brutal, bestial act. And it had been *he* who had been a coward *(Lord have mercy; forgive me, Father; Lord have mercy)*. After the gunfire, he had sat frozen at his lookout post, just off the road, unable to move. He was afraid. Afraid that what had happened had not been totally the act of men.

263

"Tell me how you came to write the note," said the chief. "Tell me everything."

He didn't want to think of it again, and it didn't get easier as he went along, but he told the chief how, toward dawn, when he finally gained his courage, he moved down off the hill and made the grim discovery, then walked the road to put the note in the nearest neighbor's roadside mailbox.

"And you did not see who did it?" The man's eyes were intense.

"No, no. It was very dark," he replied.

"And you know nothing of the other murder? Heard nothing? Saw nothing?"

"That's right," he told him, "it was dark, like I said, and I didn't come off the hill till morning."

"And then you just decided to walk into the station and tell all, is that it?"

"Yes."

"And why was that?"

"God told me to."

"God told you to come and ask for me by name? You asked for me by name, I was told."

"No . . . I mean, God didn't tell me to ask for you, but he told me to come in. You're Kyle Richards, the chief. All the . . . unfortunates know your name."

"And you're an unfortunate?"

He hesitated for a moment, searching for an answer. He had asked himself the same question many times over the past three years. Finally he said, "No. I am the Lamb of God."

"And did you kill the man you say you found out there?"

"No, I did not. I am the Lamb of God."

The big man rocked back in his chair and put both hands to his face and rubbed wearily, then dropped them to the file folder with a sigh. He leaned forward, opened the folder, and pressed flat its open wings. There were yellow papers inside.

"You know, Mister . . ." he peered at the papers in the folder, ". . . DeNapoli . . . That is your name, isn't it? Father

264

Charles Francis DeNapoli, from St. Dominic's in Chicago?"

The words were like a slap across his face with the statue of the Blessed Mother. He had given his name as Charley DeNapoli; and when they asked, told them he was from Chicago. That was all. How had they found out so much so fast? A burning from his heart spread through him. "I am the Lamb of God," he said fiercely between clenched teeth.

"They don't think you're such a lamb at St. Dominic's now, do they, Father. Sins of the flesh and all that—"

"I am the Lamb of God!"

"Sit down, DeNapoli," the chief said to him calmly, and he realized that he was standing, his arms out, his Bible and crucifix clutched in his hands. The image of the dead fetus of his child and her mother passed before him, and the nightmare. The shame. Sister Theresa. The baby. The abortion/murder. The suicide. The excommunication.

The penance: being here, and the trees.

"I am the Lamb of God," he said quietly, and lowered his arms. He had knocked his chair over and bent to pick it up. He heard the rattle of a key in the lock and the door flew open. The sergeant stood there with a black billy club in his hand. "What's the noise?" he asked.

"It's okay, Gurnell," said the chief. He waved him out. The door closed behind the sergeant and locked.

DeNapoli sat down and placed the Bible in front of him, setting the crucifix on top of it. He pulled his chair up, feeling embarrassed. He searched the surface of the crucifix for a moment to avoid the chief's eyes.

"Mr. DeNapoli"—the chief's voice was gentle now—"a man was killed out there last night. I—"

"He was your friend," he said.

The chief sat back and stared at him pensively for a moment, then answered, "Yes. How did you know that?"

"I saw you the day you made the signs. When it was safe, towards evening, I went down and looked at one. They were fine signs, very fine."

"Why are you out there so much?"

"The trees," he said simply.

"Say again."

"The trees. The dark ones out there on his land. The trees."

"What about the trees?"

"Why, they're evil, of course."

"How do you know that?"

"I am the Lamb of God. God has told me this, about the Evil, and about you. The trees . . . the Evil out there is my penance for my sins. But I am afraid, a coward. Still, that is my penance, God has told me."

"What has he told you about me?"

"That you are the Lamb of God, too."

The chief stared blankly at him, as if lost in thought. Then he spoke suddenly: "Ravana? Have you heard that word before? Does it mean anything to you?"

"No," he said simply. It was a strange word. "Why?"

"No reason," he replied and stood up, a sign of dismissal. "What I'm going to do, Mr. DeNapoli, is set you up with one of the local missions. I'm not going to arrest you at this time. You will, however, be required to call the station three times a day until further notice. If you try to leave, the mission will contact me. I will find you. And I will make you regret it. Do you understand me?"

He said that he did. The chief told him that he could stay the night in jail, and that the mission halfway house would take him in the morning. The chief turned to go.

"Kyle Richards," DeNapoli heard the words tumble from his own mouth; the voice was deep and alien. It scared him. The chief turned around. "Yes," he said.

DeNapoli stared at the chief, trying to speak on his own to tell him that these were not his words. A lightheadedness ballooned in his mind. "I am the Lamb of God," he heard his voice say, "and you are the Lamb of God." He felt his hands push the Bible, the crucifix riding on its leather cover, across the table toward the policeman. "Take these, please."

266

"No," said the chief.

"Please." He heard the entreaty in his own voice, and it frightened him. He was not in control.

"No," the chief insisted, and turned to go.

"Kyle Richards, if you do not take these because you do not believe that you are the Lamb of God, so be it. But please take them, a favor to me." The chief stopped, his back still to him. "A favor to me. Please take these, please."

Tears welled up in DeNapoli's eyes and he began to cry. He bowed his head to hide them, ashamed. He did not understand and he was afraid. "Please! Please! Kyle Richards, for my soul, take these! These! Please, O Lamb of God, for my soul!"

He began to tremble. Tears flowed in rivulets down his face, forming coin-sized puddles on the tabletop. He cried with his eyes open. He saw his face reflected obscurely off the shiny waxed surface. What a wicked wretch he was. "Please! *Please!*" he begged, not looking up, "take it!" He broke down completely and cried uncontrollably.

And as he sat there, his head bowed, his shoulders shaking, he felt the Bible slip from his fingers, and heard the far door close softly soon thereafter.

# 32

Kyle left the excommunicated priest and went to his office. He closed the door behind him and let his fatigue take over for a moment. His feet hurt, and his back was sore. It was two AM, and it had been a long day.

He felt secure in his decision to let Charles DeNapoli go. County homicide had concurred. DeNapoli was crazy in a nut way, but not in the murderous sense of the word.

Kyle sighed and put the old Bible and the crucifix on his desk, and wondered why he had taken them. His weakness again, he supposed. The ex-priest had looked so pitiful seated at the table, his head bowed, weeping and pleading—and the trees.

He had mentioned the trees and the Devil. The Evil there, he had said. Just like Dave Pickers, Kyle thought, and looked automatically at the painting leaning against his bookcase, still wrapped in a white sheet. Kyle turned to his desk and the journal lying there on top. Dave's writing referred to the trees a lot, too. And the fact was, the common thread that ran through all the events of these murders was that small forest of dark eucalyptus trees. Even the findings of the search of that area were odd: his men had covered in and around the trees, swarming like methodical insects over the ground, searching the stream, its lackluster pool, and the shale rubble in the clearing. He had even sent one man climbing into the burned-out oak to check the limbs. Nothing there. In the search they'd found no weapons, no evidence of Phael's body, not a trace of a clue. Nothing. The area of the trees itself was bizarre, too.

Compare it to any similar ground anywhere in the world and what you would find there: dead animal bones, insects, some tattered bit of rag, or littered paper—something! But not in that stand of trees. Nothing, as if cleaned by some unworldly hand. What's more, Kyle's and Black's radios had functioned perfectly when they had accompanied the larger search party. It was a strange piece of real estate, that was for sure. One thing had remained the same, though. Kyle still had felt the loathing, only a subcurrent the second time in, but there, nonetheless. And he had felt unclean. He still felt unclean.

He shook the feeling off as best he could, and picked up a cold, half-filled cup of coffee and drank deeply. It tasted like shit, which was ten times better than he was feeling right now. He was angry with Dave for dying on him. The feeling was irrational, Kyle knew that, and he felt guilty about it; but, dammit, he'd liked that old man. And now he was dead.

Shit.

The ironic kicker was that the only other person Kyle could take it out on, the murderer, was probably dead, too.

John Black had backtracked the trail of the man lying in ambush between the fallen trees, around the stand of eucalyptus to a hiding position behind a bush, then across Dave's land to Phael's car. In the trunk a bandolier of shotgun shells of the kind discovered near the murder scene were found. A pair of work boots lying next to the spare wheel compared in size to a clean sneaker print discovered in a spit of dirt near the car. There were no other tracks in the area, so all that indicated that Phael had bushwhacked Dave and cut into the trees, probably because of the passerby who had stopped and later called the station. The question eating Kyle up, of course, was why would he do it? What could he have against Dave? And in the same vein, why would anyone kill Phael? With a man like Phael, though, there were probably plenty of people with a reason, but who could kill Phael? He was one tough son of a bitch, Kyle could vouch for that.

Now Phael was dead without a clue, and the county was

working the cult angle—the comparison of Phael's demise to that of Cathy Pickers had not gone unnoticed. Nothing had turned up on that, yet. And it wouldn't surprise Kyle if nothing did. Fifteen years ago, the investigators had turned up a big zip, and that could be the case with this, just as easily.

Kyle took another swig of cold coffee, walked over to the painting, unwrapped and placed it on top of the bookcase, making an easel by leaning the top edge of it against the wall. He studied the painting for a moment. There has to be a logical reason for everything that has happened, he told himself.

He turned to his desk and opened Dave's journal to the entry from that Sunday up at the cemetery. Kyle read Dave's words silently: *Kyle is a good man, a man of his word. Today he has promised to bring my baby back to me, to lie down in peace next to her mother. God bless him for doing this for me. And God forgive me for doing this to him.*

# 33

The service was graveside, and Reverend Toland, a thin man, healthy in his late sixties, delivered the eulogy. Kyle scanned the surprisingly large number of people who had turned out on this bright, warm day. Mostly older people; people, Kyle would guess, who remembered Dave Pickers from before his life had turned dark and lonely. He saw Michele, standing next to Edgar and his wife, and looked quickly away. She had ridden with her uncle and aunt, and had asked Kyle if he would like to ride with them. He had declined, citing some awkward excuse about having something to do afterward.

But as afterward came, Kyle moved through the milling mourners, hearing more than once, "Well, he's at peace at last," and touched Edgar's arm, asking if he might have a few words with him. They made small talk as Kyle led them around the headstones, up the slope of the cemetery. They stopped close to the ivy-covered brick wall, out of earshot of the other mourners.

"I suppose this is 'off the record' too," said the newspaperman. "Am I right?"

Kyle smiled. "You are," he said. He looked down the slope and watched the people climb randomly into their cars and drive away. A few stood by the brown metal casket, talking. Edgar's wife and Michele stood clustered watching Edgar and him.

"Didn't Dave have any relatives, Kyle?" asked Edgar. "I didn't see any."

"Dave only had one," said Kyle, "a niece. We couldn't

271

reach her. Dave made burial arrangements for himself a long time ago."

Edgar murmured understanding, then said, "And what is it you want to talk to me about?—off the record, or course."

Kyle got to the point: "We don't have any real leads in this case, but it appears that Phael killed Dave Pickers, and whatever killed Phael, well, that's a mystery that I'm looking into also. What I need to know is why would Phael kill Dave? What was his motive?"

Kyle paused. Edgar stared at him noncommittally, puffing on his pipe, waiting.

"What keeps popping into my head," Kyle said, "is the thing that people, more than one, even you, said at the time I arrested him, 'He's the mayor's man.'" Edgar's eyes narrowed in interest. "'The mayor's man' by definition would do what the mayor wants—"

"Doesn't prove a damn thing," Edgar said.

"I didn't say that it does. But let's just say that it's something to be looked into."

"And you want my help?"

"Yes."

Edgar pulled his briar pipe out of his mouth and held it in a pose, a grandmaster considering a chess problem. "What kind of help do you need?"

"Answers to questions."

"About the mayor?"

"Yes. And more. I need to learn everything about him. I need everything that you know, or can find out, because if what might be true is true, I'm going to need as much information as I can get to keep from having my ass burned."

The old man considered this. Finally he said, "And why me?"

"I think you're bright enough to figure that one out, Edgar." He smiled thinly at the man. Coy was not one of the newspaper editor's strengths.

"Well," Edgar mused, "I am probably the only person in

272

town that could step around asking questions and snooping without arousing *too* much suspicion. Not too many people in town don't know my feelings about the mayor. But murder's another thing, Kyle."

Kyle glanced at the blue morning sky for an instant, where two red-tailed hawks were drifting lazily on a wind current, circling, hunting at leisure. Suddenly one of them tucked his wings and dropped from Kyle's sight behind the ivy-encrusted wall. Whatever its prey was, Kyle would never know.

He shifted his gaze over to the wizened eyes. "Do you think the mayor's capable of murder, Edgar?" he asked. "Of having it ordered?"

Edgar stuck his pipe back into his mouth and sucked on it. Kyle knew the question Edgar was contemplating was not the one he had asked. Edgar was deciding whether or not he could trust Kyle with his thoughts. And that would tell Kyle everything—whether Edgar himself trusted Kyle.

Clarice shouted from below, "Edgar, come *on.*"

Edgar ignored her, and answered Kyle's question: "Yes. In my *opinion*, if the mayor wants something badly enough, he is capable of murder."

"Thank you, Edgar." Kyle said gratefully.

Edgar acknowledged the unspoken trust between them with a nod.

Clarice's strident voice cut its way up the slope: "Edgar, *come on.* I have Lady's Auxilliary."

Edgar didn't flinch. "There was something else?"

Perceptive man, thought Kyle. "Yes. I need the number of that professor. The one in Santa Barbara."

The old man's eyes flicked down to Clarice and back.

Was there a ripple of guilt in that look? Kyle thought so.

"I'll have to look it up when I get to the office," said Edgar.

Kyle pulled a small notebook from the inside pocket of his suit. He slipped out a pen and placed it to the white lined paper. "Sometimes a number'll just come to you," he said, smiling. Edgar glanced guiltily down the slope.

273

"*Edd*-gar! Come *oo-on!*"

"She's really a good woman," said Edgar. "I do love her dearly, when she's not upset."

"*Edd-garrr!!*"

Edgar glared down the hill. "For God's sake, Clarice, hold on to your girdle, will you! You want to start an uprising!" He looked at Kyle. "If she's not careful I'm going to join these good people here so I can get a rest."

Kyle stood, his pen poised. "Off the record," he encouraged.

Edgar gave Kyle Nancy Lyon's telephone number. "Off the record," he said.

"You got it." The idea of an old fella like Edgar having an affair tickled him even on a solemn day like this. They started downhill toward Clarice. She saw them coming, got into the car, and slammed the door so hard that Kyle was sure some long-dead teeth were rattling in the graves.

Michele slipped into the back seat and said something to her aunt.

Kyle shook hands with Edgar and watched him get into his car and drive away. Then he turned to the coffin waiting to be lowered into the ground.

He and Dave were alone again.

For the last time.

Kyle moved closer to the coffin and stood, his hands clasped in front of him, his eyes tearless, his voice firm when he spoke: "I haven't forgotten my promise to you, Dave," he said. "I'll keep my word to you if I can. And don't worry about God forgiving you for what you think you did to me. God forgives you." He touched the burnished metal casket; it was cold. "I forgive you, too."

# 34

Two weeks after Dave Picker's funeral, Kyle drove to Santa Barbara and knocked at the two huge rough-hewn oak doors of Professor Nancy Lyon's Spanish-style home. Her house sat high on a hill overlooking the city and the ocean. A short Mexican woman dressed in a gray-blue work dress answered the door.

"Hello, I'm Kyle Richards," he said. "The professor is expecting me."

"*Venga*," she said, and motioned him in, closing the door behind him. She scooted past him and signaled him to follow. He did so, trying to catch a glimpse of as much of the house as he could. The professor had done very well for herself, he thought. The house was beautiful. He loved the Spanish style with its rough-lathed plaster and arched doorways. The flooring was dark oak wood, highly polished and covered with American Indian accent rugs at strategic points. The furniture was heavy dark wood in Early California motif, as were the wall and light fixtures—black wrought-iron pieces.

"*Aqui*," the maid said, quick-stepping him through the dining room and down a narrow hallway that gave out suddenly into a high-ceilinged spacious study. Three of the walls were floor-to-ceiling bookcases. The fourth opened onto a patio with wide doors.

Kyle retarded his steps, expecting a request to wait here, but the woman skitted to the doors. She stared for a moment out of one of the panes, then nodded and said, "Ah." She swung out the doors and stepped down on red oven-fired patio tiles that

275

glistened in the bright sunlight. She called out in Spanish. Kyle walked to her side and looked out over the backyard garden, a series of vine trellises and rose bushes stuck in a thick mat of lush green lawn. The rear of the yard sloped down and gave out over the city, and past that, the ocean. The view captivated him and for a moment he did not see the woman kneeling beside one of the rose bushes turning the black loamy soil at its base. She stood suddenly, and quite gracefully, Kyle thought, for a woman of her years. Early sixties, he decided. She spoke in fluent Spanish to the maid while gazing with interest at Kyle.

"Would you care for lunch, Mr. Richards?" she asked. Her voice was rich and strong, soothing. "No, thank you," Kyle said. As she approached him, he could understand Edgar Griffith's "indiscretion" with the woman. Even in her gardening clothes she was a striking woman. She wore khaki trousers and blouse, with a wide-brimmed straw hat banded by a sun-colored kerchief, her hands covered with gardening gloves and holding a hand spade. Kyle guessed her to be five foot ten. Her wide face was comely, with a prominent brow and long nose, that in some mystical way did not appear masculine, but rather noble—and sensually feminine.

"Iced tea, then, Mr. Richards? I need some myself," she said.

"Yes, thank you, Professor Lyon," he replied, finding himself wishing that she were a little closer; there was something about her eyes.

She spoke quickly in Spanish to the maid and turned to Kyle. "Please have a seat." She motioned to the round patio redwood table and chairs. "I'll be with you in a moment."

Kyle walked over to the table as the maid disappeared inside the house. He did not sit down, preferring to wait until the professor was present. He watched her as she moved gracefully over to a small gardening table littered with pots and tools. Her back was to him. When she turned around, the work gloves were gone and in their place were a pair of light, white cotton gloves. They seemed incongruous to Kyle, like touch-up paint

276

on a finely aged antique.

"The wages of sin," she said, tugging gently at the cotton gloves. "So many years of doing field work, out in the sun. Age spots." She smiled kindly at him to ease his embarrassment. He hadn't realized that he had been that obvious. "Please, sit down, sit down."

They both sat. Kyle found himself wishing that she would remove her hat, and as if she were reading his mind, she did so and set it on the chair next to her. Her hair was long, thick and iron-gray, coiled and pinned tightly on her head. Her eyes, large and set graciously apart, were a collage of blue and gray with irregular specks of rust and yellow scattered about. They bristled with intelligence.

She's waiting, Kyle realized. He said, "First of all, thank you for seeing me."

She inclined her head. "Edgar called a week ago. He . . . how shall I say it . . . 'called one in,' I believe is the correct expression."

Kyle smiled. A tinkling of glasses on a tray announced the arrival of the iced tea. Kyle laced his drink with sugar and lemon, as he continued: "Are you familiar with the murders that took place several weeks ago in Briggs City?"

She nodded, her eyes going wary.

"Well, one's cause of death is easy to see—shotgun wounds, but the other, the other is a different matter. It is grotesque and the *modus operandi* is the same as one committed sixteen years ago, a young girl named Cathy Pickers. Do the circumstances of both deaths—the heads in the trunks of the tree, the . . . " Kyle searched for a polite way to describe the butchering.

"The genitalia removed and placed in the mouth," completed the professor. "Mr. Richards, it is not necessary to mince words with me." He nodded, relieved at her frankness. "Now, what is it that you wish to know?"

"Do these murders bear any similarity to any rituals of the local Indian population?"

Her eyes flashed, as if Kyle had personally insulted her.

"Definitely not! The Laikute are among the most peaceful peoples on the face of the earth! And their rituals are never cruel, Mr. Richards!"

Kyle sipped some tea and watched her cautiously. He had stepped on a landmine with that one. Would he step on another one with his next question? "Ravana," he said. "I need to know all that you can tell me about Ravana."

The professor sat motionless, as if cut from marble, her right hand wrapped around her glass of tea, her eyes bright and pin pointed on some spot far in the distance.

"Professor?" Kyle said, unnerved by her look.

"Edgar said that you wished to know about the history of the Trees," she said, her gaze still distant.

"The Trees and Ravana are the same thing, are they not?" Kyle was guessing on this one, but thoughts of his own had been forming over the past few weeks.

"Yes." Her eyes fluttered, then focused on her white gloved hand around her tea. She brought the glass to her lips and made a token sip. "Yes. One. They are One."

"Edgar told me that you did some research a number of years back on the Laikute religion and the Trees."

"Yes, that is true."

"And that you wrote a dissertation paper on the subject."

"And a book."

"A book?"

Saying nothing she rose gracefully and left. She returned several minutes later holding a black cloth-covered book about an inch thick, and a dissertation fastened by tarnished brass brads. Kyle took the offered book from her; she placed the dissertation in front of him on the table. He read the title on its spine: *The Religious Rites and Beliefs of the Laikute Indians, by Nancy Lyon.* Kyle glanced at the title page of the dissertation, too. It read, *Doctoral Dissertation: Religious Factors and Beliefs As Functional Parameters of Communal Behavior In the Daily Life of the Laikute Indian Tribe of Central California.*

The woman sat down. "Those two should tell you everything you need to know. You can borrow them, but I expect them to be returned in good condition. Will that be all, Mr. Richards?"

"No. I'm afraid not." Why was she trying to get rid of him?

He placed the book on top of the dissertation and put them to the side as if dismissing them, then looked at the woman. "I want you to tell me about Ravana," he said, "as if I were a student."

She sipped her tea and cleared her throat. "Very well." She began to speak in a resigned, pedantic tone: "Ravana is the mythical embodiment of evil that plays a key role in the religious beliefs of the Laikute Indian tribe." She hesitated for a moment, reaching out for her straw hat and placing it on her head. Her face became dark, shielded from the sun's light. She sighed heavily, as if concluding that this bothersome policeman was not going to go away, then continued: "The Evil, Ravana, is the necessary opponent of the Priest clan of the tribe. In a way they both need each other to exist. The Evil, Ravana, needs to express Itself—to grow—and to do this rapidly It must face *and defeat* the Good, represented by the Priests of the Laikute tribe. If there is no one to face it, then Ravana's growth is slow. Without being opposed, Ravana's strength grows linearly, but with an opponent its strength increases logarithmically. Now, the function of the Priests is to physically face Ravana, *deny* Ravana's existence and pronounce it nonexistent, thus draining It of all its power.

"This must be done by each successive generation or spell the end of the world—"

"Ravana's taking over?" interrupted Kyle.

"Yes, exactly." She paused momentarily and peered at Kyle speculatively.

"It doesn't seem like such a tough thing to do," he said, trying to make his voice light, and failing at it, "just tell the Thing that It doesn't exist; unless, of course, It's going to eat your head off?"

Her expression was unreadable, but Kyle recognized the

279

distasteful tone of her voice as she spoke: "It *will* eat your head off if you have little, or no, faith, Mr. Richards. In fact, if you have little or no faith, you will never really get to face it. Most likely the *Key-ha-hehs* will get you. Those are its Legions: the dead, those who have fallen before you, or the creatures It creates. They will get you, unless you have faith, or unless you agree to face Ravana. At the point where you agree to face Ravana, the *Key-ha-hehs* cannot harm you because then Ravana wants you, wants you badly—each Priest that it defeats makes its strength grow and grow. Up until that point its Legions can kill you."

"Can they be killed, the . . .?"

"The *Keh-ha-hehs?* Yes. They are not Ravana. They can be battled and defeated by normal means; they are limited that way."

She paused a moment, remembering, then continued. "In the ritual, to face Ravana, in order for anyone to step upon Devil's Ground—the Trees, the area within—that person must be purified and swear fidelity. To prove this, the individual must lose the last joint of his little finger of his left hand—the heart hand, the Laikute call it—and have a hole drilled through it. That joint is then treaded onto the *Meh-na,* which is the necklace of bones of all those who have stepped upon Devil's Ground in the ritual of facing Ravana. That necklace has power, in the hands of a Priest to ward off the *Keh-ha-hehs.* The priest would use the *Meh-na* to make the job easier, so to speak."

"I don't see how a string of bones could really have any effect one way or the other, Professor," said Kyle, still contemplating the transformation in the professor's tone of voice, from detached when she started, to almost impassioned now.

"No more than the rosary in the Catholic religion, or *Jinta* sticks in the Panah sect in Somalia. It's all a matter of belief. Belief and belief systems. The Laikute Priests believe that the *Meh-na* would ward off the Legion, and it does. The strong

280

Priest believes that Ravana does not exist, and It doesn't—at that moment It disappears, defeated."

Kyle asked: "What about now? Today. Do the Priests still face Ravana today?"

She shook her head. "No. Even back when I did my study, Holy Eagle was concerned with the dwindling of his tribe and the sacred rites of Ravana. There was trouble at that time, even, in getting to the Trees. Owned by private parties. Stolen from the Indians long ago. They would sneak onto the land and to the Trees to perform their rites."

"And now there is nobody?" asked Kyle.

"As far as I know, no. Holy Eagle died, sometime in the sixties. And his son, to whom the *Meh-na* would be passed, was killed in the Korean War. That would leave nobody, unless Holy Eagle had a grandson, but I don't think he did. Though, I'm not sure of that point."

"And what would happen if there were not Priests to face Ravana? No one left? Then, Ravana would grow. Slowly— linearly was the word you used?"

"Yes. But not necessarily. If I may hazard a guess, I would say that Ravana would reach out and find someone to face him."

"Ravana would have the power to do this?" asked Kyle. "I thought the Devil's Ground was his turf."

"Ravana's 'turf' is the universe, Mr. Richards. In a weakened state minor things can be done. But as It gathers its strength, more and more things can be done. I support my assertion that It would go find someone, by pointing out the nature of the Beast. Throughout Laikute lore, Ravana is referred to as the Manipulator. It is a great planner, schemer. It is most proficient at this, and having an ingrown nature to expand as rapidly as possible. It would hasten the speed of its growth, if It could. In short: It would find someone, Mr. Richards."

She stood up. "Now, if you will excuse me, I am busy. I'll be leaving for New Guinea at the end of the week, and I have a lot to do." She pointed to the books on the table. "Take them. I'll be back in eight or nine months. You can keep them until then. And please don't lose them."

"I won't," said Kyle, standing. "A question, if I may. What happens when Ravana chooses his opponent. Can that opponent defeat him?"

"It would choose someone strong, brave, but with a flaw that It could exploit. If It chooses someone too weak, the power gained from the confrontation would be weak. It would need someone strong in order to gain strong power."

"And would that person have a chance?"

She dismissed him with a wave of her gloved hand, shooing him like a fly. "Only God knows that, Mr. Richards, only God."

Kyle stood his ground. "Just two more questions, Professor."

She stared silently at him.

"One: you haven't asked me why I'm asking about Ravana. It seems to me that if I were asked so many questions, I would want to know why they were being asked?

"And two: you speak of Ravana as if . . . *It* . . . is real. Do you believe It exists?"

Under her straw hat Kyle saw her wonderful eyes turn sad, heavy-lidded. Her face sagged, pained. She spoke softly in a clear, low voice. "One: I haven't asked because I do not wish to know for sure, and I will speak to you no more about that.

"Two:" She indicated the book and dissertation (Kyle picked them up). "In those you will read words that are objective, speaking of *their* beliefs this and *their* beliefs that, referring to the Laikute tribe, of course. What you must consider is the decade in which I wrote those. I was trying to get my doctorate, without being laughed out of the university. So you ask me, Do I believe in Ravana?" She raised her gloved left hand up in front of her. "In order to participate in the ceremony, Mr. Richards, one must be purified. I was young and anxious to succeed. What a small sacrifice to see what only a handful of men had seen in the history of the world." She pulled off the whie cotton glove and held out her hand to him—the end joint of her little finger was missing. "If you were to see the *Meh-na*, Mr. Richards, one of the finger bones on it would be mine."

Kyle stared at her, dumbstruck.

"Now, *good day*, Mr. Richards."

She walked into the house, leaving him alone to find his own way out.

# 35

He needed time to think. Instead of heading straight back to Briggs City, he drove aimlessly along country back roads. By nightfall he found himself driving through Solvang, a small Danish community filled with tourist shops. He spotted a gas station and pulled in. Christ, had he put the miles on today, close to three hundred, the tank was almost dry. He paid the man and hit the road heading for home.

It was nearly eight before he realized that he was close to Briggs City. His headlights cut a swath in the dark night road. He was coming in on Highway 28, and in a few minutes he would pass Dave Pickers's place and the trees. He cursed himself tolerantly. He'd meant to take the main highway and come in from the north just to avoid the trees, but he had been so lost in thinking about how he was going to handle the trees, and what he had learned about this impossible thing Ravana, that he had unconsciously missed the access to the main highway. Now, he was halfway to Briggs City, and on the road that would take him past that damned copse of eucalyptus trees. He glanced down at the book and dissertation Professor Lyon had loaned him. Perhaps they would have the answer. He looked up and felt a moment of pleasure. The lights at Dave's ranch were on. It would do him good to stop by and say hi to old Dave.

Dave is dead.

The thought floated in blackness for a second, then stabbed him with sorrow. Vandals! he thought. He sped up, at the same time reaching over and switching his police radio on. As he approached, he could see the outline of the house against the black cancerous mass of the trees. Dave's truck had been moved to the side of the house, and parked in its place in front was a white Cadillac. He felt his initial tension ease itself into discretionary caution. The look and feel of the situation was not one of robber. With the warm yellow lights from the windows, the scene was more prosaic than peculiar. He ignored the jagged pangs of memory that turning into Dave's drive brought to mind.

Before he was within a hundred feet of the house, the front door opened, the porch light went on, and Leia Conway, the councilwoman, came out.

What was she doing here?

"Hello," she said, as he got out of the truck.

"Hello," he answered. "What brings you out here?"

"Surprised, Kyle?"

There was that flirting tone Leia always had when talking to him. And why was he all of a sudden thinking of Michele and feeling guilty for no reason? "Yes," he answered her question, giving her an inquisitive smile.

"Well, I'm not robbing the place. It's been sold. I'm handling the details."

"Sold? But what about probate, Leia? Dave's not been dead that long."

She smiled, a little patronizingly, Kyle thought.

"Dave Pickers didn't own the land, Kyle. His niece owned it. To pay for his hospital stay after his daughter's murder, I guess he had to sell out to his brother. From what I understand, it provided Mr. Pickers with living money, too. His brother died, and left it to the niece with the stipulation that the land never be sold until her Uncle Dave agreed, or passed away—it was a condition of the will.

"Now that he's gone, she was anxious to sell." A bad feeling arose in his mind; he felt his heart quicken with dawning intuition. "And who bought the property, Leia?"

"Why . . . the mayor, Kyle." She pointed to Devil's

285

Ground. "See those trees over there? The mayor's going to rip those down and build a huge supermarket there, right on that spot. It is going to be the headquarters store with a huge warehouse to supply his other stores."

"Then"—she waved past the trees—"about a half a mile further on, the mayor is going to build a huge shopping mall. It's going to bring a lot of money into our town. It's wonderful."

Hate welled up deep in his being, carrying with it a name: Neil Gathers. Now he had a motive, by God. The motive for Neil Gathers to have a harmless old man murdered. Leia said something to him. He ignored it.

"Leia, did the mayor ever approach Dave's niece about selling the land before now?"

"Yes, he did. About a year ago, I think. She told him she couldn't sell unless her uncle said okay." She sounded annoyed. "Kyle, what's wrong?"

"Nothing," he said finally. "I'm sorry. I . . . I liked Dave a great deal, and his death has me upset." He felt awkward. She seemed to sense this, and tried to put him at ease. "Okay," she said. "I'm going to check the rest of the house. Then lock up. I'll be right back."

Kyle stood for a moment, looking at the trees. He thought about the mayor and Phael. Motivation—he had that: the mayor wanted the land and Dave's niece couldn't sell until her uncle was dead. The link between the mayor and Phael for the murder of Dave, that would be a tough one to prove. Phael would have to have directly left evidence that linked his act to the mayor, a letter, or something very stupid. Not much hope of that—the mayor was not a stupid man. Kyle took deep breaths of the cold night air, not moving his eyes from the trees. He thought, *You did it, Gathers, and I'm going to nail you, you son of a bitch.*

The mayor had bought the trees, and the land around them. The trees. Everything pointed to the trees. And according to Professor Lyon, that was the same as pointing to Ravana. He remembered his flow sheet: his name with an arrow jabbed on it, written in blood-red Crayola, from another name, RAVANA. And then what Professor Lyon had said about Ravana's need hit him with renewed force: Ravana needed an opponent to draw power from. Kyle heard the snakes hissing in his head. The sound rose in intensity, louder and louder, until he thought his head would explode. Stop it, Kyle!

He had control again. Thank God he did, because what he was thinking was crazy and impossible, and he just wasn't buying it.

He stood still a moment longer, letting the chill air brace him back to reality. He felt a grim pride: one more time, he'd staved off madness.

He took a deep breath. The wind shifted, coming from the trees now. And riding the night air like a demon was the stink of rotting flesh.

# Excerpts IV

May 20, 1981

He came to me today, *Ehkeh-Heh*—the Fallen Warrior, the Chosen One.

Ravana's time has come.

# Book III

# 36

The time was now, he knew it, just as he knew that since the night he had traded Cathy Pickers for his life, he had been the most miserable human being on the face of the earth.

He moaned out loud in the darkness of his car, opened the door, and stepped out into the cold night. Sacred Mountain rose before him like some monstrous black bear reaching high into the star-filled sky.

It was three in the morning, a Saturday, and he would have to hurry. The mountain still must be climbed, the fire built, and his plea made before sunrise. The groundbreaking would be in the morning sometime, and though no one would probably see him up on the white rock promontory of the mountain, he wanted to play it safe and be gone by then.

He pulled a canvas duffel bag from the car and started upward, unsuccessfully dodging memories of the first time he had climbed the mountain. He'd been so peacock proud then, to be chosen to face Ravana. If he had only known then that he was the *Heytah-nee*—the Traitor, the Fallen One, he would have run away from here till the end of time.

The climb took an hour. In his youth he had made it sprinting in less than half that time without being winded. Now, he clutched his sides and took gasping lungfuls of the cold night air. He regained his breath and stripped naked. He reached down to the duffel bag, hoisted it over one shoulder like a sailor, and climbed the last ten feet up to the Sacred Place, the white rock shelf that pouted a hard lip out from the mountain toward Ravana's ground.

Shivering, he walked to the edge and looked out. The moon had descended, finding its rest between the darkness of the night and the burning rays of dawn. The landscape stretched like a black lake beneath the star-filled firmament above. He could not see Them, it was too dark, but They were there. He could *feel* Them. And he could feel *It*, too. *It* had taken his soul and let him live, the cruelest of all things to do.

He backed away from the edge to a place deeper on the shelf, next to a mass of rounded boulders. Here he placed his bag and opened it, emptying the contents in the dark, taking inventory of them by feel: two gallon jugs of water, a leather pouch with sacred herbs and the sacred mushrooms, a large cast-iron kettle, an iron tripod with a pot hook suspended by a chain, a can of charcoal starter fluid, and dry wood for the fire.

He found the old place for the fire and gathered the small rocks that had been its border years ago, now scattered by animals or vandals. With the rocks, he made a circle with a three-foot diameter. He set the tripod up and laid the wood carefully under its iron legs. Reaching behind him, he pulled the kettle and a jug of water around and emptied the water into the pan. He lifted the kettle under the tripod and slipped it onto the chain's hook. With the help of the lighter fluid the fire caught quickly, and he moved between the flames and the boulders. The heat reflecting off them warmed his back. He grabbed the leather pouch and emptied the contents into the water. Soon it would boil, and when that happened he would start the chant, *Hey-ha-heya, Hey-ha-heya,* the summons for his dead priest ancestors, the Spirit Elders. He would chant that until they came, and then he would call forth Holy Eagle, his grandfather, and ask his questions.

He moved out of the warmth of the fire for a moment to bring in a large leather satchel. He pulled from it two clay pots, each one a size that fit snugly in the cup of both hands. He placed these beside concave depressions worn into the white rock by centuries of use, then rooted in the satchel again until he found it. Its irregular bones felt like teeth biting into the hand that closed around it. The *Meh-na*. Very slowly, his mind drowning in dark unpleasant memories, he withdrew the necklace, the talisman against Ravana. For one brief, agonizing moment, the terror of that night sixteen years ago was as real as the breath he drew that instant. To clear the feeling he quickly put the charm on, but found the bones unmercifully weighted and sharp against his skin, as if they did not wish to touch his tainted flesh.

He checked the kettle. It was near boiling now, so he ladled out some of the brew with a clay cup and filled both depressions in the rock, then mixed a part of the contents of one of the clay pots into the first depression. He stirred it with a stick and watched the white powder made from bone and ash and resin thicken up into a whitish mud body paint. He used the second depression in the same manner with the contents of the second clay pot and mixed a black mud body paint. Glancing back over his shoulder as he stirred, he saw the brew starting to boil and he began to chant, *"Hey-ha-heya, Hey-ha-heya, Hey-ha-heya,"* his naked body beginning to rock softly with the rhythm. He turned to the kettle, ladled out a small portion, and drank it. It scalded his throat. He pulled a bone knife from the satchel, held his heart hand over the pot, and sliced deeply into each of his fingers. He let his blood drip into the pot, still incanting the plea for his ancestors, careful not to betray his pain in his tone of voice.

He cupped another portion of the brew and blew on it until he could drink it without burning his throat. He set the cup down and turned back to the paint, first painting his entire body with the white. Then, using his fingers as a brush, he painted the circles of the Sun on his face, the wavy lines of the Water on his abdomen, and finally the vertical lines of the Earth on his legs. This done, he began to dance, circling the fire out to the tip of the ledge and back to the fire, chanting, pleading with his ancestors, "Hey-ha-heya, Hey-ha-heya, Hey-ha-heya."

With each circle, he drank the potion and pleaded with the

295

Spirit Elders to grant him their presence. His concept of time was lost by the fourth circle, and between that and the draining of the potion bit by bit into his stomach, his sweat poured freely, sweating through the body paint and causing it to run in streamers to his feet. The sacred rock was stained with mud-paint footprints. His mind began to crack open like a gourd: animals, dogs, wolves, elk, deer, crows, eagles spewed forth and took up position in a glowing lime-green sky. As he circled by the ledge he stared out toward Devil's Ground and saw a fountain of flame gushing up from the trees, high into the sky, out into space. The animals circled and circled, and became horses with riders, Laikute riders, his ancestors. An eagle soared on silver wings, approaching closer and closer.

The Indian danced in place now on the ledge, his arms out in supplication, calling Holy Eagle's name and thankful that he had come. The enormous bird dived with a deadly swoop and the Indian dropped to the rock. He lay there for a moment until the sound of the beating wings ceased, then he dared to look up. The boulder behind the fire had become the head of Holy Eagle, fully ten feet tall, and luminescent—the same sad eyes of old, the broken nose, the long scraggly silver hair, the same face the Indian remembered as a boy.

Holy Eagle said nothing.

The Indian approached cautiously. It hurt to look directly into those sad eyes. The last time he had seen them they were full of scorn and rage—Holy Eagle's grandson had become the *Heytah-nee*.

"I have come, Grandfather . . . Holy Eagle, because I have news . . ."

"What news would you have that we do not know, *Heytah-nee?*" Each word vibrated throughout his body, though his grandfather's voice sounded as if spoken softly into both his ears at one. The scorn in the voice bit into his heart.

He hesitated. A wind caught the fire, blowing sparks and exciting the flames to dance. Their image reflected in Holy

Eagle's large eyes, replacing the old man's pupils.

"Grandfather, the Whites are tearing down the trees. Without the trees Ravana is nothing." He heard his own voice become the pleading of a small boy. "I—I can get my happy spirit back. Ravana will be dead, Grandfather." Tears welled up in the Indian's eyes. "Please, Grandfather, help me. Please."

Holy Eagle's eyes glowered hotly. His huge lips moved: "You fool! *Heytah-nee!* You have spit on your ancestors, you have spit on me. When you die you will join your spirit with *Ravana.* If you want your happy spirit back, if you wish to regain your *Pay-Wa,* then go now and face *Ravana!* Claim your soul! Face *Ravana!*"

"I can't, Grandfather! I can't!" He brought both hands to his face. "I'm scared! *Afraid!* Please. You go for me, you go for me."

"Silence!" Holy Eagle's voice was a violent wind through a rocky chasm. It flushed the Indian's cheeks with shame.

"Holy Eagle, please. The Whites are tearing down the trees. They are going to level all of Ravana's ground and turn it into a parking lot and stores. Even *Ehkeh-heh* will not be able to face *Ravana.* Ravana is as good as gone. Without the trees, without the ground—"

The flames of the fire roared high, obliterating the face of Holy Eagle, then guttered to almost nothing.

The Indian felt woozy. When was dawn? Soon, he guessed. The fingers of unconsciousness reached up from their darkness and clenched his mind. He fought it, sinking to his knees and seeing Holy Eagle's face once more. The old man's head moved so close to him that he could reach out and touch the giant pockmarked broken nose if he wanted to. The eyes loomed huge and sad. The big lips spoke and he could smell on the old man's breath the fresh smell of mountain pines. "Fool," said his grandfather sadly, "all that is put on Ravana's ground is Ravana's. Throw a rock on *Its* ground and *It* owns that rock. Spit upon Ravana's dirt and that spit belongs to *It.* Build a fort on Ravana's ground, and Ravana is the master of that fort. These White men's tinkering means nothing. All built on Ravana's ground belongs to Ravana."

The voice faded with the Indian's consciousness.


When he came to, it was heavy morning daylight, the fire in dead ashes. The boulder was again only a boulder. He pushed himself up with both arms and flipped over, sitting up, both legs sticking over the ledge. He ached all over. Holy Eagle's last words rang in his ears: "All built on Ravana's ground belongs to Ravana." He shook his head to clean the words from his mind, but they were incessant. He looked out toward Ravana's ground and watched the Whites gather near the Trees for the groundbreaking ceremonies for Mayor Gathers's new supermarket and shopping mall.

# 37

"I kept up with the chief this morning, Mom," Curtis said to her proudly, but Michele missed the uptake, muttering "Imbecile" under her breath as she negotiated the curve of the road behind a damned yellow VW van driving ever so slowly.

"They shouldn't let people like this on the road," she told Curtis. "I hope we're not late."

"The invitation said ten o'clock, Mom. It's only nine-forty. We're almost there now."

"Yes, but I wanted to *be* there by now. If it wasn't for the incompetent driving that van, we would be."

There was a break in the unusual oncoming traffic. Michele gunned it, swung the wheel, and passed the damn van, trying not to show hostility in front of Curtis. She satisfied herself instead with a slice-of-death look at the driver out of the corner of her eye.

"Evil eye," said Curtis, laughing.

"You didn't see that," Michele responded grimly.

They drove in silence for a few moments, heading out toward Dave Pickers's old place, along with other shopkeepers and businessmen from Briggs City, at the invitation of Mayor Gathers's development company. Michele knew there would be other people there from other communities, too: Blake, Midvale, Taylorville, all at the mayor's invitation, all for a purpose. The mayor hoped to generate interest in the new mall he was building, presell store space. Her invitation had said in part, "The Gathers's Development corporation invites you to become a part of the future. You are cordially invited to

299

groundbreaking ceremonies for a new idea in public convenience, the Galleria, a complex of shops, department stores, movie theatres, supermarket, professional buildings, restaurants, family entertainment centers—everything to meet the needs of the buying public." Michele had felt elated when she had read it. This was opportunity knocking with a big Knock—Knock. If she could arrange financing, and assure herself store space, then that would be just the beginning. One successful store could lead to another, and another . . .

"Mom, there's nowhere to park." Curtis twisted in his seat, staring wide-eyed at the erratic queues of cars lining both sides of the road. As Michele searched for a place to park, a rising anxiety made her hands try to crush the steering wheel of her little VW bug. This many cars meant all those people were vying for *her* store space, and here she was outside of it all trying to find a damn parking place.

She finally found a place to park about a hundred feet from Dave Pickers's drive. Another car pulled in behind her.

Michele took Curtis's hand and hurried him along with a pull. Curtis pulled his hand away. "Mom, can I go on ahead? Please?"

She looked down at him. He was facing her walking backward as they passed the twelve-foot-high chain-link fence that separated what was now left of Pickers ranch from the construction site. A flood of warmth filled her heart. The first time she had seen that face it had been so small and pink. She had supported it in the crook of her arm and guided those tiny lips to her breast to feed it. Now, it smiled up at her. The angle of his jaw more pronounced, his whole musculature and skeleton hardening. She could see now in that face what he would look like as a young man with a wife and child of his own. And how old would she be then? Oh, time, how it passes so fast.

She waved her hand in a motion of dismissal. "May the Force be with you, Luke Skywalker," she said.

Curtis grinned. "You, too, Mom," he said, spun around, and was jogging toward the gates.

She watched him, speeding up her own pace. He ran like a man—thanks to Kyle. God had answered her prayer when he had sent that man here. Just six short months ago she had been worrying about Curtis appearing manly. After all, his primary role model was her. And now, by the grace of God, and the attention of Kyle Richards, her worry had flipflopped. Now she worried that he was too much a man, or a male, anyway, for a boy his age. He had the rolling walk of the chief, and an uncanny way of looking at her that, except for the color of the eyes, could have been Kyle's gaze.

More cars passed looking for parking, and the jagged sounds of a crowd became louder as she approached nearer to the gate. A frown pulled at the corners of her mouth. Damn. The thoughts of Kyle's influence on Curtis had snared her into that murky area of conflict that had obsessed her more and more in the last few weeks or so. How could Kyle be so blind, not see that she wanted to love him, that she wouldn't *"leave"* him like his wife and daughter had left him. He was afraid; he saw the murder of his family as them leaving him, and he was afraid to get close to her because she might leave him too. She could sympathize, of course. How it must have hurt him to discover their bodies! She had cried one night thinking about it, cried at his pain, and at how he had been affected. And she'd wallowed in confusion. If he was so afraid to get close to her, why wasn't he afraid to get close to Curtis? She sighed. Well, at least there had been no other woman. She could comfort herself with that, but she was growing impatient with that man.

She loved him, and he loved her (at least as best she could tell without him telling her directly). Perhaps she had been too passive—out of consideration for his situation—but she could feel herself leaving that behind like she had being a "helpless female" to become a competitive businesswoman supporting herself and her child. She would find a way to approach Kyle, somehow. And soon. She wasn't going to turn into an old maid just waiting for him. A little kindness and a little assertiveness (couched in feminine subtlety) was all he needed, she was sure of that.

She turned into the gate. She saw Kyle, and that sudden, almost sexual rush of pleasure she always felt warmed her. Doing the best to control her emotions, she walked toward him.

Kyle had paid the invitation little notice when he'd seen it, except for the handwritten note at the bottom asking him to be there at nine o'clock instead of the scheduled ten o'clock, signed by the mayor himself. A form of an order, Kyle supposed, and he resented it coming from that man; but it went with the territory—groundbreaking, opening of public buildings, the installment of public officers—it was all part of being chief of police.

What did surprise him was *this* groundbreaking. Instead of the few people, a silver shovel and a photographer for the press, and the five-minute ceremony that he was expecting, the groundbreaking had the air of a gala event: food and beverage stands (all free), a magician, two clowns teasing the crowd and passing out helium-filled balloons to the kids. Music blaring through a PA system. A small raised platform had been erected, a chrome-plated microphone stand and mike placed front-edge-center, gleaming like a silver spike. Off to the side of the platform stood a large rectangular table covered with a gold cotton drape that was jury-rigged by pulleys to be removed at the appropriate time.

Before Kyle could get a chance to peek under the cover, the mayor had called him over to meet the other people who had been asked to come early. The first introduction was Larry Allen, the store manager from the mayor's market, an oily-looking man of about forty with a narrow head on a beanpole neck. As Kyle moved over to shake hands with the next man, all he could remember of Allen was a slight feeling of distrust, a bobbing Adam's apple, and shiny black shoes with white gym socks. The other man was introduced as Harold Torkelson, head of the construction department of Gathers's Development Corporation. Kyle warmed to him immediately—he was actually taller than Kyle, six feet six, with a firm handshake and friendly smile.

"Going to make this an occasion to remember, Kyle," said the mayor. "Isn't that right, Harold?"

The tall project manager raised a long arm and pointed toward the west, to the heavy-duty equipment. Kyle turned and saw row upon row of industrial-yellow steel earthmoving monsters lined up and pointing toward the trees. Men in bright yellow hard hats milled around talking among themselves. "Got the bulldozers and graders ready," said Torkelson, and then pointed toward the trees. "No one there yet, but our demolition people should be over there any minute. Going to blow us up some trees for the folks."

"My idea," said the mayor. "I want this to be an event to remember, the reshaping of the future for Briggs City and all the surrounding communities. The county, too," he said expansively, waving his arms theatrically as if conferring blessings upon the land. "First I break ground with the shovel. Then an explosive boom and twenty trees fall down. Then my earthmovers roll, demolishing the trees and leveling the ground for the greatest shopping and industrial complex this part of the state has ever seen."

He dropped his arms and looked almost mystically out over the land, a seer into the future, a shaper of things to come. All Kyle could think was how they were standing on Dave Pickers's land, and how this man standing next to him probably had had him killed.

"Will it be safe blowing the trees with people this close?" Kyle asked.

"No problem there," offered Torkelson, "just enough pop to knock the trees down; we're far enough back—no danger."

The other councilmen began to arrive, along with Edgar Griffith, and seemingly hundreds of people all at once. The magician began performing, the clowns clowning; a festive air

303

reigned, bolstered by the drone of a crowd having fun, making laughter and merriment.

"I invited businesspeople from our town and the neighboring communities," Kyle heard the mayor tell the councilmen, then felt a mental tug-Michele. She would be at a function like this.

Kyle turned his head. There she was, heading for him.

Curtis intercepted his mom, holding two balloons, red and white, bouncing from strings, and began talking excitedly, walking with her, not recognizing where they were going.

Kyle waved, and Michele tapped Curtis and pointed toward Kyle. They gave him big smiles. He felt a longing for their company.

"Chief, we need you up here," said the mayor.

Kyle pointed toward the stage for Michele's and Curtis's benefit, then he stepped upon the stage.

The mayor tapped the microphone for attention and then began his speech. Kyle hoped that it was not a long one, but he glanced over at the trees and saw the five workmen with yellow hard hats and orange safety vests still seeding the trees with dynamite. That probably meant twenty minutes of bullshit from the mayor, at least.

Kyle listened with half an ear as the mayor spoke of the future development of the land here. He searched the crowd for Michele and Curtis. He found them on the periphery of the sea of people. He kept glancing at them instead of keeping his eyes, properly, on the mayor. Gathers got his attention back by pointing grandly at the gold-cloth-covered table as the mayor pointed to it and said, "Behold the Future of this fine land you're standing on. And your future too, I might add." With this, the pulleys pulled and the gold cloth reared back and a collective *"Oooh"* rose from the crowd. A scale model of the completed Galleria and business complex was mounted on the plywood table. Separate from that was a huge supermarket: Gathers's Market Headquarters Store read a sign under it. Kyle sensed the mood of the business people assembled: excitement mounting to desire; here was opportunity for profit and gain abounding. He had to hand it to the mayor. Gathers knew how to generate interest.

Suddenly there was a series of explosions. *Boom! Boom! Boom!* Then one tremendous *Boo-oommmm!*

Kyle looked to the trees.

White smoke billowed up near the woods. Five trees and five demolition men were flying in the air like nuclear missiles, coming in a arc for the crowd.

Kyle heard secondary explosions and in horror saw the trees and men burst into pieces in the air.

He leaped from the platform screaming at people to run as he ran toward Michele and Curtis. The night of his Tragedy flashed through his mind, filling him with horror. Michele! he thought. Curtis! I've got to save them! He pushed a lost man aside and there they were. Both seemed frozen in shock, staring up at the debris, not realizing that the trees and bodies would rain down on them.

Kyle grabbed them each by an arm, and ran toward the table holding the model complex. He picked Curtis up under one arm and Michele under the other and dove under the table. Branches and pieces of wood and arms and legs and unidentifiable pieces of bodies came *crumping* down. Kyle gathered Michele and Curtis together and covered them with his body just as a deafening explosion sounded seemingly in his ear. He heard wood crack; the far end of the table crashed to the dirt. *Close!* Kyle thought.

The rain of debris stopped just as suddenly as it had begun. Then the injured began to moan and cry out. Kyle rose off Michele and Curtis and crawled out through the table's legs. He helped them out.

"Are you all right?" he asked.

Michele stared up at him in tears. "Yes, I think so." She turned around, then went rigid and screamed. Kyle followed her line of sight. Sprawled over the flattened model of the future Galleria was the torso of a man, dressed in blue jeans,

305

red-checked work shirt, and orange safety vest. His head, arms, and legs were missing. The five stumps leaked blood out in red streams, covering the future of Briggs City with a syrupy red sheen.

"Go home, Michele," said Kyle. "Take Curtis and get away from here." Michele nodded, grabbed Curtis, and ran toward the road. The moans and cries for help broke through Kyle's mental fog.

God, I've got to help these people! he thought.

As he ran toward his truck and the radio, his head turned uncontrollably toward the dark trees.

They stood there, silent, and mocking.

# 38

At seven-fifteen AM Harold Torkelson stood waiting in front of the newly completed Gathers Market viewing the skeletal structures of the remainder of the shopping complex in the distance. He searched for the sensation he always felt when looking at something he was building—a sense of pride and permanency; the thrill of knowing *he'd* built those buildings and that, by God, when he died he'd have left his mark on the world.

The feeling would not come. What is it? he wondered, about this particular building that gives me the willies?

The sense of being watched poured into his mind, as heavy and cold as wet cement. He shrank back from the building to the refuge of his pickup truck, leaning against the grill and cocking a leg up on the bumper. Now the market was to his left, and the feeling of being watched came from the left.

He realized suddenly that he hated the supermarket.

The irony was that it was perfect! Perfect in every respect. Just a little too damn perfect! The explosion at the groundbreaking had left him with a bad feeling. His experience had been that however the construction began bode either well, or ill, toward its completion. If that was the case, this thing should have been hell to get done; but it wasn't. Instead, it was as if some unseen hand had guided the project. There was not one accident except the first—and he was still trying to figure how that little bit of dynamite had done that much damage—not one hitch, not one! The mayor had given him an impossible timetable and he had come in not just on schedule, but three days early. So here he was waiting for the mayor and that squirrelly Larry Allen for the walk-through, a tour of the completed project.

He whistled softly to himself, pulling a ring of keys from his pocket and bouncing them up and down for something to do. They made a jangling sound that broke the oppressive silence that seemed to come from the market.

He saw the silver Mercedes coupe coming, pushed himself off the grill, and unobtrusively straightened his bolo tie.

The car slid up carefully nose to nose with his truck and he walked forward to greet the mayor as he stepped out. He gave Larry Allen a quick wave, wondering if that fella ever wore anything but black peg-leg slacks, white shirt, and black bow tie. With his black wingtips and white (for Christ's sake) gym socks, and his Brylcreem-slick hair, he appeared frozen in the nineteen fifties. He'd have to be a good grocery manager, though, because the mayor only kept those people that made him money.

To each his own, thought Torkelson, grimly anticipating the walk-through. He shook the mayor's proffered hand and led him around to the main doors of the market, jangling out the key and unlocking the door.

As he pulled it open, a jarring alarm sounded. Torkelson smiled at the two men's surprise. "Alarm's working," he laughed, and cut the alarm with a tubular key, then opened the security mesh door with a third key, pushed it open, stepped through, and held it for the mayor and Larry Allen.

"God, it's dark in here, Harold," said Allen.

"Safety lights on," replied Torkelson as he removed the key and let the security door close. "Be careful or you'll ruin the surprise. Follow me."

The smell of fresh paint and newness filled his head. Normally, he loved that smell, and the feeling of newness, just as he normally loved the walk-through—the pride of showing off his work—but this time he found those feeling conflicting with his ingrained dislike of the market.

308

Well, he wasn't being paid to like or dislike, that was for sure. He shrugged off the feelings and led the mayor and Larry Allen past the empty checkout stands, through the section that would become the liquor department, and then to a door leading into the back room. He propped it open and told them to wait there. He stepped into the back anteroom and pulled an electrical lever, then stepped back out: "Voila!" he said, as the ratcheting sound of gears and chains pulling filled the vast emptiness of the new market. The automatic blinds (placed there to temper the rays of the afternoon sun) rolled up and let the soft illumination of the morning flood in and soak the newness of the readied structure with purifying light.

"Wonderful," said the mayor.

"Great," said Larry Allen.

"I thought you'd like it. That's why it was so dark in here; a little theatrics before the walk-through."

"What about the grate?" asked the mayor.

"Same thing," Torkelson replied, and slipped into the back and pulled the lever marked Security. He returned outside, the accordian-mesh steel grating rolling up in clanging thunder off the window and doors to wind around its hidden spindles. Within a minute the bank of front windows was clear, revealing the newer construction outside. "Now, that'll keep anybody out at night. It's the new kind of grate—even a bulldozer with a chain couldn't pull the mesh out. The market'd fall down before the grate would."

The mayor nodded his approval. "Let me see 'em drop," he ordered, and Torkelson stepped back and hit the lever. A harsh bell sounded two short bursts. "That's the warning," he told the two men, stepping back out. Then the security grating dropped in an ungodly clang, down and locked in thirty seconds.

"Same thing in back for all the doors," stated the mayor to Larry Allen, "somebody wants to get in, the only door without the mesh is the roof access, but we've got it wired with a tamper-proof alarm, right, Tork?"

"Right," Torkelson affirmed, watching Larry Allen smile that ass-kissing smile of his.

"Nobody'll get in this place when it's locked up like this," said Larry Allen.

"Let's walk through," he said. Both the mayor and Larry Allen gave him a strange look. He realized his voice had quavered. *Damn it, he wanted out of here!*

He took them first to the back room, showed them the receiving nook, the self-service deli room, the freezer (not turned on yet), and listened to them both coo about the amount of warehouse space. There was more space than that, he told them, even though they both knew, and suggested formally that they take the freight elevator. He showed them the upper warehouse space area, connected to the main floor area by a conveyor belt, took them to the large metal cage holding the compressors, and had them poke their heads in the catwalk tunnel that ran along what the customers would see as the edge of the ceiling. There were square mirrors, like eyes, every ten feet so that someone in the catwalk could spot shoplifters if and when that became a big problem for the store. He took them back down in the freight elevator, past the main warehouse to the underground storage area. This had no conveyor belt system, and would rely only on the elevator, the heavy inventory goods being stored down here.

"Are you sure there'll be no leakage?" asked the mayor.

"I rerouted the stream. We're going to use it ornamentally"—he looked at Larry Allen—"take the flow through the new mall. The mayor's idea. A nice touch, don't you think?"

"A great idea," Larry fawned.

You butt-sucker, thought Torkelson, and led the two men back into the elevator. You must make the mayor a *lot* of money.

Once again on the main level, he showed them the back rooms for produce, liquor, and meat. All were separate unto themselves, the meat having huge freezer vaults that reminded Torkelson of tombs.

Finally he took the two men back to the front of the store past the shades and security mesh switchbox and up the back room stairs to the office structures. It was composed of an outer office and an inner office. Torkelson watched Larry Allen drool over the inner one—it would be his. There was also a money room whose only entrance was from inside Larry's office. The wall of the manager's office that faced out on the customer floor of the store was all two-way mirror so that he could get a bird's eye view of everything.

The mayor walked over and touched a new microphone shaped like a tulip bulb at the end of a flexible chrome gooseneck arm. "Larry, this is so you can yell at 'em when they slow down. Sort of an electronic whip."

Larry laughed a little too heartily.

"Well, that wraps up the walk-through, mayor. I trust you're pleased?"

"Pleased as punch," said the mayor. "Let me walk you down." He turned to Larry. "Wait up here and enjoy your new office; I'll be right back."

"Sure thing," Larry said.

Torkelson led the mayor down the short hallway to the stairs and then down past the switches past the front of the store. The only thing left now was the handing over of the keys, but the mayor had dismissed Larry, so he probably wanted to talk with him. Sure enough, the mayor stopped near the first checkstand and put a hand briefly on his arm. He had that grave look—after ten years of working together, Torkelson knew the signal—a very serious matter.

"Harold, has anybody been asking you questions about me or our operation?" the mayor asked.

"No. Why?" he asked, puzzled. He had seen the mayor concerned before, but this went byond that. Gathers was *worried*.

"Nothing I can put my finger on exactly." He paused for a moment, rubbing his chin with the knuckles of his right hand and staring out at the new construction in the distance.

311

Finally, he took a breath and looked back up at Torkelson. "Somebody's been walking on my web," he said finally. "And I don't know who, but I'll find out. You just make sure that your people know that *everything* about our business, down to the number of rolls of toilet paper we buy, is confidential. Understand?"

"Understood," said Torkelson, and he did. The mayor was a prime mover, and there were a lot out there who just couldn't stand to see a man make a success of himself. "If there's anything you need, I'm with you one hundred per cent, Neil. You know that."

"Thanks. I appreciate that." The mayor took his hand and shook it warmly. "And thanks for the store," he added.

Torkelson pulled the ring of keys from his pocket and dropped them in the mayor's waiting hand. "You got a fine store here, Neil. A real headquarters store. Just the beginning."

They said good-bye, the mayor opened the door for him, and he stepped outside and savored the sound of the door closing behind him. It felt good to be in the fresh air. It felt clean out here. Fresh and wholesome.

As he climbed into his truck, started it up, and drove away from the store, he marveled at how odd he felt about that market. Never before had he had such indescribably feelings about a structure. He felt . . . felt almost *guilty* about the whole thing. *Guilty.* And as he drove away from the market another feeling came over him—relief, as if his part in something terrible was done.

# 39

Kyle eased up from his bed and dressed himself silently in the dark. The clock's dial read one AM in red digital numbers.

Why was he up? He wasn't sure. But he had an urge to take a drive.

He steered the truck out onto Highway 28, drove the distance, and turned into the Gathers Market parking lot. He parked not far from where he had turned in, and stared at the market. The parking-lot lights were extinguished for the night, so the light thrown from the windows seemed more intense. Two cars, two vans, and three trucks were parked near the building in the no-parking zone; the night crew, Kyle guessed, probably stocking the shelves.

Kyle wondered why he had stopped. Perhaps to verify for himself one more time that everything was all right, that time does indeed heal all. The market had been open now for over a month, and there had been no problems. The groundbreaking disaster had shaken his confidence in his decision not to believe what Professor Lyon believed about Ravana—but no trouble had arisen.

In fact, time had healed a lot of things in the past four or five months. He hadn't had one bad dream at all since the groundbreaking; he had heard no hissing, either. It was as if with the trees had gone the evil—or the craziness he had interpreted at first as evil. In any case, it was gone, and he was glad of it, and thankful.

Some things time can't heal, he thought. His promise to Dave Pickers still chewed at him: the list of Cathy Pickers's friends that Michele had written up yielded one name that wasn't in any of the police interviews—Melinda Belardis. According to Michele, Belardis was Cathy's best friend, and the daughter of a diplomat. She had moved overseas four months before the murder, and so was not questioned. Kyle tracked her family down, only to find that Belardis had followed in her family's tradition and was herself in the diplomatic corps, serving in Morocco. She was due back in the States for a visit soon, and her mother promised that her daughter would call him when she arrived.

Kyle grunted. He didn't expect any startling leads from the woman. It was a loose end that needed tying up so he could tell himself that he'd gone the full distance on his promise to Dave.

Then that would be that.

Kyle stared at the giant letters of the market's name: GATHERS.

He sighed. Time hadn't healed his feelings about Neil Gathers, either. It had tempered them, though, down to a simmer, because of lack of evidence, and Kyle's memory of Marcus Wendler. Kyle had handled the investigation of that murder case, and been damned pleased when Wendler got a life sentence for the bludgeoning death of his wife. Wendler had a history of domestic violence, he had a motive, and enough evidence amassed against him, thanks to Kyle's work, to nail him to the judicial cross. Wendler maintained his innocence the whole eight years of hell he spent in prison, before the conscience of Wendler's next-door neighbor, the real murderer set him free.

The pain that man had suffered in prison—separation from his children, the physical and psychological abuse of inmate life, and the horror of losing that much of his life for a crime that he didn't commit—deeply affected Kyle. He never forgot the Wendler case, and so with his and Edgar's covert investigation turning up nothing except sketchy circumstancial evidence, some of the pressure Kyle felt to "get the mayor" had vented. He had a gut feeling about it, but he'd had a gut feeling that Wendler was guilty, too. Murder was too strong an accusation to make without evidence, so Kyle would wait and watch. Maybe something would turn up. Until that time, the mayor was suspect, but innocent.

"It's only fair," Kyle said to himself, as a car drove by on the highway and broke into his thoughts.

He looked at the market and shrugged. Okay, he'd had his look. He started the truck, turned around, and headed up the road.

He glanced at the rearview mirror and started. The light from Gathers Market glared back at him, like a single, yellow-slitted eye.

Kyle looked away and looked back. It was just the market after all. Time heals all, he thought, and let that warm him as he drove home.

# 40

"Hey, clean it up down there!" yelled Larry Allen into the
microphone. "Store opens in thirty minutes!"

From inside his office his voice was loud enough, but down
on the floor he knew it sounded like the voice of God—and it
was just that in his goddamn store, you better believe it.

He loved his new office high above the liquor department,
with its nifty two-way mirror for a window so that he could spy
on the whole operation without being seen.

He caught sight of a brown arm jutting up through the ribs
formed by the tops of the shelving giving the silver rectangular
eye of his office window the finger. Aisle seventeen—canned
vegetables. He flicked on the mike.

"Lopez, it's payday today. You want me to flush yours,
smart-ass?"

Two brown arms raised up over the aisle, palms facing Larry
Allen, and semaphored a negative. Lopez had given him trouble
before and Larry had "lost" his check. Lopez got his money, of
curse, but it took an extra day to have the check written, and
Larry had told payroll to take their time about it. Lopez, who
loved to get stinking-ass drunk the night before his day off, had
been out of money and had had to stay dry that night and come
in on his day off to pick it up.

Larry Allen had one rule in his store: Don't fuck with Larry
Allen, 'cause he'll fuck you back in speckled spades, shithead;
and don't you forget it.

One little girl was about to learn that today.

Larry leaned forward and flicked the mike switch to private,

316

then pushed a button marked Booth. "Tony," he said. He watched Tony Daley, his grocery manager, pick up the com-line phone and switch the box over to private so the communication would now only be through his telephone.

"Yeah, Larry," he heard Tony say.

"Yeah. You see Lynnanne come in, you send her up to my office pronto, got it?"

"Got it. You got my check?" asked Tony.

"What check?"

"My check. It's payday, remember?"

Larry hadn't forgotten, he just loved to hear that little edge of panic in people's voice when they think they aren't going to get their pay—the almighty dollar. "In more ways than one," he said and clicked off, watching Tony grimace up at the mirrored window and hang up.

Larry rolled his chair back and laced his hands behind his head. He really hadn't had to tell Tony to send Lynnanne up, because he wasn't about to leave this window until she came in. It was payday, all right, especially for Lynnanne. She had made the mistake of breaking Larry's rule and now he was going to fuck her back in speckled spades.

He knew the secret of payback: patience. The weakness in most people is that they're impatient, and Larry knew that most people wouldn't credit him, hothead that he was, with any patience at all—but they were wrong about that. When it came to getting even, he had all the patience in the whole fucking world.

Lynnanne was going to learn that today, too. He wondered if she was bright enough to put two and two together. Shit, all he had done was grab her tits, and she'd come off the wall—kneed him in the nuts! And Jesus Christ, hadn't that hurt. But that pain wasn't what made him move against Lynnanne; it was his pride—goddamn it, women never seemed to understand men. If Lynnanne had kneed him good and let it go at that, he'd have let her slide. But no, she had gone around bragging to everybody. It was bad for his image, made people laugh at him

317

behind his back. Well, people just don't laugh at Lawrence Medford Allen and get away with it.

Lynnanne was going to pay.

That tit-squeezing incident had happened about seven months ago, and since that time he had been just as sweet as punch to her—overtime (which she wanted), lots of it. Money, money, and more money for her—more overtime. The silly bitch probably thought he felt guilty.

Larry Allen rolled forward and grabbed a styrofoam cup of black coffee off the console, spotting Rachael Macht, one of his checkers, just coming in. A quarter to eight. Lynnanne would be in soon.

He took a sip of the hot coffee and leaned into the microphone: "Let's get it in shape!" he shouted. This time it was Rachael who raised her arm and flipped him the bird. "Anytime, sweet thing. Anytime," he whispered, and forewent any animosity toward the woman's gesture. There were victims and nonvictims, and Rachael was the latter. Larry had once put the squeeze on her and she had given him a swift kick and sent her husband, Manny (six-foot-two-inch, two-hundred-and-fifteen pound Manny), down to talk to him.

So, if Rachael wanted to express herself with her middle finger, Larry's thoughts were, It's a free country. Of course, Rachael was a nonvictim.

He kicked back and waited for Lynnanne to come in as the rest of the store readied to open up for the business of the day.

Rachael Macht stood on tiptoes to put her marking gun on top of her register. That was she could keep an eye on it, so it didn't "disappear." She'd already lost two guns to the grocery department—she couldn't prove it, but they were always stealing extra guns because that weenie Larry Allen was too cheap to buy everybody one. He said everybody should just give the one they got to the people on the next shift. Nobody's gonna do that. They'd never get the gun back, they knew that.

318

Just let somebody try to take this gun.

Rachael grunted in dissatisfaction. She'd worked for Gathers Market four years in the old store, and liked it better there. She could walk to it from her home, and it *felt* safer. She could not explain the reasons for her feelings, she just didn't like the *feel* of the store. The only reason she didn't ask for a transfer back to the store in town was that the mayor had personally asked her to work at this new one. He had said that he wanted his best checkers there. And of course, she had said yes.

After flipping that greasy Larry Allen off, Rachael walked back through the swinging double doors into the back room, pulled her buff-colored time card from its slot, punched it in the time clock, and promptly went to the ladies' lounge to have her morning bowel movement. "My bowels only move on company time" she was fond of crooning anytime Tony Daley, the grocery manager, said anything about it, then adding, "If you don't like it, go talk to Larry." Of course Larry wasn't going to say a thing, not to her. Not after her Manny had had a talk with that perverted stupid bastard.

Rachael stopped in the outer part of the lounge to put her purse in her locker. Unlike some of the checkers, she dressed for work at home, wearing her orange polyester skirt and blouse to the store, to avoid the peephole she was sure Larry Allen had managed to put in somewhere in the lounge (She and Suzy Haynes had searched the lounge high and low for it, and the rest of the restroom too, finding no peephole, but Rachael still didn't trust either room).

After she locked her purse up she pushed through the swinging door to the bathroom. It had three stalls. As usual she chose the middle one, opened the creme-colored door and looked up. The small brown square of shirt cardboard that she had taped over the vent with masking tape was still in place (she was wise to that potential peephole, too). She closed the door behind her, raised her skirt and shimmied her pantyhose and pants down over her rump, and sat down, staring at the

319

picture of Eric Estrada that she had taped to the back of the stall door. She flinched momentarily against the cool round of the seat. She let her mind float from what she would buy with the small bit left over from her paycheck, to what it was like working for a snake like Larry Allen, back to swarmy feelings of what Eric Estrada's lips would feel like on her nipples. Her minor arousal was interrupted by a familiar feeling: bowel pressure, then release, and then something unexpected, an almost imperceptibly cold . . . lick? That's what it felt like—a gross, cold lick on her cheeks down between—

It's nothing, she thought. Take it easy. Even Larry Allen can't climb through the plumbing.

She stared hopefully at the picture of Eric, but other thoughts forced themselves in. Had this stall always been so dingy? It was fresh paint, but the creme color seemed dirty, and—

There it was again, a lick. Not her imagination, a goddamn lick on her cheeks and her sex.

She opened her legs quickly and stared down past her tuft of hair into the blackness of the bowl. Glowing yellow eyes stared back at her.

She gasped in air to scream, but before the first sounds issued forth from her throat, before she could scramble up, the eyes shimmered brightly and she felt the lick again, this time hard and wet and foul, across her cheeks. It left a slimy-snail's-trail feeling on her butt. Then something quickly jutted up into her sex; it burned like hell.

She felt the scream split from her throat. She scrambled up. The thing jerked raggedly from her vagina. She opened the stall door and stumbled out. She fell to the white linoleum floor, her pantyhose and pants strangling her ankles together as she grabbed the sink and struggled to stand.

The bathroom door swung open and Suzy Haynes rushed in.

"Jesus, Rachael," said her friend, "what in the hell is the matter with you?"

"In the-thee buh-buh-bowl," Rachael choked out, backing

away from the stall door.

"What!"

"There's something in the bowl."

Suzy shot Rachael a wry look, marched to the stall, threw open the door, stepped in, waited a beat, and let loose a mocking scream. She stepped back out, a disgusted look on her face.

"Well?" asked Rachael, panting and struggling with her underwear.

Suzy stared at her for a moment, then shook her head. "Rachael, there is something in the bowl, and it ain't fruit. I looked at it, but I ain't gonna flush it for you. Hey, Rache. You okay?"

Rachael didn't answer. Her vagina throbbed dully with pain. She would have to check herself and clean up, but one thing was for sure, she didn't like this store, and she wasn't going to flush the bowl either.


The rest of the night crew had already clocked out. Harold Cager thought of them, already over at the snack bar wolfing down hot, runny eggs and rashers of bacon. *Don't wait for me, you suckers,* he thought, *I'll catch up.* He inserted the buff card, closed his big baby-blue eyes, and listened for the big *snap-whunk* of the stamper.

*Snap-whunk.*

"Doan bea' me, massa," he said to the time clock, and slid his card into its holding slot. They had added paper goods to his section today, so after he threw the canned vegetable section (a heavy piece of work in itself) he had had to throw the paper load, too, meaning he was forty minutes overtime, meaning Larry Allen (the turd) was going to throw a shit fit. Well, let him. He sits up in that big fancy office and looks down at everybody. Hell, you hardly see him on the floor anymore.

Harold grabbed his coat and Pendleton shirt from his locker and tucked them under his fat arms like a security blanket. He wore his tee shirt, stained and streaked by the night's grease and heavy sweat, pulled out and tented over the fat of his stomach. He did not bother to tuck it into his blue jeans. His heavy boots made a satisfying clunking sound as he pushed through the swinging double doors out onto the main floor. He turned and plodded along the back wall toward the produce department. As he passed by, the cool from the dairy case licked out at him, chilling his after-work sweat. He avoided looking down any of the aisles. Work was over for the day and he didn't want to see any more cans of anything.

"Hi, Steve," he said, reaching produce.

The old produce man raised a meaty arm. "Like that night shift, do ya?" he teased, then laughed.

Harold waved him off in mock disgust and walked toward the front of the store to the snack bar—which was actually more than that. It had a grill and you could get a breakfast, lunch, and dinner if you weren't looking for anything fancy.

Ruby, the snack-bar manager, spotted him coming; she smiled and moved to put the quadruple order of French fries in the pneumatic fryer. Harold loved to watch the fries come up out of that thing. It was circular, and once the basket was loaded with white finger-sized potatoes, Ruby pushed a button and the basket recessed into the top of the stove, then a stainless-steel-dome pressure lid would automatically cover the top. When the fries were done a bell would sound, and the lid would slowly open and the basket raise out automatically, the oil dripping out the basket's mesh, leaving a most welcome sight, golden brown fries.

"Hey, ain't you gonna sit with us?" asked Martino as if offended. He didn't look at the others of the night crew, all sitting around one table. Suckers loved to badger him. Who cared?

Harold said, "Hi" to Ruby and sat down to await his order, which was the same every morning: four orders of fries, two eggs, six sausage patties, and two huge glasses of milk. Ruby always waited until she spotted him, then started the order, and Harold always took the center booth that gave him the bird's-eye view of the grill.

He removed his watch and sat eyeing the deep fryer—he had it timed to the second—four minutes and thirty-eight seconds before the bell would ring.

The bell dinged a moment after his eyes moved from his watch to the pressure cooker. Ruby paid no attention, busy with the sausage and eggs. The lid raised smoothly and the basket rose smoothly and Harold smiled in anticipation, then stopped breathing in shock. He looked to see if the other guys saw it, but they were busy talking among themselves, and of course when he looked back it would be gone—he'd been working too hard.

He looked back. It wasn't gone.

It sat there in the basket, oil still draining from it, blackish, brownish, the skin shriveled up on it—a human head. The eyes were wrinkled and sunk in, staring from dark hollows.

Harold opened his mouth, but no sound came out. He turned to the crew and mouthed soundless words, then to Ruby, whose back was to him. He looked again at the head. Still there.

He closed his eyes in a rush of dizziness and rested in the dark of his own mind, until the head floated by and winked at him.

He opened his eyes suddenly, staring at the basket.

"Order's up," said Ruby. She put the plate with eggs and sausage on the counter along with two glasses of milk, and went to the basket and emptied the fries into a separate plate.

"Your order's up, Harold," repeated Ruby in irritation. He was staring at the empty stainless steel basket. He had been working too hard, that was all. He grunted "Thanks," and for the first time since he had been eating breakfast here he didn't touch the fries.


At age fifty-six Steve Gorden felt the pains of thirty-four years in the produce business. The arches of his feet sagged in agony—*agony!*—his back hurt (going out at least once every three months), and his hands looked like he picked the damned produce out in the field instead of preparing it for the customers. Despite this, he considered himself a happy man. He was ready to retire in just nine more years to a small cabin in northern California with nothing to do but remember what it was like to love up his wife, Sarah, or do it to her if he still could.

But that was nine years away. Now, he was in the produce backroom. It was large and boxy, separated from the main backroom by a cement wall. It had its own roll-down ribbed-steel receiving door, which Steve kept up and open to the outside ever since what had happened to him three days ago. Cold as it was in the morning, and despite the bitching of those under him, he liked it open and kept it that way because it let the fresh, outside air in. This place needed that, at least. It was almost unbearably claustrophobic without it—ever since three days ago, when in the end he'd thrown that damn mirror out into one of the large garbage bins, and almost quit his damn job, taken early retirement, or something.

He tried to dismiss the thoughts, clutching the clipboard with the day's inventory on it. He turned away from the open door and the fresh air into the rich vegetable smells of lettuce, yellow squash, and greens. He looked at the crates stacked eight high and in rows along the cement walls, filled with fruit and produce. He counted the crates and checked them off with a stubby pencil pulled from the pocket of his green bib apron. He purposely restricted his vision of the big gray-blue industrial "bathtub" over by the entrance to the store's floor area. Done, he turned his back on the tub and moved over to the long wooden trimming table and hung the clipboard up on the nail that used to hold the mirror.

The mirror had been there like at the old store because Steve's claim to good looks was his long wavy thick hair. It had once been a silken black, now it was an even silkier silver. He liked to check and stroke it with a brush before he went out on the floor. A little vain, he knew, but that mane up top, combined with rich brown twinkling eyes and a few soft words for the ladies, had gotten him more than a few heartthrobs in his day. He'd considered that mirror almost a tradition in his career in produce—until three damn days ago. He had been standing right where he was now, checking scheduling, after putting a bunch of damn celery in an icy bath in that monstrously large tub behind him. He heard a sound in back of him. He looked up into the mirror, and could see the rest of the room plain as day. The tub, too. And the tub was filled, not with celery, but with a white corpse!—a naked man! Floating in swamp-green slime! Steve whirled, instinctively pulling his machete from its hook on the wall, facing the corpse—except now, the corpse was gone. He was looking at the celery instead.

Too much V.O. last night, he thought. He calmed down, turned back to his scheduling, occasionally flicking a look at a tub full of celery. He became engrossed in his paperwork again, then the noise sounded again, more distinctly this time—a sloshing sound, the kind made when a person sits up in a tub after soaking their entire back and head.

Steve froze, his eyes riveted to the schedule: Tom Costa, Saturday through Thursday, three to ten. He heard more washing sounds and smelled the faint odor of decaying meat. Steve jacked his eyes up to the mirror—

The corpse was sitting up.

Brackish green slime dripped down its back. It looked back at Steve with vacant, shriveled eyes. It grinned at him, then stood up—

Steve grabbed the machete. He whirled around . . .

"Hey, Chrissakes, Stever! What the fuck are you doing!" Tom Costa stood in the doorway, the hinged batwing doors swinging behind him. "What the fuck are you doing! Scared the shit outta me!"

"The celery," Steve managed to croak out, "the celery."

Tom looked over at the tub bobbing with celery bunches. "Yeah, sure, Steve," Tom said. "Sure."

When Tom had left, Steve snatched the mirror off the wall, opened the receiving door, and trashed it right then and there. Obviously, it had been a trick of light, or fatigue or something. Celery was celery, for God's sake. But from that day on, the very first thing Steve did when he walked in that back room in the morning was open that door, weather be damned. If it was hailing golf balls or shit balls that door stayed open, no matter what!

Steve turned suddenly and stared at the empty tub suspiciously. Maybe he would take early retirement: there was just something wrong here, and he didn't know what.

Gordon Hall, the meat manager, was loading the meat case when he heard Tantenbaum scream. The thought that maybe his assistant had lost another finger to the band saw crossed his mind, but then he remembered that Franky was doing the honors this morning, and that Tantenbaum was working the meat locker, getting set up for the morning's load of beef, pork, lamb, and chicken. The frosty air in the locker nips right through the arctic jacket and fur-lined gloves necessary for long-term work in there; maybe Tantenbaum was bitching again . . .

The sound of the band saw stopped. The whapping sound of the wrapping machine stopped. Gordon looked down the long line of the meat case that he had spent all early morning loading, and could see nothing. He was down at the far end, near the seafood, and although the working area of the meat department was open to the customer's view, it was blocked from his line of sight by a wall that ran half the length of the case.

He stopped for a moment, dull metal tray resting on the edge of the case, his bald head canted, listening. There were a lot of excited voices down there now. That did it! He let the tray slide into the well and marched down behind the meat case, clumping his six foot and two hundred and thirty pounds of muscle and beer-belly down on the sawdust-covered cement.

He'd see what those sumbitches were up to!

Gordon cleared the half-wall and stared into the meat department. Tantembaum's back was half to him. Franky and Audrey (the wrapper) flanked Tantenbaum, listening to him. All three occasionally glanced at the huge freezer door gaping open at them, its insides frosty with the cold ragged sight of red meat and dead white fat swinging from rollered meat hooks. It looked like the throat of some ravenous monster. Banks of fluorescent tubes bathed the cutting floor and the locker, and for just a moment, as Gordon heard the sounds of distress but was unable to understand the words, the three, dressed in their white smocks streaked with blood and gristle, looked like tainted angels amid the blood and carnage of a senseless massacre.

"What is it?" he asked in a quiet, firm voice.

Tantenbaum swung his head around and Gordon watched a flooding of relief across Tantenbaum's face, the face of a soldier reassured by the presence of an officer. The scared man reached out and gripped Gordon just above the wrists as if for reassurance, emphasizing that what he was about to say was serious, and true. "The meat moved," he said in a controlled voice, pointing toward the open locker door with his small chin. "It moved, for Chrissakes, Gordon! I swear!"

Gordon sucked in a deep breath in through his nose—no alcohol. He studied Tantenbaum's face for a moment: brown eyes, wild, dark hair disheveled from shaking his head to violently. His face twisted, anxiously beseeching Gordon to believe him.

"Okay, okay," reassured Gordon, moving his arms away to break Tantenbaum's grip. He stared at the open freezer door. "You say the meat moved?"

"Yeah," answered the scared man, nodding his head for emphasis.

"Shaking on the hooks?"

"That and more, Gordon. More!"

"All right, everybody back to work." Gordon shooed them with his hands. They stood staring at him blankly. "Back to work, I said." He raised his voice enough to let them know he meant business. "Tantenbaum—you finish loading the case. The damn store opens in ten minutes; let's get to work."

Amid mumbling they moved off toward their work, and Gordon turned around and faced the freezer door. He walked over and picked up the olive-drab arctic coat that lay where Tantenbaum had thrown it. He picked it up and put it on, then retrieved the gloves and pulled these on. Maybe the chill had gotten to Tantenbaum—working in the cold box for any length of time could freeze the bejesus out of a man. Back in '70, poor old Mark Doughty had accidently gotten locked in a locker over a weekend and died, frozen stiff like a popcicle.

As Gordon pulled the hood up over his bald head, it caught on his white safety helmet. He removed it and felt the synthetic fur warm his pate as the hood covered it.

He grabbed the freezer door with his black gloved hands and entered the box purposefully, pulling it shut behind him. He paused thoughtfully, studying the locker. It was huge—forty feet wide by eight feet long. The big sides of beef, lamb, and pork hung like human bodies from long, rollered hooks. None of the meat was moving, jiggling, or any such thing. He had cut short the powwow outside for two reasons: one, no work was getting done, and the store was about to open; two, Tantenbaum needed calming, and the best way to do that was to get him back to work; if there was anything wrong in here, Gordon would find it.

The blower booted in suddenly with an electrical whine. Involuntarily, Gordon flinched. A blast of cold air chilled his face. He looked up at the blower's vents and cursed—the damn door had been open too long, now he was going to walk around in a blizzard. The jacket or no, it was still more comfortable when it was just cold. Damn that Tantenbaum.

Gorden stepped forward, moving off to the right past a box of steer heads—brains, the Indians and some of the old

328

westerners loved the brains. The sunken, collapsed eyes of the white bovine skulls stared up at him, and dumbly he stared back at them, patting opposite arms to ward off the cold.

He pulled his eyes away from those of the dead steers and looked at the hanging meat basking in the cold fluorescent light of the box, unmoving.

What had Tantenbaum seen? Gordon wondered. There's nothing in here, but he'd better check the other end of the box just to make sure. Maybe somebody had gotten in. There was another door down there, the receiving door, kept locked, except when meat was coming in. Surely if anybody did get in here it would have to be through the front door; and besides, that Tantenbaum would have spotted someone in here. Wouldn't he?

Gordon stopped halfway down the length of the galvanized gray metal walls, trying to listen over the whirring hum of the blower. Nothing. He cursed the blower and the hanging meat blocking his view of the other side. Hell, he couldn't even get a clear view of either end of the box, the *doors* to this damn oversized coffin. The blower shut off suddenly and he jumped at the abrupt silence. He didn't like it in here. It was . . . *vile*. He wanted out, to be anyplace but here. Still he moved toward the locked end of the box. He approached it from around a hanging side of beef. It was locked. That was good. No one in from that side. He laughed nervously. The sound died flat in the cold. It's too damn quiet in here, he thought. It's too damn quiet without that blower.

He looked at the hanging sides of beef that blocked his view of the other side of the box, the side with the unlocked door in it. Jiggling. Isn't that the way Tantenbaum described it? The idea came to him quickly and he turned around, grabbing a lever on the box by the wall, pulling it, and looking up at the chain-driven track that supported the rollered hooks. The chain moved, the hooks moved, the meat moved. He threw the switch: the chain stopped, the hooks stopped, the sides of meat stopped . . . and swung, gently. In fact you could say they jiggled. That's right, they were jiggling, if you really looked at them. And, by God, that was it. A short maybe in the electrical, maybe; the chain moves slightly, the meat jiggles, and Tantenbaum goes lighting out of the box like there was a damn monster in here, for Christ's sake. Damn story had given Gordon the willies, and the damn smell was just from the blower—after all, it hadn't started until *after* that ol' blower had kicked in, had it? Nope. Better to get out of this box and get a repairman out here to look at that thing before all the meat gets tainted with the stink if it hasn't al—

A muted *thunk* echoed through the room.

The beef quarters were still by now, and that *thunk* had been a good one, like a cardboard meat box falling off a wheeled flat-top table. And hadn't he heard the scraping skitter of skull bones tumbling over themselves onto the concrete floor? Hadn't he?

He should look. But he wasn't going to. He was just going to walk on the other side of the box, right down the side there, turn left and out that d—

*Thwack. Thwack.*

Gordon started moving according to his plan, the right side of the box and down the aisle there. He tried to call out, but his mouth was dry, and his lungs wouldn't pump the damn air through his throat properly. Those second sounds he recognized. The sound of a beef quarter dropped on the cold cement floor . . .

*Thwack. Thwack. Thwack. Thwack. Thwack.*

The chain jiggled on this side of the track, the meat swung, jiggling. He stopped a quarter way down the length, and found his voice.

"All right," he said with courage as thin as butcher paper, "I know you're in here, and I'm telling you to walk out that freezer—"

*Thwack. Thwack. Thwack.*

Some dummy must be pulling them off. Gordon's view was still blocked by a triple line of beef. He hunkered down on all

330

fours. The cold from the cement floor drove up into his knees and hands like spikes of ice. The smell of wood shavings tickled his nose, a bouquet mixed with the smell of butchered meat in the room.

The sides of beef lay where they had fallen. The steer heads were scattered across that side of the floor. But no legs, no human legs. No boots, nothing.

He stood. His legs felt like tubes filled with cold rocks. He forced them to move. He was afraid he was going to shit his pants.

He heard more noises. Scratchy, whispering noises, like skulls and meat being dragged over cold, cold concrete.

By God, he wasn't going on his knees again. He was just getting the hell out of—

*Ahhh! Ahhh!*

It was a horrible, blood-freezing sound, lungless and mocking.

His legs failed him. He froze.

Don't Ahh again, he thought.

*Ahh-Ahhh!*

Fuck.

He heard scratchy, scraping sounds, gathering in the room, another *Ahh*, this time by the door. Two *Ahhs*, two diff—

*Ahh-Aaahhhhhhhh!*

Three *Ahhs* three different places. God, let me out of here, please!

Now there were more scraping sounds—stiff, scraping sounds.

He dropped to his knees, looked, and tried to scream. He couldn't.

Oh, dear Jesus God!

The things he was staring at were a mockery of his butcher's art. The left and right front and hind quarters of beef had reassembled themselves. No neck, but the beef skulls sat where the neck should go. There were three of them, the closest not thirty feet away (on the other side of the hanging meat, thank

331

God), a second next to the fallen box of heads, and the third . . . the third was down by the door.

They moved toward him, drag-scraping on the stumps of missing legs.

*Ah-Ahh-AAhhhhh!* The bellowing thundered through the locker. All three bawled at once. Their skulls turned in the neck openings to point flaccid eyes at him. They bawled again and inched their way toward him.

Gordon began to shake all over. He rose unsteadily on his feet. A long pent-up scream issued from his throat, quavering timidly at first then warbling in full, unabashed terror. He bolted, not looking, not caring, toward the door.

One of the things turned the corner of the aisle and stared at him. He heard the others, on the side, move toward him faster. Scraping along fast to catch him. The one in front of him lowed. Its skull pinwheeled on its axis, its eyes glowing yellow fire.

He screamed even louder. *Got to go past it, only one door, shit!* The other cow corpses were to his side, so he leaped All-America-Football fashion over the beast, but not quite high enough. His left boot caught and he tumbled into the meat and back around so that he faced the pursuers. He hit more hanging meat, slid, and banged up against the door and sat staring, frozen in fear. The things turned and began shuffling toward him. They were going to *get him!*

He scrambled backward, tumbled, and rolled. He landed flat on his back, still panicked until he saw Tantenbaum, Audrey, and Franky standing over him. He was outside the locker! Thank God!

"What in the fuck is going on, Gordie?" asked Franky. He looked inside the freezer. "Christ, will you look at that box? It's a mess!"

"Did it jiggle?" asked Tantenbaum.

"Look at you," said Audrey in marvelment.

Gordon regained his feet and whirled around, ripping at the gloves, then the coat. "Let me the fuck out of here!" he shouted, throwing the coat and gloves away. "You tell Larry I quit! I quit quit *quit!*"

He pulled an envelope from under his smock and threw it at Franky, hitting him in the face. It was a request for transfer back to the old store. The old, nice store. But screw that now. He quit!


After what had happened to him in that spooky lower warehouse, Coogle felt he had a right to knock back a little of mother's milk and daddy's scotch; Larry Allen could go to hell.

Coogle sat on an upended blue milk crate with his back against the cool cement wall, fifty feet from the stairwell leading up into the dimly lit upper warehouse. He cupped a white china mug in both hands, sitting on his left knee that jutted up crossed over his right. Wide lazy smoke twirled its way up from the tip of his cigar tucked between fingers of his left hand. Beside his makeshift easy chair sat a half-gallon leaker from the milk box and a pint of Cutty Sark, opened, half-full. Coogle raised the cup and knocked back the remains of his third cupful of snockered cow.

Larry Allen could go down in that basement and get the washer, he thought. He could just do that, 'cause Coogle Washington Carver wasn't going down there no more.

Coogle slipped his cigar between his lips and puffed, chewing on the end, then leaned sideways and pulled up the pint and poured a quarter-cupful of the hooch, set the pint down, and filled the cup with milk. He set the leaker down and let the cup regain its position on his knee. He was getting drunk and didn't care.

A scratching sound echoed faintly in the warehouse, way off to the left. It was dark there, of course—that dumb-ass Larry lit every seventh bulb, both in the upper and the lower warehouse, to save money. Both levels were filled with large inkwell shadows and eerie distortions. Coogle peered in that direction for a long time. This area ran one hundred yards in length and about a hundred and fifty feet wide. It was empty of goods to speak of, but not empty of everything. There were odds and ends, bones of things to be. Throughout the warehouse, roller conveyor sections raised on trestles for moving boxes of groceries around wove and snaked in and out of weak yellow blotches of light; conveyor belts—still unused—waited for the day when the mayor's other stores were open and they would be needed to handle the central buying volume. The belts descended through the floor to the main-floor warehouse, passing such a distance that the noise from below was never heard up here. Directly across the room from Coogle were the rectangular openings into the catwalk tunnels that ran around the perimeter of the display floor. It was through these that someone entered to watch for shoplifters, crouching down in the tight space and moving over to the mirrored eyes that viewed the main floor.

No one ever used them. Not yet. Theft was minimal. Word got around, about Larry Allen's store. It was a bad place to shoplift.

Coogle jerked his head back to one of the catwalk holes. Inky black. Had something moved?

He watched intently until satisfied. In moving his eyes back to his doctored milk, he noticed the bodies . . . the mannequins. They stood, about fifty of them, some one hundred feet away . . . seventy-five feet away?

He could have sworn they were further away than that when he'd come up here.

He gazed at them. They were head and half-torso models on long metal legs attached to wheels for easy mobility . . . so they can skate, he thought suddenly, skate around . . . skate closer and closer to *you!*

He sipped his milky booze and smoked, still staring at the mannequins. They were for the mayor's department store when it was complete. He'd gotten a deal on them, and had bought and stored them up here. Out of the fifty or so, eight were black. Someone had put a panama hat and sunglasses on one black mannequin and hung a sign made of cardboard and straw baling twine around his neck: *Calypso Joe*, it read. It was out in front of the others and . . . staring at him?

Coogle examined his cup. Enough of this stuff.

A scraping sound, like something wiggling, squeezing its way through a tight space, rose faintly from across the darkness. He thought he saw something move past one of the crawl-space openings, eight violet eyes gleaming all in a row, gliding by, peering out of the opening and continuing on toward the left.

Not again, thought Coogle. Earlier in the lower basement, someone had turned out the damn lights, leaving him in total darkness. The taunts "Niggah! Niggah!" came from everywhere and he'd run blindly toward the elevator, groping feeling, finding it, closing the double doors and fingering the buttons in the dark. As the elevator started up he felt relieved to be safe, and pissed off that he would be scared of whitey's taunts. Then he realized that he was not alone in the blackness of the elevator. The air was muggy and rank. He felt paralyzed as something moved in the dark toward him, its stink growing, a ragged wheezing sound swelling louder until it seemed to be inches from him . . .

And then, thank God, the elevator door had opened on the main floor and light rushed in and there was nothing there. But he'd been scared, all right. Afraid. And no one would believe him. And he knew that all that happened in the basement warehouse hadn't been a joke. He had grabbed his bottle and milk and come up here to be alone. To drink, smoke, and calm his Mississippi mule-shit nerves. And now he knew that this had been a mistake too.

With forced calm he set his cup down. He ground his cigar out with a shoe on the floor, then picked up his bottle and its cap and screwed it on, retrieved his cup, and stood up correctly.

Damn! Calypso Joe was only fifty feet away now.

Coogle hurried toward the stairs. He heard the scraping sound again, then a digging sound like something trying to come out of the crawl-space opening.

He kept moving, staring straight ahead at the stairwell. He heard wheels squeak . . . rolling? He quickened his pace. Now ten feet from the well and the descending stairs. The wheel sounds rose and he moved faster, and reached the well. He clopped swiftly down the stairs, feeling relief and release on the tenth stair, as if the evil (up there, anyway) could go no further. He knew he'd been drinking, and that could be part of it, but he also knew what he saw and what he heard. He knew he couldn't tell anyone either, no one would believe him, especially about what he saw. Now, that had to be a 'lucination, 'cause he'd seen more than just something passing by. He'd seen a leg pop out the hole and he recognized that kind of leg, and them eyes. But that just had to be a 'lucination, 'cause spiders just don't get that big. They just don't!


Larry Allen called Lynnanne up to his office even before she was fully into the store. She didn't seem to hear him, so he repeated it again gently. He saw her head swing up to his office window and point toward the back and make a gesture miming clocking in.

"I'll write you in," he said over the loudspeaker. "Come on up." Christ, this a first, he thought, she isn't carrying her Bible. Probably got a pocket one in her purse.

She smiled at him grandly, like she had been doing since he'd been giving her all the extra hours, the overtime that she needed to get that lemon-yellow VW bug she drove. She had come to him and asked for a raise, and explained why, and he'd said he couldn't just give a raise, that there were rules about that, but he could promise her overtime if she was willing to work. She agreed gratefully, never realizing that he was giving her rope to hang by. It was all part of the payback. Her father had died early this year, and Larry had asked her if she was going to be able to make it, her mother not well and her brother still only seven. Tears had popped into her eyes as she said how thankful she was to have this job and the overtime. She could just make it with that and the small pension the family got from the Gathers' grainery. Larry had said that he was glad to help.

So with a month to let that little talk cool off, he was ready, and watched her shoulder-length hair bounce around her pretty oval face as she passed by the checkstands, smiling, a happy girl.

"You shouldn't have fucked with me, Blondie," he muttered to himself as she passed into the liquor department and out of sight.

He hurried from his chair and opened the door, turned the lock on it, and, leaving the door opened, scooted behind his desk and sat down.

She knocked lightly, then entered, all smiles. "Hi, Larry!" she said.

"Hi! Close the door a minute, will ya?" He smiled back. She closed the door behind her; Larry heard it click, and felt good knowing that no one could come in.

"What's up, Doc?" asked Lynnanne. He eyed her outfit—a skirt and a zippered short-sleeve blouse that hugged the swell of her breasts and ran sensually around the curve of her hips and thighs. He felt an erection growing, pressing against his pants.

"I've got your paycheck here," he said, and raised a white envelope waving it so that it made a flapping sound, watching her pretty green eyes dance with the motion.

She reached over the desk and he handed it to her. God, her face was angelic! That pert nose, soft red lips, only a little makeup. She pulled the envelope from him, grinning, obviously relieved that that was what he wanted. "Thank you." She started to go on by.

"Got some bad news for you, Lynnanne," Larry said with false reluctance.

She stiffened. He could read her thoughts: fired. I've been fired. The fear was written on her face like the headline on the Briggs City *Review*.

He let her dangle for a moment. When he spoke, he let a little more of the false pain into his voice: "Going to cut your hours, Lynnanne. Cut back to forty . . . maybe less."

She bit her lip.

"I need that overtime, Larry. I really *need* it."

*Yeah, and I needed to squeeze your tits too, bitch, six months ago. But you had to kick me and make me look foolish. You bragged about it. You broke my rule. You fucked Larry, now he's gonna fuck you back in speckled spades, baby.*

"I know that you do," he said with sympathy, "but . . ." He hesitated, pretending to search for the right words to ease his embarrassment. "To tell you the truth I *could* keep giving you the overtime."

Her face quivered in puzzlement.

"But I got to asking myself, why should I stick my neck out for her, she's done nothing for me. I mean, there are plenty of other girls who are *grateful* for the overtime . . . overtime I can't give them because I'm giving it to you . . ." He nodded at the clear and reasonable truth of his words.

She dropped her purse on his desk firmly and leaned toward him. Her breasts hung down, lovely against the fabric. If she'd just let him touch them, he never would have had to get even, and she wouldn't be in this fix; but the truth was, he was kinda glad things had worked out this way. He could smell her lemony perfume, her trademark.

"I am grateful, Larry. Very, very grateful. I asked you about the overtime before I got the car . . . I can't make it without the money. I told you."

"Yeah, I know," he replied, "but you didn't expect me to keep it up indefinitely, did you?"

"You said you would!"

"Well, maybe if you were grateful . . ."

"I am grateful!"

"No. No. You're grateful to that wimpy greaseball Tom, that's who you're grateful to."

She started to speak, then gaped at him with dawning

understanding. Yeah! he thought. Reality time, bitch. You want *more* reality, try looking under my desk. My cock's going to explode!

"Yeah," Larry said, *"he* spends ten bucks on you for a date and you're all over *him; me?* I give you thousands of dollars in overtime and what do I get? Huh? *I* can't even get to squeeze your *tits!"*

Her face whitened with shock.

He smiled. "That's right. I never forget. You hurt my feelings, too. I liked you . . ."

"I—I—I like you too, Larry, but . . ."

"But what!"

"But . . . Tom is my boyfriend. I l-l-love him. You, you're m-m-married . . ."

"Don't talk about my wife!" he snapped. "Just think about the overtime!"

"I'm grateful for the overtime. I—I need the overtime . . ." Her body began to tremble. "I—I have to have it, my family depends on it . . ."

He stared at her chest. "The overtime's not the problem. I can stick my neck out for you, as long as I know that you're grateful . . . Christ, I've always wanted to see your breasts, y'know that?" His voice sounded husky and nervous in his ears.

She looked around at the window. The first shoppers were coming in.

"It's a mirror, remember, honey? No one can see in. The door is locked, too. Why don't you move around the desk here?" He motioned. She hesitated, then inched around. He turned in his swivel chair and beckoned her forward with both hands.

"My family needs the money," she mumbled, then balked, defiance in her face. She started to speak. He silenced her with a raised finger. The defiance faded into misery and guilt.

"I've always wanted to see them," said Larry, pointed with his chin. She hesitated, her eyes growing wet, then grasped the zipper of her blouse. She pulled it down slowly and unhooked it at the bottom, exposing her bra.

She began to cry silently.

Larry reached up and touched the lemon-colored brassiere. "Yellow's your best color, Lynnanne. Take the top off and I'll help you with your bra if you want."

"I can do it," she pouted, her mouth smacking with spit. The tears tracked down her rosy cheeks.

"I *said* I'll help you."

She dropped her arms to the side.

"Now, that's a good girl." He reached up for the brassiere. "And you're gonna do everything I tell you, right?"

She closed her eyes, and nodded.


Larry guided Lynnanne's head forward, unzipped his pants, and fed his engorged member into her mouth. God, that felt good. He rested his fingertips on her head and stared as her blond hair bobbed up and down. He'd been holding off coming as long as possible, but it just wouldn't hold too much longer. "Lynnanne," he said, "no, don't stop . . . that's it . . . ooh-ooh it feels good . . ." The trouble with you, he thought, is that you broke my rule . . . *He was ready now, almost, all most* . . . because when you-*ou* fuck with ol' Larry, you're gonna get fucked back in speckled spades.

He moaned as he came, and thought what a wonderful job he had. What a wonderful store!

# 41

Kyle heard the roar of Leo's Corvette crack the morning calm of the neighborhood. He grinned ear-to-ear. Leo was here! He ran and made the porch in time to see his old friend's yellow machine take a bump and glide into the drive. He bounded over to the car and opened the door. Leo screwed up his bullfrog face, roared with laughter, and popped out of the car.

"Key-rist," said Leo, "what a soft job you lucked into, Rookie. Clean air. Sunshine, for Key-rist's sakes. A real lay back-and-send-me-the-check job, I swear. Key-rist!"

Leo nearly shook Kyle's hand off, then pulled a fat cigar from his shirt and lit it up with a Zippo, a souvenir from the Korean War. Kyle was amazed at how little Leo had changed over the years that he had known him. At fifty, his hair, as full and rich as Kyle's, still held its natural sandy color. He'd wrapped his barrel chest in a white dress shirt, and covered his boxy hips and bantam legs with new Levi's. Western boots added a little extra stature to his five-foot-eight-inch height.

"Urban cowboy?" Kyle ventured.

Leo dragged generously on his cigar, then released a smoke screen from between his thick lips that would make a chemical-weapons engineer weep with pride. "The women love it," he bragged, "they simply *love* it."

Kyle guided his friend toward the door. "I bet they just love that cigar, too, Leo," he said.

"You know what they say, Rookie: 'Wait'll the smoke clears'—well, hell, *I* make the smoke. Without me there'd be none to clear!"

Kyle put a quick arm around his old friend, and led him into the house. He felt like a kid reunited with his best friend after a long, lonely summer. Leo the Magnificent had arrived! And Kyle had taken Thursday and Friday off just for him.

Kyle led him to the refrigerator and opened it barndoor wide. *"Voila!"* he said. "For the Ritual!"

"To the Ritual!" lauded Leo.

Kyle pointed proudly to the refrigerator contents: cases of Budweiser, pounds of potato salad, and lots of steaks. All this for the Ritual, a tradition that began back when Kyle was a rookie and Leo a sergeant, back before Kyle was married. Breakfast consisted of one filet mignon, medium-rare for Leo, medium-well for Kyle, and mounds of potato salad, and beer. Lunch would be a repeat of breakfast, except two steaks each would be consumed. And dinner a repeat of lunch, except by this time both men would be three sheets to the wind and having a good old time.

Kyle ripped out two cans of Bud and threw them at Leo, who caught each with a grunt. Kyle pulled out another two beers and closed the refrigerator door. The ice-cold cans tingled in his hands. Leo put down his cigar on the white porcelain of the sink. He popped the tabs on the cans, then drained them both. Kyle watched Leo's Adam's apple dance as the beer went down. Leo let the second can drop from his face and grimaced crazily. He held the two cans out in front of him, almost touching Kyle's ribs, crushed them, and belched, "I'm a *man!*" He threw them over his shoulders, and they clattered to the floor.

Kyle's turn. He popped the tops of his own cans. Of all the aspect of the Ritual, drinking beer in the morning was the worst. But the Ritual was the Ritual. He tilted back his first, letting fluid icicles run down his gullet. He killed the second can, belched, "I'm a man!" He squeezed their empty little bodies to recyclable death, and threw them over his shoulder. They clipped the cupboards and crashed to the floor . . .

The Ritual had begun.

Kyle loosed a couple of steaks from the refrigerator and led

342

Leo outside. Leo had given him an estimated time of arrival, so Kyle had timed the lighting of the barbecue. The coals were now hot gray in color. The weather cooperated too: seventy degrees, blue skies, and no clouds. Perfect!

"Take a chair," Kyle said as he moved over to the grill. Leo sat down in a green-and-yellow lawn chair separated from another chair by a white-topped red plastic ice chest. "Beer in there." Kyle indicated the chest with his fork as he unwrapped the meat and prepared it on the butcher-block sideboard of the BBQ. He felt suddenly uneasy, staring at the meat, punching random holes in it with his fork. He had asked Leo down here for more than a visit, more than the Ritual. Did Leo know that? He looked up. Leo was giving him that wall-eyed stare through a rising raft of blue-gray smoke. He had not taken a beer.

"Why don't we get the business out of the way first, Rookie," said his old friend, "that way we can have the rest of the day off. Is it the dream?" He sounded like an older brother.

Thank God for you, Leo, thought Kyle. He dropped the steaks on the grill—they sizzled, and filled the air with tangy smoke. "There are a number of things, Leo."

"I've got all day, Rookie."

"Most of it is business, not personal . . . except it is personal, in a way . . ."

"Uh-oh. Leave you alone for a minute, and the bleeding heart is saving the world."

Kyle smiled absently at him, the savory smoke from the steaks rising in his nostrils. His mind was away now, organizing, so he could present all the facts in an unbiased manner to Leo's trained mind. People often underestimated Leo, judging his intelligence by his looks. Some of them had gotten rude surprises, including long and nasty jail terms.

Kyle turned the steaks to seal in the juices, and began to speak. He knew that when he had finished, every detail of what he had said would be firmly in Leo's mind. By the time they'd finished their steaks he'd told Leo everything about the Cathy Pickers murder, the Dave Pickers murder, Leonard Phael's head, Kyle's belief that the mayor had something to do with the latter deaths, and finally, with great hesitation, about Lisa's ghost and, hardest of all, Ravana. During all this talking Leo said absolutely nothing.

"I'm writing all this up, Leo. Documentation. The most validation comes from Dr. Lyon's work on the Laikute. I've got to question her some more. She told me the Laikute had nothing to do with Cathy Pickers, yet in her book on their beliefs, for the Omen of Ravana's coming she describes the decapitation along with the genitals in the mouth. Also something about 'the face and loins devoured.' Dr. Lyon is out of the country. Sounds cult to me, but other than the murders, there's no cult activity around that I can find."

Kyle was finished. He watched Leo take a sip of beer, and appear to listen to a bluebird singing. Leo relit his cigar, and slipped his Zippo back into his pants pocket. "Okay," he said. "Let's take it from the top."

Kyle smiled; some things never change. 'Let's take it from the top' was one of them. Leo enumerating the items on his thick stubby fingers was another.

"One. The girl's murder. That's, what . . . sixteen years ago. To be frank, Kyle, you've got nothing new—"

"Except Melinda Belardis," interjected Kyle.

"She's—"

"The diplomat's daughter, who married a diplomat. She was Cathy's best friend. She went overseas about three months before the murder. I spoke with her mother. Now, the girl's overseas, but is expected back sometime this month. Her mother promised me that she would have her give me a call when she gets—"

"I don't see what good that will do. Face it, Kyle, the case deserved the morgue and you only raised the dead because of the old man. Bleeding-heart Kyle. It'll be the death of you and me both." Leo shook his head, then continued, "What I'm saying is; it's no problem. When the woman calls, ask her your questions and then bury it—you did your good deed for your friend. Remember what I told you about who's responsible for the world: God. Not you."

Leo's middle finger popped up next to his index finger. "Two . . . and I'm going to combine the mayor on this one. Someone killed your friend Pickers, probably that Phael guy; now investigate that, but the head-in-the-tree one, well, you've said it yourself, there aren't any clues, not a one. The cult thing, but there's no other cult activity around. Dead end.

"And Key-rist! to try and hang the old man's murder on Neil Gathers, Kyle. You've come up with nothing but hearsay evidence, and that's not even about the murder, but about " shady" deals, etcetera . . ."

"I know that he did it!" Kyle was embarrassed by the thunder in his own voice.

"Hunch," stated Leo. "A hunch."

"My hunches—"

"Yes, yes." Leo pointed his cigar at him like an accusation. "But it was the facts that got your collar convicted—not hunches!"

Kyle looked away and tried to calm down.

"No sweat, kid." He puffed on his cigar in little toots and the smoke hung in Kyle's nose. "I'll tell you what," said Leo. "I want you to think about how it is around here. How much you like it. How well do you think you would do without it? Have you thought of that, kid?"

"Yes," Kyle said. The thought had been as recurrent as his nightmare had been when he first had set foot in this town. It was as if it had replaced the dream. He knew what Leo was getting at.

"Well, how would you do without it?"

"I don't know."

"Don't skirt it, Kyle. We both know how badly you need this"—he waved around the yard with his cigar—"because this was part of the program, wasn't it?"

Kyle remained silent as the vivid memory of Leo, almost two years ago, sitting much as he was sitting now, with his gruff

345

voice and waving that damn cigar around a semiprivate patient lounge at Woodhaven, lit up in his mind: Leo talking about "the program" and how the three steps of his plan would work. He'd enumerated them on his short stubby fingers then, too. One, getting out of the hospital; two, living outside the hospital; and three, finding an environment to encourage growth and stability. All these to help Kyle rebuild his mind, his self-confidence—and this had been it, this yard, this house, this town, this job—all part of the program. Leo's program. And it had worked, Kyle knew that. Kyle felt better . . . hell, he *was* better . . . and so now what Leo had left unspoken twirled precariously around in Kyle's head, like a thousand knives let loose at once to slice into his brain if he let them. The thought: if the town and the job meant so much to him, to his stability, why was he trying so hard to bring them tumbling down around him? Why?

It wasn't as simple as that, he countered mentally, but a small nagging voice in his mind told him that it was.

"I can't stop being a policeman, Leo . . ."

"Not asking you to. I'm telling you to start acting like one. You've poked around this thing more than enough to see that if the mayor is guilty, there's no way to get him. Personally, it looks to me like you're going after him just to make him mad, and have him boot you out of paradise so you can play in the rubber room again . . ."

"Knock it off, Leo."

"No, *you* knock it off, Rookie. You've done every fucking thing in the book and by the book to follow through with the investigation and you've come up with zip. Neil Gathers is no dummy; careful as you are, he's gonna pick up on your questions sooner or later and you're gonna look fat, dumb, and unemployed. Not because you were being a good policeman, but because you put more emphasis on this than you should, because of a hunch, and/or personal reasons."

"My hunches have saved your ass a lot of times, if I may refresh your memory."

"My memory serves me fine. And you're right, your hunches have saved my ass on many a mad, mad day, my boy. But that was P-W. You know what P-W is, Rookie?"

"No."

"Pre-Woodhaven. Got it?"

"I'm better, now."

"Yeah, but you're not the same."

"I know the mayor had something to do with Dave Pickers's death."

"No, no. You *think* that the mayor had something to do with Dave Pickers's death. You *know* that your investigation has turned up zip, and that there's nowhere to go with it. Which brings me to my point about this and the whole damn thing, including your ghost story: everything points to an attempt—unconscious, I grant you—to sledgehammer the good foundation of the normal life you've found for yourself—self-destruction, believe me, and you've got to turn that around, right now."

"Let me show you the flow sheet with the writing on it. The crayon marks."

"No need. I believe there's writing on it, but what I don't believe is how those marks and that writing got on the flow sheet."

"Leo—"

"Let me finish. Let me ask you this: is there anyone else that has seen what you've seen either with you or without you?"

"No, but—"

"No, but *no!* And the crayon markings could have been written in your sleep, some form of sleep walking, and the noises . . . well, hell, Kyle. You've come a long way, and you're doing fine. The noises are a little aftershock, that's all. You've got no proof—*outside* proof—and I venture to say that's because it's all up there in that Phi Beta Kappa mind of yours. Let it ride and it'll go away."

Kyle sat with Leo in a soupy limbo for a moment, resisting the thought at first, but finally letting it anchor itself in his

347

mind. Leo made sense. All of that could have happened in Kyle's head. And it was that thought that so much *could* have happened in his mind, and yet be unreal, that made him shudder.

"What about the tree, Leo? And Dave's painting?"

Leo examined the stub of his cigar and looked out over the lawn as he speculated. "Lot of trees like that around, Kyle. You see one that looks like the one in your dreams, you look real hard, and it becomes that tree—a trick of mind. The old man's painting has you in it because you're his friend, and that thing in your dream because maybe he's read a book on the Indian devil, too. Never can tell."

"But that means I'm crazy . . ."

"No. I never would have recommended you for this job if I thought that. It's just a bad area in your mind come to surface in a peculiar way, and you'll handle it, just the way you handle the first steps of the program—it'll fade away, believe me.

"You haven't had the dream, have you?"

Kyle shook his head, almost thankfully. "Not in a long, long time," he said.

"Proof. Q.E.D."

"What do I do with what I have?"

"Just what you did. Which is just what I told you to do to get out of Woodhaven and back on your feet; you *choose* to ignore those things that are detrimental to you. You drop the investigation, you drop the fantasy, and you *choose* to live a normal life: Remember, in Mr. Rogers' Neighborhood, you can't get to the Land of Make Believe unless you take the trolley. Don't get on the trolley and you'll be fine.

"And don't worry about responsibility—*I'm* telling you to do it, Rookie, so it's my game, now. Remember the rules: I'm in charge until you are A-Okay, that was our deal, wasn't it?"

"Yes." Yes, that was their deal and it had worked so far. He was out of Woodhaven and living a normal life.

"And you agree to do what I say?"

Kyle hesitated briefly, the flutter of relief that he always felt

348

when Leo had tucked away another problem palpitating his mind. "I agree," he said.

"Good. Good," said Leo, patting him on his leg. "Now, let's get on with the Ritual—'I'm a man,' remember?"

"That sounds good," Kyle said, and scooped out a couple of Buds and handed them to Leo. "That sounds real good." The Ritual began in earnest at that point and lasted into the afternoon. When Kyle got good and drunk he told his friend about Michele, and how he really felt about her, his caring and his fear, his love for Curtis and about Pickers's niece, and how that relationship seemed to be on its last leg. Leo advised that he go for Michele, and not live in fear of what might become; even inebriated Kyle felt uneasy about the advice, because with his inhibitions lowered with alcohol, he could face the naked truth—he could love that woman, and maybe already did.

A late afternoon telephone call from the Parker Center in L.A. cut an overnight stay by Leo short. He was needed tomorrow morning, the chief was having an emergency meeting on manpower, a must call for Leo. Kyle put on a pot of coffee and they spent the next three hours sobering up, and then Leo was off after extracting a promise from Kyle to do as he had advised and drop the investigation. Kyle agreed, and when he did, relief flooded him. Leo had done it again, set him free.

Kyle hit the rack at nine, an hour after Leo had left. He fell into a contented sleep that lasted into the early hours of the morning, until he realized he was having the dream again, with the robed figure beckoning. He was terrified at first, then fearfully began to move in a circle around the tree. The figure seemed to want to show him something. As Kyle moved, it became clear what the figure had in mind. Stripped naked and hanging upside down from the lower limb of the tree were Michele and Curtis, their arms just missing the surface of the brain/ground. They were alive and wiggling, staring at him, calling out, their voices sounding distant although they were only fifty feet from him. The robed figure moved behind them, its yellow eyes burning. Michele and Curtis did not seem to see him. Kyle shouted warnings, but his legs would not move—he was too terrified. The giant snakes writhed and hissed at him from the branches. He shouted to Michele and Curtis to look out behind them, but they only shouted at him to help save them. Kyle tried to avert his head when the figure reached them, but some ungodly will beyond his own control held him rigid, forcing his eyes to remain open and watch. From the sleeves of the thing's robe, green reptilian hands with sharp black talons extended and gripped Michele's legs, then a green, scaly snout appeared from under the cowl and a mouth opened wide, exposing large razor teeth. The thing paused for a moment. Its yellow eyes glowered slyly. It smiled with wicked amusement at Kyle. Then It bit into Michele, and tore the flesh from her body, in bloody, ragged chunks.

Somewhere in the dark mist of sleep the Grateful Dead were raising the unliving with the jarring *twangs* of steel guitars and the *boom-boom-ratta-tat-tat* of a god-awful drum. Michele buried her head deeply with a large pillow and reached out with one flailing hand to strangle the group to make herself grateful and them dead. Her hand scraped the smooth wood surface of her night table and the cold glass trunk of the lamp. No radio. "Oh, God, will it ever stop," she mumbled into her mattress. Cuatiously, she raised one end of the pillow, slit an eye, and groaned at the radio, mocking her with its 6:25 AM eyes. It screamed its hard-rock obscenities from six feet away, couched like an evil cat on the mahogany rocking chair, its brown tail plugged into an exposed outlet.

Now she remembered: Yesterday she had managed to strangle the beast, so in a fit of sanity last night she had moved the monster to the rocking chair and tuned in an oldie rock station, set the switch alarm, then jacked the volume up to maximum—*Oh, Gawd!* No way around it; she would have to get up.

With a determined groan she rolled out of bed, opting to pull the plug on the thing rather than fiddle with the dials. Since she was up anyway, she might as well go through with it.

She stepped into furry pink slippers, used the toilet, then wrapped herself in her thick, warm rose-colored robe, relishing its strength against the early morning cold. She shuffled down the hall through the white batwing doors into the kitchen, where she started the coffee maker that she had prepared the night before. While it brewed she gathered up the paper from the front walk. She looked around and wondered how on earth anyone could enjoy anything so beautiful so early in the morning.

"Curtis, this is for you," she told herself, thinking about her decision two weeks ago to try to spend more time with him, by being up with him in the morning, and making him a warm breakfast. She included a little bit of exercise for herself by watching Richard Hittleman's *Yoga for Health* program on the local PBS station and trying the bending and breathing. She had to admit that she did feel better afterward. It was just the getting up in the morning that was killing her.

She poured herself a cup of coffee and sipped herself into consciousness, starting the oatmeal at a little before seven so that it would be ready at the time Curtis got in from his run. She was on her third cup and halfway through the Community Calendar section of the paper when she heard the front door bang.

"Hi, Mom! I feel great!"

"That's wonderful. I do too!" she said, and received her morning kiss with a proffered cheek and a kiss back. She hadn't had to lie too much, the third cup of coffee was the charm.

"Did you beat the chief this morning," she asked.

"No, the chief didn't run today. His friend Leo is coming to visit and the chief said he had to get ready for him."

"Oh," Michele said simply, and rose to serve the oatmeal.

"It smells so good in here, Mom. When you've been out

351

running and breathing that clean air and come in where it's warm and smells so good from the cooking, it really makes you feel like you're alive. It's so great!"

Michele spooned out two bowls of the steaming-hot cereal, enjoying a welling sense of pride and love for Curtis. Now *this* was worth getting up in the morning for, she thought, watching the healthy pink flush in her son's cheeks, and savoring the joy in his voice at being alive. She'd been missing a lot staying in bed.

"What are you staring at me for, Mom?"

"I'm not staring. I'm telling you that I love you with my big, beautiful eyes." She opened her eyes wide and batted them at him theatrically.

"Your big, beautiful hands could tell me they love me by bringing me a spoon if they want."

Michele laughed and pulled two spoons out of the drawer, gave one to Curtis, and sat down. Seeing Curtis in that running suit reminded her of Kyle. She thought how foolish she felt still loving a man who had not once indicated that he loved her back. Still, nothing that she had had come easily to her; it had all been work. And as Aunt Clarice had said after listening to Michele's account of that horrible, horrible day at the groundbreaking ceremonies, it was not important that Kyle know that he was meant for Michele, just that Michele know that Kyle was meant for her. Aunt Clarice cited her great struggle with that infamous rake Edgar Griffith in 1937, and how he never gave her a second thought the day he met her, and six months later they were engaged, and married three months after that. "He went kicking and bucking, Mishy," she said, "but he still went, and that's the most important thing."

Michele remembered her answer to that: "Well, Kyle had better see the light soon. I can tell you that." she had said. And Aunt Clarice had sat there rocking and smiling, and when Michele asked why, Aunt Clarice answered, "Because now I *know* that you love him." Michele harrumphed at that, but within a week her anger had turned to a blue mood that

352

gradually regained its hopeful color.

She had been waiting for the right moment to ask Curtis if he knew how Kyle felt about her. She would have to bring it up herself: Curtis never volunteered any comment about the subject, and Michele suspected that he knew how she felt about Kyle.

She sighed mentally as Curtis bowed his head and said a brief grace, then worked with some fervor at lacing his oatmeal with butter, brown sugar, and milk.

Now was as good a time as any, Michele decided.

"Curtis," she began.

Curtis stopped his first spoonful two inches from his mouth and let it rest there in suspended animation. Did he recognize something in her tone, the fey little guy? "Does the chief ever mention girlfriends to you?"

Curtis slipped the cereal into his mouth. Finished chewing and swallowing, he said, "I don't think he has any, Mom. He never talks about any."

"Never?"

"Never."

Curtis played with a bit of oatmeal on the spoon, eyeing her for a moment. "Mom, I think he likes you."

"What makes you say that?" Michele said, trying unsuccessfully to hold the interest out of her voice.

Curtis looked into his steaming bowl in thought. "Let's look at the evidence."

Another Kyle-ism, thought Michele with a warm smile.

"He always asks about you," Curtis went on, "and he's always telling me to take care of you, and do what you tell me to do, and to help around the store and the house. I never see him with anyone else and he never talks about other ladies. Now there has to be a reason for that." Curtis took another bite of oatmeal and searched for his train of thought. ". . . Oh, yeah, anyway, if he talks about you, there has to be a reason, and I think it's because he likes you. I know that because, y'know, like when you know I'm hiding something from you, you just

353

know it?"

Michele nodded. "But this still doesn't mean he cares for me," she said. "He may just ask about me because I'm your mom."

Curtis considered this for a moment. "He likes you, Mom," he said simply. "My instincts tell me he likes you a lot."

Michele felt a flush in her cheeks. There are no children anymore. Just young people in little bodies.

She changed the subject abruptly, asking him about the Jedi Knights of Briggs City, and as he talked she watched his man-boy face and didn't hear a word that he said. Her mind was much too busy thinking over what he had told her. And that made her feel hopeful. She felt another surge of determination. Aunt Clarice had gotten Uncle Edgar. All good things come in time. You don't ask, you don't get. Any other cliche that fit, she'd buy. The fact was that things could change, things could always get better.

Suddenly Michele knew why getting up so early in the morning was worth it. "I love you, Curtis," she said.

Curtis stopped in mid-sentence and looked at her, bemused. "I love you, too, Mom," he said.

She thought of Kyle.


That night, deep in sleep, Michele had a dream. She saw Kyle disappear into a black veil of mist and call out in pleading terror for help. His screaming woke her up, but the screaming didn't stop. She realized with exploding panic that the voice now was Curtis, screaming in mortal terror. She ran to his room. He was standing on his bed, yelling in loud spasms of fear. His body convulsed. She reached up and grappled him to the bed, slapping his face smartly twice before he awoke. She pulled him tightly to her and coo'd gently until he stopped shaking. "Can you talk about it, honey?" she asked. "Tell Mama. Tell Mama." His face was hot against hers and she could smell the salt of tears. She held him rocking gently back and forth and finally he spoke: "Something was hurting the chief," he sobbed, "suh-suh-something awful-aw-aw-awful."

"What, honey? What was it?"

"I don't know, Mama," he sobbed, "he was in a dirty cloud . . . I—I—I couldn't see him, but I heard him screaming for help and . . . and . . . and whatever it was it was k-k-killing him . . . and . . . and . . ."

"And what, dear?"

"And whatever it was, it had yuh-yellow eyes, Mama. Ugly yellow eyes . . . and it was hungry, hungry, and cold, cuh-cold like ice."


Finally, Lynnanne couldn't stand it any more. "It's not supposed to go in there!" she cried out. But he kept on doing it to her.

She winced in pain, and managed to hold back a scream.

"You'll get used to it," he grunted.

"I hate you," she choked out. She heard him laugh.

She hadn't been in the store a minute before Larry had called her up to his office and dragged her into the money room. She knew no one would hear them; it was soundproof, damn him. She felt sick to her stomach at how obscene it was: he had bent her over the counting table, her feet still touching the floor, hiked up her skirt, and jerked her pantyhose and panties down around her ankles, and started using his fingers and finally his thing—putting it where it shouldn't go—

"Ow!" she cried out.

"Shut up!" he grunted.

*God help me!* she pleaded, and clenched her teeth at the pain. She prayed for the thousandth time for this nightmare to be over. But hadn't her God abandoned her? What kind of God are you that would let this happen? she thought spitefully. No job was worth this; but her mother and brother depended on her. They needed the money to live. Where else was she going to get a job?

355

She stifled a sob. God had failed her! He shouldn't let this happen!

Larry finished with a grunt. The sharp jabbing pains stopped, replaced by a throbbing ache. He tossed a gold box of Kleenex on the table. "It'll be easier the second time," he said. She heard the electric zip of his zipper going up. "Hurry up."

He stepped out into his office, and she stayed as she was for a few moments, sobbing, trying to pull herself together. She hated Larry Allan. And God said to love thy neighbor as thyself. To hate was wrong! And she hated Larry Allen more than anything on the face of the earth! Anything!

She pushed up from the table and cleaned herself up with the Kleenex as best she could. Bending in pain, she shimmied up her panties and hose, blew her nose, and stood for a moment, her eyes closed, her head bowed, praying for strength. She forced her breath to be as natural as she could make it, then picked up her purse and walked out the door. Larry said something to her that she didn't hear . . . didn't want to hear.

She let herself out quickly through the side door to his office and scooted down the hall and the stairs in a hobbling quickstep that brought pain in every motion. Halfway down the stairs tears of humiliation burst out. She struggled not to sob out loud. She chose the back-way passage, around the meat department warehouse and into the main warehouse so as not to be seen. She breached the backroom hallway into the warehouse past Coogle Carver's janitor room. He popped out of his room and said, "Hi, Lynnanne." She ignored him and felt guilty. Coogle had always been decent to her, and she had snubbed him. The force of an even deeper depression seemed to take hold of her. She needed to be alone, to think and to cry.

She mounted the stairs leading to the upper storeroom.

As she stepped into its brooding half-light of the room, she searched for a private place. Some fifty feet away she found a blue milk case turned on end, and stopped there. The remnants of several crushed cigar butts littered one side, and from a half-gallon paper carton the smell of sour milk wafted up. Someone else needed to be alone, she thought. Another person had needed peace and quiet, and had come up here.

She tried to sit down but it was too painful, so she knelt a few feet away from the milk case, then sat gingerly back on her heels. Her physical aching receded to a dull discomfort, and she managed to hold her sobs off to metered spasms. She pulled her Bible from her purse, opened it, then slammed it shut and jammed it back into her purse. God's forsaken me! she thought. She began to cry again, and buried her face in her hands.

"Lynnanne?"

She jerked her head up suddenly and looked toward the sound of the deep voice. For a moment, she couldn't see anybody, but then Coogle spoke again and she saw him. His head seemed to float some two feet off the ground. He was on the stairs, not fully to the top, and apparently not intending to mount them any higher. He looked around the warehouse, staring intently at the dark access holes to the security catwalk, then around the floor. The darkness of the room almost made his dark skin disappear, so that a trick of her eyes made him out briefly as two floating, bloodshot eyes. "Where are the dummies?" he asked.

The question seemed so strange to her that she managed a sardonic snicker; she did not answer him.

"You all right?" he asked. He took a cautious step up, then another, looking around the warehouse warily. "You shouldn't be up here. Dangerous up here, hon'."

"I don't mean to be rude, Coogle, but I want to be alone now. Please."

He mounted a few more steps, again looking all around until he was only one away from stepping into the warehouse.

"Please, Coogle. I'll be okay; I promise."

"Not safe up here, Lynnanne." He seemed to be searching for some way to explain. "Rats," he said, peering around into the dark places of the huge warehouse. "Big rats, size of dogs." He nodded his head in affirmation. "You sure you all right?"

"Yes."

"You don't look it."

"I am. Just go—please." She watched Coogle back down the stairs, still looking all around suspiciously. "You be careful, y'hear. Not safe up here. You come down soon, hear?"

"And don't fret so much, Lynnanne," he said just before stepping down and out of sight, "nothing can be that bad."

She gave an ironic laugh. Nothing can be that bad? Well, it was! She looked around the warehouse in full awareness for the first time since she had gotten up here. The gloomy darkness hung all around. She began to feel the full force of it. What if Coogle was right, and there *were* rats up here? That skittering sound . . .

There. Again.

She heard a different nose, a squeak to her right, and turned. She breathed a sigh of relief. There were the dummies—the mannequins were what Coogle had meant—all over by the far wall . . .

She heard squeaking wheels on her left and looked. Mannequins on built-in rollers stood there now. None had been there before, she was sure of it. Fingers of fear touched her spine. This second bunch was only a half-dozen feet from the stairs. And they looked so real—like people. Staring at her, almost.

She clutched her purse and stood. Looked to the right. That group of mannequins stood closer now. A squeak to her left. She jerked her head around. Those mannequins were now between herself and the stairs. Run! she thought. The only direction open was straight ahead deeper into the dark warehouse. Her legs felt like wooden pegs under her—God, they wouldn't work! The squeaking of wheels sounded on both sides of her now. If she could reach the far wall, she could duck into one of the security openings. They couldn't get in there, she was sure.

She forced herself to look back at the—

Both groups of mannequins had merged into one.

Her heart raced. Her throat felt dry like a papery tube. She was going to pee her pants.

Wheels squeaked behind her. She turned abruptly toward the far wall, and pulled up short . . .

Fifty mannequins stood behind her, a dark brown one wearing a panama hat and sunglasses out in front. "Calypso Joe," a sign around its neck read. "Hallo, ma'am," it said in a deep, Jamaican voice that reminded her of the man on the 7-Up commercials talking about the "Un-Cola." "There no 'scapin' us, ma'ahm. Nossirmahmbob, no 'scapin' us."

Lynnanne sprinted for the black rectangular port in the side wall, a hundred feet away. The squeaking wheels rolled leisurely behind her. She heard them . . . circling? . . . she was fifty feet away from the dark access port. She could make it! They couldn't get into there! Then she could call for—

"Help!" she screamed. She stared horrified at the eight violet eyes scattered across the opening of the access port. They were iridescent, and stared back hungrily. She saw a black mass dimly behind those eyes. Her heart thudded. God, those eyes all belong to one thing! she realized. *Oh, God, help me!* She tried to scream, but her mouth was too dry. Her lungs felt empty.

An enormous spider crawled out of the port. Two of its eight black legs wiggled through first, followed by six more, pulling its huge, bulbous black abdomen through next. Its face and thorax were combined in one blocky black mass. The eyes were scattered over the top portion of the face; two wickedly curved fangs protruded out, black juice dripping from their tips.

Lynnanne froze, then backed away. The mannequins circled up around her as if to protect her, but the giant spider crawled in a facile lumbering fashion up over them, knocking some down as it moved toward her. It was ten feet away. Its black fangs clamped-and-released, clamped-and-released, in anticipation. Its eyes studied her, then it scrambled toward her.

"Cleo!" Calypso Joe's voice thundered. "No-no! Boss Mahn, he be mahd you do that!"

The spider stopped short, five feet from her. Its black shiny legs and its mandibles twitched, as if barely restrained. The grapefruit-sized violet eyes radiated lustful hunger at her. Lynnanne gasped pathetic mewling sounds.

"Doan mine Cleo, ma'ahm," said the black mannequin, "she an uppitty widow-lady. Got no mahnahs." Lynnanne turned around to face him. "Boss Mahn, he gots plahns for you, ma'ahm." His mouth smiled showing little human skulls as teeth, "Yes, ma'ahm." Suddenly, all the mannequins extended their arms. Scalpels appeared in their hands. The surgical blades glinted in the dusky warehouse light. "It be surgery you be gettin', ma'ahm. Surgery!"

She screamed, and the mannequin rolled forward in a squeaking thunder of wheels. Calypso Joe grinned tiny skulls at her—each with gleaming yellow, pinpoint eyes—then the moment of madness descended, and all that had been so carefully planned had begun.

## 42

The ringing of the telephone brought him instantly awake from his restless sleep.

Oh, great, a fucking wake-up call, thought Kyle. He grabbed his watch from the night table—six AM . . . Shit!

He threw off the covers and sat on the side of the bed, letting the annoying screech of the telephone cycle on for a moment. He'd been around police work too long not to recognize a "sorry-to-bother-you-sir-but . . ." telephone call when he heard one. He knocked the remnants of sleep and that damn nightmare out of his mind as best he could with a few shakes of his head, then picked up the receiver. "Chief Richards," he said heavily.

"Chief, this is Koger, sorry to bother you, sir, but we've got a missing girl . . ."

Kyle listened very carefully, then told Koger that he would meet him at Gathers Market. He hung up and grabbed a quick steaming shower. He toweled off, dressed quickly, and drove to the market, trying to ignore the edge put on him by the horrible dream and the bad night's sleep.

The sight of the market as he drove into its parking lot made him squirm mentally. Somehow in the early morning sunlight the huge building appeared to be waiting there, just for him. He parked next to the other police cars and was let in by the grocery manager and shown back into the warehouse, where Dwight Koger had set up a small operations room in the male employees' lounge. Fresh coffee in a Mr. Coffee drip coffeemaker and donuts sat on a small table. The grocery manager, a short, dark-haired man of thirty, poured Kyle a cup and handed him a donut and then left the two men alone.

"Black and McCulley are getting names," said Koger. "We'll have a list and pull them in one by one to talk to them. Low profile—as low as you can get in a thing like this, anyway—try not to disturb the work."

Kyle took a quick sip of the hot coffee and devoured the donut. "You waived the twenty-four hours, right?" he asked.

Koger nodded, and Kyle noted the slight shift in the sergeant's attitude—defensive posture number one—Kyle himself had used it on a number of occasions and in just this same situation. The normal waiting time for a missing person was twenty-four hours, and if Koger had waived that, there would have to be a good reason.

Koger eyed him steadily. "Suspicious circumstances, Chief."

"Okay, run 'em down," Kyle said.

Koger fished a black notebook from his brown suit coat pocket and fingered it open, sipping from his white sytrofoam cup. The man had an intensity and professionalism that Kyle admired; this would be his next lieutenant, he decided.

Koger set down his cup of coffee and squared off on his thick muscular legs like a major-league baseball player up to bat. "All right. We have a telephone call yesterday from her mother—time one-thirty. Work called her asking if daughter—Lynnanne Wilkes aged nineteen, female cauc, five six, hundred twelve pounds, blond hair, green eyes—had returned home. Mother says no, that she left for work. Work says that she came to work, but that she wasn't there now. Officer Brock tells her it's not a police matter—missing person, no suspicious circumstances, not a juvenile, twenty-four hours, then come in and fill out a missing-persons report." Koger paused and eyeballed Kyle for a second. "You can bet she had a few choice words for the department after that."

"Standard police procedure is great unless it's your own kid involved," said Kyle. "What happens next?"

"Next, we have the store manager calling us—Larry Allen's the name—telling us that the girl's mother just called and told him she'd called us, and for us not to worry because she was upset this morning over a schedule change, and that he would look for her . . ." Koger thumbed a page over and continued. "Basically the rest of the story is, we get a few more calls from the mother, we tell her what the manager said and is doing— the search—but finally in the evening, no girl, coat still in locker, car still outside the store, and nobody seen her leave, equals police involvement . . ." Koger closed his book and put it away and squared off against Kyle. "I didn't call you earlier because it still looked like she could turn up . . ."

"Don't let it get this far next time," Kyle said, carefully gauging his voice to eliminate any tone of reproach. "I know it was a judgment call, but I want to be informed."

Koger rocked back and forth and picked up his coffee. Kyle watched his face cautiously as the sergeant drank nervously and finally said, "Okay. Like I said, I thought it was going to pan out. Moving right along, we got more manpower—that added to help from store personnel—and we conducted a proper search, and early this morning turned up the girl's purse stashed in one of the security catwalks, under a running board, at which point I called you." Koger stopped, awaiting Kyle's comments.

"What condition was the purse in?" Kyle asked, indicating that they were about to take a walk with a jut of his thumb.

Koger poured himself another cup and followed Kyle out the door. "A little dirty, but according to her mother, everything was there, wallet, money, et cetera."

Kyle stopped just out side the locker room door as a forklift heavy with a load cut its way through the warehouse. The big, meaty driver called out to a wispy young man in a red butcher's apron, "Here's your deli, you faggot!" The young man, sprinting toward a large stainless steel door, screamed over his shoulder, "Your mother's a whore, Edmonds!" Kyle thought the wispy one was going to run into the deli room, but at the

363

entrance the man made an abrupt leap to his right and mounted a pallet of Delmonte pineapple juice just as the crazy forklift driver jammed the pallet of cheeses into the deli doorway.

"Fuck-head," said Koger under his breath.

"Yeah," agreed Kyle. "Why don't you show me where you found the purse."

Kyle followed Koger back through the bowels of the warehouse and up a flight of stairs. Emerging on the second-story landing next to Koger, Kyle stared out into an inky darkness barely diluted by a few lights and there. Kyle felt something familiar and uneasy, like a tidal wash of foul brine, the wave subsiding, leaving a stink in his mind.

"Yeah, I know," said Koger, and Kyle turned to the sergeant and saw that the man was looking at him. "Creepy, hunh?"

"Bela Lugosi," Kyle said, and wondered if Koger was getting the same feeling that he was—of being watched; wanted, and watched. "We got people up here?" he asked.

"Nossir."

Koger pulled a small flashlight from inside his suitcoat pocket and led him across the cement floor toward the square black access holes in the far wall.

"Christ, somebody must have moved them," Koger said, his voice echoing then dying in the darkness.

"What?"

"The store dummies. They were all over here." Koger raised his arms and wiggled them about the warehouse. "Scattered around. I told the sons of bitches not to move anything."

Kyle looked around. A palpable silence pressed heavily against him. This warehouse was so darkly cavernous, he wouldn't be too surprised to see giant bats fly out of the recesses of the rafters. He shivered inwardly. This place was cold and gave him the willies. Christ, why weren't there more lights?"

"Looked like corpses," said Koger, "laying all around; some standing. Where the fuck are they?"

"Show me where the purse was found," Kyle said flatly. He

364

was puzzled. This place had just been built and this upper room looked dingy already. Koger snapped on his light, and in its spill Kyle saw rat droppings and as they stepped in the tunnelway the foul smell of a . . . *lair* . . . why had that word popped into his head? He didn't know . . . lair was the word, though, but that was impossible . . . a lair implied an occupant, and the worst they could have up here were rats and spiders. "This place sure stinks," he said. "Smells like bad cheese."

"It wasn't me," said Koger. He was leading Kyle rapidly through the tunnellike catwalk.

"Not that, Koger." Kyle stopped for a moment near one of the two-way mirrors that gave a view over the store floor. "Wait one," he called, and Koger stopped and gave an exasperated sigh. Through the mirror Kyle could see most of the store floor, and in return a dim illumination managed to take hold of the square mirror and into the walkway for about a foot. He looked down the way they had come. Now that his eyes had adjusted, he saw similar patches of light down the length of the tunnel, until at a hundred feet's distance, darkness took a black handhold. *Lair.* The word kept buzzing in his head. "You righteously don't smell it?" he asked.

Koger shook his head impatiently. "Dusty up here, that's all," he said, then nodded into the darkness. "The purse was found down here."

Kyle followed him.

"Here it is," Koger said, stopping where the catwalk turned to cover the west side of the store. He squatted down and pointed with the flashlight beam at a rough chalk circle on the floor. "It was tucked under here." He indicated a space between two exposed joists. "Nobody caught it the first time around, but another turned it up. Nothing missing."

"You said . . ." Kyle heard his own voice trail off, as a malaise washed over his mind once more. "Let's get out of here. It stinks."

"It wasn't me, I tell you," Koger said, and Kyle laughed nervously. "Must of been a ghost, then."

Instead of going back the way they came, Koger rounded the corner to the right and stepped out through a nearby access hole. They emerged next to some heavy air compressors, huge metal gray monsters that sat idle for the moment. Kyle wondered why they hadn't walked across the warehouse and stepped through right at the spot in the first place. Christ, this place gave him the creeps.

As they neared the landing Kyle spotted an overturned milk crate with cigar butts sprinkled around like the droppings of a giant rat. To the side was a milk carton. Kyle stepped closer and smelled its sour contents. "You make this," he called to the sergeant, who was already at the landing.

"I'll have somebody up, now," he said. "Until we found the purse, it wasn't important." He disappeared down the stairs and Kyle turned back to the crate and its litter. Some of the stubs were old and some fresh. Whoever sat here had been up here more than once. Store personnel, someone seeking a little privacy; and that someone might have seen something, or know something.

As he tucked this thought away, a skittering sound violated the silence of the vast warehouse. Kyle jerked around; his hand moved instinctively for his gun. He stopped, then eased the breath from his lungs. This place had made him jittery. Standing under the lights was one of the mannequins Sergeant Koger had mentioned. Funny, though, Kyle hadn't seen it there before. In long strides, he approached the dummy. It was black and somebody had dumped a straw hat and sunglasses on it, and as Kyle got closer he saw a sign hung around the dummy's neck: Calypso Joe. Kyle walked up to it and shoved it a little, marveling at the wheels. They made a skittering sound, didn't they? A squeaky but skittering sound. He raised his eyes to the dummy's face and saw a dark reflection of his form in the sunglasses. Calypso Joe seemed to be grinning maliciously at him.

"I've had too much of this place," Kyle said under his breath, and pushed the dummy one more time. It rolled back with a squeak. Kyle turned and walked back to the stairwell. Just before he started down the stairs he looked up at the opposite wall, and stared.

Had they been there before?

Clusters of dummies attended him in dim light. Almost like jurors, thought Kyle. Standing and staring, a jury passing judgment on him.

He stood there staring dumbly back at them, then shook his head. Jesus, maybe he was going crazy again. He just didn't like it here. It felt . . . it felt evil . . . and now that smell is back. Christ.

Kyle heard a clicking sound and wrenched his head around to Calypso Joe. Had the dummy's arms been stretched out like that before?

Kyle looked around the dark warehouse. Damn, it was spooky. With an imagination anyone could paint themselves into a haunted house, he thought. After all, he hadn't seen the damned mannequins until later because his eyes hadn't adjusted to the dim light for a while, and he was concentrating on following Koger. Shit, even Koger couldn't see the damned things and he was looking for them.

Kyle rested his hand on the wooden bannister, and caught the lie right there. *He* hadn't seen the mannequins until *after* Koger had left, so there was no one to bear him witness that the mannequins had appeared where there were none before; no witness that Calypso Joe's arms had been down by his side and now they were up and beckoning . . .

Kyle's breath exploded from him; he gasped violently and shuddered, fighting to control himself as he stared at Calypso Joe who now had only one arm raised—raised in accusation, pointing at Kyle.


Patrolman Black ushered the first person into the boxlike lounge-turned-command-post. Kyle stood up with a smile and shook Coogle Carver's hand only to get a weak return on his investment. The man was afraid, Kyle realized. It was as obvious as the difference in color of their skin. The fact that Kyle was a policeman and Coogle a black meant he was used to a special kind of treatment from the law.

"Good to see you, Coogle," said Kyle, and indicated that he take a seat in a folding chair next to a card table stacked with magazines. Kyle smelled booze as Coogle passed. He examined the black man's face for the telltale signs of drunkenness. His eyes were clear enough, not watering, nor excessively bloodshot. Steady enough on his feet, too. A buzz on, maybe, but not drunk. Coogle sat his small frame down in the chair. He was dressed in a dark green work jumpsuit, his wide, normally gentle eyes darting in surly suspicion from Kyle to Dwight Koger to the floor. Kyle knew that Coogle was a proud man, and decided that a one-on-one interview with him would be best.

He sent John Black from the room, and glanced at Koger, realizing he could handle two things with one order, calming Coogle down, and finding just how out of it he himself had been with the mannequins in the upper warehouse. "Koger," he said, and the sergeant stopped fish-eyeing Coogle and turned to Kyle. "You remember upstairs, the mannequins? We didn't see them, right?"

"Right."

"Even when you went downstairs?"

Koger thought for a minute, then said speculatively, "Right?"

"You're not sure?"

Koger shook his head. "I wasn't looking for them, coming out, but I don't remember seeing them at—"

"They moves around," said Coogle.

"Who the hell asked you?" said Koger, glaring at the black man.

Kyle stood up and guided Koger by the arm out the door, telling Coogle over his shoulder he'd be right back.

"I want you to take somebody with you and check out the

mannequins," said Kyle. "I didn't see any either, and then I did. See if somebody's playing games. As you stand by the stairs there should be one to your left about thirty feet, and off to the right maybe four groups of them. If they're not like that then somebody's pulling our wangs. Seal it off and search it again."

Koger called over to Black and they took off toward the stairs as Kyle ducked back into the command post. He had taken it from a pragmatic standpoint—he had seen what he had seen, dammit—that something was going on up there. Sending Koger up to check it out was the proper thing to do. But the rub was that Leo's little speech yesterday had hit home. Nobody but Kyle had seen any of the things that Kyle had seen, or heard what he had heard. He had no intention of taking this thing lying down; the memories of Woodhaven were just too damn fresh. Maybe Leo was right; maybe he had just conjured these things up in his mind to screw himself up. Well, goddammit it, he had a good life for himself now, and he wasn't going to fuck it up!

Kyle looked at Coogle and was pleased. Getting rid of Koger had had its desired effect. Coogle wasn't the eiptome of cool, now, but he was a damn sight more relaxed.

"I figured we could talk a little better in private one on one," said Kyle. "Easier on everyone. But before we get on with the questions, tell me what you meant when you said the mannequins moved."

The black man eyed him and said nothing.

"Coogle, give me a break, would ya?" Kyle said. "You were the first man I met in this town with any sense. The girl's missing, I've got to ask questions of *every*body. It's my job, for Christ's sakes." Kyle waved his hands up to the ceiling, indicating the upper storeroom. "I would have sworn myself those dummies upstairs moved. It scared the crap outta me."

Coogle exhaled a sigh. Kyle thought that he detected a little bit of shame on the old man's face. If it were there, it had whispered by quickly and was gone. Coogle leaned toward

Kyle. "They move," he whispered. "Sometime it gets too much down here, so I goes upstairs—got me a spot—sit down, have a smoke . . ."

"Sit on a milk crate?"

"Yeah. How d'you know?"

Kyle grinned again. "I found your spot, Coogle."

The old man nodded and continued with his story. "I swears I see lotsa things move, not at first, but lately. Haints." He leaned even closer to Kyle. "Haints. Upstairs, downstairs. I don't go down there"—he pointed to the floor, his index finger rigid like a spike—"no more, no matter what. That cheap ass Larry Allen can go down there and clean it hisself, 'cause this nigger ain't going, let me tell you."

"What's down there?" asked Kyle.

"'nother warehouse, like upstairs, but it's worse downstairs, a lot worse."

"What is?" asked Kyle.

"The haints!" Coogle's eyes opened wide and Kyle thought it might be the liquor, then the fear in the man's face seeped through. "Ghosts, goblins, boogeymen, spirits—*haints!*"

"There are haunts here, then?"

"Yes. An' after Lynnanne gone like that, I'm getting out of this place. I'll work a few more days, but they better transfer me back to the town store or I'll go to the mayor."

Kyle studied Coogle for a minute. This man was serious and afraid. "You think the haunts got Lynnanne, Coogle?"

"I didn't say that. But she be nice to me all the time. Nice girl. Bit of a Bible beater, but always respectful. I told her not to go up there . . ."

"When was that?"

"Yesterday."

"What time was that, Coogle?" Kyle pulled a yellow legal pad out of his briefcase, and unobtrusively brought a pen from his pocket and began writing.

"'Bout eight o' clock."

"Morning or night?"

"The morning. I come in early in the morning."

"When was the last time you saw Lynnanne?"

"I just tol' you."

"Eight o'clock?"

"Yeah."

"Where did you talk to her?"

"Upstairs."

"I thought you said you didn't go upstairs."

"I don't, but she came whizzin' by me crying and up the stairs, so I followed her and I told her it wasn't safe up there."

"Where was she standing when you talked to her?"

"She be kneelin' down—at my spot."

"To your knowledge did you know her to go up there before?"

"No."

Kyle paused and wrote this down, too. The pattern was the same: ask the question, listen to the answer, then write it down. It made most people nervous to write while they talked. He had deliberately kept his tone conversational, and Coogle had responded in kind.

"Coogle, you said she was crying when she went by you. Did she tell you why?" Kyle paused a moment, then added an aside before Coogle could answer: "You are a big help, I want you to know that."

Coogle pursed his lips and acknowledged the compliment by relaxing more in the chair. "She tol' me she wanted to be alone, to leave her alone. She wanted to be alone, but she didn't say why she was cryin', but I think Larry Allen has somethin' to do with it."

"The store manager?" Kyle asked.

Coogle nodded. "You see, Larry likes the ladies. He be puttin' his hands all over 'em if they let him. Things like that."

"More than that?"

"Yeah. Sometimes. Get the squeeze on 'em, if they need more hours, days off and such. But Lynnanne, she a good girl. Always carries her Bible . . ."

371

"You think Larry had the arm on her?"

Coogle shrugged. "Could be. I don't know. Could be."

Kyle made a note and looked up at Coogle to see him lost in thought. "What are you thinking about?"

Coogle grimaced and stared around at the walls and up at the ceiling and down at the floor. Finally he said, "This place. This store. There's somethin' really wrong here, somethin' bad. I just *feel* it. I *feel* it in my bones." He sat up straight, crossed his small legs, and capped the high knee with brown hands folded into each, and stared into Kyle's eyes. "Don't you?" he asked.

The question hit Kyle like an arrow. He hesitated briefly, then admitted, "Yes, I feel it too."

Kyle asked a few more location questions of Coogle: if he knew where she hung out, if she mentioned anyplace particular, then he asked if Coogle knew of anyone who wanted to hurt her, or had anything against her. When he said "No," Kyle handed him his card and kicked him loose, asking him to give a call if he thought of anything else.

As soon as the small janitor left, Koger walked in with John Black. "No soap, Chief," said Koger. "I didn't see any of the mannequins from the stairs. The search turned them up way the fuck down the far end of the warehouse, all grouped together, kind of huddled together in the dark." He laughed nervously. "Spooky up there. We didn't find nobody but the dummies. Somebody could have been up there, and come down maybe. Somebody could've . . ."

Or some*thing*, thought Kyle. Some *thing*.


Kyle grunted with dissatisfaction. Here it was midafternoon, all the interviews but one had been conducted, and the till was fitted with brass coins. Nothing to go on. The assistant manager and a checker had seen Lynnanne come in; the manager said he had a lengthy discussion on her hours, and when he couldn't accommodate her she left his office in tears; Coogle had seen her, warned her against being up in the

372

warehouse; and then nothing from then on. Her purse, her car, her locker—all indicated that she hadn't left, yet she wasn't on the premises either.

In the interviews, Kyle had followed up on Coogle's remark about Larry Allen sexually harassing the help. It was a touchy subject so he used an elliptical approach, guiding the women into the subject, making them feel more and more secure, then asking them directly if there was any problem with sexual harassment in the store, mentioning no one's name in particular. The response varied from the bawdy remark of Rachael Macht—"I'd kick him in the balls if he touched me!" (When Kyle asked who, the dark-haired checker said, "That prick Larry Allen.")—to a simple denial of any knowledge of any kind of pressure from anyone in the store. Nothing to hang Larry Allen on.

Koger strode into the lounge. "I've got the last one outside, Chief," he said. "She's kinda slow"—he pointed to his head—"I mean, you could sell her the moon, if you know what I mean."

"Okay, show her in," said Kyle. "Then I want you to go see Mrs. Wilkes. Do a follow-up interview, and make sure she knows that we're doing everything possible."

Koger nodded, stepped out briefly, and ushered in a young girl of about nineteen, who took to the folding chair like a timid animal, sitting quietly looking out from under dark brown bangs with doelike brown eyes. "Chief, this is Bunny Coolins," introduced Koger. The girl said nothing. Koger shrugged his shoulders and left.

"Hi," said Kyle.

Bunny's eyes flicked tentatively up to his a few times, then, seeing that it was safe, looked at him fully. Her childlike gaze filled him with such a warm feeling of guileless innocence that he smiled involuntarily, a gesture that she mimicked happily, a small creature wanting to be loved.

"It's a pleasure to meet you, Bunny," Kyle said softly, extending his hand. She stared at his hand a moment as if honored, then reached out, shook it briefly, then nested her hands in her lap. "You're the chief," she said hesitantly. "You're a policeman, and whenever anyone needs help they should go to a police, 'cause policemen are good and they help people, right?"

Kyle hid a smile behind his hand at her request for confirmation of a truth that she had been taught in her childhood; a state in which, Kyle thought, God had chosen for her to live out her life. He answered her with a sincere "That's right, Bunny." And then added, "Did your mother teach you that?"

Beaming, the girl nodded. "She teaches me rules. 'Rules to live by,'" she recited. "That's because I'm not real smart. Mama says, 'If Bunny follows the rules she won't be a fool'; so, I follow the rules and I'm not the fool. Is that a *real* police whistle?"

Kyle followed her gaze down to the key ring at his belt. "My lucky whistle," he told her. "I've had it since the academy; brings me luck."

"It sure is nice," said Bunny. She seemed enchanted by it. "A real police whistle. If a person were ever to be in trouble, she could blow that and every policeman in the world would come, hunh?"

"That's right, Bunny. I have a few more questions for you now. If you concentrate very hard, you could be a real help on this case, okay?"

"Really?"

"That's right. Okay?"

She nodded, trying to look only at him, but her eyes kept dipping to Kyle's silver whistle on his key ring like a kid to a new toy.

Kyle began his questioning. She answered each query simply with a "yes" or a "no" where appropriate, much to Kyle's satisfaction. Most people tend to elaborate in a meaningless direction when questioned. With Bunny, Kyle could guide her perfectly to search her memory for exactly what she knew about the missing Lynnanne that might help him find her. He turned up zip on this score, so he began his questioning on his long shot: sexual harassment, and Larry Allen.

Before he started he stood up to signify that the questioning about Lynnanne was over and to give Bunny a rest. He motioned for her to stay seated, and closed the entrance door firmly. He made a show of it for Bunny's sake. Now he was going to toss her some not-so-innocent questions, and he wanted her to feel as secure and private as possible. With her, he would have to be doubly sure not to lead her into any conclusions. You have to go with what you know, thought Kyle, trying to assuage the guilt he felt asking these questions to such a childlike woman. And what he knew was that Larry had a reputation for hitting on the woman for as much as he could. As Kyle looked into Bunny's doe eyes the possibility of what could be made him shudder in dread.

He took a chair near her and began, "Bunny, do you know what sexual harassment is?"

"No," she said, her eyes shifting to his, then back at the whistle.

"Do you know what sex is, sweetheart?"

"Yes." She looked at him quickly and recited, "'Good girls save their pearl for the man that they would marry.'"

Kyle stifled a laugh, smiling instead. "Very good, Bunny.

"Now, what sexual harassment is, is . . . let's see, it's when somebody wants you to have sex with them and they tell you that if you don't, you would lose your job. Has that happened to you, sweetheart?" Kyle knew that the scope of sexual harassment fanned out a lot broader than just intercourse, but he had kept it narrow and to the point for Bunny's sake.

Bunny sat up straight in her chair, a mottled red color moved like a cloud across her face, and then she began to jabber, her tongue wagging fearfully. Finally she caught herself and yelled at him, "I didn't tell! I didn't tell tell tell! If you wanna do well, then don't tell tell tell!" Tears flooded her eyes and down her cheeks. "I'm a good good girl. I'm good! And I didn't tell!" She buried her face in her hands and sobbed and shook, rocking back and forth. Kyle stared at her, frozen for a moment by her reaction.

He slid forward on his chair and reached out and patted her awkwardly on the head. "Of course you're a good girl, Bunny. Of course you are." She quieted a bit and stopped rocking. "There, there," he cooed, "there, there." Bunny reached out for him and Kyle let her slip her arms around him. He pulled her close, comforted her, and found himself thinking of his daughter, Lisa, the time her hamster had died, and she'd been filled with guilt that somehow it was her fault. Kyle recognized the feelings behind Bunny's tears as ones of guilt, too.

He saw Larry Allen's sly face in his mind, and felt red anger erupting inside him. Still, he had to hear it from her, so he sat her down and dragged his folding chair close to her, and sat down himself, holding both her small hands in his. She sat, her head downcast, staring at her lap. When he spoke to her, she answered him talking into the top of her thighs. "Mama says to be good. She says that I'm not real smart so I should listen to my betters and be grateful that Larry Allen done give me this job 'cause I'm dumb, and dumb people can't get jobs mostly. She says that I should do what Larry Allen says, 'cause he's the boss and knows what's best for me until I get home. But Mama says a 'good girl saves her pearl for the man that she would marry' and that if I'm sinful and wicked I will go straight to hell in a handbasket; but that I should do what Larry Allen says, 'cause he's the boss . . ."

"She told you to have sex with Larry?" asked Kyle, hating the question even as he asked it.

Now Bunny turned her head up to him, her face full of denial. "No-o-o! She doesn't know and please don't tell her. Plea-ease!"

Kyle said that he wouldn't, and she looked as relieved as he felt. "Go on, then," he urged.

"I did what he said 'cause he said I could keep my job and

that it really was part of my job but that I couldn't tell nobody because it was secret."

"Would you do it anyway, if you knew that you keep your job even if you didn't, sweetheart?"

Hate clouded Bunny's face. "No," she said vehemently. "'Good girls save their pearl for the man that they would marry.'"

"And you're a good girl, Bunny. And you save yourself for marriage from now on, you hear?"

"Yes." She searched the room with her eyes for a moment, then said, "But my job. I didn't tell, but all's not well. I'll lose my job. Larry said if I tell I lose my job."

Kyle squared off in his chair and touched her on both arms, forcing her to look in his face. "You're my friend, aren't you?"

"Yes."

"So you take this card." Kyle pulled a business card out of his open briefcase and wrote on the back of it, then handed it to her. "Read it out loud," he said.

"'Bunny Coolins is my friend. Call me if she needs anything—Chief Richards.'" Bunny's eyes goggled. "Boy-oh-boy, we're friends, real friends?"

"That's right," said Kyle. "And real friends take care of each other, don't they?"

"Yes, they do," she responded softly, then more earnestly, "They do, they do."

"Now listen to me," said Kyle. "After today, Larry Allen should never bother you again. But if he does, you tell him 'No!' and you call me right away—don't worry about your job, because I'll make sure that you keep it; you just make sure that you call me. You got it?"

She nodded eagerly at him. "I got it."

"Excellent. Now we're best friends. You go on now, and don't worry about a thing."

He stood up and she did too and hesitated, then wrapped her arms around Kyle and hugged him a real bear hug, then started for the door, sparing his police whistle a parting glance.

377

"Sweetheart," Kyle called after her. She stopped. "You forgot something."

"What?"

"Your whistle."

Her eyes toyed shyly with the whistle. "That's *your* whistle."

"We're friends, aren't we?"

"Yes."

Kyle detached the silver traffic whistle from his keys, and when he looked up she was unzipping her uniform top.

"What are you doing?" asked Kyle.

She stopped the zipper halfway down. Kyle watched helplessly as she reached in her ample cleavage and flipped something out and detached it from her bra by a safety pin, handed it to him, and zipped her uniform back up. Kyle held it in his hand. The heat of her breasts still warmed the charm: a coin token, the kind Kyle used to get out of a machine for a quarter at the penny arcade, with a star in the middle and you get to stamp your name or anything you wanted on it. It read: *Bunny Coolins Is Smart.*

Kyle looked up at her and smiled, handing her the whistle. "Thank you, darling." A very fair trade, he decided; kissed her on the cheek and sent her out the door.

Then he went looking for Larry Allen.


Sweet God, how this badge protects the wrong people sometimes, thought Kyle as he stared into the scared eyes of Larry Allen.

Kyle had found the son of a bitch in his office, and with a bit of theatrics pretending to find Bunny attractive, elicited a pride-filled confession from Allen that he knew from personal experience she was "a good screw, and sucked like Old MacDonald's well pump on a Saturday night." The store manager smiled a good ol' boy smile after confessing that, then almost lost bowel control when Kyle turned suddenly dry-ice cold and said, "Yeah. Well, she said you made her do it, asshole. You told her she'd lose her job if she didn't. Makes you a pretty sorry sack of shit in my eyes, picking on a kid like that. Makes you shit in my book, anyway. And believe me, that's one fucking book you don't want to be in, shithead."

The grocery man started to get mad, but he looked in Kyle's eyes and the bravado drained out of him. He settled himself down in his desk chair, as if it gave him some power, and attached an expressionless look on his face. "I deny," he said, "I deny every word of it . . ."

Kyle saw red.

—and when his fiery rage cleared he had Larry Allen doubled over, by the sofa. He must have pull/dragged the son of a bitch over his desk: his papers and stapler were scattered everywhere, the telephone was spilled on the floor, and Kyle was shaking Larry Allen until the man's teeth clicked together. "You listen to me," he heard himself say, "you shit-for-brains asshole: If I *ever* hear one story about any form of sexual harassment in this store—and, Buddy, after those interviews, I've got ears all over this place—I'm gonna be all over you like stink on *shit!* You got that, mister!"

Larry Allen was choked with fright, but his eyes managed a "have mercy" agreement, and the smell of fear from the man loosened Kyle's hands. The store manager sank to the floor.

Kyle stood up and shook a finger at the prick. "This badge keeps me from doing what I'd like to do, but I'll promise you this, if anyone loses their job, or their hours are cut, or I hear one complaint for as much as a whispered word in their ear, I'll come for you. And you won't like what happens when I find you! You won't like it at all!"

Kyle stood, momentarily glaring at the man, until Larry started nodding his head, bobbing it up and down in submission. Then Kyle opened the office door and walked out.

As he got into his car his legs began to shake, the effect of the adrenaline bleeding off. What he had done was not ethical, and he felt ashamed in that way, but the truth was that the law was lax in some areas—sexual harassment was one. Yes, he could have presented a case against Larry Allen, but the only person it would have hurt would have been Bunny. Larry Allen would have walked free, the bastard, and Kyle didn't know if Bunny's mental makeup could have taken the abuse—God knows the sexual abuse had been bad enough.

His composure restored, Kyle twisted the key in the lock and the car fired up. He slid it into gear and started accelerating when he heard the trill of a whistle, over and over again. He looked around and saw Bunny Coolins pushing a train of grocery baskets, the whistle clamped between her teeth. She turned her head suddenly, saw him, and waved both arms at Kyle, a giant grin on her face. Kyle waved back and thought of the charm the girl had given him and, sensing that it would please Bunny, flipped on his light bar and siren.

Driving away, he started to cry for the first time in a long time, for his wife and his daughter, who were dead and never coming back to life. And then suddenly he knew why he had lost control with that slime Allen, and why the little token in his pocket meant more to him by each passing second than that whistle ever had. Because Bunny's token symbolized his future, and that damn whistle his past. If Leo were to ask him this minute how much this town meant to him, he would know what to answer now: Everything. Everything in the whole damn world.

# 43

Harold Cager knew the whole story, he had been there since the beginning:

Larry Allen had not gone home that evening, and everyone that worked in the store that night knew that meant Larry was really pissed about something. Nobody knew what. They rarely did when he got this way, but they knew enough to stay clear, and to pass the survival tip on to any benighted employee, especially at the change of shift.

By the time the store closed and the night shift had come on, no one had seen Larry except Rachael Macht, who was working a late shift for Sarah Corning, and saw "the prick" come out through the liquor department, grab a six-pack of Budweiser, march by her and go to the meat department and pull two small chickens off the self-serve BBQ spits, slap them in a foil-lined warmer bag, glide by her with a scowl, and disappear through the swinging backroom door and up to his office. She passed this tidbit on to Harold who passed it on to those of the night shift who hadn't been warned, and nodded understandingly at the spontaneous groan that issued forth from the listeners. A small powwow of the night shift was called by mutual agreement in the main warehouse backroom, where it was agreed they'd all work like there was no tomorrow until Larry Allen left. Harold brought up the fact that it was impossible to tell when Larry Allen left. Larry had the master keys and could leave by the back if he wanted, meanwhile they'd be working under the gun for no reason.

Since it was generally understood that no one but a pure

grade Triple-A fool disturbed Larry when he got like this, Johnny Simmons suggested that if by midnight no one had seen him leave, they'd each take turns checking outside to see if his truck was gone, which meant leaving the store, which meant turning off the alarms and unlocking the door and repeating the process over and over again. Then Tommy Lin told Johnny Simmons he had his head up his ass because Larry would catch on real quick, and then he'd stay all night, and then that would mean eight hours of backbreaking work for sure. They brainstormed for a few minutes more, and were about to give up when Roger Wood, the night crew's boss, finally decided that Tommy and Johnny would stage a big fight about midnight right where Larry could see, and he'd speak out if he were up in that office, that's for sure.

At midnight a mock shoving and shouting match took place, and when Larry's voice in imperative tones did not shake the cans off the shelves, the night shift started laughing and relaxing, and breaking out the pop and munchies for their twenty minute (that usually stretched to thirty minutes) break. They had already rolled the floor, putting all the cased goods that were to be stocked down their proper aisles. They took their break, then busted their humps for three or four hours slinging the entire load, getting everything up.

This done they coasted for two hours, drinking beer and playing poker until the morning shift came on, then walked out to their cars together, and gasped in fear when they saw Larry Allen's Ford truck still sitting there. Had he been watching the whole time? Were they all going to be fired? Where the hell had Larry been all night that he hadn't reamed their asses out for goofing off? He must have left with somebody, Harold suggested, but Johnny offed that remark by saying matter-of-factly that he'd known Larry Allen over five years and that he didn't go anywhere without his Chevy. In a concourse of agreement everyone nodded their heads and looked uneasily at the red truck. Finally, Roger Wood suggested that they go back in and see if he was there, but before they could reach agreement, they all heard the sirens, and watched the two police cars and an ambulance swing into their parking lot and pull right up to the front door of the market. The crew ran as a herd back to the door, and as John Black was running into the store Bunny Coolins ran out, her big eyes opened wider than kiwi fruit. The crew grappled with her, and asked what had happened. "It's Larry Allen," she cried out. "He's . . . he's . . ." She choked on her words, and began to gag.

"What the hell is it!" demanded Roger.

"It's . . . it's awful . . . he's, he's dead. He's . . ." Bunny threw her hands up to catch it, but too late. She vomited all over Roger Wood, then sank to her knees, and began to retch in dry heaves.

While Roger danced backward, his face violated with disgust, Harold watched Rachael Macht, Steve Gorden, and several more of the morning crew hurry out of the store. Inside he saw Mike Edmonds push the paramedics aside and bolt for the door. When he got outside, Mike dropped to his knees and started gasping for air.

"What the fuck is it!" asked Harold, but it was too late, the big receiver began tossing his cookies, then Harold felt grazed by an arrow as Kevin Slangheimer pushed by. The deli man turned around suddenly and pointed at the big receiver. "It figures it would happen in your room, Edmonds," he yelled in accusation.

"What!" screamed Harold. "What happened!"

The deli man stared blankly at him, his eyes opening wide, glazed in remembrance. "It's Larry Allen . . . he's, he's . . . Oh, Jesus, I think I'm going to . . ." He sank to his knees and added his contribution to the rising smell of vomit.

Harold turned to the door, but made no move to go in. Instead he watched, as everyone who could, ran out.

Larry Allen saw the night crew roll the goceries onto the floor. They moved fast, sweat popping out on their brows and soaking their tee shirts in minutes. It was for his benefit, he recognized the symptoms of "the-boss-is-watchingitis" and leered at them in a particularly nasty manner through the two-way mirrored glass of his office.

High above them like a God, he thought, except a God can get laid once'n a while, and that fucking asshole police chief had ruined his fun. By God, that was unfair! A manager manages a store, and everything in it, for God's sake, and now that asshole has come in and fucked everything up.

Larry moved away from the window, turned his back on those pricks too.

He grabbed a beer from his desk, popped the tab, and guzzled it as he paced his office, thinking. The truth was, he was scared; scared shitless. It's a wonder the way a man's life can go to ruin in a few fucking hours, but that's what had happened to him. Damn! And where was Lynnanne, anyway? Christ, *he* was worried about her, for Christ's sake! Worried about what really *had* happened to her, and what the hell she would tell Kyle Richards once she was found.

Christ, the chief acted like *I* did it, for Christ's sake, thought Larry. If Lynnanne tells that big cop about him and her—son of a bitch, it'll be all over. That man had meant business when he'd squared him off about banging the help.

Larry slammed his fist on his desk and threw his beer across the room. It hit a picture of Neil Gathers, the plate of glass shattering into a bizarre spiderweb design. "Shit," he said out loud, and then slipped out the door. He checked his watch. It was near midnight. He glided through the back room and out into the liquor department and down the aisle past the meat department. As he rounded the corner, the pell-mell rumble of voices arguing wafted over the gondolas, and he saw Roger Wood run toward the front. It sounded like Johnny and Tommy were having a real hot argument. The rest of the crew would be up there too. People are like flies, they can't help but land on shit, so the whole fucking crew would be up there, and just as well, too, because he sure in hell didn't want to talk to

384

any of them.

He slipped through the double doors and into the empty warehouse, turned right, and headed down the long aisle back toward the receiving door. It was silent, the subaural hum of the large space broken only by occasional unrecognizable sounds. Rats, most likely, he decided. The lights were cut half-bank back here, by his orders to save money, but it made the huge room dark and full of lurking shadows. He made an effort to ignore the thoughts they evoked, listening instead to the sounds his shoes made clocking on the cement floor. The sounds were half swallowed by the ink-black shadows between the tiers of the high, scaffolding pallet racks. He made his way to the receiver's room, located by the receiving door, and noted with satisfaction that he could no longer hear the sounds of the arguing night crew—soundless back here, he thought, not even the rats.

He pulled his key ring out and fished for the proper key and fit it into the receiver's room door and opened it. He entered and flipped on a small desk lamp and sat down in the cramped office, his back to the door. Larry began filing through some invoices on Mike Edmonds's desk. In a minute he'd get to the real meat-and-potatoes matter of finding the invoices that had been altered. Larry believed that by bits and pieces Edmonds had begun stealing from the store, and to a dedicated man like himself that was heresy. Even with the worry on his mind, he had to go through his routine of being the manager. Perhaps, he reflected, that's what he loved about his job: when his emotions would waver, as they frequently did, the cure had always been the doing of the mundane aspects of his job, like a blind basketweaver making unconscious motions and losing himself in the task, bleeding off the tensions of life.

Larry sighed heavily, then concentrated on the stack of papers in front of him, checking for irregularities, running his finger down the quantities column, engrossing himself so that he lost track of time. So far, if Mike had been stealing, he hadn't been covering it up by altering invoices. This puzzled

Larry. The last inventory had shown a loss, and Larry knew that it wasn't walking out the door. Security against shoplifters was nice and tight. An occasional one here and there, but Larry's reputation for dealing with shoplifters was legendary and kept losses down to a minimum.

He sat back in the chair, stretched, and rubbed his tired eyes, then quickly opened them. He hadn't heard anything, but he could smell the scent . . . that lemon scent . . .

He felt pressure against his eyes and saw only blackness. Instinctively he reached up and grabbed two arms just above the wrist. The skin was cool and clammy to his touch, and he noticed another odor at the same time, a faintly foul smell.

"Guess who?" sang a familiar voice.

"Jesus, Lynnanne . . ." Larry tried to turn his head, but her hands held him rigid. God, she's strong, he thought.

"No fair, peeking." Her voice echoed; the teasing tone of her voice was very sexy. Larry felt aroused.

"Lynnanne, everybody's been looking for you all day. They think you're dead or something."

"I've been hiding. Waiting. Thinking, really. About us. You."

Larry tried to pull her arms apart and turn, but she was wood. "God, you're strong."

"Yes, I am, aren't I?" He noted a trace of glee in her voice. "And I'm strong enough to admit that you're the best thing that ever happened to me, Larry. Me crying, whimpering like a baby, when all you were really doing was making me a woman. That's what a woman is for, anyway."

Larry relaxed, a bit relieved. She sounded sincere, and that meant no trouble with the chief when he questioned her. Still, he was suspicious. "I'm glad you feel that way. You're right, y'know. A woman needs it too. Sometimes she just has to get used to it, but this is sudden—"

She pressed harder across his eyes, her hands were cold and damp. God, it hurt a little. "Easy," he said.

"Well, you're the fool, Larry Allen"—she mocked a

Southern Belle in tone—"Here you make me do it for so long, then, when *I* come to *you*, you act like I've got lice or something."

Larry didn't want her mad; the image of Kyle Richards flashed in his mind. "No, no. It's just that it's a sudden change, that's all. Listen, I'm glad you're safe, believe me."

That damn smell of lemons and light decay worried the inner tissues of his nose.

"Then you make love to me . . ."

"Listen, Lynnanne, I'd love to, but—"

"Unzip your pants, Larry Allen, and pull that monster out, you hear me. He's getting hard now, I can tell. He's a mean ol' monster who wants to roar in my cave, isn't he?"

Larry couldn't help himself. His member swelled. God, it was getting hard. It had never been this hard before. He tried to shift in his seat but couldn't move. He had to admit there was something sexy about the situation, not to mention Lynnanne herself. Still, Chief Richards hadn't been bluffing, and this could mean trouble.

"Now, don't you worry about the chief, Larry. He'll be fucking me soon, then we'll have the goods on him, won't we?"

"How did you know that's what I was thinking?"

"I've got a friend who's got 'ears all over this place.' Bigger, better 'ears' than that old blue knight'll ever have. Have you unzipped yet?"

Larry started to say no, but realized that he had and that he was holding his member in his own hands. It was hot, engorged with blood, throbbing, and felt larger than he had ever remembered it to be. "It feels like it's going to explode."

"Only in me. Promise, Larry."

"Okay, okay, but hurry!" He thought his dick was going to explode.

"I'm going to take my hands away, but you won't be able to open your eyes until I tell you."

"Okay, I'll keep them closed. I'll keep them closed," he said, but felt vaguely unsure that he could open them by his own will anyway.

"Now your hands down to your sides, and they can't move either, Larry."

His arms moved to his side. He felt his penis bouncing from the throb.

"I'm removing my hands now, Larry . . ."

He felt cold air over his eyes and forced himself to will his eyes open. They were pasted shut. He felt her hands touch his shoulders and turn him around on the small swivel stool so he faced her. The brief stink of rotten meat made him gag, then disappeared. He tried again to open his eyes but couldn't.

"It's payday, Larry. Payday. When you fuck Lynnanne, she fucks you back in speckled spades, Larry. Speckled spades. I want to make love to you, though. You taught me to love that. You can open your eyes now, Larry. Open them big and wide, Larry. Big. And. Wide."

Now, Larry didn't want to open his eyes. He fought to keep his eyes closed. His eyelids began to shudder. To twitch. Abruptly they popped open—

Ah shit, thought Larry, relieved. It *is* just Lynnanne. Smiling closed-mouthed at him. Her hair, a little dirty, hung in stringy blond strands. Her eyes, lackluster and deep blue, devoid of passion. She wore no bra under her zippered uniform top. Jesus, they never looked so huge, like large cantaloupes, for Christ sake, and would you look at her legs? He moved his eyes, straining to see. No stockings on. The thought of her naked sex under the burnt-orange nylon skirt made him wince with pain in his loin. He tried to speak and with effort said, "I really want you. More than anyone ever before." Then he looked up at her face. Small blue eyes attached to fleshy pink stalks writhed their way out of her nostrils. They moved uncoordinated for a moment, then their gaze riveted on him. *They're looking at me!* he thought. *Seeing me!* He tried to scream but couldn't. She spoke, and when she did he could see her teeth, now row upon row of silver needles. They made a metallic gnashing sound as she spoke: "I want you, too, Larry, but first I want you to suck my tits, Larry. My titties will be so glad to see you, Larry. So glad to . . ." She unzipped her top and opened it wide. A scream crammed in his mouth, but would not issue forth, could not issue forth. Two huge eyes hung from her chest like breasts, their blue gaze hungry with intelligence—evil and malicious. They blinked and he forced himself to look at her face. She was grinning. "It's payday, Larry," she said. "Payday." And then he heard the gnashing sound, hard metallic gnashing, like nails being forced together.

The sound came from under her dress.

Oh God, no! Oh God, no! his mind screamed.

"Oh, God, 'yes,' Larry. I want you so . . ." She raised her skirt and tucked its hem into the waistband so that he could see the vertical lips between her legs peel back and grin . . .

"Tin-grin, tin-grin," cackled the Lynnanne-thing.

. . . grin and reveal the silver-needle teeth gnashing, and gnashing together.

He sat helpless on the stool, frozen, a living mannequin. The Lynnanne-thing mounted him, gripped his penis, and fed it into her vagina piece by piece. Then she began to eat his face. Toward the end she let him gurgle a little, but did not let him die until she had turned his head to a small mirror mounted on the wall, and let him see himself, his face stripped down to white glistening bone, his eyes lidless, staring at his very own skull.

# 44

Kyle sat in the five AM cold of his kitchen breakfast nook. He gave a morose grunt as he downed his second cup of coffee. Yesterday had sure taken its toll on him: the disappearance of the girl, the investigation, and taking Larry Allen to task, had all been coated with the black syrup memory of the dream about Michele and Curtis—and of that robed horror feeding on them.

God, it's a wonder that he did keep his sanity.

He'd taken steps on that last night, though, and again it was all thanks to Leo Brumagin asking those maddening questions, like what would you do if you didn't have this town, this job?

What he had done was simple—he had made a decision to put the Ravana mumbo jumbo aside. He'd tucked everything—and that included a full written report on Ravana that he had compiled, and Dr. Lyon's books—in a box and shoved it up in his den closet, secreting the Dave Pickers painting and his own flow sheet away too, way in the back of the closet.

He had no proof! Damn it! He had faced that last night. The problem was in his mind and nothing more, and by every power in his possession he was not going to lose the ground he had gained, not now, not ever. He would as soon rot in hell first as go back to Woodhaven, and he would fight every thought, every emotion, and every action on his part that would send him back there. This was his life by the goodnes of God, and he wasn't going to lose it!

Kyle found himself holding the coffee cup halfway up to his mouth, staring into the oily black surface of the liquid. He felt that odd mental wrench that always came when he realized suddenly that he had been lost in thought. His fingers began to twitch and he became aware that he was holding the cup very tightly. To calm himself he brought his other hand up and guided the cup to his lips, savoring the hot liquid running down his throat.

More thoughts popped up, nagging doubts that swirled around like waterlogged floatsam half in and half out of his consciousness. As he rose to go jogging he felt the key worry strongly. Though he pushed it down, it kept bobbing up: if he were really free of this Ravana thing, he would have thrown the stuff out and sent Dr. Lyon back her book, now, wouldn't he, instead of putting it in his closet?

Kyle rinsed the cup, then placed it in the sink and stood there for a moment thinking. He had no corroboration of any of this. Even Coogle's "haints" were really nothing—it was spooky up there, and a coincidence.

Kyle nodded his head in affirmation, but when he grabbed his beeper and exited the back door, the feeling that he was lying to himself resurfaced. "Shutup!" He said out loud to his mind, and broke into a run without warming up first, eating up his own block of Eskay Street like a madman. He turned left at the corner, and slowed down gradually to a nice ground-eating pace as his peace of mind returned. He took the first full block easily, his mind mellowing. As he entered the second block, he looked around in anticipation . . . Yes, there he was.

Curtis was waving like a pennant in a windstorm as he ran toward Kyle at full gallop. "Hi, Chief."

"Hey, sport, long time no see!" Kyle felt better immediately. Curtis slowed up, executed a little circle around Kyle's back, and fell into pace with him. "Hi," he said.

"Hi, Curtis. We've been victims of circumstance."

"What's that?"

"I've been busy, and you've been busy. It's a wonder we can run together at all."

"Yeah, I know. Boy, my life sure seems busier than ever."

"It's called growing up," Kyle panted. "When you grow up too much, it's called growing old."

"Like you?"

Kyle gave a wry smile. "Yes. Like me. And since you're being such a smart guy, if you want to get paid you better do the work—my plants are dry as a bone; I left 'em alone, it's your job."

Curtis looked up at him, a shadow of fear and guilt running across his face.

Kyle smiled to put Curtis at ease a bit. "You gotta do the work to get the pay. Why haven't you been doing it?"

Curtis was breathing hard now. "You haven't been home."

"No good, Curtis. You've got a key, remember?"

The boy was silent as they ran further. Kyle was worried that Curtis had interpreted the discussion as too heavy-handed. "You can handle it today, if you want, after the run. The plants can take it. The fish need their food, though."

Curtis was still quiet. "Whoa-oa, boy!" Kyle touched his arm and slowed them down to a halting walk, then a stop. He turned around to face Curtis, reaching out and grabbing him by his shoulders, holding him off at arm's length. The boy looked perplexed. Kyle tried one of his smiles on him to no avail, so he asked again, "What is it?"

Curtis looked diffidently down to the sidewalk, so Kyle caught a knee on the cement, letting his hands run down to hold the boy by the elbows. "Nothing you can't tell me, son," he said, his face now at an even level with the boy.

Curtis brought himself to speak. "You know how you told me how you couldn't get into a barroom brawl if you stay out of a barroom?"

Kyle said that he did.

"Well, I don't go in when you're not there because I can't go into the bedroom—you know the one you made me promise not to go into?"

"Yes, I remember," Kyle said, the short hairs on the back of his neck began to tingle. "Go, on."

"Well, I hear noises in there . . . and I'm . . ." He seemed to struggle with a word, while Kyle waited patiently. Finally, ". . . I'm *tempted*," he said, "to go into the room, that is, at first . . . I was *tempted* to go in, but then I got . . . I got *scared* to go in . . ." The boy stopped and looked at Kyle as if for permission.

"Go on," said Kyle.

"I just get scared . . ."

"Of what?" Kyle felt his limbs go weak. "Of what, Curtis? You didn't go into that room, did you?"

Curtis shook his head violently. "No, I was afraid to . . . because of the noises. They scare me, so I don't go in the house without you."

Kyle's throat felt thick, the words hard to get out: "What noises?"

Curtis's face told Kyle that the boy had mistaken the trembling in his voice for anger. "No, Curtis, I'm not mad at you. I need to know what the noises were. What they sounded like."

For the first time Curtis looked him directly in the eyes. "The little girl singing, and the record player. She called my name, too, one time. It was spooky. And the bell, sort of a rocking chair one like my grandma's, that sound with a bell. Do you know the sound?"

Kyle tried to contain himself. "Y-yes, I know that sound, Curtis. Are you sure it came from the room, though?"

"Yes."

"Did you talk to that . . . voice, Curtis."

"No. I didn't. It wasn't right . . ."

"What do you mean?"

"It just wasn't right. It scared me. I thought it was maybe a tape recorder, maybe, but it scared me, so I didn't go back in." He looked at Kyle guiltily. "Are you sure you're not mad at me, Chief?"

"Yes, I'm positive, Curtis," Kyle answered. "You've just helped me out a great deal." He let the sentence linger, because

393

the waterlogged driftwood bobbed up in his mind again, this time a different piece: if Curtis heard Lisa's voice too, then Kyle wasn't imagining it, and if he wasn't imagining it, then something very strange, but very real, had walked into his den and written a very scary word that night.

Ravana.

Kyle's beeper went off, and a premonition exploded in his mind. "Come," he said to Curtis. The nearest telephone was at Curtis's house. Kyle stood in the kitchen dialing the station while Michele, wrapped in a pink robe, poured him a quick cup of coffee. He just got the first sip when he heard Sergeant Lotito's gravelly voice say, "You aren't gonna believe this one, Chief . . . I can't even describe what they found . . . God . . . it's . . ."

"Give it to me, Sergeant!"

"Homocide. A real mess. Larry Allen, the store manager at Gathers Market. Gory . . ."

"All right. Call county on this one, then. I'll be there as soon as possible." He hung up without another word.

"What's wrong, Kyle?" asked Michele, studying his face.

Kyle felt that one swig of her coffee turn sour in his stomach. He handed the cup back to her. "I've got to go now." He paused for a moment and answered her apologetically. "I'm sorry. The store manager at Gathers has been murdered." He paused for a moment feeling foolish. "There's more to it than that, I think." He stared wistfully at her face. "Much more." He hurried out the door without saying good-bye.

# 45

"I'm beginning to feel like I live here," Koger said, waiting for Kyle at the door of the market like a public-relations tour guide.

Kyle grimaced and stepped past several puddles of vomit on the outside. "From the aroma, I'd say we got a real winner here. Bad?"

The sergeant nodded. "As bad as you can get." He poked in the direction of the crowd outside with his chin. "Those are the strong stomachs, they made it that far. Every damn body had to have a look. Most of them put their breakfast in reverse right on the spot. Pretty grim."

Koger led the way past the empty checkout stands. Kyle followed beside him, amazed at the equanimity on the sergeant's face. "Can't be all that bad. You look all right."

"Used to be a diener in the army," Koger answered, guiding Kyle down an aisle braced on each side with canned vegetables, toward the back of the store. "Did about four hundred autopsies. Even this makes me sick, though."

"I could barely stand the autopsy we had to watch at the academy. Where are we headed?"

"Back room, near the receiving doors. He's in there sitting on a stool. Unbelievable." Koger pushed through the double doors; Kyle followed, reflecting on the sergeant's tone of voice. The last word had given Koger's game away. Everyone coped in his own way. Koger's way was not to feel, at least not to let it show, and the more outwardly calm he appeared the greater his need for control. It must be quite some show back there.

As they approached the receiving door, the smell of vomit added to the dry warehouse smell. Two uniforms were outside an open door talking with the ambulance team, and Kyle's inner voice began speaking to him in soft dreading tones: *They're not looking; everybody always looks.* And that could mean only one thing: nobody wanted to look. What a way to start a morning.

He greeted the group with a nod, then quickly stepped around them and in front of the door to a small room and gasped at what he saw. Cops, he thought. We like to think that the grisly sights we see in our career harden us to almost anything, but the truth is it makes us feel it more deeply. We just bury it in the deepest pit of our minds and say, "There, now I can take anything." Then something like this comes along. Vomit pushed in a sour column up Kyle's throat. He bit it back with discipline of twenty years of service; the small detective in his head to view, assimilate, and make sense out of homicide. It was hard to do, especially when you had not a cloudy-eyed corpse staring off into space, but a grotesque caricature of a human host welcoming you to some small chamber of hell. A six-foot-by-eight-foot-deep cell, almost floating in the smell of human feces, mixed with the cupric reek of arterial blood and stench of an almost inconceivable death.

Who in God's name would do such a thing?

It was Larry Allen, all right. Kyle would have recognized him without having been told, if solely by the out-of-style bow tie around his blood-soaked shirt neck, the white socks in the black wingtips, drenched in the dried red-rust color of blood. He sat on a stool facing the door, his back propped against a desk, dressed as Kyle had remembered him yesterday. In fact it could have been him yesterday if you ignored a few minor details: there was meat on his neck enough to hold the bow tie, but all that above was white glistening bone. A skull. Grotesque because the hair remained wavy and even combed slick-oily wet in the D.A. Larry had sported, but underneath was nothing but fresh-picked facial bone. There should be some blood, but it was as if the skull had been licked cleaned. It seemed almost a mask, the face missing . . .

*(An omen will It give of its coming, that the face will be eaten and . . .)*

Kyle focused on the eyes, left in the socket as if by afterthought, regarding him with introspection, the mouth hanging open, tongueless, unable to speak to say how it felt to have . . .

*( . . . loins devoured . . .)*

Where had he heard that? Read that?

Nancy Lyon's book on Ravana.

Without really wanting to, Kyle let his eyes drop to the black slacks and the intestinal mess that draped down to the floor in ropy, dried blood, brown-red strands, like sausage. His eyes willed themselves away—anywhere but there. Kyle forced them back to search and to see. The lower portions had been eaten, or ripped away, or *devoured*. Kyle could see no penis or testicles in the mess. They could be hidden somewhere in the mess, or they could be . . .

*DEVOURED!*

Kyle reeled away from the door, clutching his face with his hands. He heard the voices of the others, but he could tell by their tones that they misunderstood. He had not turned away to vomit at the sight, but clutched at his face because the word, that word, that single, solitary word had not come into his head, but was spoken into his mind: *Devoured*. And in that word was the epitome of evil, and when it finished its sounding, the hissing began; so loud, it was as if the snakes had crawled in his ears screeching their sound . . .

And now there was silence, except for Dwight Koger's strong hands pulling him up off a pallet full of cases of pineapple juice.

"Easy, Chief," Koger said. "I know. I almost puked and I used to cut 'em open left and right."

Kyle righted himself with Koger's help. God, he'd really gone down on that one. Unbridled fear spread in him, flashing across his consciousness, then he mastered it and accepted the other men's interpretation of his actions. "Sorry." The others made motions that no apologies were necessary.

Kyle took a few small steps from the area, breathing deeply and fearing what he was feeling. Intuiting. A legend?—an insane one for an insane man? Kyle winced at the thought. He heard the clang and creaking as those cast-iron doors raised, exposing the place where the hissing sounds and the snakes of madness twined their way through the branches of that damn tree; the beckoning robed figure underneath, its yellow eyes blazing, waiting for him, waiting to drive him mad.

Kyle stopped next to the forklift and braced himself against it. He closed his eyes and continued his breathing, trying to collect and collate his thoughts. Oh, God, how the ups and downs of this thing chewed at him. Yesterday he had been just fine, the decisions made, the madness a thing to be dealt with by choice; today, madness outside of himself, and nowhere to turn. To explain to anyone what he was thinking would itself make him a candidate for the loony bin—Christ! Woodhaven! Kyle shuddered at the thought, and moved on with his thinking. What had done it for him this morning? What had made him so damn sure that he was all right? It had been verification, unsolicited from Curtis—Curtis had *heard* the noises! *Heard!* not thought he'd heard, but heard the noises, the laughter of the ghost of his little girl.

Now, what he needed was someone reliable to trust, someone local—he'd cast the thought of calling Leo out altogether: another breakdown, was all he would say. The idea came to him quickly: Edgar Griffith, an objective, fair man, who would keep an open mind. Just examine the evidence, is all Kyle would ask. Perhaps with Curtis's corroboration, and Coogle's (because it was all tied to this store, wasn't it), and perhaps some validation from Dr. Lyon, he could swing Edgar over to his side. Convincing cases have been built on less than that, Kyle tried to comfort himself. As for now, there was the investigation.

The county sherriffs arrived shortly thereafter. Kyle pointed them in the direction of Koger and the little room, then intercepted the mayor, who had stalked in, his normally white face puffed and mottled red in rage: "What in the hell is going on in my store, Kyle! I've got a girl missing one day, and a dead store manager the next! Y'know, *I* had to go by and tell his wife! I've known him for twenty years and what the *fuck* is the county doing here? *I* told you when *I* hired you that I wanted all police matters handled by *my* police! Now, what the *fuck* is the county doing in my store!"

Kyle took a stance and eyeballed the mayor. "Don't *you* come into a murder investigation without the first clue to what is going on and climb in *my* tree, Mayor! Not before you take a walk back there and see what we're dealing with! This is no simple murder! You go on back and have a look! Your store manager hasn't got a face—it's been *eaten clean to the bone!* And whoever did, ate his dick and nuts too, it looks like! Go on back! We're not equipped to handle this! There's a pool of blood a herd of rhinos could bathe in back there! Go take a look!"

The mayor stood stunned at Kyle's blast back. It seemed to have cooled his heat to a simmer. "I'll go take a look," he said, then he looked around the warehouse searching for unwelcome ears. Safe. "Okay. I take it it's bad. But, bad publicity is bad for business, and I don't want any more of it. From now on leave the county out of this. If you haven't got what you need here to do the job, then you tell me what you need, and I'll get it for you. But from now on, no county. Got it?"

"I hear you," replied Kyle, his eyes not leaving the mayor's for an instant.

The mayor didn't like his answer, and looked like he was going to address that point, then thought better of it. "No county. Just remember that," he said, and walked back toward the carnage. Kyle hoped he puked his guts out.

"Chief," said a man behind him. Kyle turned and saw the

assistant manager—Tony, he thought the name was—standing just inside the double swinging doors. "Yes."

"You got a telephone call. You can take it up at the front if you want."

"Who is it?"

"Station."

Kyle followed him up to the front, and took the phone. "Chief Richards," Kyle announced, leaning on the floor manager's podium, watching Tony disappear down one of the aisles. It was Sergeant Lotito: "Chief, you had a red flag on a return call from a Linda Connelly, in Miami. You want me to tell her to call you back, or patch her through?"

Kyle groped for the name for a minute, then found it. Cathy Pickers's friend, the diplomat's daughter, born Melinda Belardis, married name, Connelly.

"Patch her through," Kyle snapped.

"Hello," said the voice. It was light and lilting, full of potential laughter.

"Hello, Mrs. Connelly. This is Chief Richards. Thank you for returning my call."

"My pleasure, but I'm not sure I know what it's about, Chief Richards."

"I wanted to ask you a few questions about Cathy Pickers, if you don't mind."

Kyle heard her gasp. She hesitated, then said, "My lord, my lord, Chief Richards, I haven't thought about that in years. Did you catch the person who did it?" All the humor had left her voice now.

"No, but I'm just doing a little checking. I understand that she was your best friend, right?"

"Yes. My lord."

"What is it?"

"No. I was just remembering. It was quite a shock when I found out. I was overseas, and I didn't find out until almost a year after she was dead. I stopped getting letters, y'know, but didn't think . . . then, finally I got a letter from a friend . . ."

400

"Yes. Let me ask you, did any law enforcement agency get ahold of you at all?" Kyle thought not, but sometimes records got misplaced.

"No. No one," she said.

"Okay, fine. Let me just ask you a few general questions, then." Kyle proceeded, and she responded. He maintained an even pace, pushing with difficulty the current investigation out of his mind, only to have it return and nag him like a horsefly. Koger was back there and the county had a very competent team. He hated to admit it, but he just wasn't necessary enough at this time to be back there.

After a few minutes Kyle had learned nothing new, and with a feeling of relief, a weight lifted off Dave Pickers's graveside plea, Kyle was just about to hang up, when he asked intuitively, "Mrs. Connelly, I know girls, and there are always secrets between them. Can you think of anything back then that she made you absolutely promise not to . . ."

"Oh, my lord, Mr. Richards. Oh, my lord . . . Y'know, I had forgotten. You asked about boyfriends . . . Well, her father was absolutely the worst about that, and I don't know why I forgot . . . probably because I was just leaving when she got involved, but she made me promise not to tell . . . Do you suppose that's why it slipped my mind?"

"It could be," said Kyle, wishing she'd get on with it but knowing that if he pushed, he could be the loser in terms of information. "Could you enhance on it a bit, please?"

"Oh, yes. There was a boy—an Indian boy—and she made me swear up and down never never to tell; her father would have killed the boy and maybe her too—he hated Indians. Said they murdered Cathy's mother . . . My lord, I never thought about that . . ."

Kyle's mind spun. Detail: Dave Pickers had said that there had been a boy there, that he had seen a boy. A link. This could be a big link, not only to the murder of Cathy, but to Ravana.

Kyle schooled his voice, coaxing, cajoling, interrupting the woman's girlhood reminiscing as she meandered to the point.

"Mrs. Connelly, if I may ask a question?"

"Yes?"

"What was the name of the boy?"

Kyle covered the mouthpiece with his hand, and held his breath, almost crushing his ear with the earpiece.

"Let me see . . . it was . . . it *has* been a long time . . ."

"Please, lady."

"My lord, Mr. Richards. I remember now. It was Wolf . . . yes . . . Raymond Wolf Elkhart. Everybody just called him Wolf."

Kyle's mind buzzed; he thanked her, then hung up.

Wolf.

# 46

Home by four-thirty, Kyle telephoned Edgar Griffith at the *Review* as soon as he walked in. A young nasal-voiced girl told him that Mr. Griffith had left for the day, but when he told her his name, she offered him Edgar's home number, adding that he had left just a few minutes ago, and "If you have to get him right away, he walks up L Street then turns on Marlin—it's about a fifteen-minute walk." Kyle thanked her, hung up, then rustled up his report on Ravana and Dr. Nancy Lyon's book out of the closet and rushed out the door.

He found the newspaper publisher just at the corner of L and Marlin and beeped him to stop with his truck horn and a wave.

Kyle stepped from the truck with his report and Nancy Lyon's book, and walked around to Edgar, who stood there like a small statue puffing a pipe. "Understand you've been busy," he said to Kyle. There was no smile on his face, and the twinkle in his blue eyes conflicted with the serious lines of his face.

"I'm sorry to bother you, Edgar. It's important, though; I believe very important."

Edgar searched Kyle's face, then looked down at the bundle Kyle was holding in both hands. He looked up at Kyle again in silence.

Kyle felt awkward and sensed something else troubling the old man but pushed on, driven by his own needs. "Edgar, I need some help. A special kind of help. I need you to keep an open mind about something. These . . ." He offered the report and book to him. Without hesitation Edgar opened his battered leather briefcase and slipped them in. He closed the clasp on the old case. It made a brass snapping sound that somehow marred the afternoon stillness of the street.

"Now, what is it that I've accepted so quickly, Kyle?" asked the old man.

Kyle searched for a way to explain, but found himself at a loss for the right words.

The old man puffed his pipe and stared frankly at him. "That bad?" he asked.

Kyle found his voice: "It's hard to explain," he said. "It's all in the report . . ." He stared into the wise old blue eyes for an instant and felt suddenly panicked. "Look, when you read it—the report—I want you to promise me to keep an open mind. That's very important. In fact, I think it would be better if you read the book first, then the report. The book's by Dr. Lyon, it's on a weird subject . . ."

"Most of her books are," said the old man.

Kyle sensed it again, something wrong with the old man. He interrupted himself and asked Edgar straight out what was the matter, to which the newsman reacted like a person caught being rude, overcompensating for it by extreme amiable smiles. "No. You've caught me in the middle of a little ritual—my walk home," he explained. "Thrown me off guard a bit, that's all."

A lie, but Kyle stepped over it. He couldn't worry about that now.

"You were saying," urged Edgar, touching the bowl of his pipe and pulling it from his mouth.

"Edgar, I've run into something very . . . shall we say . . . irregular. It involves the murder of Phael—Dave, too—and now the murder case from today. I'll warn you, as you read it, it will seem crazy, impossible, but what I've learned lately is that a lot of things seem impossible, but that doesn't make them so." Edgar started to speak but Kyle waved him off. "Look. I'm trusting you with this because I believe you to be an impartial observer when you want to be—I *need* you to be, in this case. Before you judge—and that's after you read what I've given

404

you—I would appreciate a chance to talk to you, and your word that you will keep this in strictest confidence. Will you do that for me?"

Edgar's eyes did not move from Kyle's face. "I don't know what this is, but I must admit that you've got my curiosity up. Okay, Kyle. How soon do you need to talk about this?"

Kyle offered his hand. "As soon as you can, Edgar. Please. It's very important."

Edgar shook Kyle's hand. "I'll get back to you as soon as I can." He released Kyle's grip, and turned down Marlin Street, not looking back.

Kyle watched the old man walk away, his tweed jacket swaying on his small frame, and felt some confidence. If he could get Edgar to believe, then he'd have a chance of getting others to listen. If not, he'd be in big trouble—*fucked*, he thought, was a better word for it, *fucked*.


Edgar stopped walking, ostensibly to bat the black remnant of his tobacco from his pipe. But it was sadness that really stopped him, holding him up just a little, enough time to clear his head so Clarice would not catch on. He had learned to like Kyle in the past few months, and respect him for the work that he was doing. But how hard it had been to hold still and not say a word during that last brief encounter, when in his inside coat pocket he had a letter from David Cornish, the newspaperman who had sent him the clippings on Kyle some eleven months ago. In a short note David wrote that he had been bored, trying to keep busy, and decided to do a follow-up on the Kyle Richards story—Whatever happened to Kyle Richards?—when he came across a piece of information that was going to turn some heads around. He said that he could not reveal his source, of course, but that he had checked the lead out thoroughly and found it to be sound: Kyle Richards had spent a year in a mental institution after the murder of his wife and child—Woodhaven, it was called. Kyle had been in pretty bad shape.

Edgar sighed and put his empty pipe in its belt holster and stood there looking at his home three doors down. For the first time in a long time, he didn't know exactly what to do. It was his duty to reveal the information, but then Kyle would lose his job. Then, again, Kyle seemed normal, and if he was discharged, then the doctors most assuredly had pronounced him well—maybe.

A dilemma.

Kyle had been doing an excellent job, and Edgar had noticed no "crazy" behavior on his part. The death of a wife and child (and brutal deaths, at that) were enough to make any man need a "rest," but the question festering in Edgar's mind was what kind of "rest" had the man needed? In all due conscience, he would have to check it out with the people at Woodhaven; he could get David to squash what he was doing if Woodhaven checked out okay, and until then Kyle deserved the benefit of the doubt. After all, Kyle had said or done nothing to indicate that he was unfit for duty, had he?

No, thought Edgar, and he continued up the three doors to his house, his briefcase noticeably heavier by the new addition to its contents.

# 47

Father Charles's sleep evaporated like steam off a cauldron. He sat bolt upright from under his ragged sleeping blanket and stared starkly out through the night across the road toward Gathers Market. The store's huge plate-glass panes projected eerie neon light onto the asphalt screen of the parking lot. Traffic was nonexistent; the only cars in the lot were parked in the fire lane right up close to the door. The time? Midnight, he would guess, he had no watch, except an internal one, one that woke him up and made him stare, and feel that something terrible had just taken place. He scratched through his croaka sack and pulled out the old binoculars and turned them on the storefront. He was in the same place where he had once spied on that big police chief as he went out to see the old man. Up on a hill, just out of sight, and staring at the spot where once the trees had stood . . .

Now the market.

Nothing to see, but something had happened in the store—he could *feel* it.

He kept his distance, spying throughout the night with his field glasses. In the early morning people ran out of the market vomiting. Soon police cars and an ambulance arrived, their lights twirling, their sirens shrieking. Then the big police chief pulled up and entered the store. Several hours later, the ambulance attendants rolled a black-plastic-covered gurney out the door, with the lumpy figure of a body on it. They loaded it into the ambulance and pulled slowly away.

After he watched the ambulance drive out of sight, he turned his back on that evil place and knelt to pray.

He prayed first for the policeman, who, although Father Charles did not know in what way, was a part of God's Will in all of this; and then for the soul of the freshly departed; and finally for himself. It would be tonight, he knew that much, and he was afraid.

He passed the day in prayer, foregoing food and water, although he had both, and his stomach cried out and the lining of his mouth felt ragged and dry. *Penance. Penance.* "Oh, my God, my Father. Why am I here?" he pleaded constantly throughout the day and into the night, until his voice was hoarse. Still there was no answer, no direct answer, there never was, only the feelings, the overpowering sense of what was wanted, what must be done. That feeling rose up in him now. "Please, God. No. I'm so afraid," he beseeched. But he knew there would be no mercy.

As closing time for the market neared, he watched the men of the night crew arrive one by one, then left his hiding place and walked down the small hill and across the road into the parking lot of the store. He left everything behind, except his crucifix, a purple stole, and a small, worn leather missal.

He peered through the market window. The large black hands of the store clock read nine-thirty-five. He'd have to get in soon. As ten o'clock rolled around, the manager tended toward getting rid of customers, his eyes peeled for anyone coming in that he might have to shoo out later. Father Charles knew that for sure. He had spent many nights since the store opened, observing the routine. Why? He had never known; he had been guided, as he was guided now.

But this time he was scared.

His heart thumped harder in his chest. He felt his adrenaline kick in, but was disgusted with his weakness: he wasn't even inside the market yet, and once he was inside he didn't know what he would find—not exactly. All that he really knew was that what was in there was evil, and what he was guided to do was for his own soul. Still, when his legs began to move toward the door, he wanted to turn and run, to run and never stop. Instead, he tucked the stole in the right pocket of his tattered tweed coat, and the missal and crucifix in the left-hand pocket. He fished the three dollars that he had been saving for God only knew what purpose, and clutched them in his right hand. He marched through the pneumatically opened double doors, slid through the chrome turnstile, and headed toward the liquor department, recording the look of distaste the checker gave him.

The dark-haired man at the manager's stand with the orange vest caught a glimpse of him and wheeled around with nonchalant purpose and headed down the aisle toward him. The man adjusted to intercept him as he turned down the meat and deli aisle. There, a meat man, robed in a white smock and paper hat, was running a heavy green cover over the meat case and did not look up as he passed. Father Charles paused at the fresh fish section and looked over the bin at the wines kept there as a plus sale for the market—fish and white wine. He picked up a bottle with his left hand and pretended to examine the label.

"We got more up in liquor," said the dark-haired night manager, who had eased around the corner and pretended to be going up to the front.

Father Charles turned to him and said thanks. He watched the man's blue eyes dart down to the three bills in his hand, and saw the suspicion fade from the man's face.

"Got some good cheap stuff up front. Gallon," the man offered.

Father Charles thanked him again and the man was off. So this is what the three dollars had been about. Indigents don't come in to buy, but to steal. Understanding, he marveled at the guidance. He replaced the wine, and looked down the aisle to see the night manager going around the corner. The meat man coughly lightly and turned away from the priest, continuing the roll of the plastic cover. Father Charles pushed quickly through the swinging doors leading into the meat department and scuttled down a corridor that took him behind the walk-in cooler. He turned a corner, getting out of sight just as the swinging door crashed open. Probably the meat man. The steps walked easily away from him. He hadn't been seen.

But how long could that last?

He mounted some boxes and a crate, then grabbed the top edge of the cooler box and swung himself up. He rolled on his back as he made it, landing as quietly as he could on top in the dust and dirty grease. A blower whooshed to life startling him. He cursed the noise until he realized it hid the sounds he might accidently make.

He risked movement just one more time to wiggle his way away from the edge, and pulled his crucifix out. He clutched it to his lips, kissed it, and prayed to Almighty God for an answer to his question:

*Why am I here?*

Again no answer, and soon the lights dimmed. The meat man was leaving. After a time the store quieted except for mechanical things and that whispery sibilance of noninhabited buildings.

Occasionally, a chip of a voice from the night crew or an odd noise from their activity broke the silence, but soon he realized he had made good his entry.

But as he lay there he began to feel *It. It* discomforted him. *It* frightened him. *It* made him want to leave. *It* fouled the air with an odor no nose could detect. And he knew it was with this *It* that he would have to deal. Or *It* with him, he thought grimly.

He began a mental cleansing, a praying, then waited. After at least two hours, he was guided to climb down and head back toward the rear of the corridor to a door. He reached out and opened it slowly. A stairway—leading down. The low-wattage yellow bulbs cast a sick, jaundiced light on the cream-colored walls. It looked like the throat of a dying man. He paused, then pulled out the purple stole, kissed it, and draped it around his neck. He found his crucifix and missal, and wished for a vial of holy water. He stared down the stairwell.

*It* was down there.

His feet began to move forward. He was on the landing. The door closed slowly on its pneumatic pull; Father Charles began his descent. Dread mounted in him as he took the first and the

410

second step. When he reached the third step the terrified screams of the night crew rose in his mind, and the reek of putrid meat wafted up to him from below.


Roger locked Tony, the assistant manager, out at ten-thirty and returned to the dressing aisle that faced on the produce department. They'd come in at nine-thirty, the night crew, and Roger, who was night foreman, got the other three rolling the floor right at ten o'clock. With a lot of hump and sweat each of the men had the aisles of his sections crowded and cluttered with stacks of cardboard boxes filled with goods. With Tony gone, that left Lenny in dry goods, Corey had canned vegetables and meats, and Patrick working the milk box and paper aisle.

Roger was twenty-six, and had worked his way up from a box boy, so he knew the ropes. He knew how to handle the night crew, too. This was a good one. They had fun, and got the job done, too. That was the name of the game.

He pulled a cutter from his pocket, moved the slide to expose the blade, then began cutting the small dressing boxes open with an expertise honed by years of practice. He loved the zip sound of the cardboard as it fell to Gillette's best. He had turned that Muzak shit off the PA, and now the night crew worked to the throbbing-rhythm rock and roll of KSLM, K-Slam, 104-FM on your radio dial. That music sure made the sweat easier to take. He lined up the cut boxes in a row on a four-wheeled worktable, then checked the price book, Kraft Italian, 8oz, then adjusted his Garvey marker and slammed home the price on the top of a dozen of those skinny-necked bastards. He dropped the Garvey, and loaded the bottles into their spot on the second shelf, right next to the Kraft Thousand Island, 8oz. He grabbed the empty box and with a flourish threw it onto a four-wheeler load-cart. In twenty minutes he'd have that thing jammed with empties, then he would wheel it back and dump them by the baler, scattering them to the four points of the compass around that big overgrown trash compactor just so that Mexican Padilla would hoot and holler in the morning when he had to load all that shit into the baler.

By eleven-forty he had made four such loads, and had met Corey near the baler and told him to rebuild the holiday paper goods display that stood in the wide aisle between the meat and deli department. Pre-Thanksgiving customers had ravaged the shit out of it. Corey twisted his moon-face into a grimace. Roger said in mock contrition, "Hey, it's gotta be done, Corey." And then their talk turned to Larry Allen, and how terrible it was, and who the fuck could have done it. Roger noticed uneasily, as Patrick and Lenny joined them back by the baler for an unofficial break, that those two referred to "whatever" had done Larry in, and not "who." They had all been here last night, except Corey. And what puzzled Roger was how he had heard nothing, hadn't even noticed anything, and he had actually pulled a pallet load of Best Foods Mayonnaise for an end display from the racks not thirty feet from that damned receiving office—crap!

"You guys, listen up," said Roger, marking each one of the three separately for emphasis. "You hear anything peculiar, you give a yell. I figure last night somebody got in while Larry was going out, got him, killed him, then left the same way . . ." He looked at all their faces, seeing the effect of his speech. They looked sober enough. It was spooky in a store at night at best, and this warehouse was the worst of all, high ceiling, dark corners even in full light with the high stacks of boxes, and pallets and all. "I walked the doors with Tony before he left, we're locked up tight, so that won't happen again . . . so . . . let's get back to work, okay. Let's throw that load so we can have an easy break, okay."

"Let's move it!" He clapped his hands, and everyone laughed. A whip-cracking foreman he wasn't. He smiled at them and pulled his four-wheeler, weighty with cartons of pickles and relish, out to the dressing table. He stopped the cart, and had started to pull his cutter out when he noticed the double doors to the produce back room swinging slightly.

412

He grinned.

He was an old hand at grocery-store practical jokes, from over-inking a guy's marking gun so when he stamped prices he got sprayed with fine dots of indelible ink, to "unofficial" schedule changes that got you in a lot of trouble, and a phone call at home asking why you hadn't shown up to work. One of the others, probably Lenny, had run like hell and beat him over here.

A moan, lingering and baleful, issued forth through the stainless steel batwing doors: *Whoh-OH-OOH.*

"Yeah, right, Lenny," Roger spoke to the door, then with a gleeful smile ran over to the wet rack of the produce department and reached under the protective cover and pulled out two heads of lettuce, laced nicely in plastic netting, round and green, like vegetable bowling balls. He waited for the moaning to start.

*Whoh-oh-ooooh-oh!*

"Oh-oh your ass, Leonard!" he screamed with glee, and heaved the green heads through the clear section between the top of the batwing doors and the top of the door frame.

The moaning ceased. Roger heard the crash of boxes falling.

"Hey fuckhead," he cried out, and rearmed himself with two more of the green cannonballs, then approached the door. He paused outside and took deep breaths to a silent count to charge: one, two, *three!* He rushed inside.

The room sat empty, except for the heavy waxed cardboard boxes of vegetables, the stacked crates of apples, oranges, and other fruits. "Come on, Lenny, I got ya," he said out loud, searching frantically with his eyes. He had to be back in the corner, behind that double stack of apple boxes. Roger moved toward the stack, his back to the preparation table and the industrial tub. Where are the heads of lettuce? he thought as he reached the back wall; then he heard a wet slimy sound, like someone getting out of a bathtub . . .

He twirled around.

The dead man stood erect in the tub, dripping the green slime that pooled knee deep around him. In mirror-image

413

mockery he was holding out the two heads of lettuce Roger had thrown in the room. They dripped with slime.

Roger stood, a statue on rubbery legs.

*No! No!* he wanted to scream, but his jaw seemed locked.

"Yeah-ss, yeah-ssss." The voice, cracked and ancient like a Cro-Magnon death rattle, mocked his thoughts.

*It can read my mind.*

"Yeah-ss, yeah-ssss." The corpse tossed the slimy heads of lettuce, first one, then the other, at him like Roger threw a rubber ball to his four-year-old-son. "C-catch-ch," the dead man said, and stepped out of the tub. The slime dripped in slow gooey globs, forming puddles at its feet.

Roger's heart triphammered in his chest and throat and he cursed the fear that held him fast. If that thing moved toward him . . .

It moved, but not toward him. It sidestepped in stiff, sticklike steps, and blocked the door.

*Shit!*

The sound of something surfacing the muck in the tub forced Roger's eyes to the tub. Another corpse sat up, a female this time. She turned her head toward him and grinned. She stood up and stepped out. He heard the mucky surfacing sound again . . .


Corey stood with his hands on his hips in the aisle formed by the meat department on one side and the self-service deli on the other and made a *tsch-tsch-tsch* sound with his tongue against the inside of his mouth. What a mess shoppers could make out of a display. The display stood mid-aisle (this was the widest aisle in the store), and held holiday goods: plates, cups, napkins, paper tablecloths, all stacked to form a rectangular block. A block of different forms of paper, dyed in autumn colors of brown, orange, and rusty red. Stuck in the middle of the display impaled on a white cardboard pole was a three-dimensional paper turkey sporting a black pilgrim's hat replete with a black hatband and silver buckle.

414

"Look what they did to your display, Tom," Corey said to the paper turkey. "Fucked it up is what they did."

He squatted down by the nearest corner where a tower of napkins leaned precariously out toward the cheese in the refrigerated deli bin.

"Excuse me, young man, where might I find the tomato sauce?" said a voice behind him.

Corey kept right on doing what he was doing, shoving a recalcitrant package of napkins back in toward the display where he hoped it would stay, ignoring the fucking customer. It happened a thousand times a day. They act like you aren't working or something; that's why he liked working at night, no fucking customer to inter—

Hey, this *is* the night, he realized, and pulled both hands away from the display and in toward his body in a protective position. The tower of napkins began to fall, then fell, cascading on the floor. He did not turn around.

"Excuse me, young man . . ."

Corey turned his head, with a sort of grin forced on his face to whoever the fuck it was behind—

He pushed back and twisted at the same time, falling into the display and scattering it all over the aisle.

A skull, dirty, floating without benefit of neck or body or anything, hung there in midair thirty-six inches from his face. Just floating. It tilted down to accommodate Corey's sprawled position. The jaw opened, and it spoke to him in stench-filled shit-brown puffs of gas: "Excuse me, young man. Where might I find the tomato sauce?"

Corey began a backward crab-walk through the paper goods. "Help," he said weakly. It was hard getting the air out.

The skull moved toward him in a bouncing fashion, in a manner suggesting it rested on an invisible body that had just walked forward.

"Fucking hel-el-ellllppppp me-eeeeee!" screamed Corey, moving backward on his hands and feet, toward the back wall, slipping on packages of paper cups and napkins. A shopping cart rolled past him pushed by a skeleton woman, wearing a ragged purple sundress. Ropy strands of dirty black matted hair hung down stiffly around her skull. A small child's skeleton sat in the cart's kid seat. She stopped by the meat bin, reached under the green night cover, and chose a package of hamburger, picked it up and put it in her cart.

The floating skull moved closer. "Excuse me, young man . . ."

"*Hel-elppp! Oh-oh hel-ellppp!*" screamed Corey, mounting speed on his backward crawl.

"*Oh hel-lpp! Oh hel-lllppp!*" screamed the skull, and around the corner of the gondola flew a formation of twenty bodiless skulls, their ragged hair caught by the rush of air from their forward movement, their mouths open.

"*Hel-elllppp! Hel-elllppp!*" they screamed, heading straight for Corey.

"*Oh fuh-uh-uhhhhckkkkk!*" screamed Corey.

"*Oh fuh-uh-uhhhhckkkkk!*" screamed the skull.

"*Oh fuh-uh-uhhhhckkkkk!*" screamed the squadron, closing fast.

Corey flipped over, and started to scramble toward the back wall and safety. If he could get back there and around the corner, maybe he could get help, or at least into the back room, lock himself in a freezer or something . . .

He slipped.

His feet caught a package of napkins each, his hands slid on packages of paper cups. All four slipped out from under him at once. His jaw crunched the floor. He tasted the copper taste of blood and looked up. The wind was knocked out of him. He struggled to breath, his vision preternaturally sharp. Standing before him was a giant boar. It snorted through a snout guarded by vicious curved tusks. Stiff bristle-hair covered its brown hide. It glared at him through small deadly eyes.

Still out of breath, all he managed to say was a weak, "Oh shit."

"*Oh shi-iiitt!*" screamed the skull.

"*Oh shi-iiitt!*" screamed the squadron, now practically upon him.

The boar lowered its head and charged.

Patrick was pushing a 48-oz. Campbell's Pork and Beans that he had just priced onto its space on the canned vegetable aisle when he heard Corey's first scream. He turned his head slightly, then began to rise, but was brutally knocked to the floor, by something that dropped from above. His shoulder burned as if on fire. He reached back and felt warm liquid. He pulled back his hand; it was smeared with fresh red blood. He righted himself and stood up, numb with shock. Still staring at his hand, he opened his mouth to cry out, but a scuttling-hopping noise made him look up. He spotted gray membranous wings and huge silver eyes as it leaped at him, cracked open his chest, ripped out his heart, and feasted amidst a gushing wellspring of rich red arterial blood.

Lenny's big gold-frame glasses slipped down on his acne-pocked nose, so he pushed them back up with a sigh. God, there was a lot of work to do tonight. He leaned his short skinny frame into the pallet framework in the backroom, pulling out Del Monte peaches for a display stack. His long brown hair dropped around to his face so that he habitually shook his head to keep it out of his eyes as he loaded cases onto a two-wheeler dolly. He was putting the fifth case on the stack when he thought he heard the thread of a scream from somewhere out on the floor. He thought nothing of it; a lot of practical jokes were pulled on the night shift, he was used to it. Probably Roger with one of his two-cheeked Moon Over Miami shots from the top of a gondola, or something just as gross. But the sound had made him stop, his hands still on the case. He looked up and gasped in fright. He recognized it, of course. He had once worked for his uncle's extermination company, and when you did that kind of job you couldn't help but run into more than a few spiders. The red hourglass design on the belly gave it away right quick—a black widow.

417

"Screws its mate, then *eats* him," Lenny's uncle used to say everytime they came across one, then would smile wryly at him and finish with a chortle. "Have to be one good fuck for that price, let me tell you, let me tell *you*."

It emerged fully from the eight-foot-square opening in the ceiling, where the conveyor belt fed through from above. The front legs first, then some more legs; the front thorax, then the bulbous black behind scraped the sides of the opening as the spider pulled herself through. She walked across the ceiling in that gravity-defying way of her kind, legs feeling ahead, catching the gray metal scaffolding of the three-tiered pallet racks. Getting purchase there, she crawled down and around toward the floor.

The floor between Lenny and that long stretch of warehouse that led to the doors to the shopper's floor.

Lenny thought his heart was going to burst with terror. That *fucking* spider's body as big as a *fucking* cow.

He struggled against his fear. It wouldn't do him any good to panic. The only thing he could think up to justify the spider's size was a mutation—a mutant spider. They grew giant vegetables, didn't they? And babies from test tubes, and things. Somehow, this was a mutant spider, and one thing he knew how to do was kill spiders—that is, if he had D-7 or some other kind of spray . . . or a fucking flamethrower. Christ! The fucking body is *bigger* than a cow by a good couple a feet!

The spider was almost to the ground now.

He shot through his options. He could get into the scaffolding and hide, but what chance would he have? The other choice was to kill it—squish it! Automatically he scanned the warehouse area left to him—the forklift.

The spider hit the floor and stood there, staring. Eight iridescent violet eyes watched him. Don't panic! Lenny grunted. The forklift! The forklift! He could spear it with the front forks of the lift. The protection bars that went over the cab to keep falling objects from hitting the driver would offer some protection. He could ram it and get the hell out of here anyway, out to the front.

Lenny glanced back as he started for the forklift. Violet eyes. They always had seemed black to him before. Then again, the spiders he'd seen were all small fry compared to this one. And they were dumb, he remembered that. But these eyes unnerved him, because they weren't dumb eyes; a flicker of intelligence moved across the eight of them. They studied him. When he moved toward the forklift, it crawled to a space of warehouse floor and took up a strategic position; now Lenny could not get back to the scaffolding to hide, and could not pass around the creature without being an easy kill.

Trying not to spook the creature, Lenny forced himself to walk slowly, keeping his eyes on the spider. The other side was bare wall, the back side the corrugated steel of the warehouse receiving door. He might have a chance with the receiver door, although it still had the yellow Crime Scene sticker on it: Do Not Enter, and it was always kept locked. The receiving door was beyond hope. It would take an act of God to open that.

He was almost to the forklift when the electric whine of its motor started up. He looked quickly. No one in the damn thing. The lights on the machine came on like giant yellow eyes opening.

*Crap!*

The forks on the lift raised themselves to his chest level.

*No!*

He scuttled toward the lift.

Its engine revved viciously and the thing lunged at him.

He jumped back, his attention fully on the new adversary. He felt himself snatched quickly from behind. God, the spider! Pain rushed through him as its fangs punctured his chest, injected the venom; the spider began twirling him around with her legs, wrapping him in sticky silk.

Lenney was still conscious, paralyzed now. He knew his fate—he had learned about spiders working for his uncle. Their venom was really digestive juices, and so as his consciousness faded all he could think of was the rest of the story, that once the venom dissolved his innards, the spider would stick his fangs back in him, and through them suck back up all the juices, like soda through two sharp curved straws; and all that anybody might find of him would be a dried up skin-sack filled with bones wrapped in glistening wet white silk, like a present for the devil.

Father Charles approached the bottom step slowly, stepped down, and faced the door. The smell was terrible down here. A stink of shit and rotted flesh. He stared at the door that led beyond, and knew that It, whatever It was, lay behind that door. He reached out and opened the door. A rush of even fouler air assaulted him, accompanied by the howl of some distant ethereal wind. It was black in there. He had no light . . .

*The light of God shall lead thee . . .*

Why am I here? Why? For my soul?

He thought of turning and running. The thought seemed sound to him now. More sound and healthy than going in there.

A bray of demonic laughter sounded from within. Then a voice: *No brides of Christ to fuck in here, Priest. No souls for sale here, only bought, Priest. Only bought, only bought.*

"In the name of the Father, and the Son, and the Holy Ghost," incanted Father Charles. Now he felt moved to enter and he did so, then cried out, "Oh my God, no! Please, God, no!" But his feet shuffled toward the darkness, into the darkness. The door closed behind him. He was not alone. When he cried out in prayer, "Why, God? Why?" It was not God who answered him . . .

*Oh Ye of little faith . . .*

but the Other . . .

*Mine is the light of the World . . .*

who spoke to him the answer to his plea:

*Sacrifice! You, wasted Priest, are the Sacrifice, the Blood of the Lamb!*

# 48

Dormant until now, the black heart of the Beast began to stir.

Sunday:

Tony Daley, the assistant manager, pulling extra duty since Larry Allen's death, and hoping to be made the new manager, opened up and found the night crew missing; Harold Cager, fresh off a hot date and no sleep, arrived just a little bit early to have his morning french fries. He watched in horror as Corey Bondahl's head rose out of the automatic deep-fryer, staring at him with puffed burned skin and collapsed jelly eyes; Jorge Padilla cursed the fucking *gringo* night crew leavin' their damn boxes all over, then pushed the red compress button on the baler and watched wide-eyed, screaming *Madre mia!* as Patrick Bartrow's bodily fluids gushed out from the steel plates of the baler, and all over Jorge's brand-new eight-dollar Nike running shoes; Wally Tantenbaum in the meat department pushed the green forward button beside the walk-in meat locker door and stood stunned as two headless naked human bodies came chugging out, gaffed in the back by the hanging hooks like any other piece of prime meat; Steve Gordon, in produce, tiptoed carefully back into his back room to find Roger Wood floating face up, grinning in rictus, hair waving lazily in the mixture of dirty water and his own blood.

Up until then, the black heart of the Beast had slept, dormant but never content. After that point it began not only to beat, but to gain rhythm, and the contractions increased in strength and frequency, until it throbbed, shaking with anticipation as It sat there staring west toward the town, the town where The Chosen lived. Staring with the plate-glass panes of its eyes, and calling, calling with all the voices of all the lost souls of the damned and condemned of Hell for the *Ehkeh-Heh*, the Chosen One, *Ehkeh-Heh*, the Fallen Warrior, *Ehkeh-Heh*, the One Who Will Surely Fail.

*Ehkeh-Heh, Ehkeh-Heh, Ehkeh-Heh, Ehkeh-Heh,* intoned the grotesqueries in convulsive beat, but they soon picked up another chant: *Kyle! Kyle! Kyle! Kyle! Kyle! Kyle!* and in town, the police chief woke up braying, clawing at his ears, and ramming his head repeatedly into the cherrywood headboard trying to make it stop, *make it stop! make it sto-o-opppp!*

# 49

"Koger, where the hell's the county?" Kyle ran a hand through his hair. He felt unclean, though he had showered thoroughly this morning. It's this damn market, he thought. It makes me feel dirty.

He had come down as quickly as possible and given the station an order to call county sheriff's homocide, the mayor be damned.

"I'll find out." Koger said. He turned to go, but stopped.

"The county's not to be called, Chief Richards." The mayor's wheezy voice came from behind him. Kyle turned and glared.

"I thought I made that perfectly clear," Neil Gathers continued patiently, "yesterday. No outsiders."

"We're talking about murder, here." Kyle pointed to a thick rust-red smear of dried arterial blood that had spurted and pooled itself around a half-empty case of Campbell's Pork and Beans. "Not simple stuff like a clean shotgun blast, but wholesale murder; decapitations, a man smashed in that machine back there, another's throat's slit and stuffed in a bathtub, for Christ's sake. Some poor dumb kid was waiting for breakfast when his best friend's head popped up in the deep fryer like a Pop-Tart at the snack bar! You want a treat? Go over to the meat department and look at the two bodies—sans heads, I might add—hanging like beef on hooks. And to make matters all fucked up, we've got four bodies, two with heads, two without. We found one of the heads, the other's missing. Your man Tony tells me that none of the bodies are small enough to be of his cousin Lenny, who worked last night.

"To give you the short version: four clocked in, and we've got substantial evidence that there were five people here last night. We've got to find the fifth, and go over each murder with a fine-tooth comb . . ."

The mayor raised his hand in protest; when that failed he raised his voice and interrupted. "I told you to buy what you need . . ."

"I need a forensic lab!"

"Then contract the forensics out to the county, but keep the investigation city, got it?"

Kyle glanced back at Koger, who had backed away, observing intently with his dark eyes. Kyle turned back to the mayor. "The county is in, or I'm out, got it?"

Neil Gathers shrugged. "If that's the way you want it, Kyle, it can be arranged."

Kyle stiffened. His mind seemed to cease except for one clear image, a fleshy canvas of skin, and from that, swelling up like fresh bruises, the word, "Woodhaven." Somewhere, not so distant now, snakes hissed, and though Kyle could not see them, he *felt* them, twisting, squeezing, slipping their oily firehose bodies over and against one another, writhing to be free, to slip and untangle themselves and drop, drop down into his—"Let's talk about it in the office, shall we?" said the mayor.

Kyle wanted to punch the mayor in the mouth, but instead he looked away to Koger, who took a sudden interest in the varieties of green peas on the second shelf of the opposing aisle.

"Koger knows the score, don't you, Dwight?" said the mayor. He smiled his unctuous smile at Kyle and Kyle remembered that Koger was an "outside" recruit, and that brought one thought to mind: "mayor's man."

Kyle fixed his eyes on the mayor's sharkskin suit and followed it up to what had been Larry Allen's office. The mayor took the same seat Larry Allen had taken when Kyle had put the fear of God into him, and threw his feet up onto the desk. "Close the door," he ordered.

Kyle closed the door.

"Let me be blunt, Kyle," began the mayor, "this is *my* town. And it may be *correct* police-wise to call in the county, but I don't want any *outsiders* in this thing. *Control* is what I'm after, *control* is what it's all about—"

"What about the murders? We haven't got *control* of them, and in my professional opinion we're going to *need* outside help."

The mayor removed his feet from the desk and rolled up to the desk, a businessman listening to a propositon: "You have something on this?" he asked as if his interest was piqued.

"Yes." Kyle hesitated. Letting anybody know his thoughts about what was really going on in the market would be a task; telling the mayor, impossible. But there was really no choice here, was there? If what Kyle believed was happening was happening, then the mayor would be the man who would be the most help. If only Kyle could get the mayor to believe him. A chance in hell on that one, but he had to try. Slowly and deliberately he told Gathers everything. When he had finished, the mayor sat motionless, his pudgy hands clasped together resting on his desk. Then, he rocked back in his chair and gave a loud, barnyard laugh: *Har-Har-Har.*

Kyle wanted to shove his foot down the man's throat.

The mayor stood and leaned toward Kyle. "Sounds to me like maybe they let you out of Woodhaven too soon, Kyle," he sneered. The mayor watched him for a reaction. "That's right. I've known all along. Had you checked out. Doctor's cleared you, okay, but from that story you made up they could have made a mistake. You must want the county in here pretty bad."

Kyle's gut twisted in the grip of invisible iron fingers.

The mayor raised both hands. "Don't get me wrong. I would never have brought you on board if I didn't think you could do the job—and you have—you've done a marvelous job, but it's time you recognized the god of the well from whence you draw

425

your water, Kyle."

"I'm telling you that there are going to be more murders, and I'm telling you—"

"And I'm telling *you*—Gathers slammed his hand hard on the desk; the telephone's receiver jumped, the phone's bell jingled briefly—"that I don't want to hear any more about this. There's a murderer out there, and your job is to catch him—end of job description." He pointed a fat finger at Kyle. "Now, I'm telling *you* to either get your ass out there and do your job, or go back to Woodhaven along with your devils and your demons. I don't know what you're trying to pull with that one. I know that that's bullshit. And I know you know it's bullshit, too. So, by God, I want an answer now. Are you going to do it my way and live the nice comfortable life I've provided for you, or resign and get the hell out of my town? Which is it going to *be*?"

Kyle heard the snakes hissing. Dear God, the mayor had known all along. He'd held that trump card until he needed it and then played it like a pro. There was only one question now: Did he give in to the mayor or get his assed kicked out of town? Kyle realized with disgust that he was actually debating the question. But was it really so bad? The quality of an investigation was a subjective thing anyway. "I'm waiting."

Kyle could not look the mayor in the face. "It is my professional opinion," he said, "that the interest of the community would be better served by the involvement of the county homocide team, but in light of your insistence and my desire to stay here, I'll make do with what we have here and contract the lab work out to the county."

There, he'd said it. He'd knuckled under. His face flushed hot with shame.

The mayor walked around the desk, a good winner. "There, there, Kyle. That's the way." His tone became consoling, and Kyle hated that. "I understand what you want, Kyle— excellence. That's what I want too, but from within, from within. Enough of this devil talk—I've forgotten it already—I hated to bring out that other thing, but it's a tough job running a city, a tough job. The publicity on this is going to be bad enough the way it is. It's no good for business, or Briggs City. At least if *we're* handling it we don't have to worry about *undue* worry, *unwarranted* concern . . ."

The mayor droned on as he guided Kyle out of the office, but Kyle wasn't listening. Inside his head a vile and disgusting phrase was turning over and over in a bed of shame: *mayor's man, mayor's man, mayor's man.* There goes *the mayor's man.*


The investigation continued into late afternoon. Koger was a godsend under the circumstances. Kyle sent him to play "Meet the Press," and do the preliminary follow-up work. Kyle sensed that Koger knew the score, that the mayor had something on him too.

The shame hung on him like a suit of mail. Toward the end of the afternoon they found the head. It matched the body of the corpse hung upside down on the meat hooks, with its genitalia cut off. It was found down in the basement, stuck in a head-sized hole that had been gouged out of the support. Officer Black had found it stuffed in there. It was the head of Father Charles DiNapoli. His penis, unnaturally filled with dried blood so that it was erect, was stuck in his opened mouth, just the way Kyle had found Leonard Phael's head; and according to Nancy Lyon's book, was just the way the legend of Ravana dictated the work of its Devil principal should be marked.

# 50

At four o'clock Kyle left Koger in charge of the investigation. He had to get out of there. He pulled out of the Gathers Market lot and drove home.

Kyle walked in his front door and started slightly. Michele was standing in the doorway leading into the hall. She held a green watering can in her right hand, an embarrassed look tacked on her face.

The weight of the day seemed to lift from his shoulders.

"Well, hello, Michele," he said. "I didn't see your car in the drive."

"It's a small town. They'd have me 'with child' by the time I got home." Her face reddened. "If they saw the car. I walked, actually. I'm watering. Curtis told me about your talk yesterday."

"Is he here?"

"No. An emergency meeting of the Jedi Knights. I'm sorry . . . I . . ."

"Please. No, Michele. Don't feel embarrassed. I'm . . . I'm glad to see you." He indicated the sofa with both hands. "Please," he said, hearing the pleading in his voice.

Michele gave him a concerned look. "What's wrong, Kyle?"

"Nothing much," Kyle grunted. "I just stopped being a policeman today, that's all . . ."

"Oh, Kyle. Did you quit?"

"No." He moved to the sofa and sat down, looking up at her. "Sit here, would you?"

She placed the watering can on an end table and sat down

next to Kyle on the sofa, facing him at an angle. Her knees were less than four inches from his leg. He felt comforted by that closeness. He wanted to touch her knee, tell her that he cared for her, that he had run from her in fear—but the words would not come. She looked into his eyes now. She reached out and put her hand on his arm, a light delicate pressure. She let it rest there. "Tell me, Kyle," she said softly, and began rubbing his arm gently. There was nothing sexual in it and everything comforting.

Kyle found himself talking before he knew it. He told her about almost everything, hesitating only slightly when it became necessary to mention Woodhaven. "I was very critical of myself. The guilt got to me, I guess. But it wasn't my fault. I know that now, but I didn't know it then, and so gradually—or not so gradually, really—it affected me so badly that I needed help. Leo helped me see that. But I'm okay now, except for the dreams . . . those *damn* dreams—"

"What dreams, Kyle?" she asked. When he hesitated she squeezed his arm reassuringly. But he felt he'd told enough people about Ravana for one day. He still wasn't sure how she was taking the news about his stay at Woodhaven, and he did not think he could bear rejection from her, so he said, "Nothing, bad dreams about Susan and Lisa." He felt immediately guilty about the lie, and moved to make up for it with a more important truth: "When I got out," he said, "I rested up in L.A., just getting used to being out, but I needed something, and this job, this town and . . ." He stopped fully and put his hand on hers, afraid beyond words that she would pull it back. She turned her hand upward to hold his. He slipped his arm around her and pulled her close, then continued. "And you and Curtis were that thing. I've loved Curtis for a long time and wanted to let myself love you, just as much. But I was *afraid, so afraid.*"

"Yes," she said. "You think you killed the last woman you loved. But you didn't."

He stared at her, astonished by her insight.

He pulled her closer to him. He could feel her warm breath on his neck. He kissed her. Her lips lingered on his lightly at first, then, as he pressed harder, she opened her mouth and received his tongue. He stood up, pulling her with him, and lifted her up and carried her into the bedroom. She let him undress her and watched as he undressed, and then they made love. Slowly and steadily, building and building until Kyle felt himself flow into her and the pain and suffering flow out of his soul. They lay in the bed naked, holding each other.

Kyle stroked her hair gently and gazed into her eyes. His other hand lifted her breast gently, caressing it with his palm. "Do you think I'm crazy?"

"No. You needed help and you got it. I think you've done a wonderful job here. All I want to know now is why you said you're not a policeman anymore."

Kyle's pleasure in their lovemaking evaporated, pushed out by a pain deep inside his chest. "There's being a cop," he said, "and being a *good* cop. Being a good cop is a lot more work, but you sleep a little easier and can look yourself in the mirror in the morning and shave yourself without wanting to slit your throat. A good cop doesn't do a half-assed job on a murder investigation—murder is murder no matter who or what does it. I let Neil Gathers back me down today. When I did that, I became less than a good cop, and in my book, that's no cop at all."

Michele sat up cross-legged, facing him. "Kyle, why don't you do what you have to do, and if they fire you—"

"They'll fire me, all right. The mayor will—"

"The city council will have to—"

"The city council is *controlled* by the mayor, Michele."

"I don't believe that."

"Trust me."

Michele pursed her lips tightly, thoughtfully. "Okay. Let's assume that. I'm not sure that we should, but let's assume that. What have you got to lose? At least you go out like you came in—a *good* policeman. You'll be miserable any other way,

Kyle. You know that. I know that, even if you don't." She smiled. "Trust *me*."

He could not help but smile back. "Why?" he teased.

Her face grew serious. "Because I love you, Kyle. Very, very much."

Kyle gazed at her, proud of her, ashamed of himself. "I love you, too," he said, and kissed her. Suddenly everything was crystal clear: There was a murder investigation. *He* needed to be there, now. He sat up, picked up the phone, and dialed county homocide: "Yeah, Tom, this is Kyle Richards in Briggs City. Yeah, yeah. Listen. How about a little mutual assistance from the county, buddy-buddy? That's right, homocide. Five. Gathers Market, the new one, Highway Twenty-eight. I'll meet you there."

Kyle dressed quickly, savoring Michele's approving gaze. He kissed her, then brushed her breasts with his lips. "Sweet," he said.

"I'll be here when you get back," Michele said. "I'll put Curtis with Aunt Clarice."

"I'll be late," he cautioned.

"That's okay. I'll be here."

Kyle left feeling scared—and happier than he had in years.

# 51

Michele sat there staring at the empty bedroom doorway for a long time after Kyle had left. He had left a lot happier than he had come in, that was for sure—in more ways than one, she laughed to herself.

She lay in the bed for a few minutes more trying to regain that "glow," but that was futile. The clock by the bed read nearly four-thirty. She sat up and slipped off the bed and gathered up her clothes. The clothes that she had worn to church this morning, she chided herself. Well, she loved the man, and she wasn't going to feel guilty about that. She dressed quickly. There was much to do. She had to arrange for Curtis to stay with Aunt Clarice and Uncle Edgar for the night; go down and pay Jilly and then lock up the bookstore; and be back here. She wanted to be here when Kyle got home. He might need her.

She was just finishing brushing her hair when the doorbell rang. Her first thought was that it was Curtis, but he wouldn't be done until after seven, Mrs. Gathers had said. She thought of not answering it, but she stuffed her comb in her purse and went to answer the door.

"What a surprise," she said, opening the screen door and stepping aside.

"I might say the same thing," replied Uncle Edgar, walking in. He was wearing his tweed sports coat and perennial maroon bow tie and carrying his leather satchel bag. "Where's your car?" he asked.

"People talk," she said, and kissed him on the cheek. "I was watering the chief's plants for Curtis. He's busy being a Jedi

Knight today."

"Better mind your p's and q's, young lady, that'll be front page news tomorrow. I'm a newspaperman, remember?" He moved to the sofa and sat down like this was his own home.

Same old Unk, she thought.

"Where's Kyle?" he asked. He was looking at her, up and down, and she felt that somehow he knew that Kyle and she had made love. She felt guilty as she answered, "He's at the market."

"Oh, the murders," acknowledged Uncle Edgar. "I thought that would be wrapped up by now. I've got young Baker on that story; let him flex his wings a bit, y'know."

"Kyle was understaffed," she said.

"He's been here?"

"Yes, but he left. What did you want, Unk?" She sat down beside him and he pulled his satchel bag close to him and opened it up. He pulled out a thin black book, and a manuscript. "I'm returning these," he said. Michele did not miss the weary tone in his voice.

Michele shifted positions to better see Uncle Edgar's face without strain. She was in the same position she had been with Kyle this morning, and Uncle Edgar seemed to be in the same down mood as Kyle. Instant replay, she thought. She reached out and tugged at his sleeve. "Unk," she said, "What's up?"

Uncle Edgar offered a book and a manuscript.

Michele took them and sat them in her lap, bringing the worn black book up and reading the title: *Laikute Indian Ritual and Religion,* by Nancy Lyon; then she glanced down at thirty or so pages of typing paper in her lap. It too had a title: *Justification for Belief of Supernatural Happenings* by . . . "Kyle!" she said so loud that Uncle Edgar jumped.

"It's a report," Uncle Edgar said, "a weird, fantastic report correlating the events and prophecies in the book in present time: he speaks of devils and demons and spirits as if they were real. He asked me to read the report, and for what purpose? I suppose for my support, but it's mad, absolutely mad, Michele.

433

The concise, quantified misinterpretation of current events, guided, if my guess is correct by Nan—Professor Lyon's book."

"He's not mad, or crazy, or any of that, Uncle Edgar." She spoke the words low and with more vehemence than she had meant to. Uncle Edgar continued on as if she had spoken in a normal tone.

"Kyle was in a mental institution, Michele, for a number of months—"

"I know, Uncle Edgar. Kyle told me everything, and I don't care."

"He told you about this devil, this Ravana."

She had to admit that he hadn't, and the message Uncle Edgar was pressing across in his tone and his eyes was getting her mad.

"Michele, take a few minutes and read that. I'll wait. It won't take long. And then tell me if you don't think Kyle has a very large problem."

She started to protest.

"Are you afraid to read it, Michele?"

"No!" She glared at him. "I'm not afraid to read it! I don't have to read it! Kyle is as sane as you or me! If he says there's something there, then there's something there!"

"I'm not so sure about that . . ."

The noise came from the hall. Michele twisted all the way around. What was it? A rocking sound, and a bell: rock-*brrring*, rock-*brrring*, rock-*brrrring*.

"What the hell!" Uncle Edgar struggled to his feet and walked toward the hall. Michele followed him. Faint music, and a child's voice, singing, "Mares eat oats, and does eat oats . . ." filtered down the hall.

Rock-*brrring*, Rock-*brrring*, Rock-*brrring*.

Uncle Edgar said, "Hello." His shoulders blocked her view. That door hadn't been open while she was watering, she was sure. Now it was, and wide. Uncle Edgar hadn't opened it. She'd seen him approach the doorway. A girl child's voice said,

"Why don't you believe my daddy? He's not crazy."

"What's your name?" Uncle Edgar asked again. Michele touched his shoulder and pushed him into the room, following after.

"Hi," she said, smiling at the little girl rocking back and forth in the chair. Rock-*brrring*, rock-*bring*, that was the noise. My God, she thought, has he been hiding his daughter all along? Or was she a second daughter? Was Kyle's condition this bad? Another piece of evidence that Kyle needed help. Michele's heart lumped up in her chest.

The child's eyes were softer than her father's, softened by the mother's influence, Michele guessed, but still sharp and green—Kyle's eyes. Pale-gold hair braided in long pigtails topped a perfectly oval face. She wore a pink fluffy sundress and black shiny patent-leather shoes. She was about eight years old, Michele thought.

The little girl stopped rocking and stared intently at Michele. "My daddy loves you," she said. "And he *needs* you."

"I—I love him," Michele said, shocked by the girl's question. "And I will help him, dear. But, who are you?"

"Yes," said Uncle Edgar, "Who are you, young lady?"

"Daddy's-little-girl, that's who, and *I* believe him. You should, too." Her eyes shot accusations at Edgar. "He *needs* you. God says so. God says you should help him." Her little face blotched scarlet in her excitement.

"What's your name?" asked Uncle Edgar again with such a quaver in his voice that Michele glanced at him. His normally calm face was caught midway in change, a mask frozen halfway to understanding, an understanding he definitely found terrifying.

"What's your name, honey?" Michele felt her expression twist into a caricature of her uncle's dread.

"Lisa," the little girl said. The words struck Michele's ears with an unnatural pristine clarity that chilled her blood.

"No, no, dear. Lisa is dead," Michele said. Her heart thumped against her ribs. Uncle Edgar said nothing.

"My daddy needs you, and you think he's crazy." The little girl's face contorted in anger. "If you love him—"

Both Michele and Uncle Edgar began backing toward the door.

The door slammed shut behind them, cutting off their retreat.

"You can't go until you believe Daddy!" she screamed. "Ravana wants Daddy! It will take Daddy if you don't believe him!"

Uncle Edgar grabbed the doorknob and yanked his hand away instantly with a scream. "It's *hot*," he yelled. He spun around, pressing his back flat against the door facing the little girl. Michele crowded beside him.

"Ravana killed me and Mommy, too! Not *men! Ravana!* You wanna see? You'll believe!"

A swirling ephemeral mist suddenly filled the room and the little girl evaporated in white light, then apeared tied spread eagled to the four-poster bed. Wavy dark inhuman figures lay upon her, snarling, violating her with horned phalli until blood poured from between her legs. She screamed hysterically. The two figures righted themselves, howling through glowing, red fangs. The weird light began to flicker and the little girl was abruptly hanging from the light fixture. She was naked, her back to them; blood flowed down her small white legs in glistening red ribbons, dripping down onto the floor and pooling.

Michele opened her mouth to scream. But then the fixture pulled partially from the ceiling, plaster sprinkled to the floor in fine dust. The girl's body twisted around, faced them, blood ran in a sheet from her hairline. She opened her mouth and asked calmly, "Do you believe me now? See what Ravana did to me? See-ee-*eeeeeeee?*"

There was a wet, tearing sound and Michele's screams burst free at last. Uncle Edgar covered his eyes. The tearing sound drew out unbearably then snapped into silence as the scalp separated from the skull, leaving Lisa's hair dangling on the end of her pigtails, her body crumpled on the floor. Her large green eyes opened suddenly and she began to speak: "My daddy loves you. Help him, help him, help him. Now, do you believe? Do you believe? Do you believe . . .?"

"I—I—I believe," croaked Uncle Edgar.

"Yes-yes-yes-Yeah-esssss, we believe," screamed Michele. "Please stop! Please stop!"

And it stopped. Lisa's apparition faded. The room returned to normal. And both Michele and Uncle Edgar believed. Oh, God, how they believed.

# 52

When Kyle arrived at the market, the mayor was gone and not expected to return. That meant he thought he had Kyle under control. Hell, *I* thought he had me under control, Kyle thought, until I got home and saw that sweet vision Michele— God, how I love her. He sighed. He would need that love in the next few weeks, the next few years, because the mayor was surely going to try to fire him for bringing the county in on this one.

Kyle didn't care.

Not now. He had Michele and Curtis, and he would make out somehow. The important thing at this moment was that he had regained his self-respect, his perspective. And he wasn't above lying to make the medicine go down, either. He told Dwight Koger that the mayor had succumbed to his plea for outside help, and that explained the county. He emptied the store of nonessential personnel and kept a tight rein on communications.

The mayor called twice during the investigation, and each time Kyle talked with him, assuring him that all was well, the investigation going fine. When the mayor said that he had been "concerned" when Kyle had taken off, Kyle told him that he just had to get his head back on straight, and that it was back on straight, "After all, you do pay my salary, right, Mayor?" he said. The mayor was glad that Kyle understood "from whence the water flowed" and Kyle laughed with him, thinking what a son of a bitch he was the whole time, watching Kent Wickham from county sheriff's homocide carefully filling out his reports. Tomorrow the shit would hit the fan, but by God he was a policeman again, and not somebody's damn flunky.

By nine-thirty Kyle wrapped up the investigation and he sent the county homocide team off with grateful "Thanks." He dismissed his people, sending Koger off with a pat on the back and a big smile, knowing that sooner or later the mayor was going to check with him, and when Koger mentioned the country, it was going to be all over. But between that time and now, Kyle was going to do everything possible to gather proof for his claim of Ravana.

John Black had told him where Wolf lived. Up over the hardware store. Kyle turned into the alley and parked beside an old Chevy truck. It was dark back there except for the dim porch light at the top of a scaffolding of wooden stairs. Kyle started up, chastising himself a little for the hour, and the approach. What was he going to say? "Excuse me, but weren't you witness to a monster murder fifteen years ago?" Great.

His knock went unanswered, so he tried again, harder this time and standing to the side of the door. After a few minutes he heard steps and saw the door curtains push aside and dark eyes staring up at him.

"Who there?" came a female voice through the door.

Kyle produced his badge and held it up. "Police. Open up."

The eyes flicked to the badge and the curtain closed. Kyle heard the metal clicking of the lock's tumblers, and the door opened up, held by a chain. "Lemme see the badge again," the woman said. Kyle pushed it closer. The woman seemed satisfied. The door closed; he heard the chain slide, then the door opened wide. A short, fat Indian woman with a worn robe and pink mules stepped aside and told him to come in.

"Are you Mrs. Elkhart?" he asked.

"Yes," she answered.

Kyle guessed the woman to be in her early thirties. Her hair was shiny and black, gathered up near the head by a leather-and-wood clasp and running down the back of her robe like a river. Her eyes shone black, a glitter of fear in their questioning stare. "What is it you want?" she asked, closing the door behind him and indicating a seat at a small kitchen table. Kyle did not sit, but pointed through the kitchen toward the rest of the house. "I'm looking for you husband," he said. "I'd like to talk to him, please."

"Wolf? He's not here."

"Can you tell me where to find him? It's important," he added.

"I don't know where he is. He's not been home a while . . . a couple of days."

"I need to talk to him about what's been happening in the market. It's very important, ma'am."

She became very agitated and pointed toward the door. "Get out," she said, "He got nothing to do with the market, nothing. Go get out."

Kyle stood his ground. "I don't believe he did anything there either, but I think he can help me prevent more murders, Mrs . . . ."

"Dove," she said, suddenly softening. "My name is Dove."

"Thank you. I should have introduced myself. I'm Kyle. Pleased to meet you." He extended his hand. She hesitated, then took it briefly. Her hand was soft and warm. Kyle continued, hoping to keep the advantage. He pulled the kitchen chair out and waited.

"Sit down," she said, and he did. She moved around and took a seat. "What's this about the murders and Wolf?" she asked. Kyle decided to tell basically the truth. "This may seem strange to you, but I don't believe men are responsible for what is happening at the market," he said. If she was shocked she made no sign. "I think it has something to do with the old religion and the old trees and whatever else was out there before the market. I think Wolf—"

"Holy Wolf," corrected Dove. "He is Holy Wolf, son of Holy Crow, and grandson of Holy Eagle." She said this with some pride, Kyle noted. "He is a priest, or was to be . . ." Her voice fell silent, then her black eyes shimmered defiance. "What do you want from him?"

"Holy Wolf is a priest. Then he would know of Ravana, the Evil One—"

"Yes, he would know." She reflected a moment. "He is *Heytah-nee*—" She stopped again, searching for the right word.

"The Traitor," Kyle said in a low tone, trying to soften the impact of that word. He needed her help, and he was sorry the minute the word left his lips. Dove looked up at him in surprise. "You know?" she asked.

"I know a little, Dove. But I have to know more. I believe, but I need others to believe, and that cannot be so if I don't have help. Many others may die. Your people shop there too, Dove. Please. If you know where Holy Wolf is, please tell me. Please."

Kyle let the words rest with her. She sat thinking, staring down at the tabletop. Finally she looked up at him, this time with sad, sad eyes. "I will take you to him, policeman, because I believe you," she said softly; then with a snake's whisper in her voice, added, "but if you have betrayed me, I will curse you into the very arms of *Ravana* Itself."

She rose and made toward her bedroom to change.

## 53

Kyle followed the red beacons of Dove's Chevy's tail lights along an empty two-laned highway, little used after Highway 28 had been built, into the dark night. The road wound north for only a few miles then turned south, the hills and mountains now buffering the two trucks from the town. The condition of the road was poor. Kyle hit a few spots of decaying asphalt and bounced in the night, his eyes carefully on the truck ahead. He was conscious of the lack of the radio traffic from his radio. He had deliberately left it off: the mayor would be a problem best dealt with in the morning. They moved in tandem down the road for another twenty minutes until Dove slowed down and turned left to a barbed-wire gate where she stopped the car, got out, and opened it. She drove through, Kyle followed, then she stopped ahead, got out and closed the gate, passing by Kyle without looking at him or saying a word. She looked like a shawled phantom.

Kyle watched her slip up into the cab of the Chevy and drive toward the dark hulking shapes of the mountains. For a moment he felt removed from the action, an observer, the red beacons traveling toward the mountains, glowing red eyes of some monster retreating into its sanctuary of the night.

He shook his head to clear the sensation, and cautioned himself to exercise more control over his thoughts. Ones like that had a way of growing in the shadows of the mind until they were so huge that the shadows could not hide them. Better not to think like that, Kyle thought.

The dirt road bucked both trucks with its ruts and ridges, but soon they were at the foothills and going up, up, and up, stopping when the road ended, halfway up the mountain. Kyle got out, reaching behind the seat for his warm nylon field jacket and his flashlight. He turned it on, its strong beam of light catching something rectangular and black in the well behind the seat. Kyle reached out and touched it—the Bible the bum had given him, and next to it lay the crucifix. Kyle touched the cross and thought of the disgraced priest, and how he looked in the end, his head stuffed in a hole hewn out of a cement pillar. God, what was it he had witnessed before his death? Kyle trembled to think of it.

Dove handed Kyle a pillowcase. "There's water and some apples in it. It's for you," she said in her high, sweet voice. "Wolf will not eat. Not now. He may not talk to you. He may not be able to talk. He may be dead." Kyle's flashlight illuminated the rocky ground. Her voice came from a black, featureless oval barely distinguishable from the velvet dark of the night, and intoned the words without emotion.

"Where is he?"

"Up the mountain. Use your light to follow the path. He is way up. Follow the path; it will take you to him."

Kyle directed the light's beam toward the mountain, its jarring yellow blade cutting the darkness until the worn path evidenced itself. Kyle held the light on it.

"That's it?"

"Yes," she said.

She moved to go and Kyle stopped her. "Wait," he said. "Dove, why is he here? Why now?"

The dark silhouette stood silent, as if counting seconds and listening to the rustle of the leaves in the wind, then spoke: "He's been up here for several weeks now. He has come to ask the Elders for his soul back. It has to do with what has happened at Devil's Ground this day. This is Holy Mountain. It is a Indian holy place. You go now."

"No. Wait. Can the Elders give him back his soul?"

The wind soughed against the mountain; she was silent

443

again. Kyle waited. When she spoke, her voice trembled in sad emotion, like a mother speaking of her dying child: "No. They do not have his soul. He is *Heytah-nee*, and it is not the Elders who hold his soul."

"Then why has he gone to ask them?"

"Because, it has begun now, and he has no place else to go. In the end *Ravana* will keep his soul. But he must be this place this night, as it is foretold. It has begun, and Wolf must be here."

"What has begun?" asked Kyle, sorting through her words judiciously to find the proper question.

Silence again. The wind picked up suddenly seeming to twist and swirl into Kyle's ears, then dropped just as suddenly, dead still.

"The end of the world, policeman. The end of everything."

She quickly moved to her truck, mounted it, and soon the tail lights disappeared down toward the flatland and out of sight.


The path, narrow and rocky, jutting back and forth, climbed always upward until near the top. Here Kyle followed it around toward the east side, and if his belief was correct he would be facing Highway 28, though where along it he would be he could not guess.

He struggled up to an area of high rounded boulders and brush; the beam of his flashlight made shadow monsters of the latter against the curved stone surface of the former. His light danced ahead as he walked the narrow path, catching the stricture of brush and stone that seemed to swallow the trail. Upon closer examination Kyle found that was exactly what had happened. The trail stopped. He rested for a moment, then played the beams upon the rock, and picked his spots—he was meant to climb here. He sighed, and wished he didn't have the damned pillowcase with him, a nuisance he disposed of by tying it to his belt. Then he began his climb. It was a short climb.

About fifteen feet up he was on top of a wide ledge, walled off to his right and pinching down to a small walkway around a huge boulder on his left. Around that boulder lay the direct east side of the top of the mountain. Kyle played his light along the tawny-orange stone path, cautiously examining the ledge there: it dropped away into darkness. Bad footing and it was all over, except for a brief flight into darkness and a jamming splat on the rocks below. Kyle started around.

At the narrowest portion he was stopped abruptly by the view. The east view. He knew exactly where he was now. Below him shimmering in the ghostly sodium arc lights of the parking lot squatted the market. This holy place overlooked the market . . . Devil's Ground, as Dove had called it.

A flutter of cold wind brought his mind back to the business at hand and he walked the fifteen feet around the boulder trying his best to ignore the dark emptiness just inches from his shoes. He came onto a large flat area, white rock worn smooth by time. The convex of the boulders' surface formed a wall against which the flat area reached out, tongue-shaped, toward the darkness, and Devil's Ground. Kyle found Holy Wolf sitting propped against this wall.

Kyle thought the man was dead.

He was naked and painted ash-white, his face made fierce by designs drawn in black paint. The black marking darkened the eyes and transformed the Indian's visage into a demon. His eyes were closed. He was slumped back against the boulder unmoving. A small fire, burned down to practically nothing, waned in front of him. On the rocks that surrounded that fire rested a black iron kettle. Kyle shined his light into it. The concoction was the color of watery mud and it boiled. He wondered how it could boil with so little fire. He shined the light on Holy Wolf's face. The paint, or whatever it was, was thick, and less frightening up close. It was dried and cracked in places.

Kyle reached out to touch his neck, to take his pulse.

"Do not touch him, *Ehkeh-Heh!*" said an old voice, thick and papery yet filled with power and command. It was not Wolf's voice, but the words came from his mouth. Kyle pulled back his hand, then squatted down slowly before Wolf.

"I wish to speak to Wolf," he said. "I need—"

"*Ehkeh-Heh,* your needs are known."

Kyle stared at Wolf's face for a moment. Was the man in a daze, speaking in such a tone because of his ordeal up here, or—

"*Ehkeh-Heh,* I am Holy Eagle."

Kyle remembered what Dove had said, then looked around. No one else was here. "Are you an Elder?" he asked.

Wolf's dead mouth opened again. "Yes, *Ehkeh-Heh.*"

"Where is Wolf?"

"*Ehkeh-Heh,* his body is here, his spirit is black and with *Ravana.*"

"I am—"

"*Ehkeh-Heh.*You are *Ehkeh-Heh.*"

"I need to know about Ravana?"

"First give me your left hand, *Ehkeh-Heh.*"

Kyle hesitated, lifting his left hand speculatively. The corpse's right hand lashed out and grabbed it and slammed it to the ground with unhuman strength. Its left hand came around equally fast, holding a knife with a blade of chipped obsidian. Kyle stared in horror and shock as the obsidian blade flashed to the end segment of his little finger and severed it cleanly from his hand. Kyle screamed in pain and tried to pull away, but the corpse's grip was like an iron manacle. It dropped the knife and picked up a burning stick of wood and quickly stuck it against Kyle's bleeding finger stump. He heard the sizzle and smelled the burning flesh. Still he could not break free. The corpse stuck the wood back into the fire, and the left hand scooped the loose fingertip up like a man catching a bug and tossed it into the boiling kettle.

Kyle jerked back, screaming, and went flying, rolling back dangerously close to the edge of the cliff. He grabbed his hand and looked at it. Pain throbbed up his hand. He could barely make out the stump of his finger in the campfire light. It was black. "You son of a bitch, you son of a bitch!" he screamed at Wolf, but the big Indian was slumped back like before. Kyle began to regain control of himself. That grip that had held him he could still feel, in spite of the pain. It had been cold, deathly cold; and the entire time Wolf had never opened his eyes. Never fucking opened his eyes.

Because he didn't need to. He's dead. And had been for some time.

"*Ehkeh-Heh*, you scream like a woman, *Ehkeh-Heh*," said the voice issuing forth from Wolf's corpse.

"You cut off my finger," Kyle responded, his jaw slack with amazement—he was talking to a dead man.

"Thank the Great Spirit that the ritual doesn't need one of your *huevos, Ehkeh-Heh*. You must give before you receive, *Ehkeh-Heh*, and the price of the finger buys you a second chance for your life."

Kyle gained his knees, then sat back, clutching his left hand with his right. The throbbing pain had subsided to an aching, like shattered glass embedded in his hand. He consciously took assessment of himself, and of his mind. This was crazy, talking with a corpse—but he was doing it, and it was talking back. And damn it, he should be afraid. Deathly afraid. Yet, he wasn't. Scared, yes. But terrified like in the dreams, no. And the voice, the Elder, Holy Eagle: there was tone there, a humorous, nonmalignant timbre, almost as if Kyle were a small child the voice was teaching. The tone carried a mentor's love for his favorite student.

"You're dead," Kyle said half to break him from the hold of this spell, half to reassure himself that it was a hallucination.

"*Ehkeh-Heh*, Wolf's body is dead, but his spirit is with *Ravana*. My body is dead, and my spirit is here. Nothing dies, *Ehkeh-Heh*, it only changes; like a rock to dirt to dust in the wind, it only changes."

"I'm scared."

"Then you are smart, *Ehkeh-Heh*. Wolf never would admit he was scared, that's why he is *Heytah-nee* instead of Priest.

That's why *Ravana* is free today. Why you are here today. But come closer, you must drink."

Wolf's corpse crawled forward in stiff, jerky motions and picked up a clay bowl and dipped it in the bubbling muddy brew, and offered it out. "Drink, *Ehkeh-Heh*, drink."

"My finger's in there, for God's sake!"

Wolf's body sat silent, holding the bowl out in offering.

"I'm crazy," he said out loud. "My God, I *am* crazy."

"You are *not* crazy, *Ehkeh-Heh*." The voice startled Kyle. Loud and stern. "You *believed* what *Ravana* wanted to make you believe, so you *thought* you were crazy. But your beliefs are the truth to you as each man's are to himself. You must see the falseness of *Ravana's* lies to face and defeat It. You are only crazy as long as you *believe* you are crazy, and *believe Ravana's* lies. Now, drink, *Ehkeh-Heh*, drink."

Kyle stood up, walked over and knelt down, just out of reach of the offered bowl and the Indian. "I am not *Ehkeh-Heh*."

"Take the cup, *Ehkeh-Heh*."

Kyle reached out and took the bowl, jerking back out of grabbing range of the Indian. He sat back on his heels, holding the bowl on his right thigh. He could feel the heat through his pants.

"Now, drink, *Ehkeh-Heh*."

"I am not *Ehkeh-Heh*."

"The Chosen One, *Ehkeh-Heh*."

"Chosen for what?" asked Kyle, knowing and dreading the answer.

"To face *Ravana*."

"Why?"

"To save the World, *Ehkeh-Heh*."

"Why did you choose me?"

"We did not choose you, *Ehkeh-Heh*."

"Then who chose me, Elder?"

"*Ravana* chose you, *Ehkeh-Heh*."

"Why me?"

"You are *Ehkeh-Heh*, the Fallen Warrior, the Chosen One. He

448

chose you because you are worthy and strong, but also because he believes you will weaken in his presence. You will fall to him and make him stronger many times more than he is now."

"I don't believe in magic."

"*Ehkeh-Heh*. Do you believe in Good and Evil?"

Kyle thought this over carefully. "Yes," he said.

"Then you believe in magic."

"I don't understand."

"Drink *Ehkeh-Heh*, and you will understand."

"No! Tell me, now!"

"As you say, *Ehkeh-Heh*—"

"Stop calling me that!"

"Good and Evil are not two but one. That you believe in two, that is magic; in one, that is Truth. When you face the Devilthing, you must know Truth—One—and that is how you will defeat him. You must deny him and accept him at the same time, and know that he cannot harm you, and that all he shows you is a lie. Deny him, but accept him at the same time, and you will make him fall—"

"I don't understand!"

"Then drink, *Ehkeh-Heh*, and you will understand."

"I am afraid, dammit!"

"Drink, *Ehkeh-Heh*."

"No!"

"You will drink of the blood, *Ehkeh-Heh*, and you will do it now—"

"No! I—"

"—because since the day *Ravana* murdered your squaw and girl child—"

"What!"

"—you were destined to drink the blood and save the World—"

"Ravana killed Susan and Lisa?"

"Yes, *Ehkeh-Heh*. And this day is its day, and it will kill many more in the fat man's toy . . ."

"The Market?"

449

"Yes, *Ehkeh-Heh*. Now drink the blood. The time is short, perhaps too short, and too late. Drink it all."

Kyle raised the bowl to his lips and drank, drank it all. It tasted thick and bitter, poisoned mud. When he had finished, he set the bowl down on the rock beside him and waited patiently, fighting the rising tide of nausea.

Nothing was happening to him. Nothing. He was thinking this when the sky turned purple and Wolf turned carbon black and on the rocks around him stood Indians. Priests all, chanting, naked, painted as Wolf had been. A short Priest, with a large head and long gray hair, came forward and spoke: "Come, *Ehkeh-Heh*."

This is Holy Eagle, Kyle realized.

He rose and followed the figure to the edge of the promontory and looked out into the blackness of the night that now had a roiling texture to it. A fiery lesion glowed where the market should have been. The wail of lost souls rose from that place building into a crescendo. Fire and lava geysered out, up high. The Priest pointed to it with what was somehow a noble gesture. "Remember, *Ehkeh-Heh,* deny it all/accept it all. Tell *Ravana* it is a lie, that it cannot harm you, that there is not Two, but One, and embrace him as One unto yourself—tell It to its face that he does not exist, and save the World!"

The ledge began to shake and buckle. The night split into rolling balls of flaming orange fire. The ground melted lavalike away from him, and in his mind he heard the hissing—loud, unabated. Then for the moment the Universe ended, and all went deep and thickly black, vortexing into a nothingness beyond unconsciousness beyond mind and Kyle knew nothing, the blackness, the nothing.

Nothing.

ted Wolf. Now drink the blood. The time is short,
too short; and too late. Drink it all."

And the bowl to his face and drank, drank it all. J

# 54

First he heard sounds. The singing of birds. The rush of
wind. The distant blare of a car horn. Of traffic..

Then the dull pain in his hand, the bone-aching stiffness
throughout his body, reached his brain. He lay on his stomach,
his arms outstretched in supplication, dangling over the
tongue of the white rock. His eyes fluttered open and Gathers
Market stared at him from the distance. Its parking lot glinted
silver sun needles off the chrome of hundreds of cars jammed
into its confines. More cars streamed in, while others left.

The market.

The market was important, Kyle remembered, but in the
haze of gaining consciousness he could not remember why.

The sun hung halfway down in the western sky. He was
baking on the rock like a lizard. He struggled to his feet and
looked out over the precipice at the market and the cars.

What was it? What about the market?

His head, a dried leather gourd splitting in several places, let
one thought through the pain, one memory of last night's
ordeal: Today belongs to Ravana. And so whatever was going to
happen was going to happen in the market. Holy Eagle had said
that many would be killed. Today! And look at those cars,
people in the market. Hundreds of them. No matter what, Kyle
had to close it down. Make the mayor believe and close it down.

He struggled to his feet and turned, stifling a scream.
Whatever justification he could have had in believing that last
night was just a nightmare, a dream, was diluted to nothingness
with the evidence: Wolf lay dead against the boulder. Green

451

horseflies covered the body completely in a shimmering, buzzing green coat; the kettle on the rocks, the muddy brew cool now over a dead fire; and Kyle's little finger was missing a joint.

He moved in jolting steps toward the pillowcase, blessing Dove as he rinsed his mouth out, then drank deeply from the jar. He washed as best he could, drank deeply again, then left as fast as he could, not looking back. He was halfway down the mountain when he noticed it. He stopped and touched his chest, up high around his neck. A roughness, a necklace. He held it up and looked at it: ancient and old beads, but he knew what they were: bones, the fingertips of the Elders, the Priests. He rotated the necklace and found what he was searching for, a fresh white tiny bone—his!

He moved on and gained his truck and headed for town and the dark glass and chrome marvel, the Gathers Corporation Building, and the mayor.

"Shut it down!" Kyle glared at the mayor as he spoke.

"You *are* crazy, Richards!" said the mayor. "Ghosts, goblins, like it was Halloween or something!"

"Ravana is going to murder some more people today. You have to close it down!" Kyle had caught the mayor in his office alone, by brushing by the secretary, and slamming the door shut. He was here, but how could he get this man to believe him? "Shut it down!"

The mayor slammed his fist against his desk. "Like hell, I will. You are through, Richards. Washed up. We're sending you back to the loony bin where you belong! You're crazy! Crazy! Do you hear me?"

The words had a sobering effect on Kyle. He righted himself and forced himself to breathe deeply. It calmed him down and helped his thinking. "I'm sorry," he said to the mayor, "you're right, I am crazy." Kyle drew his gun and pointed it at the mayor's fat face. "Call the market and shut it down."

452

The mayor fish-eyed him, not a hint of fear in his face. "Won't work, Richards. You'll be arrested and the market'll be open in a few hours."

"Just make the call," Kyle said calmly. It was the first time in his career he had ever drawn his weapon to commit murder, but that's just what he would do if this man did not pick up the telephone.

The mayor picked up the telephone and dialed, saying, "You're crazy, Kyle."

"Put it on the box." Kyle indicated the conference-call speaker on the shiny wood desk. The mayor flipped the switch and turned the volume up. The ring of the telephone blared tinnily into the room..

"You're crazy . . . Monsters . . . Jesus save you, Richa—"

But then the telephone was answered and the mayor's words were drowned out by a blaring, tortured chorus of hideous screams, magnified by the speaker-box, and filling the room like death.

# 55

The market teemed with holiday shoppers, and its time was now.

It felt it, and so called forth its Legion.

The Creel appeared first, huge, gray, batlike creatures hanging upside down from the ceiling, their enormous protruding silver eyes heat sensors, choosing their food carefully, the body temperature very important. The larger, older Creel would go for the bowels; those medium-sized for the liver, lungs, and heart; and the youngest (and there was only one of those) would go for the brain. Because it was small it needed a soft skull.

Below it a human woman pushed her young in a stroller, dragging a shopping cart behind. A newborn, its skull not yet formed. A soft spot on top. Pulsing. Throbbing. The young Creel yearned to drop, but was restrained, whispered a juicy promise, *Soon, my pet, soon.*

In the upper storeroom Calypso Joe rolled slightly, with a minute squeak of his wheels. "Now, Bossman?" he asked. *Soon, soon,* came the sibilant whisper. "Oh, Bossman, please!" *Soon.* Calypso rolled an inch in anticipation. His army behind him rolled an inch. The noise echoed through the empty warehouse. "Please, Bossman! Please" *Soon.* Calypso Joe began to roll. His army rolled behind him. Faster and faster and faster, around and around the warehouse, until the noise of their motion echoed into a deafening din, so much so that the vibrations disturbed Cleo, who moved from her eggs down the catwalk to spy out, then returned, not surprised to see the first of her children eating its way out. They would be small, but ready. And as if he understood her need, Calypso Joe screamed out in joyous exultation: "Soon, Cleo, soon! Bossman, He say soon!"

And in the receiver's room, Charley Mahl, the new receiver, sat at his desk, and sniffed lightly, smelling an ancient odor, the odor of death, and . . . lemons? . . . Yes, lemons. And what was that sound? Just out of reach . . . a gnashing sound, like metal teeth.

*Soon, Lynnanne, soon.*

Now the headless, ball-less man appeared. His tatooed hands clutched his shotgun as he marched within the back room scaffolding, looking for targets, human targets.

*Soon, Phael, soon.*

And from the foul water of the produce tub, the first of many of the water dead sat up, stood up, and stepped out. Followed by another and another and another and another until thirteen were their number. They moaned for pity with gargling throaty pleas, "Let us feed, Master, let us feed."

*Soon soon, very soon.*

Then came the bonemen, and the boars, and the flying skulls, screaming, screeching, to eat, to eat. *To eat, to fee-eed!* And in the thundering pleas of the damned of hell Ravana reveled in the agony and pain, screaming *Now Now Now Now Now Now-Ow-Owww!* and in the name of all that is Evil the horror began:

Mary Deere, having just left the market, was the first to notice. Her son Tommy begged for a quarter to put in the giant jawbreaker machine, and he ran back inside to get his prize. To her amazement, the sunblinds rolled down over all the windows of the store, like a giant green eyelid closing, then a muffled rumble began and she watched the security mesh roll down, across the doors, too, locking Tommy and everybody else inside. She left her basket and walked up to the door, but now it was covered by a white butcher's apron. She began pounding on the door. "Tommy! Tommy!" she screamed, then her eyes dropped to her feet and she began screaming in earnest, not a name but a soul-rending wail. Sluicing out from under the market door and around her sandaled feet was frothy red blood, fresh and warm and sticky wet. In less than ten minutes she had screamed herself into shock, and so the noise from within, so grotesque and so inhuman, fell on deaf ears, as did the mounting wail of police sirens in the distance.

# 56

The fear in his own men's faces could be no worse than that in his own; they were clustered, all eight of them, twenty feet from the gaping black mouth of the roof hatch, decked out in black bulletproof vests, and robin's-egg-blue riot helmets with clear plastic face shields kicked up like jet-fighter canopies. They checked and rechecked their weapons, handguns and shotguns, trying to ignore the muted screams that came from below.

"Christ! Can't you do something about that?" asked the mayor, his face red and pleading.

"I could have done something about it yesterday," replied Kyle. He let the words sink in as he watched Harold Torkelson climb over the roof rise from the fire ladder built into the market's outer east wall. He carried huge scrolls of blueprints scrunched under his arms. The market blueprints.

Kyle turned to greet Torkelson. The old man's grim blue eyes moved involuntarily toward the hatch. He said nothing, but squatted down and rolled out the blueprints on the black tarred roof, fighting the curl of the three sheets.

"Wait a minute," said Kyle. A fire ladder appeared on the horizon of the roof with a clunk. Koger came into view and over the lip of the roof's edge. He was wearing suit pants and white shirt and tie, black flak jacket and blue riot helmet. Across his chest a bandolier of clips hung heavily for the M-16 automatic rifle that dangled from his shoulder.

Joe Lotito, the duty sergeant, followed him, similarly attired, followed by two California highway patrolmen. County sheriffs were on their way, too, Kyle knew, among others answering his mutual assistance call to all surrounding agencies. He recognized the Chippies, Louis Sawyer and Jim Steadman. They were loaded for bear too. Good. They'd need it down there.

"What have we got?" asked Koger, then jerked his head to the muted screams wafting from the open hatch.

"I don't know," said Kyle. "I sent McCulley and Salom down there. No radio contact, and they didn't come back."

"God."

"We go down en masse, now."

"Why not the front door?"

"All normal ways are covered by the riot grates. It's that new Marvel Mesh kind—you can't even pull it out with grappling hooks and trucks. The locks are fused together, and the fucking mesh is electrified."

"We can turn off the power."

"Then it'll be dark in there. The damn sunblinds are down tight, and we can't get to them because of the security mesh."

"Shit."

"Shit's right."

Torkelson cleared his throat. "Even if you turned the power off, we've got emergency generators in the basement. They'd kick in."

"We want to get the people out of there," said Kyle. He winced in agony as moans rose up from the hatch. Those were his people down there: his people. He wanted to fling himself down the hatch. But to rush down without a plan would be foolhardy. "How do we get the mesh up?"

"The grates have mechanical cranks. Your best bet is to go here"—he jabbed at the blueprint, the northwest corner—"that's the liquor department. In back is the power switch box for the entire store. Just outside the door is the crank for those side grates. You'd have to send someone into the lower warehouse, though"—he pulled the bottom print from the bottom of the stack, and jabbed at it—"the southwest corner,

458

the emergency generators . . . They'd have to be shut off, too. Big red levers. Pull 'em down and you'll be set."

"Thank you," said Kyle. He turned to Lotito. "Joe, I want you to stay up here. You come down with reserves, and anybody else you can find, same plan. No less than six men, though. Keep someone up here to direct new arrivals, and tell Gurnell to group the firemen and any extras by that northwest door. You got it?"

"Got it."

Kyle turned to the men. "Hart, Studwell, Higgins, Gunn, you're with Koger once we're on the main floor. Head for the liquor department and do your thing. Be sure to pull down the blinds to get some light in there. Get that gate open and get those people out of there fast."

Koger moved over toward his men. Kyle said, "Go down and secure the bottom of the ladder." He jabbed toward the hatch with his fist.

"Let's move it," said Koger, pulling the M-16 off his shoulder. He led his group over to the hatch, then stepped over and onto the ladder leading down into the belly of the market.

"Okay, you—Boylan, Harris, Stevens, Steadman, Sawyer— you're on me." Kyle walked over to the hatch. He pulled his romote radio unit from his belt. "Koger?" No response. "Koger?" No response.

Kyle stuck his head into the hatch. "Koger?"

"All secure down here, sir. Remote's all scratchy. Radio's useless."

"Gotcha. Waddya see?"

"All clear."

Kyle headed down, first strapping his shotgun over his shoulder. He mounted the lip of the hatch and climbed down. He felt like he was stepping down in a swimming pool, a long, long ladder into deep dark, vile waters that would drown him.

Darkness surrounded him as his feet touched the floor of the upper warehouse. Kyle touched his flashlight for reassurance. If the lights went out in this place he sure in hell wanted

459

a flashlight.

His eyes adjusted to the same dim light that had haunted the warehouse on the previous investigation: low-wattage bulbs spaced ungodly distances apart. Inky black shadows mottled the huge warehouse, along with patches of gray and too few spots of the weak yellow light.

Muffled screams, intermittent and horrifying, filtered up from down below.

"Hurry up!" Kyle shouted, as the troops clammored down the ladder. "We are going to double-time it to the central stairwell, then down. Koger's group takes the front and we go for the cellar. Let's move it!"

The men formed two columns.

"Sir, what's that!" shouted Hart, his flashlight playing against a far shadow, catching two silvered sacks? hanging from silver ropes?

Kyle drew his flashlight and double-timed the men toward the shadow area. "Koger! With me."

Koger held his M-16 at the ready, while Kyle approached the . . . sacks? No. Cocoons. Semitransparent cocoons hanging from thick silken cords, suspended some four feet off the floor. And through the glossy silver sheen Kyle spotted a huddled, withered figure, manlike . . . the beam of his light caught something that twinkled—a badge! Kyle raised the beam and caught the blue of a helmet and the desiccated face of a man, McCulley or Salom, he couldn't tell which.

Kyle looked up. The cords disappeared into the inky black darkness above.

Crap!

"It's Salom and McCulley," he said.

"What the fuck?" Koger eyed the sacks, and then he too looked up into the inky black. He wasn't just looking up, he was looking out.

"No time," said Kyle. "Move it!" he screamed at the men and their thundering boots resounded throughout the warehouse. Fifty yards remained between them and the center stairwell, when a rolling clamor arose from the far shadows.

Hundreds of human figures came rolling out of the far darkness. Mannequins! They gained speed, each raising one arm, the passing yellow light glittering off a hundred scalpel blades. "Bossman say kill!" came a cry. "Kill kill kill kill!" chorused other voices.

"Spread out!" shouted Kyle. "Fire at will!"

The left column flanked left, the right column flanked right. Shotgun barrages boomed. Koger emptied a clip from his M-16. Mannequins exploded, crashing down, sliding forward on momentum, tripping other mannequins. But others were still rolling, arms raised, scalpels glittering, loud papery voices screaming, "Kill kill kill kill kill!" rolling faster and faster, closing on them, in and out of the inkwell shadows, fear and death rolling before them in a roiling hot wave.

The men reloaded and fired again at the mass of mannequins less than one hundred feet in front of them. Dummies tumbled, exploding, shattering. Kyle ducked a severed mannequin arm, the wicked scalpel blade clenched in its hand missing his head by inches. Other scattered debris flew by as the men kept firing, and then the mannequins were upon them and the fighting was hand-to-hand. Kyle swung his shotgun like a club, no time to reload. Others were doing the same, buying time for a few, who ducked behind the skirmish line to reload; thank god the rolling mannequins got tangled in the debris of their comrades, slowing them up. Kyle butted a mannequin in the head, rocking him back and down. Koger stepped beside him and emptied a clip that cleared a small area in front of them. The other reloaders stepped through and blasted away, clearing gaping holes in the ranks of the mannequins.

"Retreat! Retreat! Bossman say retreat! Retreat!" chorused the broken ranks of the mannequins. They circled up and headed back toward the far darkness, Kyle's men firing after them.

"Cease fire!" Kyle ordered, and looked to his left in time to see Harris being dragged into the access port by a giant black spider. The cocoons! Spider! Fucking giant spider.

"Hold it!" Kyle commanded to men turning back toward the access port. "He's dead! We've got to save those who still have a chance. Any wounded among you?"

Steadman staggered forward, cupping his upper left arm with his right hand. Blood flowed between his fingers in rivulets.

"Make a tourniquet!" Kyle told Hart, who detached his shotgun sling and began cutting off the blood above the Chippie's wound. Kyle looked Steadman in the eyes. "You can go back on your own or with us, it's up to you. We gotta keep moving."

Steadman turned his head back, wincing as Hart tightened the tourniquet, took in the long, dark distance between his position now and the shaft of light columning down around the hatch ladder. He cocked his eyes toward the access port that Harris had been dragged into. "Uh, I think I'll stick with you," he said, "I can still use my gun." He patted his revolver.

Louis Sawyer stepped over to him. "I'll take care of him."

"Okay! Let's get moving before our friends regroup." Kyle spared a longing look at the access port. There was no time, and a good man had died. The rest of the injuries, aside from Steadman, were minor.

"Move out!"

They made it to the center stairwell and started down. The moans and screams from below galed hideously up to them now, clear and unabated. Kyle led them down in a trummel of boots. The whine of the box-baling machine rose to meet them, mingled with screams and the snap of crushing bones, the dull pop of exploding human skulls.

Kyle hit the floor firing. Ten rotted corpses were flinging living human beings, stunned into immobility by the unreal horror of it all, into the open mouth of the baler. The shoppers, most women, milled and whimpered and cried. They cowered at the walking deads' threatening gestures, and stared in shock

462

at the glistening, wet bales of crushed human bodies.

Kyle rushed forward with the mass of his troops, blasting away at the ten risen dead men and women, blowing their legs out from under them and blasting off their arms.

Kyle left Steadman and Sawyer to guard the group of some thirty people still living, ordering them moved away from the bales . . .

*(How many people does it take to make a bale? Enought to Make A Hundred Mothers Wail. HEE-HEE-HEE!)*

The words sliced through his mind, alien; vicious.

Kyle turned from Steadman, ready to lead his men out onto the floor, when he saw the lid on the boxy white floorwashing machine begin slowly to lift. Black was nearest to it, his back an easy target.

"Watch it!" screamed Kyle. He brushed Black aside and poked his shotgun level with a wet black head, raising slowly out of the dirty wash water.

"Don't shoot!" said a voice, and Kyle found Coogle Carver's round white eyes staring up the barrel Kyle was sighting down.

Kyle gave a hysterical laugh of relief.

"Is it safe, yet?" asked Coogle.

"No. Stay." Kyle pushed the man's head down and closed the lid. "Let's go."

They reached the double swing doors. Kyle stopped. "Koger, take your men up front." He turned to his crew. "Boylan, Stevens, Black, follow me."

Kyle pushed through the swinging doors, and found himself standing twenty feet from a dirty, razor-tusked boar. The creature was dining on the entrails of an elderly woman dressed in green stretch pants and white blouse soaked in her blood. The beast seemed not to notice Kyle. It snorted into the woman's abdomen, frothing the blood in her body cavity. Then it turned its monstrous snout and obscene pig eyes on Kyle and the other men piling in through the doors.

The boar lowered its head, pawed the blood-slick floor, and charged.

Kyle fired from the hip, multiple blasts, sidestepping down an aisle. Others opened fire. The distance was twenty feet. The lead tore gaping holes in the mammoth boar, but its strength and momentum kept it coming. The men scattered. The boar slashed with its tusks, catching Higgins in the leg and bringing her down. Then it lowered its head and burrowed into her, its head twisting, gouging large slabs of skin out of her body, spraying blood in glistening red sheets. Koger emptied a clip into its heart and it dropped, right on Higgins, crushing her body.

The men struggled to shift the boar off their fallen comrade.

"No time, she's dead," said Kyle. "Move it—"

The shrill trilling of a police whistle cut him off. Kyle turned around and looked up toward the front. The whistle sounded again. Kyle scanned past a dozen blood-mangled bodies. At the very front he searched, eyes jittering, and then he saw. The eight-by-eight-foot stainless steel bottle basket was flipped upside down, coke bottles and cardboard all, but a small arm was sticking out and pointing toward the ceiling.

"Chief! Look up! Look up!" screamed Bunny Coolins.

Kyle obeyed instantly.

Roosted in a cluster were gray batlike creatures, watching with huge quicksilver bubble eyes. They hung upside down, grinning cavernously with triangular silver teeth.

"Scatter!" he screamed, watching in horror as the gray mass dropped, and five or six dog-sized spiders tumbled out of the broken mirror spyhole like a litter of black death, to join in the carnage.

Kyle twisted and jerked back, tripping and rolling and coming up on his knees next to the corpse of a headless RC Cola salesman. The man's wet blood soaked into the pants of Kyle's uniform. A large gray thing, stomach bulging from other kills, hop-waddled down the aisle. Its wings fluttered a little with the effort. Its silver talons, razor sharp, clacked against the floor; its eyes, bulging and jiggling, reflected a distorted image of Kyle on their convex surfaces, making it seem that some grotesque aberration of himself was attacking him.

Kyle raised his shotgun, and pulled the trigger.

The gun clicked. Empty.

The thing hop-waddled faster toward him. Jesus—four feet!

Kyle dropped the shotgun and rocked back to gain his feet while drawing his automatic. Arms grabbed him around his legs. The headless corpse had him. Kyle's automatic cleared his holster. He fired into the beastly eyes of the bat-thing. They exploded in sprays of blood and white writhing maggots. Kyle emptied his gun into the gray hide of the creature. It rocked backward and fell on its back. As the gray thing fell, Kyle turned his attention to the hug of the headless corpse. An image burned into his brain—Dwight Koger, face twisted with disgust at the spider wrapped around the barrel of his M-16 like a normal-sized spider might around a twig. Koger shook it around, trying to dislodge it, finally smashing it against the shelving, its body popping like a black water balloon filled with motor oil.

Kyle wrestled free of the corpse, extracted the empty clip, jammed a full clip into his automatic, and jacked the slide to feed a round into the chamber. He lunged past the bloodied gray carcass, retrieved his shotgun and fed shells into the tube, then jacked a round into the chamber. When this was done he holstered his handgun.

"What the fuck is this!" someone bellowed.

Kyle turned and was glad to see some reinforcements. Lotito pushed a wounded Stevens aside and opened fire on a winged monstrosity. Behind the sergeant three reserves and a deputy sheriff flowed out of the swinging doors and joined the melee. Kyle stared in shock. Within seconds, Boylan, Studwell, lay sprawled, eviscerated by the things; Gunn lay slumped against the milk case, spider fang marks on her throat, her neck swollen, face turning purple; Stevens sported wicked claw marks down the front of his shirt. His badge had been ripped off. He stared at George Boylan's lifeless body; they had been friends. Koger's left arm, mangled and dripping blood, hung limply at his side; blood drooled down the left side of his face.

"Ruined my fucking shirt," said Koger.

"Lotito, we need medics," Kyle said.

Lotito tore his gaze from the gray bloody creatures lying about. "Black's on . . ."

Black pushed through the double doors, two paramedics following him.

"Get Koger and Stevens," Kyle told the paramedics, deliberately steering them away from Gunn. He fought a horrible tide of guilt. It was like Vietnam, fucking 'Nam, when you patched up those that could be put back into battle first, then helped the mortally wounded. No time.

"Fleshwound," Koger was saying, the fire of battle still glowering in his eyes.

Hart, the only one in the original force besides Kyle uninjured, looked at Kyle. "Let's get moving!"

Kyle pointed to Lotito: "Go with him, Joe. Keister, Lasocco, you too. And check under that bottle basket in front and pick up the girl—she's alive." He sent the medics along with them. That left him four men.

He led them along the dairy wall past a woman missing an arm and crying in terror as a small boar charged her. Kyle got it with a blast and kept on moving, trying not to slip in the blood. The floor was slick with the blood of other people, and he and his men kept hurdling over corpses.

They reached the meat department and saw a different sort of butchering going on. Men and woman were gaffed on the rollered hanging meat hooks, while bonemen in butcher aprons and sanitary hats used meat cleavers and bandsaws on the meat. At the wrapping machine, one skeleton, his white paper sanitary hat cocked at a jaunty angle, grinned sardonically as it slapped steaks of human meat onto styrofoam trays, sent through the machine to be sealed in cellophane and weighed, then pulled the self-sticking label from the printer and pressed it on the package.

"Stevens, Kelly," ordered Kyle. "Get 'em!"

Petersen and Black started to follow Kyle, then the air filled with the screech of banshees, the men turned around, and down the corpse-littered meat aisle a squadron of skulls came flying, teeth gnashing, screaming: *"Eat! Eat! Ea-ea-eatttt! You-ou-ouuouou!"*

The doors to the meat department's back room opened, and undead Legions marched out.

Petersen opened fire on the skulls, while Kyle and Black blasted at the trooping corpses.

Even the fervor of battle did not keep the stench of slimy rotting flesh from making them all gag. Petersen took out most of the skulls, but three got through, and they circled him as he batted them with his shotgun. Kyle saw one zip in between Petersen's flailing arms and take a huge bite out of his face. The corpses moved in and grabbed Petersen, and Kyle couldn't get to him in time. If he fired, he'd hit the man.

Ravana's Legions poured out of the back room. Christ, how many? Too many! Kyle's shotgun was empty. Black's too.

"Run!" Kyle screamed, and they bolted back toward the batwing warehouse doors, reloading on the run.

Kyle heard Black scream, stopped, turned, but it was too late. One of the gray bat-things had dropped from above, knocking Black to the floor. Before Kyle could fire, it ripped Black's chest open, pulling his heart out with its claws. Blood geysered up from Black's body and sprayed the creature as Kyle blasted it apart.

The army of corpses was closing.

Kyle wheeled around: more were coming from the other direction, and down the aisles. His only chance was to get into the back room with Steadman and Sawyer, and hope they could hold off until reinforcements came.

Koger and the rest couldn't have made it, not with this many creatures to fight.

Kyle dove through the batwing doors and heard shotgun fire. He stepped from behind some boxes, and saw Sawyer take a blast to the chest from a headless corpse—Phael! Kyle realized. Kyle raised his shotgun, and fired three rounds into it, blowing its legs out from under it, and one arm out of its socket. Phael's shotgun skittered under the pallet frame, out of reach.

The batwing doors burst open, and the corpes began shambling in. Kyle held his fire. Bonemen came from the warehouse. Kyle whirled around.

He was surrounded.

Kyle made a slow pivot around his left foot.

Ravana's Legions encircled him, then stopped dead cold.

Slowly, Kyle stopped his pivoting. They weren't going to harm him. Ravana *wanted* him. What was it Holy Eagle had said? The same thing as Professor Lyon, wasn't it? Ravana needed to face Kyle in the ritual to enhance his power. If not, Ravana's power would increase more slowly.

But Holy Eagle was banking on Kyle to win, and Kyle knew he would lose. Let Ravana choose another, Kyle decided, someone more worthy. Maybe with all that has happened, someone can figure out a way to beat this thing.

Kyle pulled his handgun from its holster, placed it against his temple, cocked the hammer, and screamed, "Hey, Ravana. Fuck you!"

*Wait!*

The command was hot and wild; it writhed in his mind.

What the hell, he had the time. "What the hell for!"

The sea of walking corpses and dead men parted, forming a path to the freight elevator.

Kyle felt his blood run cold. Was Ravana Itself coming up to see him? Kyle heard the hissing of snakes in his mind.

The gauntlet of corpses shuffled nervously in place.

The elevator stopped.

Kyle put slight pressure on the trigger. No way was Ravana getting him.

The elevator doors opened, and there, being held by two risens, were Curtis and Michele.

# 57

Neil Gathers walked across the market roof, and stared at his daughter. "Christa Marie, what are you doing up here?" He turned to Sergeant Powell, who had escorted her up. "Have you lost your mind?"

"Daddy! Listen! Little Neil and Curtis were going to the market after school. I found their bikes down on the other side."

"Oh, my God!"

"I think Mrs. McKinney may be there, too. She called looking for Curtis before all this happened, and when I told her they had gone to the market, she freaked."

"Does your mother know about this?"

"No. I rushed here after I heard something was happening."

"Okay. You go tell her. And you stay at home, until this is over. I'm going down and get Little Neil."

Craig Powell coughed. "Sir, there are no more reinforcements. More will be here in a few minutes."

"You and Mead are going down with me!" he bellowed. "You use the shotgun, let me have your pistol."

"Yessir," said Powell.


Neil Gathers, with Sergeant Mead and Sergeant Powell at his side, stalked through the gloomy, dim light of the upper warehouse. It was quiet. Too quiet. Dread chewed at his guts. What should he do now? More help would be on the way, but they couldn't wait. Little Neil was down here! He had to come

469

down, too.

"Over there," said Powell, his flashlight beam cutting a swath into one of the inky pockets of darkness. A silver-threaded cocoon, the size of a duffel bag, hung from a silver rope that dropped from the darkness above. The cocoon and rope were wet, scattering the lights' beams in a cold, glittering sparkle.

"That doesn't look good,", said Powell.

"What is it?" asked the mayor fearfully.

"It's the way we found Salom and McCulley," said Sergeant Mead. "Cut it down, Powell." Powell laid down his shotgun and pulled out a pocket knife. With Mead lifting him up, he managed to grab the sticky cord above the sack and worry the knife blade through it. The mayor caught it instinctively and regretted it at once. The wet, woven threads of the cocoon were cold and sticky. He felt the fluid on the threads dripping, soaking through his shirt and tee shirt to his bare skin, cementing the godawful cocoon to his own body. "Get it off me!" he screamed, the weight and angular shapes of what he was holding beginning to register—a child's body, but lighter than it should be. Powell and Mead began to pull at the sack, twisting it. It stuck like taffy. They pulled and twisted, trying to screw it off the mayor, getting more entwined themselves. "Shit!" Mead yelled in disgust. He pushed the cocoon back toward the mayor. The sack stuck to Neil Gathers's face, its hard contents bumping his cheek. When Mead pulled back sharply, a patch of the cocoon pulled free on the mayor's face, exposing the contents. Gathers moaned, building into a mournful wail. "Oh *God,* my son, my son!" Gathers could not tear his eyes from the shriveled face of Little Neil. His son's skin was sucked down to the facial bone, the eyes sunk deep down in the sockets. The lips were dried back around the teeth, forming a sardonic grin.

"Run, Mayor, run!" screamed Mead. The mayor barely heard him. Shotgun fire exploded, and the mayor danced around, holding tightly to his son. The rolling roar of squeaky wheels filled the warehouse. The mass of mannequins charged with a roll of thunder from the far side of the warehouse, gaining speed, arms extended, scalpels in hand.

Mead and Powell ran backward, firing rounds, scattering a few of the mannequins.

The mayor broke into a shambling run behind them, heading for the distant ladder, encumbered by the cocoon.

There was an awful whisper, then a clatter of steel, and the mayor realized with horror that the mannequins were hurling their scalpels. He felt pain in his back, but kept running. Two of them buried in his back. Ahead of him Mead looked like a pin cushion, twenty scalpels punching deep into his back. He dropped, his dead body skidding up to the base of the ladder, hitting it with a *thunk*. Powell took one in the ankle and screamed; he was halfway up the ladder. The mannequins were gaining on the mayor. Powell scrambled out the hatch just as the mayor reached the metal rungs and started to climb. He held his son's spider-silk-wrapped body in the crooks of his arms and tried desperately to climb. He glanced down and saw the mannequins surrounding the bottom of the ladder, but he was twenty feet up by then, and could catch the glimpse of sunlight admitted by the hatch: a rectangular patch of blue. No more looking down. Just climb, *climb!* He scrambled up another ten feet, another five. Scalpels flew by him. Missed, thank God! Four more feet to go. A man's face appeared in the opening, his arms reached down, and the mayor knew he had it made—

The hatch slammed down shut, decapitating the man, and cutting both his arms off just above the elbow. The red-haired head and bloodied stumped arms hit the mayor in the face and bounced, falling to the mannequin crowd below. They cheered.

The mayor continued upward, watching in horror as the hatch glowed, fusing itself in fiery heat to its frame. He was sealed in, stuck on the damn ladder.

He began to sob, then clenched the ladder, getting hold of himself. The mannequins couldn't reach him up here. And help would come, bring a blowtorch. That was it. All he had to do was wait.

After a minute he braved a look below. The mannequins were clustered around the base of the ladder, their arms reaching up. They were silent. Defeated.

He heard banging above his head. Rescuers were taking axes to the hatch. It wouldn't work, the hatch was too tough, the mayor knew that, but at least the banging meant they were trying to get him out. If he just held on they'd have a blowtorch soon enough. He was home free . . .

"Cle-ee-ee-o-o-o-o!" chorused the mannequins in a lilting, teasing summons. "Oh-oh, Clee-ee-ee-o-o-o-o!"

Who the hell was Cleo? A mannequin that could climb a ladder?

He heard a noise and looked off into the dark of the ceiling. Eight violet eyes glowered at him. The spider crawled out of the darkness along the heating ducts. Neil Gathers felt his bladder go. Warm urine ran down his leg. Trapped! He clutched his son's body with both hands and dived headfirst into the sea of mannequins below.

Kyle clutched his shotgun, seeing them all—Ravana's Legions between him and the two he loved—knowing even then it was useless. "Michele," he said. She looked up. "Kyle," she said.

"Fuh-fight!" Curtis choked out.

"No," said Kyle. He stared out at the ghoulish horrors around them. Every dead thing in Ravana's Legion: walking corpses of men, woman, and children, dirty and black with slime; bonemen; boars; and hanging from the rafters, those batlike creatures. And all silent. Silent. Shit!

"Ravana!" Kyle screamed. He put his handgun up near his head again. "A deal: You let me take these two out. I'll stand at the base of the ladder. Just let me see them out, and I will face you! If not"—Kyle placed the gun to his head—"I'll blow my brains out, and you can find yourself another *Ehkeh-Heh*. That's my deal! Take it or leave it!"

For a time there was silence. Ravana's ghouls stared at him with the stillness of death, the hunger of absolute evil.

*Agreed!*

The word buzzed in Kyle's head like a thousand flies. He took the gun from his head and walked through the gauntlet of corpses. They reeked of rotting flesh. Without wanting to, Kyle caught glimpses of an eyeless socket, and maggoty meat hanging in a flap from a jawbone.

"Get out!" Kyle yelled at the corpses holding Michele and Curtis. They shambled past Kyle. He entered. The door closed. The motors began a throbbing hum. The elevator started moving. "I want you both to know—" Kyle stopped speaking and began pounding the door with balled-up fists. "Son of a bitch. Son of a bitch . . ."

"What is it, Kyle?" asked Michele.

It's going down. Down! Down! The elevator's going down!

Kyle stopped pounding on the door. There was not much time. "It is better to be dead," Kyle said, "than to belong to *It*." He handed his handgun to Michele, and was glad that she took it without argument. "I'm going to face that thing. If I win, we go free. If I am defeated, shoot Curtis in the head, then yourself." Michele began to protest; he cut her off. "It's the only way, Michele, believe me." Kyle pulled the necklace of bones from around his neck and handed them to her. "These will protect you from his creatures, they shy from them, wave them—"

"But you?"

"I forgot to use these up there. None of them can touch me now, anyhow; Ravana knows I will face It. I was hoping to get you out first. With you in the balance, I'll face It. If I fail, or if that necklace is knocked out of your hand, then one shot to Curtis, one to yourself. Remember that." He turned to Curtis. "If she can't, take the gun and shoot her, then yourself, Curtis. It's an act of love, do you understand me?" Curtis nodded his

473

head, his eyes filled with fear.

You're not the only one, Kyle thought. He felt his own stomach knotted up, his breath labored. If he could defeat *Ravana*, he could save them. But God, how he feared that evil thing.

The elevator ground to a noisy stop and the doors began to open. Kyle handed Curtis his shotgun. "Michele, once we're outside, keep your back to the wall, Curtis behind you. Hold the necklace out, and forget that shotgun, it won't do you as much good as the bones. I love you both." He turned and led them out the terror of his dream, now a living, breathing reality.


He had to be strong for them. He led them out onto his own brain: the floor was pink and convoluted brain matter, slippery like wet clay. He positioned them near the elevator door, Curtis, the smaller, behind Michele, Michele with the necklace outstretched in her left hand, the automatic in her right. Bonemen and ragged corpses immediately closed in, moaning, Michele shooed them with the necklace, they recoiled, but even then, one reached out with a naked, disembodied leg and tried to bat it from her hand. She parried and warded it off with a thrust of the necklace and a fierce scream. "Get away!" screamed Curtis. And that is the way Kyle left them, screaming and fighting for their lives. Kyle knew his only way to truly save them waited beneath the gnarled, char-black scrub oak.

The "sky" shown ultraviolet purple. A glowering, burnt-orange moon glowered an evil eye at him, and Ravana's Legion, standing between Kyle and Ravana, parted, a sea of undead souls manifested as putrifying human corpses. The air lay heavy and humid. The stench of reeking, rotting flesh was unbearable. Yet he bore it. The hissing of the snakes wailed in his ears, and he saw them, twisted and coiled in the limbs of the tree, a writhing Gordian knot that somehow was unraveling—as was his nerve—

No! That way lay insanity, the abyss! Oh, God, help me!

"Acknowledge your fear, *Ehkeh-Heh!*" commanded a voice in his mind—Holy Eagle. "Then release it! Fear not Ravana, nor its evil. Its only power is your own fear of It.

"Fear is Man's homage to the Devil, *Ehkeh-Heh!* Without fear this vile Thing does not exist! *Ehkeh-Heh,* face Ravana for all Mankind.

"Face its Evil, but know that It does not exist if It does not exist in your own mind! Cleanse your mind, *Ehkeh-Heh!* Release the darkness within, know that It is not true! Face Ravana, *Ehkeh-Heh!* Cleanse your mind, *Ehkeh-Heh!* Your mind! Cleanse your mind and go forth and kiss the illusion, the kiss of death! Pull back its robe and kiss It! Cleanse your mind and kiss It!"

Then a dark voice filled his head: *You are the Fallen Warrior, a failed man who left his wife and child to die! Your fault, Kyle Richards! Your fault! Listen to them scream, failed man! Watch them die because of you!*

Kyle's mind exploded with the vile words. The area under the tree became the living room in Kyle's old home. Susan, his wife, was tied to the glass coffee table, naked. Cloven-hooved, horned-skin, menlike creatures with gargoyle faces pranced around the table, taking turns kneeling behind her and driving their spikelike members into her vagina and rectum, roaring laughter as she screamed and screamed, and blood gushed out. One held Kyle's own utility blowtorch, lit it up, and raked her body with the blue jet flame. Smoke curled up from seared, burned lesions across her body. She screamed hideously. Her head bounced and bounced until it cracked through the glass coffee table, gashing her throat. Blood geysered up from her wound. One creature reached down and drove her head through the jagged glass plane of the table with a side-to-side sawing motion, until it hung down half severed off, dangling almost, those blue eyes he so loved upside down and staring, accusing . . .

"It was not my fault!" roared Kyle.

"Yes, it was," said Susan's head. "It was all your fault."

Had she blamed him? Was this the truth of her thoughts?

"No, *Ehkeh-Heh!* All is in your mind! Cleanse it! Face Ravana!"

*Now the bedroom, failed man! Your child! Or bow before me! Come forward and bow before me! You are mine, Fallen Warrior! Plead with me! I will set you free!"*

It raised its robed arm, holding out a huge green-scaled claw. On what served as its ring finger, a yellow sentient eye stared up at Kyle.

Kyle's fear rose wildly in him. His legs began to tremble, and moved forward, against his will: "No! No!"

*Yes!*

Ravana's iridescent yellow eyes waxed with anticipation.

"Help me! Help me, please!" Kyle's feet moved him closer. He willed them to resist, but he had no control. He threw his hands up to cover his eyes. He felt his mind exploding in slow motion. He was almost to Ravana.

"*Ehkeh-Heh!*" Holy Eagle's voice filled his mind. "know that this is false! Do not resist! Do not fear! Do not kneel, *Ehkeh-Heh!* Yet do not resist! Unrobe it! And kiss its face!"

Kyle felt his mind slip now, sliding into that crevasse. Not just on the edge, but going over. His thoughts moved like taffy. He knew he was at the robe monster. He felt his knees begin to shake and bend; he began to kneel. He couldn't help it. His mind screamed in agony. His consciousness heightened and filled with shame . . . but he would do it, he would do it because he was crazy, he had to be crazy to be living this, this . . . A wave of self-hate washed over him like molten lava. He pulled his hands away to stare into the yellow ring eye on Ravana's taloned hand. It stared back gleefully. He was crazy. His hands moved toward the claw, his mouth pursed to kiss it, and he knew that he was lost . . .

Two sharp sounds cracked through the black fog of his horror. Two shots. One for Curtis and one for Michele, he remembered. The two people he loved most on this earth dead! Not because of him, but because of this Thing! This godless creature!

Kyle saw red.

Rage filled his soul. He grabbed the green claw in both hands, wrenched it, and yanked. It came off in his hands and disappeared in flames. Kyle regained his feet. "Holy Eagle, guide me!" he cried out.

"Cleanse your mind! Cease your hate! Know that It is not real!"

"Teach me!"

"Learn!" A white, swirling mist appeared. Holy Eagle's face showed grim in its center. "Become, *Ehkeh-Heh!* Become!"

Kyle's vision filled with shimmering rainbow colors, expanding and dissipating, leaving a brilliant snow-white mist now, occupying his entire consciousness; and the Light became all, the darkness not darkness, but a differentiation of the Light; and all that was in this Light was all that was, his emotions, his fears only as real as he chose them to be, the only Truth being the Light—

And Kyle became the Light—

Then was back in the warehouse, Ravana's warehouse hell.

Ravana's glowering, yellow eyes waned. Kyle smelled the fear in It now. He gained great confidence in that.

"Remove its cowl, *Ehkeh-Heh!*"

Kyle reached up to the cowl. "You are not real," he said to the yellow eyes. A snout appeared from the black recess of the cowl, flashed silver teeth, and bit deeply into Kyle's hand. He felt pain . . . no, not pain . . . It was in his mind . . . "You are not real," he said, and removed the cowl and kissed . . .

Nothing!

He felt a rumble, then the room around exploded in flames. A hissing, howling sound rose up, joined by a chorus of ear-shattering moans. Flames danced across Kyle's eyes, and he felt himself consumed, consumed in a purifying flame. Beside him stood the old Indian Priest: "*Ehkeh-Heh,* you are *Ehkeh-*

*Heh*, Great Spirit Warrior, The Chosen One," said Holy Eagle. "Live long in peace, Great Spirit Warrior, and know that you are loved."

The warehouse was suddenly empty, the silence deafeningly loud. Kyle was alone, except for thousands of human bones. Ravana had given up its dead. The dry dusty smell of crypts filled his nose. He felt void of everything. At his feet lay a small headless skeleton. Without question he knew whose it was.

His mind was pristine clean, and though he felt like wailing for the loss of Michele and Curtis he buried the emotion. He had a promise to keep. Something he wanted to do. He was clean now. Clear. And empty. He would mourn later. He knelt down by the bones, touched them tenderly.

He purposely did not turn around; he could not bring himself to look upon Michele and Curtis, their heads blown—

"Kyle? Are you all right?"

Kyle whirled around. Michele and Curtis stood by the elevator door, dirty and dusty, but alive, *alive!*

He rushed to them. "I thought you . . . I heard shots, two shots . . . I . . ."

"I fired at one of the things," said Michele. "It tried to grab the necklace."

Kyle pulled them both to him and began to cry.

478

# Epilogue

Kyle glanced in the rearview mirror. The market was fast
receding. The green plastic garbage bag lay on the floor
between his heels and the seat; it was the only thing he could
find to carry them in. He felt Curtis's small weight on the seat
next to him, and beyond, the luminous presence of Michele.
The truck hit a bump and he slowed to make the turn. "I was so
afraid something had happened to you," he said to Curtis. He
looked across to Michele, ". . . and to your mother. I love you
both very much . . ." Michele gazed back at him, her face
radiant. "Yes," she said, "I love you, too. We both do." She
reached around Curtis, laying a warm hand on Kyle's shoulder.

Kyle made his turn onto the narrow, little-used back road,
and drove up the hill, barely noticing the mayor's smoked-glass
monument in the distance. Since the confrontation with
Ravana, his mind had seemed as clear as mountain air—a
blessed relief.

He steered the truck through the red-brick and black-iron
cemetery gates. The bag at his heels settled; he pressed it back
against the bottom of the seat with his left foot. He guided the
truck to the spot where, so long ago, it seemed, he and Dave
Pickers had parked to pay their respects to the old man's wife
and daughter.

"Wait here," Kyle said solemnly. He got out of the truck
and reached down to pick up the green plastic trash bag, and
closed the door.

He threaded his way past granite tombstones until he found
the Pickers marker. In the bright afternoon sun the stone

479

seemed to shine. He stood, the bag held by both hands, the contents rattling dryly as the bag shifted against his legs.

"David," he said, "I've kept my promise. I've got Cathy's . . ." he faltered, not knowing how to say it, ". . . I've brought your baby back to you, David. I'm not sure of the procedure, but I'll have her buried as soon as possible . . . I'm sorry about the bag . . . I'm sorry . . ." His words trailed off; the tombstone shone brightly, reflecting the sun.

A gust of wind blasted him, pressing the bag against his legs and forcing wholesome air into his lungs. He ached with a solemn joy as he turned to see Michele and Curtis. They stood beside his blue truck, Michele's arm around Curtis's shoulder. They watched him. They waited for him. They loved him. He was no longer alone.